PEACH COBBLER MURDER

It didn't matter what she thought of Shawna Lee personally. If her cookie competitor was hurt or in trouble, Hannah had a responsibility to do what she could to help.

Once she'd made up her mind, Hannah moved quickly. She raced to the back door of the bakery, but when she turned the knob she found it unlocked. She pushed the door open, praying that the two holes she'd seen in the kitchen window weren't bullet holes, the shoe behind the counter had no foot in it, and the peach cobbler on the floor meant nothing more than a slip of an oven glove. But where was Shawna Lee? And why hadn't she shut the oven door and cleaned up the mess?

"Uh-oh," Hannah gasped, skidding to a stop as she rounded the corner of the kitchen counter. Shawna Lee was down on her back on the tile floor and there was a huge blossom of what looked like dried strawberry syrup on the bib of her white chef's apron. There was also a neat hole in the middle of the blossom and Hannah knew that there was no point in continuing to contaminate what was surely a crime scene. Shawna Lee had been shot in the chest and anyone with an ounce of brains could see that she was dead . . .

Books by Joanne Fluke

Published by Kensington Publishing Corporation

A HANNAH SWENSEN MYSTERY WITH RECIPES

PEACH COBBLER MURDER

JOANNE FLUKE

KENSINGTON BOOKS
KENSINGTON PUBLISHING CORP.
www.kensingtonbooks.com

KENSINGTON BOOKS are published by

Kensington Publishing Corp.
850 Third Avenue
New York, NY 10022

All Kensington titles, imprints, and distributed lines are available at special quantity discounts for bulk purchases for sales promotions, premiums, fund-raising, educational or institutional use.

Special book excerpts or customized printings can also be created to fit specific needs. For details, write or phone the office of the Kensington Special Sales Manager: Kensington Publishing Corp., 850 Third Avenue, New York, NY 10022. Attn. Special Sales Department. Phone: 1-800-221-2647.

Kensington and the K logo Reg. U.S. Pat. & TM Off.

ISBN 0-7582-0155-9

First Hardcover Printing: March 2005
First Mass Market Paperback Printing: February 2006
10 9 8 7 6 5 4 3 2 1

Printed in the United States of America

This book is for my GoldenRuel.

ACKNOWLEDGMENTS

Thanks to our kids, who aren't shy about saying, "What's this *supposed* to taste like?"

Thank you to our friends and neighbors: Mel and Kurt, Lyn and Bill, Gina and the kids, Jay, Bob M., Amanda, John B., Trudi, Dale, Adrienne, Dr. Bob and the Bobbettes, and Mark Baker.

I can't thank my editor, John Scognamiglio, enough. Some people have a guardian angel; I have John S. And thanks to all the other talented people at Kensington who keep Hannah Swensen baking and sleuthing.

Thank you to Hiro Kimura, my cover artist, who tastes every title dessert for inspiration before starting in on the artwork. *(It shows!)*

Many hugs to Terry Sommers and her family for critiquing my recipes and lending the kind of moral support only Cheeseheads can.

Thanks to Jamie Wallace, my Web expert, for MurderSheBaked.com

A big hug for Sue Ganske who explained *Kransekake* to me.

And thank you to everyone who e-mailed or wrote to share their lives, recipes, and feelings about Hannah and Lake Eden with me. I created a special treat for you, the Chocolate Overload Cookie Bars. *(They're really incredible . . . and Hannah agrees!)*

 # Chapter One

"**D**ick Laughlin just went in!" Lisa Herman stood behind the café curtains that covered the bottom half of the plate-glass window and peered out across the snow-covered width of Main Street. "And Barbara Donnelly's right behind him. She looked this way and I think she saw me, but she still followed Dick inside."

"I think I can live without a running head count," Hannah Swensen told her young partner, resisting the urge to object as Lisa pulled out the tall stool she used when she operated their cash register and repositioned it so that she had a clear view of the Magnolia Blossom Bakery across the street. The stool was no longer necessary since their bakery and coffee shop, The Cookie Jar, was as empty as one of Hannah's cream puffs before it was filled with vanilla custard.

"I know it's depressing, but I'm setting up a surveillance post right here. We need to keep an eye on the competition." Lisa grabbed one of the steno notebooks Hannah kept handy and hiked herself up on the stool, no easy task for a petite young lady who only topped the five-foot mark when she was wearing high heels. "Uh-oh!"

"What now?"

"Charlotte Roscoe just came out the door carrying a big bakery box. Today's the weekly teachers' meeting and she always comes in to get cookies from us!"

"Once the novelty wears off, they'll be back," Hannah repeated what had become her personal mantra, chanted at least a dozen times a day during the two weeks since Shawna Lee Quinn and her rich, widowed sister, Vanessa, had opened their new bakery.

"You always say that, but are you sure?" Lisa looked a bit doubtful. "I mean . . . what if their baked goods are better than ours?"

Hannah was shocked. Lisa had never questioned the quality of their sweet treats before.

"Sorry." Lisa read the expression of betrayal on Hannah's face and immediately backtracked. "I'm sure ours are better. They're bound to be better. We're professionals and they're just doing it because Shawna Lee always wanted to own her own business and Vanessa gave her the money to indulge her. I don't think either one of them can bake worth a hill of beans, but I wish I could taste something, just to be sure."

Hannah curbed her first impulse, the one where she told Lisa to bite her tongue, and forced herself to be reasonable. It was true that they'd never tasted anything from the Magnolia Blossom Bakery and it would be a big relief if their cookies tasted like sawdust and their piecrusts were tough. On the other hand, what if the two sisters had somehow managed to produce superior baked goods? Was it better to go on in blissful ignorance, taking their own expertise on faith and believing that their bakery was better? Or should they put it to the taste test and close their doors if Shawna Lee and Vanessa had managed to win the Main Street dessert war?

"What's the matter, Hannah?"

"Just having a mental debate with myself."

Lisa broke into a smile. "Who won?" she quipped.

"I did. Why don't you take some money out of the register and run over there? You could try their Southern Peach Cobbler. They call it their signature dessert."

"I couldn't!" Lisa looked properly shocked. "It would be disloyal!"

"Not if you were just comparing their desserts to ours."

"I'd still feel like a traitor. Couldn't you go in and order something just to be friendly?"

Hannah's eyebrows headed skyward. "I should be friendly to the woman who talked her rich widowed sister into financing her so that she could open up right across from us and steal almost ninety percent of our cookie business?"

"Well . . ."

"Do you really want me to walk across Main Street and pretend to be neighborly with the person who undercut our dessert catering and left us with sixteen cancellations?"

"Seventeen," Lisa corrected her. "Rose McDermott's cousin canceled the cookies for the baby shower this morning. I had a feeling that was going to happen when Shawna Lee and Vanessa ran their catering ad in the *Lake Eden Journal*."

"I saw it. *Fifty percent off of your total first order.* If

Shawna Lee ever challenges me to a fight, I'm going to choose grammar as my weapon."

Lisa laughed, but she quickly sobered. "I don't blame you for being upset, Hannah. I'd be seeing red if Shawna Lee made a play for my guy."

"Which guy?"

"Herb, of course."

"Not *your* guy. I was talking about my guy. Which one?"

It was a legitimate question and Hannah waited anxiously for Lisa to answer. She was currently dating two Lake Eden men, something her marriage-minded mother found immensely satisfying. The thing that Delores Swensen did *not* find satisfying was that Hannah had been dating both men for over a year and neither one of them had proposed.

"Well . . . I don't know for sure that Shawna Lee's making a play for him," Lisa said, waffling a bit. "I just *think* she might be."

"Which guy?" Hannah repeated.

"Uh . . . Mike."

Hannah took a deep breath to combat the sinking feeling in her stomach. Mike Kingston was chief detective of the Winnetka County Sheriff's Department and more handsome than any man who didn't make his living in front of a camera had a right to be. Hannah had long suspected that Shawna Lee and Mike might be more than merely friends, former coworkers, and apartment complex neighbors, but Mike had denied it. Since she had no proof of any hanky-panky, Hannah had done her best to believe Mike preferred his women with frizzy red hair, a sarcastic sense of humor, and some extra pounds—never mind how many—that came from sampling her own baked goods.

"Nobody called to tell me," Hannah complained, her stomach reaching rock bottom with the force of an elevator whose cable had snapped. If anyone in Lake Eden got the goods on Shawna Lee and Mike, they were honor bound to call Hannah immediately. That was how small towns worked. You got all the news that was fit to print in the *Lake Eden Journal.* The news that wasn't fit to print was conveyed by phone on the Lake Eden gossip hotline.

"That's because Herb and I are the only ones that know about it. Why did you ask me which guy it was? Norman would never even look at Shawna Lee. He's completely loyal to you."

"He is?" Hannah gave a slight smile as she thought of Norman Rhodes, local Lake Eden dentist and son of her mother's partner in the antique business. Norman couldn't come close to Mike's sexy good looks, but he was bright, funny, and solidly dependable.

"I've seen you with both of them and Mike's got a roving eye. He always checks out the other women, even if he's with you. Norman doesn't do that. When he came in this morning, he couldn't take his eyes off you."

"That's because you and I were the only ones here and you're a bride-to-be."

Lisa looked radiant for a moment and Hannah knew she was thinking about her wedding, only twelve days away. Hannah's younger sister, Andrea, was making all the arrangements and she'd called every day this week to consult with Lisa about flowers, color schemes, and last-minute decorations.

As Hannah watched, Lisa's expression changed to one of worry. "I'm sorry, Hannah. I shouldn't have said anything about Shawna Lee and Mike. It was just one sighting and it could have been nothing."

"*Sighting?*" Hannah smiled, but it didn't reach her eyes. "Did somebody spot a UFO at the same time?"

"Of course not."

"I didn't think so. Extraterrestrials are supposed to be brighter than we are. They'd wait until summer to land in Minnesota. Now tell me what makes you think that Mike's involved with Miss Blonde-To-The-Bone."

Lisa burst out laughing. "Blonde-To-The-Bone?"

"That's what I call her when I'm being petty. And I feel petty a lot of the time when it comes to Shawna Lee. She's the kind of shallow Barbie-doll blonde that gives real honest blondes like Andrea a bad name."

"Shawna Lee's not a natural blonde, is she?"

"Andrea says definitely not. She spotted her out at the new beauty shop at the mall, getting her roots redone." Hannah answered Lisa's attempt to change the subject, but then she zeroed in on what she really wanted to know. "What about this sighting? Who saw them? Where was it? When was it?"

"Herb saw Mike's Hummer parked in the lot behind the Magnolia Blossom Bakery last night."

Hannah nodded, accepting the statement at face value. Herb Beeseman, Lisa's fiancé, was the only law enforcement officer on the city payroll. Herb not only enforced parking and driving regulations within the Lake Eden city limits, he ran security checks on the local businesses before he went off duty at night. Hannah knew her former classmate at Jordan High was completely reliable. If Herb said he saw Mike's Hummer behind the Magnolia Blossom Bakery, then Mike's Hummer had been there. "What time did Herb see it?"

"Eleven. And Vanessa was out of town until this morning. Herb thought maybe Shawna Lee had a problem and she called Mike to fix it."

Hannah doubted that, but she supposed it might be true. "Well . . . Mike did part-time work as a handyman when he was in high school. I guess Herb could be right."

"I don't think so. What kind of problem would Shawna Lee have at eleven at night with the lights out?"

"Electrical?" Hannah guessed, going for the humor and trying not to show how upset she was. "Seriously though, if the power went out and Shawna Lee didn't know how to reset the circuit breaker, she might have called Mike."

"The power didn't go out. Herb saw dim light from a lamp in the apartment over the bakery."

Hannah hated to ask, but she had to know. "Which room had the lamp?"

"Shawna Lee's bedroom."

Hannah gulped. This was serious. There was only one thing Mike could have been doing in Shawna Lee's bedroom and it had nothing to do with his handyman skills.

"I asked Herb to go back and check at midnight, and Mike was still there. I guess there could be some reasonable explanation, though. If you go over there and nose around, Shawna Lee might let something slip."

Hannah shook her head. "Forget it, Lisa. If I set one foot in that bakery, they'll know right away that I'm checking out the competition. What we really need is . . ."

"Andrea," Lisa interrupted.

"Andrea? As in my sister, Andrea?"

"Yes. I'm sure she'd be willing to go over there and check out the baked goods."

"That's a great idea! Andrea can find out their profit margin, their operating costs, their sales, and their average customer profile in less than five minutes. And they'll never know they told her. She's perfect for the job."

"She's certainly good at getting people to talk about themselves."

"She learned that from Mother. And Mother could have been a star CIA operative. I'll go call Andrea right now."

"Don't bother. She's here." Lisa slid off her stool and headed toward the kitchen. "She turned the corner a minute ago and she should be at the back door by now. I'll let her in."

Hannah headed for the coffee urn and filled three cups. She carried them to the back booth, frowning slightly as she walked past the empty tables. They'd had a total of twelve customers all day and that didn't bode well for the future of The Cookie Jar.

Andrea pushed through the swinging door that separated the kitchen from the coffee shop. "Did you hear? That famous groundhog back East saw his shadow. That means winter's over!"

Lisa exchanged glances with Hannah. "Not me," Lisa said. "You tell her."

"Tell me what?"

"It's the other way around, Andrea. If it's a beautiful sunny day and the groundhog sees his shadow, we'll have six more weeks of winter."

"Really?" Andrea started to frown. "That doesn't make any sense! If it's a beautiful day today, why won't it be a beautiful day tomorrow? And the next day? And the day after that? And before you know it, all those beautiful days will turn into spring."

"That would be nice, and it makes as much sense as choosing one day and dragging poor Punxsutawney Phil out of hibernation."

"That's what I think." Andrea shrugged out of her winter coat and glanced around with a puzzled expression. "Where is everybody?"

"Across the street," Hannah told her. "Lisa counted twenty-three people who went into the Magnolia Blossom in the past hour."

"That's just because they're the new kid on the block." Andrea placed her coat and gloves on a nearby chair and twirled around. "What do you think?"

"You're all dressed up," Hannah responded, noticing her younger sister's wine-colored pantsuit. Andrea's high-heeled suede boots matched the color perfectly and her shining blonde hair, done in an elaborate twist, was secured in a clasp studded with wine-colored stones.

"Not that. What else?" Andrea struck a pose that would have done credit to a model on a fashion show runway.

Hannah was stymied. What did Andrea want her to say? She hesitated and finally settled for the tried and true, "You look gorgeous. Is that a new outfit?"

"No, I got it last January. They were having a sale on designer originals out at the mall. But my pantsuit's not what I wanted you to notice. Just look at me! I lost every ounce of weight I put on when I was pregnant with Bethany!"

"Good for you," Hannah replied, trying to sound both supportive and enthusiastic, something she would have achieved only if she'd been an Academy Award–winning actress. Bethany had been born in December, the night of the Lake Eden Christmas Buffet. Now, just two months later, Andrea was back to the same size she'd worn all the way through high school. To Hannah's way of thinking, that just wasn't fair. It took her forever to lose a pound or two, and her sister shed weight as easily as a wet dog shaking off water.

"How did you do it?" Hannah asked, even though she wasn't sure she wanted to hear Andrea's answer.

"I joined the new gym out at the mall and the minute Grandma McCann gets up to take care of Bethany, I drive out there and go to an early morning exercise class. It's fun!"

Hannah made a face. The only early morning activity she'd dislike more would be flogging. And come to think about it, the two had a lot in common.

"I knew I had to give myself an incentive so I'd go every morning. You know how it is."

Hannah nodded, although she'd never even considered driving to the gym every morning before she went to work.

"I figured that if I looked really good while I was exercising, I'd go. So I bought myself a cute little exercise leotard. It's bright pink spandex trimmed with black. You should see it. It's just darling."

"I'll bet it is," Hannah said and she meant it. Why was it that only people who didn't need to exercise looked good in exercise clothing?

"Anyway, now that I'm down to my regular weight, I decided to go back to work on a part-time basis. With Tracey in school and Grandma McCann taking care of Bethany and doing all the cooking and everything, there's nothing for me to do at home. And besides, I want to pull my own weight financially." Andrea turned to Lisa. "I sold your neighbor's house this morning."

Lisa waited until Andrea had taken a seat at the back table and then she sat down beside her. "Which neighbor?"

"Dora Lambrecht."

"That's great news! It's been vacant ever since she moved out to Colorado to live with Mary Jean, and we miss having a neighbor on that side."

Andrea took a sip of her coffee. Then she noticed the bare tabletop and her pleased expression changed to one of concern. "There aren't any cookies?"

"There are," Hannah reassured her, "but we thought you might like something different for a change. How about critiquing some pastry?"

"That sounds like fun! Now that I don't have to diet, I can splurge a little, especially if it's for a good cause. Bring it out."

"I'm afraid you'll have to go and get it." Hannah delivered the news with a perfectly deadpan expression. "Lisa and I have to stay here."

"I can do that. Is it in the kitchen?"

"No, it's across the street at the Magnolia Blossom Bakery. We need one of everything on their menu, including a half pan of their Southern Peach Cobbler."

Andrea looked completely baffled for a moment, but then she started to grin. "You want me to go get takeout from your competition? And not let Shawna Lee or Vanessa know I'm bringing it back here?"

"That's right. Are you willing to be our spy for the day?"

"I'll do it!"

"I'll give you some money from the register." Hannah pushed back her chair.

"No need. I made a nice commission on the Lambrecht sale and I can afford to treat you. I'll just go out the back door and take my car. That way they won't know I've been in here. And then I'll bring everything right back to you. Just call me Gypsy Rose Lee."

Gypsy Rose Lee? Hannah was stymied for a moment. Her sister had obviously made some sort of connection between the famous stripper and her own role as a spy, but Hannah had no idea what it could be.

"Hold on a second." Hannah caught up with Andrea as she was about to push open the swinging door to the kitchen. "What's all this about Gypsy Rose . . ." The light dawned and Hannah finished her question with a laugh. There *was* a connection, an erroneous one. "You said Gypsy Rose Lee. Do you mean Tokyo Rose?"

"That's it! I always get those two names mixed up. Keep my chair warm. I'll be back in a flash with the goodies!"

* * *

Hannah had just poured herself another cup of coffee when she saw a familiar face at the front door. It was Norman, and he was carrying a package wrapped in bright red paper printed with gold hearts and tied up with a pretty gold bow.

"Hi, Norman," Hannah greeted him when he stepped in. "I thought you had back-to-back appointments at the clinic this morning."

"I did, but Mrs. Barthel called to reschedule. Her husband's gone and her car won't start. She said by the time she called around and found someone who could come and get her and bring her to town, her appointment would be over anyway."

Hannah understood. Helen and Ed Barthel lived at least seven miles from town and most of it was on narrow country roads that were plowed barely wide enough for two cars to pass.

"Coffee, Norman?" Lisa called out.

"Yes, thanks. And a couple of your best cookies."

"Why don't you wait and taste the pastry from across the street?" Lisa suggested. "We sent Andrea over to bring back one of everything."

"Okay, but I bet it won't be as good as your cookies."

"You mean you haven't been over there yet?" Lisa sounded absolutely astounded.

"Not me. I don't see any reason to go there when I'd rather come here." Norman hung up his coat and walked to the back table with his package. "This is for you, Hannah."

"Thank you! But isn't it a little early for Valentine's Day?"

"It's not a Valentine. That's just the only paper I could find at the Red Owl."

"Well . . . thank you," Hannah said again, hoping she didn't look as flustered as she felt. Why was Norman giving her a gift? It wasn't her birthday.

"Open it now. It has to be kept refrigerated."

Hannah gave him a smile and ripped open the package. Life was too short to save paper and ribbon. She stared at the object inside for a moment and then she turned to Norman with a puzzled expression. "Breakfast sausage?"

"Right. After all, today's a special day."

"It is? The only thing special about today is that it's . . ." Hannah stopped in mid-sentence, gave a hoot of laughter, and leaned over to give Norman a big kiss right on the lips. "Breakfast sausage. *Groundhog* Day," she said and then, because it had been so much fun the first time around, she kissed him again.

Chapter Two

"At least the lid is suitable for framing," Hannah commented, eyeing the box that Andrea had just brought back from the Magnolia Blossom Bakery. The two southern sisters had gone all out to make sure anyone who saw their bakery box would remember it. It was gold foil cardboard with a cluster of pink and white magnolia blossoms stamped on the lid.

Lisa stared at the box for a moment. "I thought magnolia blossoms were yellow."

"They can be yellow, pink, or white . . . or any combination of the three. Vanessa told me. They chose the pink and white for their primary colors and carried out the theme inside."

"Pink walls?" Hannah guessed, envisioning a room the color of a piece of bubble gum.

"Creamy white. They used pink on the curtains. There's a mural of a magnolia tree in full bloom on the back wall and they picked up the dark, glossy green from the leaves and used it for an accent color on the counter and the tops of the tables."

"Sounds nice," Hannah said, even though she hated to admit it.

"It's gorgeous. But then again, it should be. Shawna Lee told me they hired a decorator from Minneapolis and she commissioned an artist to paint the mural and the border of magnolia blossoms around the top of the walls."

"Sounds expensive," Norman commented.

"And beautiful." Lisa looked impressed. "I wonder how much it cost."

"Too much for us," Hannah told her, hoping that Lisa wasn't getting any ideas about redecorating The Cookie Jar right in the middle of their current financial slump.

"I can tell you exactly what they paid." Andrea preened a bit, something she always did when she was about to impart inside information. "The decorator's fee was five thousand dollars and that doesn't include any of the furnishings."

"Furnishings?"

"Things like mirrors, tables, chairs, and light fixtures. When I asked about the mural and the borders on the walls, Vanessa told me that the artist charged twelve hundred to paint it. And they paid him another five hundred to design the lid of their bakery box."

"That's a lot of money!" Lisa looked shocked. "It adds up to six thousand, seven hundred dollars."

"Without the tables and chairs, and the other furnishings," Hannah reminded her.

"You're right. I forgot about that." Lisa looked around The Cookie Jar. "At first I was a little envious, but I like our place just the way it is."

Andrea slid one perfectly manicured nail under the tape on the bakery box. "All this reporting is making me hungry. Let's taste their pastry. I can tell you everything else I found out while we're eating."

Hannah wasn't quite sure what she expected, but it wasn't what Andrea uncovered when she raised the lid on the bakery box. There were tartlets nestled in little paper cups, cake doughnuts with various toppings, frosted cupcakes, slices of pie encased in triangular plastic containers, a fudge brownie, several kinds of cookies, and a half pan of Southern Peach Cobbler.

"What's the matter, Hannah?" Norman asked her. "You look disappointed."

Hannah shrugged, examining the array of standard bakery treats. "It's not what I thought it would be, that's all. I guess I was hoping for really different baked goods."

"Like what?"

"Things I've never tasted before, like Shoofly Pie and Apple Pandowdy."

"From the song," Andrea commented, pausing in her effort to remove the baked goods from the box without getting fruit, frosting, or filling on her fingers. "What is Shoofly Pie and Apple Pandowdy, anyway?"

"What *are*," Hannah corrected her. "They're two separate desserts. Shoofly Pie is an open pie filled with molasses and a sweet crumb mixture. Flies are attracted to molasses and that's how it got its name."

"How about Apple Pandowdy?" Lisa asked, clearly fascinated.

"That's similar to an apple pie or a cobbler, except it's made with molasses. It was originally associated with New England, but they make it in the southern states, too."

Andrea looked as if she didn't quite trust her elder sibling. "How do you know all that?"

"I looked up Shoofly Pie and Apple Pandowdy in the dictionary. It was when I was in second grade, right after Miss Gladke taught us the song. I wanted to know what kind of desserts would make my eyes light up and my stomach say howdy."

"The only thing that looks 'southern' in here is the Peach Cobbler," Norman said, eyeing the plastic container that Andrea had set on the table. "And that's only because it's got a little sticker saying it's made with real Georgia peaches."

"Norman's right," Lisa said with a smile. "The cupcakes are just cupcakes like everyone else makes. And the pies are just pies. That makes me feel better already!"

Hannah gave her a warning look. "Don't crow too soon. We haven't tasted anything yet."

"You're right. I don't want to jinx us." Lisa got up to get a knife and cut each portion into four pieces. Then they began to taste each item and Andrea made good on her promise to tell them everything she'd learned about the Magnolia Blossom Bakery.

"They don't know their profit margin." Andrea swallowed a bite of pie and took a sip of her coffee. "They're not bothering to keep track because Vanessa is willing to underwrite the bakery for the first year."

"Must be nice to have an angel," Hannah said, using the term theater people used to describe their backers.

"That's what Bill said when he walked me out to the car."

"Bill was there?"

"Sitting at the counter with Mike. I rode him up one side and down the other for not coming here, but he said they only went there to check out your competition."

Hannah's brows knit together in a frown. According to Herb, Mike had been with Shawna Lee at midnight and perhaps he'd even spent the night. Wasn't that more than time enough to check out her competition?

"Maybe I shouldn't mention this, but it was standing room only and the line at the cash register reached all the way to the back of the room. That's why it took me so long. I had to wait in line."

Thanks for telling me they had a lot of customers, Hannah thought. *It makes me feel much better.* Of course she didn't say what she was thinking. She'd asked Andrea to report on the competition and that was exactly what her sister was doing. "What else did you find out?"

"Shawna Lee didn't make her bed last night and she's got a see-through peignoir set." Andrea glanced at Norman and looked a bit embarrassed. "Sorry, Norman. I forgot you're a bachelor. A peignoir set is a . . ."

"I know what it is," Norman said quickly.

"You do? But how do you . . . ?"

"Tell us more," Hannah interrupted, before her sister could stick her foot any further down her throat.

"Okay. Well . . . she wears tinted contacts. I knew nobody ever had eyes that green! And she takes diet pills prescribed by a doctor in Minneapolis. Do you want to hear what I found out about Vanessa?"

"Sure," Hannah said, indulging their personal spy.

"She's got three raw silk dressing gowns and every single one is printed with magnolia blossoms. She must really have a thing for magnolia blossoms."

"That's interesting, I guess," Lisa commented.

"But it's not really important. The important thing is, Vanessa had at least a dozen pairs of Manolos and they were scattered all over her bedroom floor."

"What are Manolos?" Lisa asked.

"Manolo Blahniks. Designer shoes. Very expensive. I think there might have been a couple of pairs of Louboutins mixed in, and maybe a Choo or two, but I didn't get a chance to really look."

Hannah was amazed. "How do you know all *that*?"

"I snooped. Shawna Lee and Vanessa were both busy at the counter and I had Mother hold my place in line."

"*Mother* was there?" Hannah gulped out the words. Not only had her not-so-loyal customers deserted her, her own mother was patronizing their rival!

"Relax, Hannah. Mother was doing the same thing I was. Luanne and Carrie were waiting for her back at Granny's Attic and she was in line for takeout. They talked about it this morning and they decided to check out your competition."

"Who else was in there checking out my competition?" Hannah asked the critical question.

"Cyril Murphy. He was ordering a box for his mechanics at the garage. He's going to let me know what everyone thinks of their baking."

"That's very . . . helpful. Anyone else?"

Andrea turned to Lisa. "Your dad was there with Marge. I can see a difference already, Lisa. He didn't have trouble remembering who I was and he mentioned you and Hannah by name. I think those new Alzheimer's drugs are working."

"They seem to be," Lisa said, looking very happy until she remembered the other part of Andrea's comment. "Wait a minute. What were Dad and Marge doing *there?*"

"They were sitting with Herb at a table."

"*My* Herb?"

"That's right."

Hannah was beginning to see a pattern and she voiced it as a question. "They told you they were just checking out our competition?"

"That's right! How did you know?"

"Just a guess," Hannah said, trying not to sound too sarcastic. Every once in a while, Andrea could be incredibly naive. "Just for the record, how many people told you they were there to check out our competition?"

"Well . . . there was Dick Laughlin, Kate Maschler, Vera Olsen Westcott . . . she's married now, you know. And Stan Kramer, Charlie Jessup, and Doc Bennett. They were sitting at a table together. Babs and Shirley Dubinski were there. They were half finished and they told me that your fudge cupcakes were a lot better. I talked to a lot of people, and everyone said they were there to try it out so they could tell you. You have some good friends, Hannah."

Hannah sighed and an old saw flashed through her mind. With friends like that, she didn't need enemies.

"What's the matter? You don't look happy."

"Think about it, Andrea. All those friends, the ones who were helping to check out our rivals, were buying their baked goods and paying for them. How much do you think our friends put into the till at the Magnolia Blossom Bakery?"

"I . . . don't know. A lot, I guess. I didn't think about that."

"Lisa and I took in a total of twenty-six dollars and thirty-five cents today. We still have to bake, pay our bills, and keep up on the rent while our friends are across the street stuffing their faces at our competitor's."

"Hannah's right," Norman said, reaching out to pat her shoulder. "I can see going in there once, just to look around and taste something, but a real friend wouldn't abandon you the way they're doing."

"That's what I mean!" Hannah exclaimed. "How many servings of Southern Peach Cobbler do they have to eat to critique it? We've been operating in the red ever since Shawna Lee and Vanessa opened their doors and our *friends* are going to put us right out of business."

Andrea was silent for a moment, and then she sighed. "You're right. But Shawna Lee and Vanessa's desserts aren't that good. At least I don't think they are."

Hannah glanced down at Andrea's plate. She'd only taken one bite of blueberry pie and it was one of her favorites. Another of her favorites, a chocolate cupcake, was intact except for a tiny little nibble mark on the top.

"Andrea's right," Lisa spoke up. "I just tried one of their molasses cookies and they taste like the ones they have at the hospital in the vending machines. I don't think they're fresh-baked."

Hannah reached for a chocolate chip cookie and tasted it. Lisa was right. The cookie part was dry with no discernible flavor, and the chips tasted more like carob than chocolate. "It's not the cookies, or the pies, or the cupcakes," she said, glancing around at the partially eaten pastry.

"Maybe it's the Southern Peach Cobbler," Norman suggested, pointing to the only dessert they hadn't tasted.

"Maybe," Hannah said, and turned to her sister. "Do you know if they serve it hot? Or cold?"

"Hot. They scoop it out into a bowl, stick it in the microwave to heat it up, and top it with a scoop of vanilla ice cream. I watched Vanessa do it before she served it to Bonnie Surma."

Hannah gave a little whimper. Bonnie Surma was one of her biggest supporters, ordering cookies for her Scout troops, and desserts for every party and group meeting she hosted. And now Bonnie had defected to the Magnolia Blossom Bakery for a bowl of their signature dessert!

"We should serve it the way they do, or it won't be a fair test," Lisa said as she picked up the pan and stood up. "I'll go heat it and put on some ice cream."

Once Lisa left, Andrea reached out to take Hannah's hand and give it an affectionate squeeze, a rare occurrence for sisters who'd been raised not to be overly demonstrative.

"What?" Hannah asked, noting the suspicious moisture in Andrea's eyes.

"Do you really think you might lose The Cookie Jar?"

"I hope not, but it doesn't look good."

"Then you're worried?"

"Oh, yes. I just don't want to say much in front of Lisa. She's about to marry the man she loves. I don't want her to have to worry about business."

Norman slipped his arm around Hannah's shoulders. And then he said something he'd never said before. "That's one of the reasons I love you, Hannah. You're always thinking of other people, even when you're in trouble."

"Bill and I talked before he went back to the station." Andrea gave Hannah's hand another squeeze. "If you need to borrow money, we'll take out a line of home equity on the house."

Hannah was so touched it took her a moment to find her voice. "I couldn't ask you to do that, not when I know that Vanessa can afford to run their business at a loss for a whole year. Don't even consider it. You and Bill and the kids come first."

"I'm not married and I don't have kids," Norman said. "I've got some savings and I'll lend you enough to tide you over."

"Thank you, but no," Hannah said forcefully enough to erase all doubt that she'd change her mind. "Both of you are really sweet to offer, but throwing money at the problem won't help. If our business at The Cookie Jar doesn't pick up by the end of the month, it's not going to pick up at all."

"What are you going to do if it doesn't?"

"Liquidate. We'll sell the capital assets and I'll give Lisa her share in cash. She'll be able to find something else, and even if she doesn't, Herb's got a good job."

"But that's just awful! Mother's got money. She

could . . ." Andrea stopped in mid-sentence after one glance at Hannah's expression. "Okay. Forget that. There's no way you want to ask Mother. But family is supposed to stick together and . . . I don't know what else to do! If I could figure out a way to get rid of Shawna Lee and Vanessa, I'd do it in a flash!"

There was a note of panic in Andrea's voice that worried Hannah. Her younger sister was really upset. "Take a giant step back and wait for the Southern Peach Cobbler. If it's good, we have cause to worry. If it's not, we can relax a little. Then the Magnolia Blossom Bakery is just a flash in the pan and our customers will be back when they get tired of inferior baked goods."

As if on cue, Lisa appeared bearing four bowls of Peach Cobbler with vanilla ice cream melting in rivulets on the top. "Here you go. I hope you hate it!"

Hannah laughed. Lisa, who never said anything bad about anyone and seldom criticized anything, was already giving the signature dessert a thumbs-down. "Did you taste it?"

"I had a bite in the kitchen, but don't let that influence you. Make up your own minds."

Andrea raised the spoon to her mouth and took a bite. "This is really good ice cream."

"It's Bridgeman's. Taste the cobbler."

Andrea spooned up a bite of cobbler and tasted it. She chewed, swallowed, and shrugged. "It's funny, but I've got the strangest feeling I've tasted this somewhere before. And before you ask, today's the first time I've ever been in the Magnolia Blossom Bakery."

"But what do you think of it? Is it good?"

Andrea frowned slightly. "There's nothing *wrong* with it. It's . . . okay."

"Just *okay?*" Hannah asked, feeling pleased when Andrea nodded. She tried a spoonful for herself and decided that her sister was right. It was generic peach cobbler, acceptable, but no better than that. "What do you think, Norman?"

"It tastes like the peach cobbler you'd get at a twenty-four-hour coffee shop. There's nothing really wrong with it, but I wouldn't go out of my way to order it again."

"Then we all agree," Hannah said, giving a little sigh of relief. "But this place is empty and theirs is full. If it's not the baked goods, why have all our customers deserted us for the Magnolia Blossom?"

"Do you think it's the outfits they wear?" Norman asked.

"I thought you said you'd never been in there!" Hannah frowned at him.

"I haven't, but Vanessa came in for a checkup and she was wearing her work clothes."

"I should have mentioned their outfits before. It probably has something to do with it." Andrea gave a quick little nod.

"What do they wear?" Hannah asked.

"Short dresses with full skirts and low-cut necklines. And they bend over a lot when they're serving customers. That could be one reason most of the men go there."

"How about the women?" Lisa asked.

"The women go where the men go," Hannah answered. "It's human nature."

"Then there's the contests," Andrea went on.

Hannah frowned. This was the first she'd heard about any contests. "What contests?"

"The ones where you get your order free. If the theme song from *Gone With the Wind* comes on the loudspeakers while you're paying, all you have to do is say, *Frankly, my dear, I don't give a darn!* and whatever you were about to pay for is free."

"I don't give a *darn?*" Hannah asked.

"They changed it because of the kids. Shawna Lee and Vanessa didn't want them running around repeating the real word."

"Of course not."

"Then they've got the flower mug. That's the contest I won."

Hannah groaned. There was a lot Andrea hadn't told them. "What's the flower mug?"

"They serve coffee in white mugs and a couple of them have pink magnolia blossoms painted on the bottom. When your mug is empty, you turn it over to look. If you've got a magnolia blossom, your order is free. I didn't have to pay at all today because my coffee was in one of the magnolia blossom mugs."

"Cute," Hannah said, a trifle sarcastically. "Contests like that are fun for the customers, but they're expensive for the owners."

"Oh, I know. Shawna Lee told me they give away almost three hundred dollars of baked goods every day."

"A lot of new businesses have contests for the first few weeks as part of their grand opening," Lisa said.

"They're doing it for longer than the first few weeks. Vanessa decided they should have two different contests every day for the first three *months* and then gradually taper off. She hired a marketing consultant to think up the contests."

"Oh, boy!" Hannah breathed. There was no way a small, shoestring operation like The Cookie Jar could begin to compete with the Magnolia Blossom's unlimited financing.

Lisa gave a dejected sigh. "We can't afford to give away three hundred dollars of free baked goods every day. And there's no way I'm going to serve coffee in a short, low-cut dress and bend over a lot!"

"No need for that," Norman spoke up. "Not that it wouldn't be scenic, but the way to a guy's heart is through his stomach and your baked goods are a quantum leap better than theirs."

"Then what do you think we should do?" Hannah asked, moving a little closer to Norman's side.

"Just hang on and don't do anything." Norman smiled down at her and then he repeated her personal mantra. "Once the novelty wears off, they'll be back."

 # Chapter
Three

Hannah unlocked her condo door and braced herself for the onslaught. Her cat, Moishe, had been alone since daybreak and he would be eager for food and company.

"I'm home!" Hannah announced, pushing the door open and oofing a bit as her twenty-plus-pound, orange and white tomcat jumped into her arms. This was one of the few times she could baby her normally independent feline roommate and she nuzzled his fur with her chin. "Did you miss me?"

"Yow!" Moishe said, licking her nose.

Since Moishe was purring with the same intensity as a lawn mower stuck on rough-terrain speed, Hannah knew he'd been waiting for her to come home. She shrugged out of her parka coat, juggling Moishe from one arm to the other in the process, and kicked off the moose-hide boots that had earned her a black mark with the Bambi lovers who'd never come within a mile of a moose.

"Dinnertime," Hannah announced, carrying her one-eyed friend into the kitchen and setting him down by his food bowl. Then she headed for the

broom closet where she kept Moishe's food, unlocked the padlock she used to secure the door,
and frowned as she noticed the new bite marks at
the corner of the narrow wooden door. It wouldn't
be long now. Her food-loving cat had chewed
through the veneer on the corner of the door and
he was well on his way to demolishing the wood. *A
lock is only as good as the door.* Hannah remembered
her father's words, the wisdom he'd imparted to
his customers at Lake Eden Hardware. The padlock had Moishe stymied, but he was smart enough
to concentrate his efforts on the hollow-core door.
Her cat was remodeling her broom closet by adding
his own cat-size passage to the mother lode.

Hannah estimated she had about a week before
Moishe invaded the cat food stronghold. It was
time to start thinking about another solution, pre-
ferably one that didn't require an armed guard.
She couldn't really blame Moishe for trying to get
at his food. He'd lived on the street, not knowing
where his next mouse was coming from, and he'd
been half starved when he'd arrived at her door.
Even though almost two years had passed since
that winter day and his girth had doubled with regular meals and then some, he still went into a
panic if he could see Garfield's picture on the bottom of his food bowl.

"Kitty crunchies, or braised liver tidbits?" Hannah
asked her furry roommate. "Or would you like
both?"

The moment Hannah had given him the third
choice, Moishe's purring intensified to a rumble
so loud, she could hear it across the room. Hannah
interpreted that to mean that her feline friend
wanted both liver and kitty crunchies. She would

serve them separately, of course. Moishe fancied himself a gourmet and he didn't like to mix his dry food with his wet food.

Once Moishe had gobbled down his liver tidbits and was happily crunching his dry food, Hannah headed for the bedroom to get into her at-home clothes. In the summer they consisted of lightweight pull-on pants in a nondescript shade of gray and one of several oversize short-sleeved T-shirts in her favorite color, bright red. The red color of the shirts clashed with her frizzy red curls, but there was no one except Moishe to complain. And even if cats were color-blind, a fact that she sometimes doubted, he was content with Hannah's appearance as long as she kept his food bowl full.

"Time for *my* dinner," Hannah announced, entering the kitchen again. She was wearing her winter at-home outfit, a cardinal red long-sleeved sweatshirt with matching drawstring pants. "Are you going to be a pest if I have a Klondike Salad?"

Moishe regarded her with the most innocent of expressions, as if he had absolutely no interest in what she was doing as she took a can of red sockeye salmon from the cupboard and opened it. Hannah harbored no illusion that his disinterest would last any longer than the first whiff of fish-scented air that reached his nostrils. Moishe loved salmon, especially the most expensive kind the Red Owl Grocery had to offer.

True to form, Moishe was rubbing against her ankles before Hannah had drained the salmon. She scraped off the silver skin to save for him, along with the soft column of backbones. Then she flaked the salmon into a salad bowl and put a small bag of frozen green peas in the microwave.

While the peas were cooking, she grated a quarter of an onion and added it to the salmon. Then she peeled and chopped two of the hard-boiled eggs she always kept as a staple in the refrigerator, cooled the cooked peas by immersing them in ice water, and added everything to her bowl. Mayonnaise was next, mixed with a little sweet pickle juice for flavor. A few grindings of pepper from her pepper mill and her salad was finished.

Hannah carried her salad to the living room and took her favorite seat on the couch. Moishe, merely to be friendly of course, jumped up to sit right next to her and leaned over so that his nose was only inches from her bowl.

"I wonder why they call it Klondike Salad," Hannah mused, picking up her cat and moving him a safe distance away. "I guess it's because a lot of salmon comes from Alaska."

Hannah savored every mouthful and Moishe watched her do it. This went on for several minutes until Hannah couldn't stand seeing Moishe track her fork from the bowl to her mouth and then back again one more time. She got the scraps she'd saved for him and put them in a bowl on the coffee table. She was just sitting down again when her phone rang.

"Is it Mother?" Hannah asked the cat whose tail had suddenly swelled into a bush. Moishe wasn't fond of Delores Swensen and he'd shredded several pairs of her panty hose to prove it. As the phone rang again, Moishe's hackles rose and he arched his back like a Halloween cat. It was definitely her mother, Hannah decided, and she reached for the phone. "Hello, Mother," she said.

"Hannah! I'm so glad you're home!"

Delores was breathing hard, in loud little gasps, and Hannah went on instant alert. "Are you all right?"

"No! Something horrible happened and I'm still reeling in shock! I came within an inch of having a coronary!"

The mother who was not known for understatement sounded truly panic-stricken, and Hannah's pulse sped up to crisis rhythm. This could be a real emergency. "What happened?"

"There was a mouse in my hall closet! I just went to hang up my coat and it . . . it ran right over my foot! You've got to help me, Hannah!"

"I see," Hannah said, although she didn't. What did her mother expect her to do? Drive over and chase the mouse out of her house? "Don't panic, Mother. A mouse can be a nuisance, but it can't hurt you."

"I know that. It's just that it *touched* me! You don't know how that makes me feel, Hannah. My skin is just crawling!"

"I'm sorry it upset you, Mother. Do you still have that package of traps Dad kept in the garage?"

"They're on the shelf, but I just can't bring myself to use one. Mousetraps are so cruel."

"Not if you bait them right. Put a little glob of peanut butter right in the center of the bait tray so the mouse's neck is in the right position. Then when he nibbles, the bail snaps forward and . . ."

"I don't want to hear it!" Delores interrupted her daughter's description. "I refuse to use mousetraps, Hannah. They're inhumane."

"Whatever you say, Mother. But you said you wanted my help. What do you expect me to do?"

"I thought you could bring Moishe over here

and he could take care of the problem. It's only a few miles and you told me he was a good mouser."

"You want Moishe to catch your mouse?" Hannah couldn't believe her ears. The woman who thought mousetraps were inhumane preferred letting Hannah's mean feline killing machine loose on her tiny rodent?

"I'll make it worth his while. I've got a package of shrimp in the freezer. You can take it with you when he's done and he can have a nice treat when he gets home."

Hannah started to chortle. "You want to hire my cat as an assassin and pay him off in frozen shrimp?"

"You don't have to put it quite that way. But really, dear . . . I've always hated mice and I won't get a wink of sleep tonight knowing that it's running around loose."

Hannah sighed. That was probably true. The sleeping mind could play all sorts of tricks. Her mother might dream that she was being chased by a giant rodent and *really* have a heart attack.

"Hold on and I'll talk it over with Moishe," Hannah said, unwilling to cave in too easily and encourage more requests for help from her mother. Coaxing Moishe into his traveling crate wasn't easy, and listening to him complain as she drove to town wouldn't be pleasant.

"You have to talk it over with a *cat*? For heaven's sake, Hannah! You're acting as if he's your child!"

"He's better than a child. Think about it, Mother. Moishe doesn't ask for an allowance, he eats cold food straight out of the can, he toilet trained himself, and he's never going to need money for college."

There was silence for a moment and then Delores started to laugh. There were times when her sense of humor won out over her oh-so-proper exterior. Hannah was grinning as she turned to her cat, who was sitting on the coffee table grooming his tail. "What do you say, Moishe? Are you in the mood to do a little mouse hunting for hire?"

As she said the word *mouse*, Moishe's ears tipped toward her, swiveling like miniature satellite dishes. Hannah turned back to the phone. "He's definitely interested," she reported.

"Then you'll come?"

"Of course I'll come," Hannah said, wondering why out of three daughters, a son-in-law, and a whole phone book of friends, Delores always called her when there was a problem.

"Why is he hissing like that?" Delores asked, leaning down to peer into the cat carrier. "Do you think he smells the mouse?"

No, he sees you, Hannah thought but she didn't say it. It was probably best if her mother didn't know how much Moishe disliked her. "He's not fond of traveling," Hannah excused her bristling, hissing pet. And that was a masterful understatement, since her ears were still ringing from Moishe's nonstop yowls of protest all the way from her condo garage to her mother's driveway. "Where's the mouse?"

"In the guest room. He dashed out of the closet and ran in there. I chased after him and shut the door."

Hannah lugged Moishe through her mother's living room, a pale blue room filled with museum-quality antiques and artwork. It was immaculate, as always. Delores didn't clean it herself. Marjorie Hanks, Luanne's mother, came in to polish, dust, wash, and wax every Tuesday and every Friday. In high school science, Hannah had learned that nature abhorred a vacuum and the same could be said for her mother.

"Is it heavy?" Delores asked, as Hannah set the carrier down in the hallway for a moment to get a better grip.

"Yes," Hannah answered, not mentioning that it was one of the more inane questions she'd ever heard. She hoisted her hissing burden, carried him to the guest room door, and set him down again with a grunt. "Okay. He's ready to go."

"He doesn't look very happy about it," Delores said, peering in through the grate again.

"He'll be okay once I let him out of the carrier, but I'd better supervise to make sure nothing gets knocked over. And I think we should shut the door behind us so the mouse can't escape."

Hannah glanced up at her mother. She was a bit concerned about what would happen when she let Moishe out of his carrier. If Delores was in the room with them, he might just decide to shred her stockings before he hunted down the visiting rodent. "You don't want to come in with us and watch, do you?"

"Good heavens, no!" Delores looked horrified. "I'll go put on a pot of coffee. You can come and get me when it's over."

Chapter Four

"It just about killed Moishe not to go for that mouse, but he sat there like a miniature statue of the Sphinx and let it run circles around him," Hannah reported to Lisa as they had an early morning cup of coffee at their favorite table in the back of The Cookie Jar. "I know he wanted it. He was making that excited little ack-ack sound in his throat, the one he always makes right before he pounces on a bug."

"That's really strange, especially because he's such a good mouser. Do you think the strange surroundings threw him off?"

"I guess that could have been a factor, but I don't think so. I'm almost positive he knew he'd be catching that mouse as a favor to Delores."

"And he didn't want to do a favor for someone he didn't like?"

"Right. Do you think I'm crazy for attributing such a complicated motive to a cat?"

Lisa shook her head. "Moishe's not just any cat. He's the smartest cat I've ever met and it wouldn't surprise me a bit if you were right. Was your mother upset when he didn't get rid of her mouse?"

"She doesn't know. I told her she didn't have to worry about the mouse anymore, and I made sure the guest room door was open when we left. I'm hoping it'll go out the same way it got in."

"How about if she sees it again?"

"She'll think it's a different mouse. It's not like they wear name tags, you know. And that might be enough to convince her to let me come over and set traps."

The phone shrilled sharply and Hannah exchanged glances with Lisa. It could be someone with a catering order, but there hadn't been any catering orders for at least a week.

"Your mother?" Lisa asked.

"Mother," Hannah said at the very same time.

The two friends and business partners laughed. Then Hannah got up to answer the phone, hoping that the call had nothing to do with reappearing mice. "Hello, Mother."

"How did you know it was me?" Delores asked. "It could have been someone with a catering order."

"I don't think there's much chance of that."

"You're right, and that's why I called. I was in the Magnolia Blossom Bakery yesterday and it was wall-to-wall people. They're cutting into your business, aren't they?"

"You could say that."

"That's what I was afraid of. We tasted their cobbler and it wasn't anything special. I think that you should make a peach cobbler and give those two a run for their money."

Hannah was silent for a moment. The idea of fighting fire with fire appealed to her. The population of Lake Eden in the winter wasn't large enough to support two bakeries and that meant the Magnolia Blossom had to go.

"What do you think? Will you do it? The Lake Eden Quilting Society meets tomorrow afternoon and I'm in charge of refreshments. I thought I'd order a pan of peach cobbler from Shawna Lee and Vanessa, and a pan of peach cobbler from you. We can serve them side by side and the girls can compare."

"I'll do it," Hannah said. She was spoiling for a showdown, just like John Wayne in *The Shootist.* "This town's not big enough for the both of us."

"The meeting's at one, so I'll pick up the cobbler right before I leave Granny's Attic."

"You don't have to do that. I can deliver it."

"But isn't that your busy time?"

"Not anymore."

"Oh. Well, maybe we can change that. One other thing, dear . . . I picked up another package of shrimp for Moishe. He enjoyed it, didn't he?"

"There's nothing left but the empty package." Hannah told the absolute truth, but not all of it. Moishe had refused to touch the shrimp and Hannah had ended up making shrimp gumbo for tonight's dinner.

"I can't tell you how much I appreciate the way he got rid of that mouse!"

"And I can't tell you what fun he had," Hannah countered. That was true, too. She *couldn't* tell her mother about the fun that Moishe hadn't had.

After Hannah had said good-bye and hung up the phone, she turned to find Lisa staring at her curiously. "Sorry, but I couldn't help but overhear your part of the conversation. Did your mother just give you a catering order?"

"Yes, for peach cobbler. She's ordering one pan from us, and one from the Magnolia Blossom Bakery. The ladies in the Lake Eden Quilting Society are going to compare them."

"It sounds like a Bake-Off where the contestants all have to make the same dish."

"With one important difference," Hannah said, looking slightly abashed. "I was so excited at the prospect of facing down Shawna Lee and Vanessa, I forgot that I'd never made a peach cobbler before in my life!"

"Definitely better," Andrea said, popping another spoonful of Hannah's peach cobbler into her mouth. "You won, Hannah!"

"What do you think, Tracey?" Hannah asked her five-year-old niece, who'd just gotten out of school.

"It's yummy." Tracey nodded so hard, her blond curls bounced. "Can you bake this for my birthday, Aunt Hannah?"

"Sure," Hannah promised. Tracey's birthday was in September and this was February. Tracey would probably change her mind several times in the interim.

"But I always make you a Jell-O Cake for your birthday," Andrea reminded her, sounding a bit hurt.

"I know, Mommy. And that's what I want for my regular birthday cake. Your Jell-O Cake is my very favorite. But I was wondering if maybe, since it's my birthday, I could have two desserts."

"Well . . . I think that might be arranged," Andrea said.

Hannah noticed that her sister was all smiles

again. She'd long thought that her niece would make a great candidate for the diplomatic corps and now she was even more convinced.

Every chair at the back of the coffee shop was filled for this important taste testing. Lisa had called in Hannah's most ardent fans. Lisa's husband-to-be was there, of course. And once Herb had learned the purpose of Lisa's urgent summons, he'd stopped at the community center library to pick up his mother, Marge Beeseman, and Lisa's father, Jack Herman.

"Here comes Daddy!" Tracey called out as Bill Todd, the new Winnetka County Sheriff, came in the front door. Sheriff Todd was accompanied by his former partner and the man who made Hannah's pulse approximate a ragged drumroll, detective Mike Kingston.

"Are we too late?" Mike asked.

"Just in time," Lisa said, dishing up two more bowls. Correctly interpreting that Hannah had been rendered momentarily speechless by the warm smile of greeting Lake Eden's most-wanted bachelor had given her, Lisa told both men to pull up chairs by Delores and Carrie, who'd dashed in from Granny's Attic next door. Winthrop Harrington the Second, Hannah's mother's significant other, sat between Delores and Carrie, and Norman, who'd dropped in between dental appointments, completed the roster of taste testers.

"You're here to compare our peach cobbler with the peach cobbler they serve at the Magnolia Blossom Bakery," Lisa repeated the instructions Hannah had given the others. "We need to know if you think it's better, the same, or not as good."

"Like anybody's going to say it's not as good with Aunt Hannah sitting right here," Tracey said "Sorry, Mommy. I know we're supposed to give our honest opinion, or it won't help. Hi, Dad."

"Hi, sweetheart." Bill pulled his chair in next to Tracey and gave her a kiss. Then he accepted his bowl from Lisa and dug right in.

"Yours is better," Mike said, after taking only one bite. "Their peaches are too mushy."

"That's exactly what I was going to say," Bill added. "Theirs taste like canned, but yours taste like fresh. Where did you get fresh peaches in February?"

"I didn't. They're frozen. The trick is not letting them thaw all the way before you bake them."

"I must remember to tell my cook that technique when I return to England." Winthrop gave Hannah a cordial smile. "It's brilliant, my dear. And your peach cobbler is simply exquisite."

"Thank you," Hannah said in her best effort to be gracious. Winthrop had been the soul of geniality at their infrequent meetings, but she just couldn't seem to warm up to him. She still missed her father and seeing Delores with anyone else was a jolt.

"I think your spices are just right, dear," Delores offered up her opinion.

"Perfect," Carrie agreed. "Their cobbler has so much cinnamon, you can't even tell you're eating peaches. It could be . . . practically anything at all."

"Soda crackers," Jack Herman said, winking at Lisa.

"What?" several in the group chorused.

"Soda crackers," Jack Herman repeated. "Lisa's mother used to make something called 'Mock

Apple Pie.' It used soda crackers and there wasn't an apple in it."

Hannah noticed that Lisa, Marge, and Herb all turned to smile at Jack warmly and that made her feel good. The experimental drug-testing program was working. It wasn't a cure. He still had Alzheimer's and nothing could change that. But his memory had improved and it was no longer such a struggle for him to communicate.

"You know that recipe, don't you, Hannah?" Lisa asked.

"I don't think so. But apples are available all year in Minnesota. Why would anyone want to make a mock apple pie when they could use real apples?"

"Just to see if they could," Norman answered promptly. "It's like training a dog to walk on his hind legs. It's not that he can do it well . . . it's that he can do it at all."

"Samuel Johnson. But it wasn't a dog," Hannah countered, remembering the story of the woman preacher and bristling slightly.

"Tracey has that book, but there's nothing in it about dog training," Andrea said, looking confused.

"What book?"

"*Sam Johnson and the Blue Ribbon Quilt*. It's a picture book Mother gave her. It's about a man who loves to quilt."

Hannah and Norman locked eyes. The message that flashed between them was clear. Neither one of them wanted to embarrass Andrea by explaining that they'd been referring to Dr. Samuel Johnson, not a character in a children's book. Hannah was fairly certain that the closest their eighteenth-century literary figure had come to quilting was to sleep under one.

"Sounds like a good book," Hannah said, because the silence that greeted Andrea's remark was deafening.

"I liked it a lot when I was little," Tracey spoke up. Then she picked up her bowl and turned to Lisa. "Can I have seconds, Aunt Lisa? It's really good!"

Lisa scooped more cobbler into Tracey's bowl and went around the table with second helpings. When she reached Bill, he watched while she broke the crust with the tip of her serving spoon and lifted it out to top the peaches in his bowl. "What's the topping? It tastes a little like something I've had before."

"It is," Hannah said with a laugh. "It's a variation of the topping on your mother's coffee cake. I tried to think of what qualities I wanted, and that was the first taste that popped into my mind."

"Is that how you come up with new recipes?" Carrie wanted to know.

"Yes. I always start out thinking about what it should be and go from there. I decided that this topping should be halfway between a sugar cookie and a sweet biscuit."

"That's exactly what you got," Marge said, plunging her spoon into the topping and smiling as it gave a satisfying crunch. "It's just perfect, Hannah. Really."

"Let's start the poll," Herb suggested, taking out the small notebook he carried in his pocket to write down the license plate numbers of cars that failed to observe city traffic regulations. The first time a plate number appeared in Herb's notebook, the owner got a warning. But if the plate number reappeared, Herb issued a ticket. "The three categories are better, the same, or not as good?" He turned to Lisa for confirmation.

"That's right. Let's start with you, Herb. What did you think?"

"Better. I'll mark myself down."

"Mike?" Lisa continued, going around the table in order.

"A *lot* better."

Mike looked over at Hannah with a smile. Hannah smiled back politely, hoping he hadn't heard her heart thudding in her chest. Mike might think that flattery could get him everywhere and perhaps it could with most women, but Hannah wasn't about to melt down into a little puddle of gratitude every time he decided to pay attention to her.

"If theirs is a one, Hannah's is a ten," Bill said.

"Much, much better," Delores said, turning to smile at Hannah. "The quilting club ladies are going to just love it, especially when I tell Regina that you got the idea for the topping from her coffee cake. It's good of you to give her credit, dear. Some people wouldn't, you know."

Hannah basked in her mother's approval. It didn't come that often and when it did, she enjoyed it immensely. Then she noticed that Delores had cleaned her bowl until it was practically spotless. For the woman who believed that it was polite to leave a few morsels on her plate, this was high praise indeed!

One by one, Lisa went around the table and Herb jotted down the answers. The unanimous result was no surprise to anyone. Hannah's peach cobbler won, hands-down, over Vanessa and Shawna Lee's signature dessert.

"You might know it," Bill said, as his cell phone chimed. He glanced down at the readout on the screen and frowned. "We've got to run, Hannah. There's a three-car pileup out on the interstate."

That was the signal to break up the party. Winthrop left along with Bill and Mike, and Delores and Carrie pushed back their chairs.

"We left Luanne to run the store," Carrie explained, "and she hasn't had her break yet."

"Thanks for coming." Hannah smiled at both of them. "I'll see you out."

Lisa put her hand on Hannah's shoulder. "Sit. I'll walk your mother and Carrie to the kitchen and give them the bowl of peach cobbler I set aside for Luanne."

Once Lisa was back, Hannah smiled at the friends who were left. "You've really been a big help. And as long as you think my peach cobbler is good just the way it is, I'll write up the final version and put it in my recipe book."

"What are you going to call it, Aunt Hannah?" Tracey asked.

"I haven't even thought about that." Hannah knew Tracey wouldn't have broached the subject of naming the peach cobbler unless she had something in mind. "What do *you* think I should call it?"

"Minnesota Peach Cobbler. That way people will know it's from here, and not from someplace else."

"Good idea," Hannah said, giving her niece a thumbs-up. The name was pure genius and it tapped directly into the issue of Minnesota pride. Only a traitor would prefer Southern Peach Cobbler to something from his or her home state.

"Do you think we should have some Minnesota Peach Cobbler at the reception?" Herb asked Lisa.

"That would be wonderful, but Hannah might be too busy to . . ."

"I'll do it," Hannah promised, interrupting her partner's attempt to lighten the wedding workload. She was already making two kinds of cookie cakes, but she'd gladly bake all the desserts for the buffet table if that's what Lisa and Herb wanted.

"Could you bake one for me tomorrow?" Jack Herman asked. "Marge is taking me in for my final dose of brain juice, and I want to give something nice to the nurses."

"Brain juice is what Dad calls the drug cocktail they give him in the clinical trial," Lisa explained, even though everyone had guessed what Jack meant.

"My memory gets better after I take it, and there's only one drawback as far as I can tell."

"What's that?" Andrea asked.

"It makes me remember all the dumb things I did *before* I took it."

"That's ridiculous, Jack." Marge was the first to defend him. "Your memory wasn't the best before. We all know that. But you've never done anything dumb."

"Oh yes, I have. And it's something I'm probably going to regret for the rest of my life."

Jack looked very serious and Hannah reached out to pat his arm. "I'm sure it's not as bad as you think it is. Tell us about it and maybe we can help."

"I don't think anyone can help. You can't unring a bell."

"I know that one!" Tracey spoke up. "I heard a lawyer use it on Court TV, but the judge ruled against him."

"What particular bell are you talking about?" Hannah asked, quite amazed that Lisa's father was speaking figuratively. Before the clinical trial had begun, Jack had taken everything literally.

"I was so excited that Lisa and Herb were getting married, I invited someone who wasn't on Lisa's guest list."

"That's okay, Dad," Lisa was quick to assure him. "There's always room for one more . . . right, Andrea?"

"Absolutely," Andrea responded with a smile. "Don't concern yourself for a second, Jack. St. Peter's can seat over two hundred and I reserved the whole restaurant at the Lake Eden Inn for the buffet reception."

"Oh, I figured there'd be room for one more at the church and the reception. That's not the problem. It's just . . . I don't think Lisa wants this person at her wedding."

Lisa gave a merry little laugh. "I don't know who you could be talking about, Dad. I invited practically everyone in Lake Eden already."

"Not this one. I checked the list."

"Really?" Lisa frowned slightly. "Well . . . if I forgot someone we know, it's probably a good thing you remembered. I don't want to hurt anyone's feelings."

Andrea set her laptop computer on the table, unzipped the carrying case, and powered it up. "Really, it's no problem, Jack. Just let me pull up the file. This laptop comes in so handy. I absolutely couldn't live without it!"

Hannah just shook her head. Although there were things she'd hate to lose, food and oxygen were the only two she absolutely couldn't live without.

"Here we are. I pulled up the guest list," Andrea announced, after a symphony of important-sounding multi-toned beeps. "Just give me the name and I'll add it. And then I'll hand-deliver an invitation this afternoon."

"Okay, if you say so." Jack glanced at his daughter. "You're not going to like this."

Lisa gave him a reassuring smile. "Sure I am. One more guest is no trouble at all, and I like everyone in town. Who is it?"

"Someone I invited before I knew I shouldn't."

"I understand, Dad. Just tell us who it is."

Jack took a deep breath and let it out again. Then he cleared his throat and complied. "Shawna Lee Quinn." And when Lisa's smile slipped, he said, "I'm sorry, honey. I knew you weren't going to like it."

MINNESOTA PEACH COBBLER

Preheat oven to 350 degrees F.,
rack in the middle position.

Note: Don't thaw your peaches before you make this—leave them frozen.

Spray a 13-inch by 9-inch cake pan with Pam or other nonstick cooking spray.

10 cups frozen sliced peaches
    (approximately 2½ pounds, sliced)
⅛ cup lemon juice *(2 Tablespoons)*
1½ cups white sugar *(granulated)*
¼ teaspoon salt
¾ cup flour *(no need to sift)*
½ teaspoon cinnamon
½ cup melted butter *(1 stick, ¼ pound)*

Measure the peaches and put them in a large mixing bowl. Let them sit on the counter and thaw for 10 minutes. Then sprinkle them with lemon juice and toss.

In another smaller bowl combine white sugar, salt, flour, and cinnamon. Mix them together with a fork until they're evenly combined.

Pour the dry mixture over the peaches and toss them. *(This works best if you use your impeccably clean hands.)* Once most of the dry mixture is

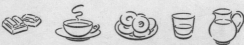

clinging to the peaches, dump them into the cake pan you've prepared. Sprinkle any dry mixture left in the bowl on top of the peaches in the pan.

Melt the butter. Drizzle it over the peaches. Then cover the cake pan tightly with foil.

Bake the peach mixture at 350 degrees F. for 40 minutes. Take it out of the oven and set it on a heat-proof surface, but DON'T TURN OFF THE OVEN!

TOP CRUST:

1 cup flour *(no need to sift)*
1 cup white sugar *(granulated)*
1½ teaspoons baking powder
¼ teaspoon cinnamon
½ teaspoon salt
½ stick softened butter *(¼ cup, ⅛ pound)*
2 beaten eggs *(just stir them up in a glass with a fork)*

Combine the flour, sugar, baking powder, cinnamon, and salt in the smaller bowl you used earlier. Cut in the softened butter with a couple of forks until the mixture looks like coarse cornmeal. Add the beaten eggs and mix them

in with a fork. For those of you who remember your school library with fondness, the result will resemble library paste but it'll smell a whole lot better! *(If you have a food processor, you can also make the crust using the steel blade and chilled butter cut into 4 chunks.)*

Remove the foil cover from the peaches and drop on spoonfuls of the topping. Because the topping is thick, you'll have to do this in little dibs and dabs scraped from the spoon with another spoon, a rubber spatula, or with your freshly washed finger. Dab on the topping until the whole pan is polka-dotted. *(Don't worry if some spots aren't covered very well—the batter will spread out and fill in as it bakes and result in a crunchy crust.)*

Bake at 350 degrees F., uncovered, for an additional 50 minutes.

Minnesota Peach Cobbler can be eaten hot, warm, room temperature, or chilled. It can be served by itself in a bowl, or topped with cream or ice cream.

 # Chapter Five

Valentine's Day dawned bright and clear, and Hannah was up with the first pale rays of winter sun that crested the snowbanks. She made short work of feeding Moishe, chug-a-lugging a mug of strong coffee, and showering before she was fully awake. She pulled on jeans, donned a vivid red sweater in honor of the holiday, and grinned at her reflection in the mirror. Her curly red hair was sticking out like Little Orphan Annie's, but there was no need to pull it back to accommodate a health department mandated hair net today. The Cookie Jar was closed.

The Cookie Jar customarily did a booming business on Valentine's Day, selling heart-shaped cookies with red and white icing, pink frosted cupcakes with hearts drawn on the top in red, Cherry Pies with crusts cut out in heart designs on the top, Strawberry Flips, the cookie that Hannah had invented for last year's holiday, and Cherry Bombs, maraschino cherries baked in cookie dough and dipped in powdered sugar. This year Hannah and Lisa had sold their treats early and while their profits hadn't come close to that of past years, several dozen of their regular customers had come back. Hannah wasn't sure if this was due to her mother's efforts, or if the locals simply wanted to come in the day before Valentine's Day to see how Lisa, the imminent bride, was doing. It didn't matter why they'd come in, just that they had. The Cookie Jar had almost broken even for the first time since the Magnolia Blossom Bakery had opened, and that was a step in the right direction.

Today was Lisa's wedding and there was no way Hannah was going to let her work on this most important of days. That was why she'd put a notice in the *Lake Eden Journal* to tell everyone that they'd be closed. Lisa deserved to sleep in, relax all morning, and think of nothing but the happiness that awaited her.

"I know," Hannah said to the orange and white tomcat that sat on her bed. "I never wear this unless I'm staying home, but we're closed today."

"Owwww," Moishe howled, staring at her for a moment and then turning his back. Since Hannah wasn't sure whether that was a comment about the way her sweater clashed with her hair, or a reminder that his food bowl was empty, she didn't reply.

Fifteen minutes later, with Moishe breakfasted for the second time and Hannah the first, the industrious part-owner of The Cookie Jar got ready to leave. While it was true they were closed, Hannah still had baking to do for Lisa's wedding and their industrial ovens would hold a lot more than the small oven she had at the condo. The wedding cakes were ready. She'd done that last night, preparing a bride's cake and a groom's cake. They weren't fancy and they hadn't required any baking at all, but she was almost positive that Herb and Lisa would love them.

The project had taken a little research. Doing her best to be surreptitious, Hannah had asked about Lisa's favorite cake as a child. The answer had surprised her, as had the answer Marge Beeseman, Herb's mother, had given. Both Lisa and Herb had liked what was known in Lake Eden as "Cream Stacks," one of the easiest cakes to make since there wasn't a bit of baking involved.

Cream Stacks were cookies stacked up like little skyscrapers with pudding between the layers. They were refrigerated overnight so that the cookies could soften and the pudding could set, and then they were frosted with whipped cream. Lisa had preferred graham crackers held together with chocolate pudding mortar, while Herb had favored chocolate wafers cemented with vanilla pudding. Once Hannah had learned all that, she'd started to ponder the question of how to make Cream Stacks festive enough for a wedding cake.

Hannah was nothing if not resourceful and she'd experimented for several days with the ingredients. It was like playing with building blocks and she'd enjoyed herself almost as much as she had as a child. But even though she'd come up with some interesting shapes, including a tower that was worthy of Rapunzel, the Cream Stacks still weren't special enough to serve at the wedding reception.

The solution to her problem had come several nights ago. She'd been watching a cable cooking show with Moishe, and the featured dessert had been an English trifle. As Hannah watched the too-slim-to-have-tasted-any-of-her-own-cooking pastry chef dish out the trifle, the lightbulb went on over her head. There was no reason in the world why she couldn't make Lisa and Herb's Cream Cakes in trifle bowls, unmold them, and frost the resulting layered domes with whipped cream.

The official wedding cake, the one that would appear in the photographs, was being created by Sue Ganske, Lisa's cousin twice removed. Since everyone on Lisa's mother's side was Norwegian, it would be a towering, twenty-layer *Kransekake*, the traditional wedding cake of Norway. As Sue had warned, when she phoned The Cookie Jar with her offer to bake the wedding cake, "You'd better plan on having another cake to serve. *Kransekake* is a sculpture dessert like the French *Croquembouche*. It's so beautiful, nobody wants to eat it."

Hannah could understand that. She'd seen *Croquembouche*, the French dessert made with miniature cream puffs coated with caramel syrup and arranged in a pyramid. Usually displayed on a fancy serving plate, it was drizzled with more caramel syrup spun out into golden threads and then dusted with powered sugar. The elaborate dessert had been displayed at a formal catered dinner Hannah had attended while she was in college. It had looked scrumptious, but none of the guests had tasted it. The *Croquembouche* had made it through the entire party intact, since no one had wanted to be the first to break off a piece.

That college party had taught Hannah an important lesson, and it was the reason the meringues on her pies weren't absolutely symmetrical, and her cookies were usually slightly irregular. When a dessert crossed the line from pretty to a flawless masterpiece, people were afraid to touch it. Hannah had no doubt that the same *Croquembouche* was still making the rounds of the formal college parties, and if anyone ever worked up the nerve to take a taste of the petrified pastry, they'd need extensive dental work.

"I'll be back by three at the latest," Hannah announced to the cat whose head was buried up to his ears in his food bowl. "I have to get dressed for the wedding. You won't mind eating dinner that early, will you?"

Moishe's head snapped up and he stared at her with an expression Hannah interpreted to mean, *Are you kidding? I'll eat any time you feed me. And speaking of food, why don't you fill up this bowl before you leave?*

"Okay, okay." Hannah unlocked the broom closet door and filled his bowl with kitty crunchies. Then she tossed him a salmon-flavored treat shaped like a fish, relocked the door, and shrugged into the long green parka coat Andrea and her mother had given her for Christmas. Once that was zipped up, Hannah clamped a matching knit cap on her head, pulled it down to cover her ears, retrieved her car keys from the saddlebag purse she then slung over her shoulder, and pulled on her fur-lined gloves. Although this whole process had taken less than three minutes, she was already overheated inside the quilted parka, and it was a relief to step out the door and into the sub-zero freezer that Minnesota provided for its residents free of charge during the winter.

The first thing Hannah did when she got out of her car in the parking lot at The Cookie Jar was to unwind the extension cord that was wrapped around her front bumper. One end of the cord was attached to the head-bolt heater that was installed under the hood of her cookie truck. She plugged the other end into the strip of outlets on the outside of her building and mentally congratulated herself for remembering. She'd caught the tail end of the weather on KCOW radio during her trip to town. The current temperature was minus eighteen degrees and the predicted high for the day wasn't expected to reach the zero mark.

It took Hannah several tries to get her key in the lock, but she didn't take off her gloves. Her palms were sweating a bit inside the fur lining and she knew how painful it could be to grasp the metal knob with a moist hand. The moisture would freeze almost instantly upon coming into contact with the cold metal. Then, when Hannah removed her hand to step inside, the top layer of skin on her palm would stay on the outside of the doorknob.

Once inside, Hannah headed straight for the kitchen coffeepot. She'd invested in one with a timer when they'd gone on sale right after Christmas and it had been money well spent. Hot coffee awaited her and it was just what she needed after her long, cold commute.

Hannah was about to take her first sip of coffee when the phone rang. Should she answer it? It couldn't be a business call. Everyone in town knew they were closed for Lisa's wedding day. It had to be someone she knew. And that meant she practically had to answer. Hannah took a quick sip that burned her lip and reached for the phone on the wall. "Hello?"

"You didn't say, *Hello, Mother.*"

Hannah was silent for a moment. Perhaps they had a bad connection, or maybe she was still half asleep. But to her ears, Delores had sounded almost disappointed. "Every time I do that, you tell me that I shouldn't answer the phone that way."

"That's true. You shouldn't. But you've done it so often I've come to expect it. I called to ask you an important question, dear. How's business?"

"There isn't any. We're closed today."

"I know that. When I said business, I meant business in general. I need to know if all the public relations work I've been doing at my clubs is working."

"I think it is," Hannah answered reluctantly. She really hated to discuss her business with Delores now that she was an adult living on her own. But her mother was concerned and Hannah knew she had her best interests at heart. "It's a whole lot better than it was, Mother."

"But it's still not good enough."

"You're right," Hannah admitted. It seemed that the unexplainable mother-daughter radar was working again, and Delores had caught the worry behind her daughter's words. "A couple dozen of our regulars are back, and that's good. And quite a few of the ladies from your groups came in."

"So every day a few more of your former customers come back?"

"That's right. Yesterday was a pretty good day. Everybody that came in wanted to wish Lisa well before the wedding."

"So you showed a profit?"

Hannah opened her mouth to answer in the affirmative, but she'd never been able to lie to her mother. "Not exactly."

"Did you at least break even?"

"Not quite."

There was a long silence on her mother's part and then Delores spoke again. "Maybe it's a passing fad. I just read a report that said most bakeries are suffering because everyone's counting carbs. People just aren't eating as much bread or as many sweets right now."

"I don't think that's got anything to do with it, Mother. Customers are still streaming in across the street at the Magnolia Blossom and they're not featuring low-carb desserts."

Delores was silent again and when she spoke she fairly hissed the words. "Those two *lightskirts!*"

"Mother!" Hannah was shocked. She knew precisely what the phrase meant in the Regency romance novels that her mother liked to read.

"I'm sorry, dear. But Shawna Lee's been trouble ever since she set foot in Lake Eden and her sister's no better. If I don't miss my guess, all this has to do with Mike."

"Mike!"

"Yes. Shawna Lee wants him and you're in the way. She opened her bakery to discredit you and drive you out of business."

Hannah considered that for a moment. Could her mother possibly be right? Jealousy was a powerful motive. "Maybe I should march right over there and tell her that if she wants him, she can have him."

"Oh, don't do that, dear," Delores said quickly. "She'd just deny it."

"Then what do you think I should do?"

"Just announce your engagement to Norman, and that'll leave the field clear for her with Mike. I bet that within two weeks she decides the bakery is too much work for her and she closes it."

Hannah laughed. She couldn't help it. Accepting her mother's advice was a bit like accepting Moishe's offer to baby-sit for a lizard. It was bound to end up in disaster. "Forget it, Mother. For one thing, Norman hasn't asked me to marry him. And for another thing, I'm not sure I'd accept if he did. The best thing for me to do is hang on and hope for the best."

"I suppose you're right"—Delores gave a little laugh—"but it was worth a try. I'd love to see you married to Norman. Mike's all wrong for you. But I do wish there was something I could do to help you stay in business. Can you think of anything?"

"Nothing that's not illegal." Hannah gave a short laugh. "Don't worry, Mother. Things'll work out, one way or another."

Once Delores had signed off, Hannah hung up and returned to her now-lukewarm coffee. The situation at The Cookie Jar was dire, but she didn't want her mother to know precisely how dire.

In desperation last night, Hannah had placed a call to a lender she'd seen advertised on television. OneDay Lenders promised cash within twenty-four hours if you had equity in a house or a condo, and all Hannah had to do was call back after nine o'clock this morning and OneDay's automated system would tell her whether it was a go, or a no. If it was a go, they could hang on for a while longer. If it was a no, Hannah had enough savings to keep them afloat for another two weeks and then they'd have to close shop.

Hannah sipped her coffee and watched the clock. Eight fifty-six. Four minutes to go. She turned to survey the row of empty glass cookie jars on the counter, wishing they were full of freshly baked cookies and there were customers to eat them. Then she glanced back at the clock again. It was still eight fifty-six. Her Grandma Ingrid had been fond of saying that a watched pot never boiled. Was it also true that a watched clock never ticked? And if time flew when you were having fun, did it stall out when you were miserable?

"Oh boy!" Hannah muttered, getting up to pour fresh coffee in her mug. Pondering weighty questions like this before downing at least four cups of coffee was risky. On her way back to her stool, she glanced up at the clock again. Eight fifty-eight. Time *was* passing. All she had to do was kill two more minutes and she could call.

The next two minutes seemed to pass with the speed of epochs, but at last the big hand was on the twelve and the small hand was on the nine. Hannah waited until the second hand had clicked off another thirty and then she dialed the number for OneDay Lenders. The moment her call connected, a recorded voice resounded in her ear. *Your call is very important to us. Our automated loan approval line is in use at the moment, but please remain on the line and your call will be connected in the order in which it was received.*

While Hannah waited for her turn to come, she thought about that recorded voice. Was it true that some grandmother in Iowa had recorded almost all of the messages that companies used on their automated telephone services? And if it was true, did she get residuals like actors whose shows were rerun on television? What would she have carved

on her tombstone, *Please hold and a representative
will be with you shortly?*

At four minutes past nine, her call was connected and Hannah punched in the number she'd
been given the night she called. And the same
recorded voice spoke in her ear, *I'm sorry, but your
loan has not been approved. More documentation is
needed before OneDay can process your request. Please
call the following toll-free number for a detailed explanation.*

Hannah jotted down the number and dialed.
This time she was connected immediately, but the
voice on the phone sounded as if he were reading a
script. "Are you a real person?" Hannah asked.

"I like to think I am," the male voice answered,
and he actually chuckled. "My name is Perry and
I'm your personal loan expeditor. Could I have
your application number, please?"

Hannah rattled off her number and waited.
And while she waited, her pulse raced at break-
neck speeds and her blood pressure reached new
heights.

"Miss Swensen?"

"That's me," Hannah said. "What did you find
out for me, Perry?"

"We need a recent profit and loss statement before we can process your loan."

"You do? They didn't say anything about that
when I applied over the phone last night."

"I know. It's just that since you're self-employed,
we need more information."

"Okay," Hannah said, wondering if she could
get Stan Kramer to come in on the weekend and
prepare one. "From when to when?"

"From the first of January to the current date."

"Uh-oh," Hannah said under her breath.

"What was that, Miss Swensen?"

"Never mind. This profit and loss statement is supposed to show a profit, right?"

Perry paused for a moment; he'd obviously never been asked this question before, and then he answered, "That's right."

"Well, it won't," Hannah said, frowning as her last hope circled the drain and went down. "If it showed a profit, I wouldn't be applying for this loan. But how about my equity in the condo? Is that enough to get any money at all?"

"Not much. Your down payment was minimal and your loan is only two and a half years old. It's a thirty-year and you're paying mostly interest at this point."

"So I'm dead in the water?"

"Pretty much," Perry answered, and then there was a long silence. "You should drop it, Miss Swensen. Go to someone you know and ask for a loan. You sound like a nice person and I don't want to offer you the high-interest loan from OneDay."

"What high-interest loan?"

"When an applicant doesn't qualify, we're supposed to offer a loan that you can't possibly pay off because the payments are too steep. Then, when you default, OneDay takes your property and you end up with nothing."

"Thanks a lot for telling me," Hannah said, and she meant it. Perry had gone out on a limb for her. "So tell me, Perry . . . is OneDay a good place to work? Or can't you tell me?"

"It's horrible. I can tell you that because I just decided to quit and go back to college."

"Good for you!"

"It'll mean moving back in with my parents to save on expenses, but it'll be worth it. For the rest of the day, when anyone calls in, I'm going to tell them the secret of high finance."

"What's that?"

"If you really need a loan, you won't qualify. And if you don't need a loan, all the lenders will line up to give you money."

Hannah thanked Perry and hung up the phone. She had the feeling she'd learned an important truth, but it didn't help her in her current situation. Unless Shawna Lee curled up and died before the next week was out, or Vanessa decided to suddenly pull the plug on her sister's financing, the Magnolia Blossom Bakery was going to drive The Cookie Jar out of business.

 # Chapter Six

Hannah was about to take the peaches out of the freezer when there was a knock at the front door. She ignored it. Everyone in town knew they were closed. But the knocking persisted and after a few more seconds of the noise, Hannah headed for the swinging door to the coffee shop to see who was pounding on the door.

The sight that greeted Hannah's eyes made her smile. There was a deliveryman standing at the front door and he was holding a bouquet wrapped in gold paper. His bright blue truck had a familiar logo painted on the side and Hannah knew he was from Bouchard's Bouquets, the florist based out at the Tri-County Mall.

As Hannah headed for the door to let him in, she wondered if she ought to tell him to move his truck. Main Street had nose-in parking and he was parked parallel with the curb, occupying three full spaces. Then she remembered that Mayor Bascomb and the Lake Eden city council had given Herb a full day off to get ready for the wedding and he wouldn't be giving out traffic tickets today. Since they hadn't hired anyone temporary to fill in for Herb, the deliveryman was safe.

Hannah made short work of opening the door. It wasn't often that anyone sent her flowers. "Come in and warm up. Are those for me?"

"If you're Hannah Swensen, they are." The deliveryman stepped inside and handed her the bouquet. "The guy that called in the order said you were closed today, but you'd be here anyway."

"Which guy was that?"

"Kingston. It's on the card."

Hannah's smile grew wider as she reached for the card, but she didn't open it. She'd wait until she didn't have an audience. "How about a cup of coffee, Kyle?" she asked, reading the name that was embroidered over the florist's logo on the breast pocket of his parka. "I've got a pot on in the kitchen."

Once Kyle had been seated at the workstation and taken his first sip of coffee, he gazed around the kitchen. "Nice big place you've got here. My wife, Judy, would go crazy for ovens like that. She's always saying hers is too small. You're not baking?"

"Not today. I've got some cookies from yesterday if you don't mind eating day-olds."

"I don't mind," Kyle assured her. "I've never been in here myself, being from Elk River and all, but a lot of people say you've got the best cookies. When the Lake Eden Gulls played the Elks last Friday night, your coach brought our coach a bag of your Walnuttoes."

"I didn't know that!" Hannah was pleased and she made a mental note to thank Jordan High's new head coach, Drew Vavra, the next time he came into The Cookie Jar. "Do you like strawberries, Kyle?"

"They're my favorite fruit."

"Good," Hannah said and headed for the walk-in cooler. "We made Strawberry Flips yesterday. Let's see how you like them."

The light coating of powdered sugar had melted into the cookie during the refrigeration process, and Hannah dusted the cookies a second time. It made them a little sweeter, but Kyle looked as if he had a sweet tooth. Then she carried the plate to the table and waited for Kyle to taste them.

"Mmm, good!" Kyle said after his first bite. "These look like the strawberry tarts my mother used to bake, but they're smaller and they taste a lot better."

"Better not let your mother hear you say that!" Hannah warned him, prompting a discussion of how mothers always wanted their children to like their cooking best.

Kyle had a second cup of coffee and ate another three cookies as time ticked away. Hannah knew she had to get to work soon. Once the peach cobbler was baked, she had to run out to the Lake Eden Inn to deliver the wedding cakes and consult with Sally about when to frost them.

"Would you like to take the rest of these cookies with you for the road?" Hannah asked him in an effort to nudge him out the door.

"You bet!" Kyle took the hint and stood up while Hannah packaged the cookies. "I'd better get a move on or the truck'll cool off and the rest of my flowers will freeze. That bakery across the street is open, isn't it?"

"Yes, it is."

"Good. I've got a delivery for the lady that owns it."

Hannah almost stopped in her tracks as an extremely unpalatable possibility occurred to her. She'd have to be careful how she phrased her question so that Kyle didn't realize he was telling tales out of school, but suspicious minds needed to know.

"It's a good thing he got flowers for Shawna Lee this year." Hannah put on a big smile for show. "Last Valentine's Day all he did was send a card and she wouldn't speak to him for at least a week."

"Yeah, the ladies expect more than a card. And let me tell you, a dozen roses don't come cheap this time of year, especially when they're a color we don't normally stock. Kingston wanted yellow, because they're her favorites. And they're twice as expensive as your red ones."

Hannah gritted her teeth and managed to hold on to her smile until Kyle had left. If she'd known he was carrying a bouquet for Shawna Lee in his truck, she would have kept him talking until her rival's expensive yellow roses turned into ice cubes. She had half a notion to dump the bouquet Mike had sent to her in the trash, but that was a waste of good flowers.

Even though she was upset, Hannah found a vase for her roses. They were beautiful, and their lovely scent wafted out to permeate the whole kitchen. Perhaps Mike hadn't known that Shawna Lee's flowers would be more expensive than hers. He'd probably just rattled off his credit card number and assumed that all roses were equal, even in the off-season. But why had he sent Shawna Lee roses in the first place? Was it merely a friendly gesture toward the woman who'd once been his secretary? Or did it mean more than that?

Hannah reached for the little white envelope that had come with her bouquet. She pulled out the card, read the message, and immediately felt a whole lot better. The card was a preprinted one that proclaimed *Happy Valentine's Day* in flowing red script, but Mike had dictated a note on the back that said, *I volunteered to work during the wedding, but I can make the reception. Save the first and last dance for me? I've got something special for you and I'll follow you home.*

At least Mike wasn't taking Shawna Lee to the wedding. Hannah let out a relieved sigh. And it was nice of him to volunteer to work so the deputies who'd known Lisa and Herb all their lives could attend the ceremony. The second half of his note pleased her even more. It meant that he wasn't taking Shawna Lee to the reception either, since he wanted to dance the first and last dance with her and follow her home. And what was the *something special* he was going to give her?

Hannah gave a little shiver of excitement as she considered the possibilities, none of which she would have discussed with anyone other than herself. Then, rather than spend her morning speculating on something that might or might not come to pass, as pleasant as that speculation might be, she headed to the freezer to get the peaches.

She'd taken all of two steps before the phone rang. Hannah turned around to glare at it balefully, but she reached out to answer. It could be

Mike and if it was, she wanted to thank him for her roses.

"Hannah? I'm so glad I caught you!" It was Lisa and she sounded panic-stricken. "You haven't made your peach cobbler yet, have you?"

"Not yet. What's the matter?"

"We've got a problem. I just found out she's bringing *her* peach cobbler."

"Who is?"

"Shawna Lee. She called the Lake Eden Inn to tell Sally she wanted to bring us three pans for a wedding present, but Dick answered the phone. And when she asked him if there was room for her cobbler on the dessert table, Dick checked the diagram of the table that Sally drew up and he said there was a spot for peach cobbler right in the middle of the table."

"And it was my spot?" Hannah asked, guessing the rest.

"You got it. I just got off the phone with Sally. She offered to throw out Shawna Lee's peach cobbler and serve yours instead, but yours looks different and Shawna Lee's bound to notice. Do you think I should just bite the bullet and call Shawna Lee, and tell her not to bring her peach cobbler?"

"You can't."

"Why not?"

"Because it's a wedding present," Hannah said, remembering her mother's advice to be gracious about accepting gifts, even if you didn't want them. "If you want to be polite, you're going to have to accept her peach cobbler with a smile and thank her. I haven't started baking yet, so I'll just forget about bringing mine."

"But we like yours better!"

"I know and I'll bake it for you any time you want it . . . just not today. There's enough trouble at big weddings without asking for more."

"That's true. Aunt Ruth's called three times to complain about the seating arrangements. She thinks she should be at the head table."

"But that's just for the wedding party, and the bride and groom's immediate family."

"I know, but she doesn't think Dad should be sitting with Marge. She said it's bad enough that everyone knows they're going to be living in the same house, and appearing at the head table as a couple is just rubbing it in."

"I think your Aunt Ruth needs a nose-ectomy. Then she couldn't stick it where it doesn't belong."

"That's funny!" Lisa said, and promptly burst into giggles. "Just wait until I tell that to Herb."

Hannah felt good as she signed off and hung up the phone. She'd given Lisa good advice about the cobbler, and she'd made her laugh in the midst of what sounded like crisis mode at the Herman residence. As far as Hannah was concerned, big weddings were more trouble than they were worth. You could think things out very carefully and do your best to plan for any contingency, but some guests always ended up with hurt feelings before the day was over.

"No big wedding for me!" Hannah said, heading to the walk-in cooler to get the wedding cakes. But she'd taken no more than a step before the phone rang again. It was probably Lisa, calling back to find out if she absolutely, positively had to accept Shawna Lee's peach cobbler.

Hannah lifted the receiver and said, "Yes, you have to accept the cobbler. Your wedding consultant, an authority on matters of good taste, will tell you the same thing."

"What!"

Hannah laughed as she recognized the voice that had uttered the bewildered comment. It was Andrea, not Lisa. "Sorry about that. I thought you were Lisa."

"What's all this about good taste?"

"Lisa wanted to know if she had to accept a wedding present, even if she didn't want it. And I said she did. What can I do for you?"

"I just found out that I can't use white doves and I don't know what to do!"

"Why were you going to use them?" Hannah asked, envisioning a flock, or whatever you called the dove group, of white doves flying to the top of the church and cooing at the people.

"They're a symbol of the transition between girlhood and womanhood. When Lisa steps out of the church as Herb's wife, the handler was supposed to set the doves free."

"What happens to them after they fly off?"

"Oh, they don't. They're trained to circle around until they find their cage again and get back in. There's food in there and the handler makes sure they're hungry."

"Okay. I get it. Why can't you use them?"

"Because it's below zero and the handler won't let them out in such cold weather."

"That's reasonable."

"I know. I don't want to see them catch a bird cold, or whatever might happen if he brought them. But I need something else to take their place. Can you think of anything I could use to symbolize the transition between girlhood and womanhood?"

"Oven cleaner," Hannah replied promptly, but Andrea didn't laugh. Her sister was really upset about the doves. "Forget that. What's wrong with using little bags of rice? People always throw rice at a wedding."

"But that's supposed to symbolize children, and Lisa and Herb don't want children right away."

"Mother will bring rice anyway. She always does."

"I know, but I can't control Mother. I just want something else, something nice."

"Let me think," Hannah said, kicking her brain into high gear. "How about flower petals? They're nice to handle, they're clean, and they're environmentally friendly."

Andrea was silent for a moment while she thought it over. "That would be wonderful," she said at last. "I can just see all those bright flower petals against the snow. But what do they symbolize?"

"The natural progression from a rosebud to a bloom exactly parallels the rite of passage from a girl to a woman," Hannah said, making it up as she went along. "The petals mingle as they fall together and that signifies the union of marriage."

"That's beautiful!" Andrea breathed.

"I thought so. Do you think it'll work?"

"I don't see why not. You just made that up, didn't you?"

"Yep."

"Well, it's brilliant. I'll call Father Coultas and ask him to mention it during the ceremony. Thanks, Hannah. You saved me."

"Anytime," Hannah said and hung up the phone, wishing someone would save her. If there were any more phone calls or knocks on the door, she'd never get anything done. She headed for the pantry, and this time she got almost all the way across the kitchen before she heard a knock at the back door.

Should she answer it, or shouldn't she? Hannah debated that question for a moment. And then she called out, "Who is it?"

"Norman. Let me in, Hannah. It's cold out here!"

Hannah wasted no time unlocking the door and ushering Norman to a stool at the workstation. "You look half frozen. Coffee?"

"Please. Maybe it'll thaw me out. The sun's shining, but it hasn't warmed up yet, and I didn't drive the car far enough to take off the chill."

"If it doesn't get any warmer than this, people had better use the plug-ins on the poles in the church parking lot. Father Coultas tends to get wordy at weddings."

Norman clasped both hands around the mug of coffee that Hannah brought him and after a moment he flexed his fingers. "They're working again."

"Yes, but can you hold a drill?"

"I don't have to. I just finished my last appointment of the day." Norman reached into his pocket and pulled out a small box wrapped in shiny pink paper. "This is for you. Happy Valentine's Day."

"Thanks!" Hannah reached out for the box with pleasure. "You didn't have to, Norman."

"I didn't? Then maybe I'd better take it back."

"Over my dead body," Hannah announced, tearing off the pink paper in one well-placed swoop. And then she was perfectly silent as she gazed at the blue velvet-covered jeweler's box she'd unwrapped.

"Open it," Norman urged her. "If you don't like it, you can exchange it. I got it at the jeweler's in the mall."

Hannah gripped the hinged lid with shaking fingers. What if there was an engagement ring inside? She did love Norman, there was no doubt in her mind about that, but did she love him enough to marry him?

"Go ahead. I want to find out if I guessed right."

Hannah steeled herself for what was about to come and lifted the lid. Inside, on a pillow of white satin, rested the most exquisite heart pendant she'd ever seen. She gave a relieved smile, half glad and half sorry that it wasn't an engagement ring, and took a closer look. The pendant was made of brushed gold and it was attached to a thin gold chain. In the center of the heart was an incredibly beautiful, elaborately faceted, dark red stone.

"Do you like it?" Norman asked and Hannah thought she heard a slight note of anxiety in his voice.

"It's the most gorgeous thing I've ever seen! But it must have cost a lot of money and I shouldn't accept something that expensive as a gift. That's not a real ruby, is it?"

"Would you feel better about accepting it if I told you it was synthetic?"

Hannah thought about that for a moment. "I think I would."

"It's not a real ruby. Put it on, Hannah. I've been imagining you wearing it ever since I bought it."

Hannah took the pendant from its bed of satin and grinned when she noticed the length of the chain. It was just long enough to slip over her head, eliminating the need for a clasp, and just short enough so that it wouldn't get in the way when she was working. Either Norman had gotten lucky at the jewelers, or he'd put a lot of thought into buying the perfect present. Knowing Norman, it was the latter rather than the former.

"It looks perfect on you," Norman said. And then he grinned as Hannah leaned across the stainless steel surface of the workstation and gave him a grateful and enthusiastic kiss. "If I'd known you'd kiss me like that when I gave it to you, I would have tried for a twofer."

Hannah laughed and kissed him again, and this time he kissed her back. The moment was perfect until the phone started to ring.

"Are you going to get that?" Norman asked.

"I suppose I should. It's probably Sally, wondering what time I'm going to get there. I promised her I'd drive out before noon with the wedding cakes."

"If it's Sally, I'll drive you."

Hannah was about to say that she could handle it when she recalled her long, cold trip into town. The interior of her Suburban was so cavernous there were areas that never seemed to warm up. And her left foot, only inches from the heater vent, was directly exposed to a draft of freezing air from a hole that Cyril Murphy and his chief mechanic at the garage had never been able to plug.

"Thanks, Norman. I'll tell her we're coming out together," Hannah said, reaching for the phone. Norman was generous, considerate, thoughtful, and timely. And even more important on this frigid winter's day, the heater in his car worked perfectly.

STRAWBERRY FLIP COOKIES

Preheat oven to 375 degrees F.,
rack in the middle position.

1 cup melted butter *(2 sticks)*
1 cup white *(granulated)* sugar
2 beaten eggs *(just whip them up with a
    fork)*
⅓ cup seedless strawberry jam
1 teaspoon strawberry extract *(or vanilla,
    if you can't find it)*
1 teaspoon baking powder
½ teaspoon soda
½ teaspoon salt
1½ cups chopped walnuts *(or pecans)*
3 cups flour *(not sifted)*

small bowl of powdered *(confectioner's)*
    sugar
1 bag frozen strawberries for garnish***

****If fresh strawberries are available, they'll be fine
in this recipe.*

Melt the butter and add the white sugar. Then
add the eggs and the strawberry jam. When the
jam is fully incorporated, add the strawberry ex-

tract, baking powder, soda, and salt. Then add the chopped walnuts and the flour, and mix well.

Roll dough balls with your hands about the size of unshelled walnuts. *(If the dough is too sticky, chill it for a half hour or so and then try it again.)* Roll the dough balls in the powdered sugar and place them on a greased cookie sheet, 12 to a standard sheet. Make a deep thumbprint in the center of each cookie.

While the strawberries are still partially frozen, cut them in half lengthwise. *(If your berries are too large to fit on your cookie balls, cut them in quarters instead of halves.)* Flip the cut piece over and place it skin side up in the thumbprint you've made on top of each cookie.

Bake at 375 degrees F. for 10 to 12 minutes. Cool on the cookie sheet for 2 minutes, then transfer to a wire rack to finish cooling. Dust the cookies with powdered sugar and place them on a pretty plate before serving.

Yield: 7 to 8 dozen cookies.

The tart strawberry pieces are wonderful with the sweet cookie. Carrie Rhodes just adores these.

As a variant, you can also makes these with seedless raspberry jam and whole fresh raspberries on top.

 # Chapter
Seven

Hannah arrived at the front door to St. Peter's Catholic Church out of breath. Her lungs felt like they were on fire from breathing in the frigid air while racing up all twenty-seven steps to the massive carved wooden door. She pulled it open, dashed inside, and slipped out of her boots on one of the long woven mats that had been placed in the foyer for that purpose. Except that it wasn't called a foyer when it was in a church. It was called—Hannah frowned, trying to remember—narthex. That was the correct word, but she'd never actually heard anyone call it that.

There was a bench just inside the door, and Hannah switched to the shoes that were dyed to match her dress. It was an indigo blue knit that her downtown neighbor, Claire Rodgers at Beau Monde Fashions, had chosen for her.

After several gulps of the warm air inside the narthex, Hannah pushed open the double doors that led to the nave, and glanced around for her sister. Andrea had called Hannah at the condo, begging her to come to the church early. Hannah had complied, dressing in a flash, changing the gravel in Moishe's litter box to prevent any acts of feline disobedience that might occur if it wasn't pristine, and rushing out the door. She wasn't sure what Andrea needed, but her sister had sounded at the edge of panic.

"Andrea?" Hannah called out, shivering slightly. The sun had fled while Hannah was getting dressed and the skies had turned to slate gray. Even though it was still daylight, the interior of the church was full of shadows. The lights were off and the muted stained glass windows in the nave didn't add much illumination. Being alone in a cavernous church without lights was grist for the horror movie mill.

"Andrea?" Hannah called out again, jumping slightly as she heard footsteps above her.

"I'm up here in the choir loft, putting some finishing touches on the garlands. Go out and close the door. And then wait for me to call you in again. I want you to get the full effect."

"You want me to wait in the narthex?"

"The *who?*"

"The narthex. That's what they call the foyer in a Catholic church."

"Oh. Yes, wait in the whatever-it-is. I'll call you when I'm ready."

Hannah did as she was told. Andrea sounded very serious. She stood outside the door for a minute or two, until she heard Andrea calling her name.

"I'm coming," Hannah called back and pushed the door open. She took one step inside and stopped in her tracks as the full effect her sister had mentioned hit her. The interior of the church flickered with light from dozens of candelabras holding multiple candles in every conceivable shade from snow white to deep blood red. They sat on wrought-iron pedestals along the church walls and they were interspersed with tall white wicker baskets of pink, white, and red roses.

"Incredible!" Hannah murmured, breathing in the heady scent of the entire rose garden that had given up its blooms for her sister. "It's just gorgeous, Andrea!"

"I know. It would have been even more impressive if I'd used real candles, but Father Coultas didn't want to take the chance with all the old wood in here."

"The candles aren't real?" Hannah was surprised when she stepped closer and saw that the candelabras were plugged into a power strip on the floor. "You fooled me, and I bet you'll fool everybody else, too."

"I hope so, and that's why I needed you to come early. The lights are on a dimmer switch and I need to get the level just right. If they're up full, people are going to see the power cords, but if they're too low, they won't see the flowers or the rest of the decorations. I'd do it myself, but the dimmer switch is in the office and I have to keep running back and forth."

It took a few minutes to get it just right, but at last the dimmer switch was set to Andrea's satisfaction. Hannah raided the office to find supplies and taped the knob in place so that no one would mistakenly change the level of lumens they'd taken such pains to achieve.

"I'm going to run home and get dressed," Andrea said, slipping into her coat. "Do you want to come along? Immelda's coming in early to run through the music, but nobody else should be here for at least forty-five minutes."

"I'll stay here and admire your decorations. It's like sitting in the middle of a rose garden and I'm enjoying it too much to leave."

Once Andrea left, Hannah headed to the ladies' room to repair the damage the winter wind had done to her appearance. That didn't take long. All she had to do was shake her head back and forth a couple of times, fluff her curls up with her fingers, and pat them into some semblance of shape again. As she headed back into the main part of the church and took a seat in the back pew, Hannah realized that there was an advantage to having unruly curls. Her coiffure looked the same whether she'd stepped out of a gale-force wind, or just finished brushing it.

The church was dim and restful, and the electric candles really did look real. Hannah closed her eyes to more fully appreciate the illusion of a garden and breathed in the perfume of the roses. She imagined it was summer, not winter, and the air was heavy with promise. The furnace, far below her in the basement of the church, gave off a faint hum that reminded her of the lazy droning of honeybees as they meandered from blossom to blossom.

Hannah smiled as she imagined a brightly colored butterfly flitting between tall stocks of hollyhock, pausing to alight on one for a moment and then fluttering away. She could feel a light breeze blowing, just enough to make the tendrils of hair at her temples quiver and tickle the skin on her arms.

Time passed and Hannah's imaginary garden changed with it. As dusk approached, long shadows made the sunflowers seem to sway on their stems, their large open blossoms too heavy for the thinner, cooler night air. Their petals furled, tips gathering to the center as the last rays of sunlight faded to darkness and the moon replaced the sun.

Fireflies came out to play and Hannah glanced down to find that she was dressed for a garden wedding under the stars. The familiar strains of Mendelssohn floated up toward the sparkling stars that dotted the heavens and guests began to arrive to sit on white cushions on the carpet of smooth grass. Hannah was in bridal white, a vision of loveliness in her spotless baker's apron. She held a lace-covered cone of cookies, each one resembling a flower, and Tracey was there with a similar cone, passing out cookies to the guests as they arrived. There was a circlet of baked meringue on her head to hold her gossamer veil in place, and the veil itself was made of spun sugar that shimmered in the moonlight. And then the music swelled and it was time for her to walk to the latticework gazebo that was made of gingerbread to join her groom.

Hannah took her place and glanced to the side to see the face of the man she was about to marry. But her veil had turned translucent and although she could see his form, she couldn't make out his features. As she squinted, desperately trying to see who it was, the music grew soft and the ceremony started.

It was a strange ceremony. The familiar phrases were indistinct and more like the music of muted

horns than any language she recognized or re-
called. The officiate wasn't anyone she knew, not
Reverend Knudson, or Father Coultas, or Reverend
Strandberg from the Bible Church. It wasn't even
a male, as Lake Eden tradition practically dictated.
Instead, the minister was a girl, a mere child, and
she said, "And I now pronounce you man and . . .
Aunt Hannah."

Aunt Hannah? Even in Hannah's dream state,
she knew that wasn't part of the ceremony. But
then, as she was about to supply the correct
phrase, the child minister said it again.

"Aunt Hannah."

Hannah jerked fully awake and blinked as she
found herself looking up into her niece's anxious
face. It had been a tough week and she must have
dropped off to sleep.

"Are you okay, Aunt Hannah?"

"Fine," Hannah said, gathering herself together
as best she could. "I was meditating on the meaning of marriage."

Tracey grinned. "No, you weren't. You were
sleeping. But that's okay. Nobody saw you but me."

"Did you drive here alone?" Hannah asked, recovering enough to tease her favorite five-year-old.

"Yes, but I let Daddy take over once we stopped
at the church and he's parking the car. Mommy's
downstairs, checking to make sure she's got
enough pins for the flowers that the men have to
wear. What are they called again?"

"Boutonnieres."

"That's right. And it's because they go in the
buttonhole. I looked it up in the dictionary you
gave me for my birthday. Everything's in there, even

the German words Karen's grandma and grandpa used when they talked about her Christmas present."

Hannah's brows shot up at this reference to Tracey's best friend, Karen Dunwright. "Karen remembered the words and you looked them up in the German-English section of your dictionary?"

"That's right. It was just great, Aunt Hannah. Karen knew what she was getting before she even opened her present. I did it for Calvin, too. His grandparents speak French."

Hannah sent up a silent prayer that the grandparents of Tracey's friends never found out, but she grinned as she got to her feet. She was vindicated. Delores and Andrea had thought she was crazy buying the massive unabridged dictionary as a present for Tracey, but Hannah had been sure that her niece would use it.

"Do you like my dress?" Tracey whirled around, an exact imitation of the model's turn that her mother had given in The Cookie Jar the other morning. She was wearing a wine red velvet dress with an empire waist and white roses embroidered around the neckline and the hem.

"You look lovely. That's a beautiful dress and it makes you look very grown-up."

"That's silly, Aunt Hannah. I'm not any older than I was before I put it on."

"I know. It's just that it looks like a dress an older girl would wear. And you're wearing lipstick."

"Only because the lights are dim here in church. Mommy said it was like makeup for a child actor, not like makeup for when you're old like she is. I have to take it off before we go out to the reception."

"That's probably wise," Hannah said with a nod. "You wouldn't want to look too old, or people might think you were the bride."

Tracey laughed, an action that made her blue eyes sparkle. Hannah's niece was already a beauty and she had the classic features that would grow even more attractive as time passed. It wouldn't be long before the boys would notice how pretty Tracey was, and Hannah didn't want to see her grow up too fast.

"Come on, Aunt Hannah. Mommy said to bring you downstairs so she can put some makeup on you. She wants you to look good for the wedding."

Hannah knew there was no use arguing. Andrea was already a ball of nerves from imagining the catastrophes that might happen during the ceremony and the reception, and she'd only get more nervous if Hannah didn't cooperate.

"I'm right behind you," Hannah said, sliding out of the pew and following Tracey to the steps. "But do you really think I need makeup?"

"It's not that you *need* it. You always look beautiful to me. But Mommy thinks you need it, and we want to keep her happy, don't we?"

"Absolutely," Hannah said, feeling more like Tracey's co-conspirator than her aunt as they hurried down the steps to the dressing room where Andrea was waiting for them.

"I now pronounce you man and wife. You may kiss the bride."

Hannah blinked back tears as Herb folded back Lisa's veil and kissed her. She wasn't sure why she always cried at weddings, but she did. She glanced at Andrea and saw that her sister was wiping her eyes on Bill's handkerchief. A glance at their mother confirmed that crying must run in the family, because Delores was dabbing at her eyes with a white lace handkerchief.

She was about to turn back to listen to the rest of the ceremony when she realized that Winthrop was no longer sitting at her mother's side. Had he decided a small-town wedding was so boring, he'd taken a powder and risked alienating his ladylove? But then she saw him slipping in through the door of the church and walking forward unobtrusively until he reached the pew where Delores was sitting.

Where had he gone? Hannah wondered, knowing it could have been anywhere including the men's room downstairs. Delores looked up as he slid into the pew and handed her a silver tote bag Hannah recognized. The tote was filled with several dozen small packets of rice that Delores and everyone surrounding her would toss at the new bride and groom. The mystery of Winthrop's disappearance was solved. Delores had left the rice in the car and she'd sent Winthrop back out to the parking lot to retrieve it.

Delores reached out to take Winthrop's arm and Hannah wished that she'd turned away a few seconds earlier. Her mother's face was radiant. It was apparent that she cared about Winthop a lot more than Hannah and her sisters wanted her to.

For Pete's sake, Mother. He just went to the car. It's not like he was out slaying dragons for you, Hannah thought, frowning a bit. She stared, willing her mother to turn and pay attention to Lisa and Herb, but the mother-daughter radar must not have been working because Delores just smiled and slid a bit closer to Winthrop's side.

"And now I give you Mr. and Mrs. Herbert Beeseman," Father Coultas announced, turning Herb and Lisa around so they faced the congregation and giving the signal for Immelda Giese at the organ to play the recessional.

As the newlyweds began their walk down the aisle, stopping every foot or so to exchange words with friends and relatives, Hannah saw Andrea beckoning to her frantically from the rear of the church.

Me? Hannah indicated her question by tapping her chest and Andrea responded with several definitive nods. And then she gave another signal for *Come here right now*, by opening her mouth in a silent yell and beckoning frantically again.

Hannah wasted no time sliding out of the pew and rushing down the side aisle to the back of the church. When she reached Andrea's side, her younger sister grabbed her by the arm and rushed her into an alcove.

"What is it?" Hannah asked, resisting the urge to yelp as Andrea's nails dug into her arm.

"The chauffeur slipped on the ice when he got out of the limo and broke his arm. Doc Knight had to take him to the hospital, and now I need a substitute driver."

"Bill?"

Andrea shook her head. "He has to lead the procession in the squad car, and Mike's out at the station filling in for everybody else."

"How about Norman?"

"His car is all packed with photography equipment so he can take candids at the reception.

You've got to help me, Hannah. I called the company and they're sending a replacement driver, but he won't be here for at least an hour. The newlyweds and their parents will be here any minute and I need *somebody* to drive them to the reception!"

"And you want that somebody to be me?"

"Yes! I'm in a terrible spot, Hannah. Say you can do it."

"I can do it."

"But can you, really?"

"Of course I can. Too bad I don't have the uniform. I could do it in style."

"I've got the driver's cap," Andrea said, pulling it out of the large carryall at her feet and clapping it unceremoniously on top of Hannah's curls. "I grabbed it before Doc Knight drove him away. I just wish I'd thought to ask for his uniform."

Hannah laughed. She couldn't help it. Andrea was used to getting her way and she'd think nothing of asking the poor limo driver to shed his pants and his jacket, and go off to the hospital in his underwear.

"He left the limo running and the keys are in the ignition. Go see if you can find something good to play for the drive out to the inn. They were supposed to provide music as part of the limo service. And I'll open the door when the bridal party gets there. I don't want to take a chance on losing *another* limo driver!"

Hannah was chuckling as she opened the driver's door to the white stretch limo and slid in behind the wheel. She'd never driven a limo before, but how hard could it be? She'd driven everything else on wheels or runners, including a tractor, a snowmobile, a powerboat, and a school bus. The only thing she hadn't driven was an eighteen-wheeler and as long as she didn't have to do anything tricky, she figured she could drive that, too.

The wedding couple's trip down the aisle was taking a while, and Hannah used the time to her advantage. She checked out the passenger compartment, opened the champagne bottle, and set out four glasses. There was a selection of music for them to peruse and Hannah picked something innocuous to put on the sound system until they'd made their own choice. She was just checking out the intercom and the glass partition that separated the compartments when the church doors opened wide.

Hannah tipped the driver's cap down low over her eyes and waited for Lisa and Herb to emerge. People were already lining up on the steps, preparing for the newlyweds' exit. Once everyone was outside, there was a flash of strobe lights and then Lisa and Herb appeared at the top of the steps. They stopped for a moment to pose for a photo, and then they descended in a shower of rice and flower petals. Her partner looked happier than Hannah had ever seen her, and Herb almost missed a step because he was so busy admiring his beautiful bride.

Andrea opened the back doors of the limo and Lisa and Herb got in. Marge Beeseman and Jack Herman were right behind them, and Hannah waited until Andrea had closed the doors before she keyed the intercom that connected her with the backseat. "Congratulations from Celebration Limos, Incorporated. You'll find a complimentary bottle of champagne and glasses on the mini bar.

That's our way of wishing you a happy life together and many rides from Celebration in the future."

"Thank you," Herb's voice answered her from the back and Hannah grinned as she realized that he'd left the intercom open and she could hear their conversation as the champagne was poured.

"We've got a woman driver," Lisa said. "I'm glad they hire women."

"Her voice is familiar," was Herb's comment.

"You're right." Marge sounded thoughtful. "She reminds me of someone, but I can't think who."

"Hannah?" Jack guessed.

"Her hair even looks like Hannah's," Lisa said.

"That's because it *is* my hair," Hannah said, turning to face them with a grin.

Chapter Eight

"This is the best wedding cake I've ever eaten!" Sue Ganske complimented Hannah as she came back for a second piece. "I just love having a choice, chocolate with vanilla filling, or white with chocolate filling. And they're absolutely gorgeous when they're sliced. Your cakes are every bit as pretty as my *Kransekake* and they taste a lot better."

"Thanks, Sue," Hannah said, accepting the compliment graciously. Hannah hadn't tasted the *Kransekake* and neither had anyone else. Plates and a cake knife were there for those who wished to sample it, but Sue's cake was still untouched. Even though Hannah had no firsthand tasting experience, she was almost positive that Sue was right. The layers were made of ground almonds, powdered sugar, and egg whites that were kneaded together and baked until they were set. And while there was nothing wrong with that combination of ingredients, Hannah knew the result wouldn't be particularly flavorful. On the other hand, the *Kransekake* was beautiful and it made a perfect decoration. Sue had drizzled the golden brown layers with white icing and decorated the resulting cone-shaped edifice with miniature Norwegian flags and colorful frosting roses.

Hannah was in a slightly pensive mood as she gazed around at the wedding guests. Had the traditional Norwegian wedding cake been created to make a point about marriage? The exterior was gorgeous, but the inside would be disappointing to those expecting a perfect treat. It was precisely what not to look for in choosing a bride or a groom, and it reminded Hannah of Shawna Lee Quinn. The southern sister was gorgeous on the outside but she was a pretty shell without an ounce of taste or substance. She'd promised Dick that she'd be there with her peach cobbler in plenty of time for the dessert buffet, and the prime space in the center of the table was still filled with the vase of flowers that Sally had stuck there while they were waiting for her to arrive.

"You're doing a great job, Hannah." Sally, who was stationed behind the dessert buffet to help people dish up the things they couldn't reach, sidled closer to Hannah's wedding cake station at the end of the table. At the same time Sally, the perfect hostess, kept up a running conversation with the guests who were trying to decide which desserts to take. "*Oh, hello, Gail. Did you try the Pineapple Whip? Marge brought it and it's absolutely delicious.* So, where is she?"

It took a moment for Hannah to realize that Sally's question was aimed at her. "Which she are you talking about?"

"The one you don't want to see. *How about some fresh strawberry pie, Sam? I know it's your favorite.* I'm talking about Shawna Lee."

"I don't know. You'd think she would have called if she'd had car trouble."

"Maybe she's stuck on the road," Sally suggested, turning to look out the series of picture windows that overlooked the lake. "It's coming down a little harder now. *Would you like me to help you with that chocolate mousse, Lucille?*"

Hannah looked out at the snow on the ground. Barely an inch had fallen and anyone could drive through that. "No way she's stuck. She just got a brand-new SUV with enough power to go through a lot more snow than what we've had today."

"I forgot about that. *A big piece or an even bigger piece, Ed? It's made with butter from Lake Eden cows.* Well, maybe she changed her mind and she's not coming."

"You think?" Hannah felt a surge of hope.

"Not really. She loves the chance to impress people and there are a lot of people here. *Let me put that in a parfait glass, Eleanor. It's so pretty that way.* I thought for sure she'd show. Do you think I ought to try to call the bakery and ask her if she's coming?"

Hannah thought that over and then she shrugged. "It can't hurt. Maybe she's tied up or something."

Sally gave Hannah a sharp look as she spooned caramel sauce on top of a serving of custard. "*Whipped cream on that, Joyce? I didn't think so. I thought I remembered you liked it plain.* Mike's not here yet, either. And didn't you say he asked you to save the first dance for him?"

"Yes."

"Do you think they might be together?"

"Your guess is as good as mine," Hannah said, visions of Shawna Lee and Mike in a clinch to end all clinches dancing on the screen of her mind.

"*You don't have to choose, Barbara. You can have a little of each.* Just as soon as this line ends, I can call the bakery."

"What good will that do?"

"If she answers, I'll listen for the sound of someone else in the background. You know . . . like breathing or coughing, or anything like that. Do you want to know? Or would you rather not know?"

"I want to know if you don't hear anyone in the background, but don't tell me if you do."

"Got it." Sally waved over a waitress to take her place. "I'll be back in a couple of minutes."

As Sally headed off to the phone in the kitchen, Hannah was already regretting her words. She really didn't want to know if Mike was with Shawna Lee, at least not right now. And she'd set herself up without realizing it. If Sally came back and said nothing, it would mean she'd heard someone in the background. Why hadn't she instructed Sally not to tell her, either way? That would have been the smart thing to do.

"Your truck's parked in the lot," Andrea said, arriving at the cake station without Hannah noticing her.

"Andrea!" Hannah gasped, jumping slightly and feeling a bit foolish for doing so. "You startled me."

"Sorry. Here's your key ring. The limo driver thought your heater was broken, but I told him it was always like that. What's the matter? You look like you just lost your best friend."

"I may have. At least one of them."

"Mike?" Andrea asked, proving that as the consummate wedding consultant, she knew precisely which guests had not arrived. When Hannah nodded, she reached out and patted her hand. "I noticed that, and she's missing, too. But that doesn't necessarily mean they're together. Don't forget that Mike had to work. If there was an emergency, they might have asked him to stay on longer at the station."

"Right."

"Well, that *could* be it."

"Absolutely. And since he's right near the phone and he knew I'd be disappointed when he didn't show up for the dance he asked me to save for him, he called out here and told me he'd be late."

"He did?" Andrea asked, starting to smile. "Well, that's okay then!"

"I was being sarcastic. He didn't call. And it's not okay."

"Well . . . try to lighten up a little. This is a wedding and everybody's supposed to act like they're having a good time, whether they are or not."

As Andrea walked away, Hannah thought about what her sister had said. How many other wedding guests were smiling on the outside and frowning on the inside? Actually, her own situation wasn't that bad. Norman was here and he'd danced with her. She had enjoyed that. And even though Hannah knew that Delores had sent him over, Winthrop had arrived at the cake table to ask Hannah to take what he'd called "a turn around the floor."

Hannah wasn't enthusiastic about the man who'd caught her mother's interest, but she had to admit that Winthrop was an excellent dancer. He'd held her confidently, led with assertion, and made the waltz they'd danced into a showing worthy of a dance competition. It pained Hannah to admit it since her father had been an excellent dancer, but Winthrop Harrington the Second was even better.

Norman, dressed formally in a dark suit, white shirt, and tie, walked up to the cake table with his digital camera. "Say, *Don't you dare take a picture of me!*"

"Don't you dare take a picture of me!" Hannah said, laughing over the absurdity as he snapped the picture.

"Works every time. The minute people say the words, they laugh. This is a good one of you . . . want to see?"

Hannah took the camera Norman handed her and peered at the small preview screen. It was a good picture, perhaps the best anyone had ever taken of her. Her eyes were sparkling, her smile was genuine, and she looked highly amused. Norman had been right to replace *Say Cheese* on his photographer's vocabulary list.

"I think I got some great shots so far. Do you want to see them when the reception's over? I could follow you home and hook my camera up to your television."

Hannah laughed. "That's a pretty sneaky way to ask for an after-party date."

"You're right. I would have asked you before, but I thought you'd be with Mike."

"You did?" Hannah frowned slightly. "Why did you think that?"

"Because he told me he asked you when I ran into him this morning."

Hannah began to do a slow burn. "Did he tell you I said yes?"

"Not exactly. I just assumed . . ."

"Assumption is the mother of misunderstanding," Hannah interrupted. "Never assume."

"Yes, ma'am. So did you say yes when he asked you?"

"No. I haven't talked to him since then and it doesn't matter anyway, because he's not here. So yes, I'd love it if you followed me home and showed me your photos after the party's over."

The next few minutes were busy at the dessert buffet. Guests had finished their first helpings and were back for seconds or thirds. Lake Edenites, or whatever collective noun the language pundits assigned to the residents of Hannah's hometown, loved their desserts. When Tracey was three, she'd looked up at her aunt and asked, "Why don't we have dessert for breakfast?" Hannah had figured that was a legitimate question, especially in Lake Eden.

When Andrea had sent out the wedding invitations with the announcement that there would be a dessert buffet at the reception, she'd received hundreds of calls from people who'd wanted to bring a dessert. Andrea had told them all to bring whatever they wished, and there were pies, cakes, puddings, custards, fruit bowls, pastries in all shapes and forms, and frozen desserts that matched the temperature outside. Hannah had no doubt that the calorie count from the collective treats on the table and in Sally's kitchen waiting to be served would be enough to feed a small country for several weeks.

"Hi, Miss Swensen," Amber Coombs greeted her. She was wearing one of Sally's waitress uniforms and Hannah assumed that she was working out at the Lake Eden Inn on the weekends during her senior year of high school.

"Hi, Amber. How's your mom?"

"She's great. She got a promotion out at Cost-Mart and she manages the whole cosmetic section now. I'm supposed to relieve you so you can have fun. Sally said."

"Thanks!" Hannah was delighted to be relieved. She'd been standing behind the wedding cake station for almost an hour and the unaccustomed high heels she was wearing made her feet hurt. "Where's Sally?"

"In the kitchen. Dick's showing her how to work the new cappuccino machine. She told me to hurry out here and tell you not to worry, that no one answered the phone. Does that make sense?"

"Somewhat," Hannah said, giving Amber a wave and walking gratefully away from the table. She was free to mingle, and even more important, she was free to sit down!

After sinking into the first unoccupied chair she encountered, Hannah thought about Sally's message. She was almost positive that Shawna Lee would have answered the phone if she'd been at the Magnolia Blossom Bakery. After all, a phone call might be a catering order that she could shove down Hannah's throat. No answer meant she wasn't there and that meant Shawna Lee and Mike weren't closeted in her apartment above the bakery. This was a big relief and Hannah spent several enjoyable moments imagining that Shawna Lee had set out for the reception on time, but a careless driver had run her off the road. The other driver had kept on going, not realizing that she'd gone in the ditch, and now Hannah's rival in both business and boyfriend was freezing her tail off, hiking to the nearest farmhouse in her party clothes.

When Lisa spotted Hannah at the table, she made a beeline for her friend and partner with her new groom in tow. Hannah noticed that she'd changed to her "going-away" outfit, a red woolen dress with a matching jacket, even though they wouldn't be going away. Neither Lisa nor Herb wanted to be far away from her father and they'd decided to stay in the honeymoon suite at the Lake Eden Inn for a week, rather than hop a plane to Hawaii, or Tahiti, and worry about him the whole time they were gone.

"I'm glad you're finally sitting down," Lisa said, giving Hannah a smile.

"Me, too," Herb echoed Lisa's sentiment. "We saw you standing there for over an hour cutting those incredible wedding cakes."

"Do we have a lot of leftovers from the buffet?" Lisa asked.

"Two more wedding cakes, one of each kind, and seconds of almost every dessert that was out on the table. Practically everyone in town brought something."

"That's so nice," Lisa said with a smile. "Herb and I noticed that there was quite a lot left, and we thought we should donate it to charity."

"The soup kitchen, the retirement home, places

like that," Herb explained. "We were wondering if you'd . . ."

"Say no more," Hannah interrupted, using one of her favorite lines from an old Monty Python routine.

"Pull out anything you'd like and take it," Lisa offered.

"No, thanks. It was all wonderful, but my hips don't need it."

"How about Moishe?" Herb asked. "Do you ever give him dessert?"

"Only ratberry pie and chocolate mouse," Hannah replied, her quip earning a merry laugh from both bride and groom.

"Thanks, Hannah!" Lisa reached out to give her a hug, an action that was unusual for her. Although Lisa was a warm and loving person, she seldom made affectionate gestures in public. "This was the best wedding in the whole world and none of it would have happened without you and Andrea!"

After a few more moments of chatter about the wedding and the reception, Lisa and Herb joined the dancers on the floor. Hannah leaned back in her chair—it was surprising how comfortable a folding chair could be when she was too tired to feel the metal digging into her back—and wiggled her feet out of her shoes.

Wishing for a foot massage, or the luxury of a steaming Jacuzzi, Hannah made do with flexing her feet under the table. She winced slightly in the process and a moment later, Delores and Winthrop came rushing up to her table.

"Are you all right, dear?" Delores looked concerned.

"I'm fine, but my feet aren't. I'm not used to wearing high heels."

"Speaking of heels, have you heard from Mike?"

"What do you mean?"

"I'm talking about your date with him, the one he asked for on the card with your flowers."

"How do *you* know about that?" Hannah stared at her mother in shock. She'd told Lisa about the flowers Mike had sent and his clever way of asking her for a date, but she hadn't mentioned it to anyone else.

"The deliveryman told me when he brought the bouquet that Winthrop sent, beautiful pink tea roses in a crystal vase."

"That's nice," Hannah said perfunctorily, giving Winthrop a polite smile. "How did the delivery-man know what was on my card?"

"Kyle was the one who wrote it down," Delores explained. "Mike phoned in his order and dictated his message."

"Oh." Hannah gave a little sigh. So much for privacy. Her mother was a charter member of the Lake Eden gossip hotline and by now, everyone at the wedding reception knew that Mike had asked her for a date and he still hadn't shown up.

"He's not here, is he?" Delores asked.

"You know he's not."

"And he hasn't called you?"

"No, he hasn't tried to contact me at all. I think it's safe to say that he stood me up."

"Perhaps he's involved in urgent police business and he hasn't had a moment to call you," Winthrop suggested, making an attempt to defend his sex. And then, when both Hannah and Delores turned to him with incredulous looks, he shrugged. "Then again, perhaps not."

"Are you going to let him off the hook if he shows up before the reception's over?" Delores wanted to know.

"Not if he's ambulatory, and he won't show up if he's not. I'll tell him that since he didn't bother to call to say he'd be late, I concluded that he wasn't coming, and I accepted a date with someone else."

Winthrop gave her an approving nod. "Excellent, my dear! A gentleman should never take a woman for granted. It's just not done. Detective Kingston owes you an apology and if I were you, I wouldn't be too quick to accept it. Informing him that you arranged another date when he failed to appear is a marvelous tactic."

"It's not a tactic."

"It's not?" Winthrop looked surprised.

Hannah smiled and felt good for the first time that evening. "I *do* have a date after the reception. With Norman Rhodes."

LISA'S WEDDING COOKIE CAKE

*This cake must be refrigerated
to set up—make it the night
BEFORE you plan to serve it.*

8 small packages of chocolate pudding
   mix***
10 cups *(2½ quarts)* whole milk *(or Half 'n
   Half if you want to splurge)*
2 one-pound packages of graham crackers
4-quart bowl

Sweetened whipped cream for frosting
   and topping

***Read the yield on the pudding package—
it should be 2 cups per package if you make it
according to the package directions. You can
use sugar-free instant, regular instant, or the
kind you have to cook. All will work. *(You can
also use 5 larger packages of pudding, each package
yielding 3 cups of pudding—if you do this, use 2
cups of milk or Half 'n Half for each package—as
you can see, this recipe is very flexible.)*

Line the inside of your bowl with long strips
of plastic wrap, leaving enough wrap to fold
back over the top when your cake is finished.

Cover the bottom of the bowl with graham crackers, all the way out to the sides. You can break them in half or quarters if you want, but it's also okay just to overlap them. *(Unlike a jigsaw puzzle, it doesn't matter if some pieces don't fit together exactly.)*

Make the first two packages of pudding using 2½ CUPS OF MILK, not the 4 cups called for in the directions on the box.

Pour approximately a third of the pudding over the layer of graham crackers in your bowl. Gently spread it out with a rubber spatula. *(It doesn't have to be perfectly smooth, just not wildly uneven, that's all.)*

Put another layer of graham crackers on top of the pudding in the bowl. *(Again, it doesn't have to be perfect—the pudding will soak into the graham crackers and all will be forgiven.)*

Put half of the remaining pudding on top of the second layer of graham crackers. Spread it out so it covers them.

Lay down another layer of graham crackers and top it with the remaining pudding. Spread

out the pudding and lay down another layer of graham crackers. (*Don't bother to wash out the bowl or pan you used to make your pudding. You're just going to make another batch.*)

Using another 2 packages of pudding and another 2½ cups of milk, make your second batch of pudding.

There are more graham crackers to cover now, since the bowl is wider. Use half of the pudding to cover the graham crackers. Smooth the pudding with your rubber spatula, lay down another layer of graham crackers, cover it with the remaining pudding, and top it with another layer of graham crackers. (*I'll bet you're already guessing what the rest of the cake will be like!*)

Make the third batch of pudding using 2 packages of mix and 2½ cups of milk. Put half on top of the graham crackers in your bowl, spread it out, and top it with more graham crackers. Now use the rest of the pudding and top it again with graham crackers.

One more time! Make the final batch of pudding using 2 packages of pudding mix and 2½

cups of milk. Spread half the pudding over the graham crackers, smooth it, and cover it with more graham crackers. Put on the rest of the pudding, smooth it, and this time cover it with a **DOUBLE LAYER OF GRAHAM CRACKERS.**

(Wasn't that easy? Even if you don't bake, you can make this cake.)

Fold in the edges of the plastic wrap to cover the contents of your bowl. Find a plate that will fit inside the bowl on top of the cake. Put it in right side up so that it'll push the cake down when it settles. Set a weight on top of the plate. I use a can of fruit.

Refrigerate the cake until time to serve.

When you're ready to serve, remove the weight and the plate, peel back the plastic wrap, and center a serving platter, right side down, over the top of the bowl. Invert the bowl, lift it off, and peel off the plastic wrap.

Frost your cake with sweetened whipped cream. *(Hannah whips her own cream, but you can use the kind in the can if it's easier for you.)*

Slice the cake as you would a pie, in wedge-shaped pieces. Everyone will ooh and ahh when you do. Pass a dish of sweetened whipped cream for those who want more, and enjoy!

HERB'S WEDDING COOKIE CAKE

*This cake must be refrigerated
to set up—make it the night
BEFORE you plan to serve it.*

8 small packages of vanilla pudding
   mix***
10 cups *(2½ quarts)* whole milk *(or Half 'n
   Half if you want to splurge)*
2 pounds chocolate cookies wafers****
4-quart bowl

Sweetened whipped cream for frosting
   and topping.

***The yield should be 2 cups per package if
you make it according to the package directions. You can use sugar-free instant, regular
instant, or the kind you have to cook. All will
work. *(You can also use 5 larger packages of pudding, each package yielding 3 cups of pudding—if
you do this, use 2 cups of milk or Half 'n Half for
each package—as you can see, this recipe is very flexible.)*

****(If you can't find chocolate cookie wafers in
the cookie aisle of your grocery store, try the section
where they keep ice cream toppings and ice cream cook-*

ies—that's where Florence Evans at the Red Owl in Lake Eden keeps them.)

Line the inside of your bowl with long strips of plastic wrap, leaving enough wrap to fold back over the top when your cake is finished.

Cover the bottom of the bowl with chocolate cookie wafers, all the way out to the sides. You can break them in half or quarters if you want, but it's also okay just to overlap them. *(Unlike a jigsaw puzzle, it doesn't matter if some pieces don't fit together exactly.)*

Make the first two packages of pudding using 2½ CUPS OF MILK, not the 4 cups called for in the directions on the box.

Pour approximately a third of the pudding over the layer of chocolate cookie wafers in your bowl. Gently spread it out with a rubber spatula. *(It doesn't have to be perfectly smooth, just not wildly uneven, that's all.)*

Put another layer of chocolate cookie wafers on top of the pudding in the bowl. *(Again, it doesn't have to be perfect—the pudding will soak into the cookie wafers and all will be forgiven.)*

Put half of the remaining pudding on top of the second layer of chocolate cookie wafers. Spread it out so it covers them.

Lay down another layer of chocolate cookie wafers and top it with the remaining pudding. Spread out the pudding and lay down another layer of chocolate cookie wafers. *(Don't bother to wash out the bowl or pan you used to make your pudding. You're just going to make another batch.)*

Using another 2 packages of pudding and another 2½ cups of milk, make your second batch of pudding.

There are more chocolate cookie wafers to cover now, since the bowl is wider. Use half of the pudding to cover the cookies. Smooth the pudding with your rubber spatula, lay down another layer of chocolate cookie wafers, cover it with the remaining pudding, and top it with another layer of cookies. *(I'll bet you're already guessing what the rest of the cake will be like!)*

Make the third batch of pudding using 2 packages of mix and 2½ cups of milk. Put half on top of the chocolate cookie wafers in your bowl, spread it out, and top it with more cook-

ies. Now use the rest of the pudding and top it again with chocolate cookie wafers.

One more time! Make the final batch of pudding using 2 packages of pudding mix and 2½ cups of milk. Spread half the pudding over the chocolate cookie wafers, smooth it, and cover it with more cookies. Put on the rest of the pudding, smooth it, and this time cover it with a DOUBLE LAYER OF CHOCOLATE COOKIE WAFERS.

(Wasn't that easy? Even if you don't bake, you can make this cake.)

Fold in the edges of the plastic wrap to cover the contents of your bowl. Find a plate that will fit inside the bowl on top of the cake. Put it in right side up so that it'll push the cake down slightly. Set a weight on top of the plate. I use a can of fruit.

Refrigerate the cake until time to serve.

When you're ready to serve, remove the weight and the plate, peel back the plastic wrap, and center a serving platter, right side down, over the top of the bowl. Invert the bowl, lift it off, and peel off the plastic wrap.

Frost your cake with sweetened whipped cream. *(Hannah whips her own cream, but you can use the kind in the can if it's easier for you.)*

Slice the cake as you would a pie, in wedge-shaped pieces. Everyone will ooh and ahh when you do. Pass a dish of sweetened whipped cream for those who want more, and enjoy!

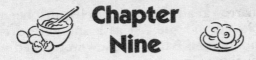

Chapter Nine

Hannah's teeth were chattering by the time she got to the end of the driveway. Dick had started her cookie truck to warm it up, but even though he'd turned her heater to the highest setting and put the fan on full power, the only thing that had accomplished was to make the buttons on the radio a little less icy.

The gravel road that led out to the highway was smoother than it had been when Hannah had driven in. The new layer of snow that had fallen during the reception had filled in the ruts. Hannah was still careful. She had precious cargo. Sally's waitresses had filled the back of her truck with leftover pies, cakes, puddings, and pastry, and she was driving into town to The Cookie Jar to put them in the walk-in cooler. Lisa and Herb had given her a list and in the morning, Hannah would deliver them to Reverend Sandburg's soup kitchen at the Bible Church, the Lake Eden Convalescent Home, the Lakeview Senior Apartments, and the new Meals on Wheels program Pam Baxter and her seniors at Jordan High were running out of her home economics classroom.

The narrow road Hannah traveled had been recently plowed and she felt as if she were driving through a tunnel. Banks of snow were piled high on either side of her, there was darkness above her with no moon in sight, and the night stretched out into infinity beyond the reach of her headlights. As she navigated the winding turns, Hannah kept a sharp eye out for stalled cars, or drivers who could have lost control and slipped off into the ditch. The road was isolated and there were no houses nearby. If she came across someone in trouble, she would offer to help in any way that she could. It was an unwritten law in the winter in Minnesota.

As Hannah reached the end of the winding gravel road and turned onto the wider paved road to town, she was grateful she hadn't encountered Shawna Lee in the ditch. Of course she would have stopped. That was a given. But she wouldn't have been happy about it. Thankfully, the problem hadn't arisen and she appreciated the turn of fate that had spared her the necessity of playing Good Samaritan to her competitor.

By the time Hannah turned into the alley behind The Cookie Jar, the toes on her left foot felt frozen. She vowed to buy the auxiliary heater that Cyril Murphy promised would solve her problem, and have the whole front end of her truck reinsulated if that's what it took to plug the leak and keep the temperature even.

Hannah pulled into her regular parking place and got out of her truck, stamping her left foot to drive feeling back into her five frozen metatarsals. She didn't bother to plug in her truck since she'd be leaving before it had time to ice up, and she clumped her way to the back door, unlocked it, and stepped into the warmth inside.

As always, a delectable assortment of scents greeted her. Hannah identified vanilla, chocolate, molasses, cinnamon, and nutmeg. There was even a hint of strawberry and cherry from the Valentine cookies she'd baked with Lisa. Hannah breathed deeply and a smile spread over her face. It was a lovely gourmet bouquet. If she could ever figure out how to bottle it, she'd be an instant billionaire.

The first thing Hannah did, even before she hung up her coat, was to put on the coffee. Norman would be here soon and he'd promised to help her unload. While she was waiting for him to arrive, she took a mug of life-sustaining caffeine into the coffee shop, sat down at her favorite table in the back, and sipped the fragrant brew.

Nothing was moving outside the large plate-glass window and Main Street was deserted, just as she'd expected it to be. No businesses in town were open past nine at night. Even the Quick Stop, out on the highway, closed at midnight.

Hannah sat back and sighed with contentment, admiring the wet flakes of snow that fell softly to the pavement. Everything was frosted with white fluff, from the roofs on the neighboring buildings to the tall pine across the street that Hannah had always wanted to decorate for Christmas. The old-fashioned streetlight on the corner cast a yellow glow and the light made the snow glitter like flakes of gold as it fell. Hannah thought again of how picturesque a winter scene could be. Artists painted it and writers wrote about it, but they did it from the comfort of a heated room. Although it was pretty, winter could be deadly for those who weren't prepared to weather it.

As Hannah's gaze shifted to the other end of the street, she began to frown. The streetlight was out on that corner, but a bright splash of light was reflecting on the snow and it was coming from somewhere.

It was a puzzle and Hannah sat there for a moment, attempting to figure it out. The light looked slightly blue and that meant it was probably fluorescent. Although she used incandescent light in The Cookie Jar because she liked it better, most of the businesses in town had banks of fluorescent lights to better display their wares. Either some business was open on the far side of the street, or someone had left the bright shop lights on. The only two businesses she couldn't see from her vantage point were Lake Eden Realty and the Magnolia Blossom Bakery.

Hannah jumped up, forgetting completely how tired she was, and headed to the front window for a better look. Lake Eden Realty was dark except for a dim night-light near the desk Andrea used when she wrote up listings. The bright lights were coming from the Magnolia Blossom Bakery, spilling out the front window and illuminating the whole end of the block. Hannah pulled aside the curtain and squinted. She could see the counter and the front row of tables, but as far as she could tell, no one was moving around inside.

Perhaps Shawna Lee had forgotten to turn off the lights when she'd locked up for the night. A good neighboring business owner would call and tell her. Hannah thought about that for a moment and decided she had much to gain and nothing to lose. If she called and got the answer phone, she'd leave a message and get credit for being thoughtful and courteous. If she called and Shawna Lee answered, Hannah would keep an ear out for signs that someone was there with her, just as Sally had tried to do earlier.

Hannah didn't have to look up the number. She'd seen it enough times in the ads Shawna Lee and Vanessa had run in the *Lake Eden Journal.* They'd even done a cable TV spot featuring the two southern sisters standing outside their bakery saying, "Y'all come in now, y'all hear?"

The phone rang once, twice, three times, and then the answer machine kicked in. *Hi, y'all. This is Shawna Lee at the Magnolia Blossom Bakery. Our hours are nine to six every day except Sunday. If you're calling during business hours and we don't answer, we must be real busy dishing up bowls of our special Southern Peach Cobbler. Y'all come on down and get a bowl for yourself. Or leave us a message to order a whole pan. Wait for the beep-beep-beep.*

Hannah, who'd gritted her teeth at Shawna Lee's syrupy voice and southern accent, almost had trouble opening her mouth when she heard the triple beep.

"Are you there, Shawna Lee?" Hannah asked. "Shawna Lee? Pick up the phone. It's Hannah across the street. It's past ten at night on Valentine's Day and your bakery lights are still on. You must have forgotten to turn them off. Just thought I'd tell you and save you a big electrical bill, that's all."

Hannah felt good when she hung up the phone. She'd done her civic duty. But what if Shawna Lee had a separate number for the apartment over the bakery? If she were in bed, sound asleep, she wouldn't hear the phone downstairs.

It didn't take long to look up Shawna Lee's personal phone number in the Lake Eden phone book. Strictly speaking, the phone book didn't belong solely to Lake Eden. Several other small neighboring towns were listed in the slim volume. But even with the addition of the extra towns and the yellow pages at the end, the local phone book wasn't something you could have a visiting child sit on to bring him up to table height.

Hannah dialed, half expecting to get an *I'm sorry, that number is no longer in service. If you think you have reached this recording in error, please hang up and dial again,* since Shawna Lee had moved out of her single apartment at The Oaks and into new living quarters over the bakery almost a month ago. But Shawna Lee must have kept her old number, because the call connected.

After four rings, Shawna Lee's personal answer machine kicked in. Hannah hung up before the outgoing message had finished playing. If her rolling pin rival was still out on a Valentine's night date, she'd see the lights when she eventually came home . . . unless she didn't come home at all, a distinct possibility since neither Shawna Lee nor Mike had shown up at the wedding reception.

At least she wasn't sleepy anymore. Hannah paced between the back table and the window, waiting for Norman to arrive. A glance at the clock told her she'd have a while to wait. Only fifteen minutes had passed since she'd arrived at The Cookie Jar, and Norman had to take his mother home before he could join her. Under normal circumstances, that wouldn't take long. Norman's mother lived only a few blocks from The Cookie Jar. But Carrie was always, without fail, the very last person to leave a party and Lisa and Herb's reception at the Lake Eden Inn would be no exception.

Since pacing the floor was boring her silly, Hannah decided to bring in some of the desserts while she was waiting for Norman. That way, when he got to The Cookie Jar, they could leave for her condo without delay. She carried in the extra wedding cakes, feeling a proud glow at how well they'd been received.

Unloading desserts was something Hannah could do in her sleep and before she realized it, she'd come close to emptying her cookie truck. There was only one load to go and she carried in the four cream pies that one of Sally's waitresses had placed in a cardboard box. They needed to go in the walk-in cooler and as Hannah stashed them on a shelf, she experienced an uncomfortable feeling of anxiety.

"*Déjà-vu*," Hannah said out loud, deciding that being locked in the walk-in cooler with the air vents plugged up once was enough for one lifetime. Even though she knew her mind was playing tricks on her, she shoved the box of pies on the nearest shelf, and rushed out of the cooler into the safety of the kitchen.

Another cup of coffee was in order and Hannah indulged herself with a piece of Shirley Dubinski's Poppy Seed Cake. Shirley had checked with Hannah, and since both of them had predicted that the dessert buffet would be a prime example of sugar overload, Shirley had decided to dust the three cakes she'd contributed with a light coat of powdered sugar instead of icing them.

Hannah glanced at the clock. She'd unloaded her cookie truck in only ten minutes. The earliest that Norman could arrive was five minutes from now and that was probably optimistic. She went back to her favorite table, but she couldn't seem to relax. There was something about the bright lights glaring in the interior of the Magnolia Blossom Bakery that made her nervous.

Perhaps there'd been a robbery. The moment the idea occurred to Hannah, her imagination was off and running. If the robbery had happened during the day, the robber might not have realized that all the lights were on. At this very moment, the cash drawer could be open and the Magnolia Blossom Bakery could be minus the day's receipts. A good citizen of Lake Eden, one who could put aside petty jealousy and hold the welfare of a neighboring business paramount, would check to make sure the cash register at the Magnolia Blossom Bakery was intact.

Hannah groaned. The last thing she wanted to do was put on her boots and her coat, and walk across the street to make sure no burglar had invaded her competitor's bakery. But basic decency demanded she do so, and she liked to think of herself as a basically decent person. Hannah stuffed her still-aching feet into her boots and slipped into her parka coat, zipping it up all the way. She scrawled a note to Norman, *Across the street at Shawna Lee's—maybe a burglary?* and taped it to the outside of the back door. Then she hurried around the side of her building to see if there was a problem with the Magnolia Blossom Bakery.

The wind had teeth and shards of ice pelted Hannah's face as she left the protection of her building. She turned up her collar and held her hand up to shield her eyes as she dashed across Main Street. She ducked under the pseudo-Jeffersonian portico of Lake Eden Realty and peered in the plate-glass window of her cobbler challenger.

Andrea's description hadn't done the Magnolia Blossom Bakery justice. It was gorgeous and Hannah would be the first to admit it. The magnolia tree mural the Minneapolis artist had painted was spectacular, all the tables and chairs matched, and everything was new and shiny. The color scheme was incredibly appealing and everything Hannah saw fit in perfectly. The homemade decorations at The Cookie Jar couldn't hold a candle to the decorator embellishments at Shawna Lee and Vanessa's bakery.

Hannah sighed. She didn't like feeling second-rate, even in the category of decorations. Comforting herself with the knowledge that at least her baked goods were better, she took another less envious and more appraising look, and came to the conclusion that absolutely nothing was out of place. The cash register drawer was pushed in, there were no signs of vandalism, and everything looked ready and set to go for business in the morning. But something about the bright lights really bothered her and she felt she should check further. Even though there wasn't much petty crime in Lake Eden, it was possible that a group of teenagers had waited until Shawna Lee had left, and then broken in to steal whatever pastry they could find in the kitchen. The lights were on in there, too. She could see them blazing through the diamond-shaped window in the swinging door.

Hannah wished that Norman were with her, but no cars had driven past and he was probably still doing what they not so jokingly called "mother duty." She didn't relish going inside to check out someone else's kitchen, but she couldn't just stand here and do nothing. She tried the front door, hoping it would save her a trip around the back, but it was locked securely. If pastry bandits were to blame for turning on the lights, they must have entered and left by the back door.

"Shawna Lee?" Hannah called out, knocking loudly on the front door. When that didn't work, she balled up her fists and hammered loudly, doing her best to wake anyone who might be sleeping upstairs. No one was inside. She was certain of it. Only the dead could sleep through the racket she'd made. Hannah pushed that very unwelcome thought aside and decided she'd have to go around to the back to see if that door was open.

Keeping a sharp eye out for broken or pried windows, or any other signs of unauthorized access, Hannah walked around the side of the building. Everything looked secure, but a glance in the kitchen window made her frown. There was a colorful pink and green box on the counter and the label read, *Betty Jo's Frozen Peach Cobbler, a division of Macon Foods*. Shawna Lee claimed that her Southern Peach Cobbler was made from an old family recipe. Maybe that was true, but it was Betty Jo's family recipe, not Shawna Lee's.

Hannah's gaze moved toward the ovens and what she saw made her frown deepen. A pan of peach cobbler was on the floor next to the open oven door. It was a mess, a jumble of sliced peaches and biscuit topping strewn over a puddle of sticky juice on the white tile floor. Had Shawna Lee simply dropped the pan as she was taking it from the oven? Or was there a more sinister reason for the baking disaster?

A glance at the other kitchen window gave Hannah an unwelcome answer to her question. There were two round holes in the glass and each hole was surrounded by a spider web of cracks. She was no expert, but they looked like a couple of bullet holes to her!

Hannah swallowed hard as she pressed her nose against the glass and held her breath so it wouldn't fog up. Was that a shoe she saw peeking out from behind the work counter?

There was the wise thing to do and the foolish thing to do. Hannah knew the wise thing would be to call for help, or wait for Norman, or do anything other than go into the kitchen to check it out by herself. But the time it took to do the wise thing could spell the difference between life and death for whoever was wearing that shoe.

Maybe the best thing to do is nothing at all, the not-so-nice side of Hannah's psyche whispered in her ear. *What difference would it make if you just went back to The Cookie Jar and pretended you hadn't seen that shoe? Who would know?*

"I'd know," Hannah answered out loud, accepting the burden of her own good character. It didn't matter what she thought of Shawna Lee personally. If her cookie competitor was hurt or in trouble, Hannah had a responsibility to do what she could to help.

Once she'd made up her mind, Hannah moved quickly. She raced to the back door, fully prepared to kick it in if that's what it took, but when she turned the knob she found it unlocked. She pushed the door open, praying that the two holes she'd seen weren't bullet holes, the shoe behind the counter had no foot in it, and the peach cobbler on the floor meant nothing more than a slip of an oven glove. But where was Shawna Lee? And why hadn't she shut the oven door and cleaned up the mess?

"Uh-oh," Hannah gasped, skidding to a stop as she rounded the corner of the counter. Shawna Lee was down on her back on the tile floor and there was a huge blossom of what looked like dried strawberry syrup on the bib of her white chef's apron. There was also a neat hole in the middle of the blossom and Hannah knew that there was no point in continuing to contaminate what was surely a crime scene. Shawna Lee had been shot in the chest and anyone with an ounce of brains could see that she was dead.

Chapter
Ten

Hannah took several deep gulps of the frosty night air. It helped somewhat, but her knees were still shaking. She leaned against the closed door for a moment and attempted to breathe more like a normal person and less like a trapper being chased by a pack of wolves. She had to calm down so that she could go back to The Cookie Jar to call the police. While it was true that there was a phone only a few feet away on the kitchen wall of the Magnolia Blossom Bakery, there was no way she could force herself to go back inside and use it.

She was about to take a step away from the wall, to see if her legs would support her, when she heard a faint voice calling her name. It was Norman and she gave a relieved sigh. Norman could call the police. She wouldn't have to do anything except stand here.

"I'm here!" Hannah managed to gasp out, hoping the faint voice that hadn't seemed to belong to her would carry to the front of the building. And it must have, because she heard Norman coming down the walkway that led to the back.

As she stood there and waited for him, bright

lights came down the alley. It was a squad car and Hannah began to frown as it pulled into the bakery lot and Mike got out. She hadn't called the police.

Both men strode toward her. They wore identical worried expressions as they spotted Hannah outside, leaning against the back door.

"Did she get burglarized?" Norman asked, arriving at Hannah's side.

"I don't know for sure. It didn't look like anything was missing, but I've never been here before."

"Shawna Lee's not here?" Mike asked.

"She's here," Hannah answered. Her voice shook a bit, but Mike didn't seem to notice.

"Where is she?"

"In the kitchen."

"And she was here when it happened?"

Hannah swallowed hard as a picture of Shawna Lee's body on the tile floor flashed through her mind. She wasn't sure she could speak, so she nodded emphatically.

"Then it was robbery, not burglary," Mike explained. "Robbery takes place when the victim is present. Burglary happens when the victim isn't home. If Shawna Lee was here, the crime was robbery."

"More than that," Hannah managed to say.

"What do you mean?" Mike turned to Hannah with a frown.

"I mean maybe it was a robbery, but there's more . . ."

"What else could there be?" Mike asked. And then his frown grew deeper. "Is Shawna Lee all right?"

"Not exactly." Hannah, never the queen of tact under the best of circumstances, could do nothing except blurt out, "I only went in as far as the counter and the only thing I touched was the door-knob and the oven door when I shut it. I'm pretty sure the department has my prints on file from the last body I found."

"The last *body?*" Mike asked, turning a shade paler when Hannah nodded. At least Hannah thought he turned a shade paler, but it was diffi-cult to tell under the weak illumination from the streetlight at the other end of the alley. "You mean Shawna Lee is . . . dead?"

"I'm pretty sure she is, although I didn't check to make sure. I didn't think I should disturb the crime scene."

Mike's lips tightened and he went in the back door without another word. Almost immediately, Norman moved to Hannah's side and put his arm around her shoulders.

"Do you want me to go get the car so you can sit down?" he asked.

"No, that's okay. When Mike comes out I'll just answer his questions and then we can go."

"I wish I'd been with you," Norman said, giving her a comforting hug. "Maybe I could have helped. And I'm sorry this always seems to happen to you."

"It's my personal curse. I attract dead bodies like moths to a light."

"That's funny."

"Not if you're the light, it's not."

Norman didn't say anything. He just held her tightly until she stopped trembling and Hannah was grateful for that. It was surprising how much better things could get when you were with some-one who understood.

When Mike came back out several moments later, Hannah was calm. But Mike wasn't. Hannah noticed that his hands were shaking and a fine bead of sweat lined his forehead.

"She's dead," he said, visibly pulling himself together as he turned to face Hannah. "Why did you come over here in the first place?"

"I was across the street, waiting for Norman, and I saw that all the lights were on. Since I didn't see anyone moving inside, I wanted to make sure that everything was all right, especially since Shawna Lee said she'd bring three pans of peach cobbler to Lisa and Herb's wedding reception and she never showed up."

Mike took out the notebook he always carried in his pocket and jotted down a few notes. "Did you call anyone to say that you were coming over here?"

"No, but I taped a note to the outside of the back door for Norman."

"What did it say?"

"I don't remember exactly." Hannah turned to Norman. "Do you still have it?"

Norman pulled the note out of his jacket pocket. "Right here," he said, and handed it to Mike.

"Across the street at Shawna Lee's. Maybe a burglary?" Mike read it aloud and then he turned to Hannah again. "What made you think it might be a burglary?"

"I called and no one answered the phone."

"You called the bakery number?"

"I called both numbers, the bakery and Shawna Lee's personal line. Since she didn't answer, I figured she wasn't home and someone had broken in."

"So you went running over here half-cocked to see if you could catch a couple of burglars?"

"Of course not! I looked in the windows. If I'd seen anybody inside, I would have run back to The Cookie Jar and called the sheriff's station. As a matter of fact, that's exactly what I was going to do when you and Norman got here." Hannah turned to Norman. "Did you call the sheriff's station when you got my note?"

Norman shook his head. "No. I probably should have, but I just rushed straight over here."

"I'm glad you did!" Hannah said, and then she turned back to Mike. "There's something I don't understand. If I didn't call the sheriff's station and neither did Norman, what are *you* doing here?"

"Me?" Mike repeated, looking very uncomfortable. "Um . . . well . . . I had an appointment with Shawna Lee at my apartment and she didn't show up. It wasn't a date or anything like that, just a personal talk we needed to have to get things straight between us. Then I was going to drive out to the reception before it ended and hook up with you."

"I see," Hannah said, wondering if Mike had planned to tell Shawna Lee that he had another *appointment* after hers.

"I got a little concerned when she didn't show up and she didn't answer her phone. I mean, Shawna Lee's not the most punctual person in the world, but she usually calls to say she's running late."

"Unlike you," Hannah muttered under her breath, still burning about the fact that Mike hadn't bothered to contact her, but he'd phoned Shawna Lee.

"When she didn't show by nine, I tried calling

again. And then I called every fifteen minutes after that. At ten-fifteen I decided that I'd waited long enough and I drove over here to see what was the matter."

"That was very considerate of you," Hannah said, barely concealing her sarcasm.

"Well, hey . . . you were considerate, too. You didn't have to walk over here to check it out. I just want you to know that I'm sorry I never made it to the reception. I was looking forward to that last dance with you."

"As a matter of fact, so was I," Hannah said, meaning every word of it. It would have been their very last dance, especially if Mike had told her the reason he'd arrived late!

"Are you all right, Hannah?" Norman asked, the moment they stepped into her condo.

"I am now." Hannah glanced at the clock on the wall. "I wonder if I have time to make a pot of coffee before Mother calls."

Norman laughed. "Let's see . . . we left the minute Bill and Rick Murphy arrived and it took us twenty minutes to get here. I'd say you've got at least five minutes."

"Two," Hannah said, grinning at him. "Loser has to pick up the tab the next time we go out to dinner?"

"Deal. Where's the big guy? He usually meets you at the door."

"Tries to knock me over, is more like it." Hannah gave a little laugh, remembering how surprised she'd been the first time she'd opened her door and Moishe had jumped up into her arms.

"He must be in the bedroom sleeping on my pillow. Why don't you go check while I start the coffee?"

Hannah had just put on the coffee when Norman came into the kitchen carrying Moishe in his arms. It never ceased to amaze her when her independent tomcat let Norman carry him cradled in his arms, belly up. If Hannah had tried that for more than a few seconds, Moishe would have turned into a flurry of claws and teeth. But when Norman held him in his very least favorite position, he just purred contentedly.

"Rowww," Moishe complained, looking up at Hannah accusingly.

"What?"

"Rrrrrroooow!"

"It's his food bowl," Norman interpreted. "Just look. It's empty."

"So you speak cat?" Hannah couldn't resist teasing him a bit.

"Not really, but that's the only thing he gets really upset about, isn't it?"

Hannah nodded and unlocked the padlock to her store of cat food. Once Moishe's bowl was filled to the brim, Norman set him down. Hannah's resident feline gave Norman's thumb a quick lick, and then he headed straight for his favorite spot in the kitchen, the place mat that contained his food and water bowls.

"Looks like I won," Norman said, glancing up at Hannah's apple-shaped kitchen clock.

"No, you didn't. It's been only four minutes and you said at least five." Hannah poured two mugs of coffee and handed one to Norman.

"But four minutes is longer than the two minutes you guessed."

"I know. As it stands right now, neither one of us won. Let's have our coffee in the living room. It's more comfortable."

"You just don't want me to see the clock," Norman grumbled, but there was a grin on his face as he carried his mug to the living room and sat down with Hannah on the sofa. "What do we do if the phone rings right now and we both lose?"

"Then we each pay for our own dinner." Hannah craned her neck so she could see the kitchen clock. "But I don't think that's going to happen. All you've got left is twelve . . ."

The phone pealed loudly, interrupting Hannah's prediction.

"Aha!" Norman crowed. "If that's your mother, I win."

"It is."

"How do you know?"

"Look at Moishe," Hannah said, gesturing in his direction.

"What's the matter with him? His hair is standing up."

"He always gets like that when Mother's on the phone." Hannah plucked the receiver from the cradle before it could ring again. "Hello, Mother."

The sigh Delores gave was so loud, Hannah imagined that she could feel it tickling her ear. "I *really* wish you wouldn't do that, dear. Unless you have caller ID. You don't, do you?"

"I have my own version," Hannah said, glancing at her puffed-up cat. "I take it Andrea called you."

"That's right."

"And Bill called her?"

"Correct. I do wish you'd stop finding bodies, Hannah. It's unladylike. Now people will start calling you names again."

"People called me names before?"

"Yes. It all started out when Mike called you his corpse catcher and Barbara Donnelly, out at the sheriff's station, overheard him. She told Bertie Straub when she got her hair done at the Cut 'n Curl, and Bertie told everyone who came in the door that she thought Mayor Bascomb ought to give you a badge and call you the Lake Eden corpse catcher."

"Really," Hannah said, being as noncommittal as possible. Actually, she thought it was pretty funny.

"People think they're being so clever. I shudder to think of what names they'll come up with this time."

Hannah could think of several that might apply, but she wisely remained silent. Delores was upset and the last thing she needed at this point was further aggravation. "Don't worry about it, Mother. It'll all blow over in a few days."

"I hope so, or I'll never be able to hold my head up in this town again!" There was a moment of silence and when Delores spoke again, she sounded more curious than angry. "Andrea mentioned that Bill said Mike told him that you gave an excellent description of the scene. Tell me everything, dear, from the moment you left The Cookie Jar right up until the time you found her."

Hannah related the story for the second time, leaving out any graphic details she thought might disturb her mother's sleep. When she was through, Delores sighed.

"I'm sorry she died. It's frightening to think

that someone we all knew ended up as the victim of violent crime. But at least it wasn't anyone I liked."

Hannah bit back a burst of startled laughter. Leave it to Delores to say precisely what she was thinking!

"So how do you think Vanessa will react? Will she go back to Georgia?"

"I don't know, Mother."

"Well, I hope she does! With your competition gone, you won't have to worry anymore."

Hannah was thoughtful as she said good night and hung up the phone. She hadn't really thought about what Shawna Lee's death would mean to her personally. Delores was right. If the Magnolia Blossom Bakery closed its doors, all of her former Lake Eden customers would be back.

"What's the matter?" Norman asked, noticing Hannah's frown.

"I was just thinking that . . ."

The phone rang again, interrupting her thought, and Hannah grabbed it. This seemed to be the night for phone calls. Since Moishe was no longer bristling, it couldn't be her mother, and Hannah answered normally. "Hello?"

"Hello, Hannah. I hope I'm not calling too late."

"You're not," Hannah said, recognizing Carrie's voice. "I just finished talking to Mother."

"Then I'll get all the details from her. Norman's there, isn't he?"

"Right here. Would you like to speak to him?"

When Carrie answered in the affirmative, Hannah handed the phone to Norman. There wasn't much she could glean from his end of the conversation since it consisted entirely of "Okay," "I'll do that," and "You too, Mother."

"She didn't ask you about Shawna Lee?" Hannah asked after she'd replaced the phone in the cradle.

"No, she had something else on her mind. She wanted me to ask you for a favor."

Every suspicious bone in Hannah's body twinged. There was no way she'd agree to a favor before she knew what it was. When she was in high school, Andrea had used that tactic and Hannah had ended up chaperoning Andrea and five giggling friends at a rock concert. The headlined band had been called Hearing Impairment and they'd lived up to their name. "What does Carrie want?" she asked.

"Delores mentioned what a good mouser Moishe was, and my mother has a mouse that she's been trying to get rid of. I'm supposed to offer you a package of frozen shrimp if you'll bring Moishe over tomorrow so that he can catch her mouse."

"I hope Mother doesn't tell anyone else what a good mouser Moishe is, or everyone in Lake Eden will want to hire him," Hannah commented, tearing open a package of her favorite Bavarian pretzels and dumping them in a bowl. "I can't believe I'm hungry after all that food at the buffet."

"I can. What did you eat?"

"Let's see . . . I had . . ." Hannah stopped and a surprised expression crossed her face. "Actually, I don't think I ate much at all. I filled my plate and took a couple of bites, but then Lisa asked me to clip some flowers before she tossed her bouquet."

Norman looked confused. "Why did she do that?"

"She's going to press them in the microwave and keep them as mementos."

"You can press flowers in a microwave?"

"I can't, but Lisa can. She read about it in a magazine. All I had to do was put the flowers in a plastic bag and stick them in Sally's cooler. I know it didn't take me more than a few minutes, but when I came back my plate was gone. One of Sally's waitresses had cleared it."

"So you went back for more?"

"I was going to. I even had a fresh plate in my hand. But Sally came up and recruited me to serve the wedding cake."

Norman laughed. "That's exactly what I thought! Did you have anything from the dessert buffet?"

"No. I was too busy serving cake. By the time Sally sent someone to relieve me, I'd lost my appetite. I had a piece of Shirley's Poppy Seed Cake after I unloaded the truck, but if I'd come straight home and gone right to bed, I would have forgotten all about eating." Hannah stopped speaking and looked thoughtful.

"What?" Norman asked her.

"I think I just discovered a new weight loss program. I'll call it the Busy Day Diet, open diet centers all over the country, and make millions by giving people so much to do that they won't have time to eat."

Before Norman had time to respond, the phone rang again. This time it was Andrea and she wanted to know exactly what Hannah had seen when she'd entered the Magnolia Blossom Bakery.

Hannah gave Andrea the same description she'd given their mother with one added fact. "And guess what I saw on the counter."

"What?" Andrea sounded intrigued.

"A box of Betty Jo's Frozen Peach Cobbler."

"I knew it!" Andrea exclaimed. "Remember when I said I thought I'd tasted that peach cobbler before?"

"I remember."

"And do you remember when Norman said it tasted like something you'd get at a twenty-four-hour coffee shop?"

"I remember that, too."

"Well, Betty Jo's is a chain of coffee shops in Georgia. The Jordan High cheerleaders stopped at one once when we went to that national competition in Atlanta."

"How about that!" Hannah exclaimed. "Just wait until I tell Norman he was right."

"Right about what?" Norman asked.

"Shawna Lee's peach cobbler tasting like the kind you'd get in a coffee shop. It was from Betty Jo's and Andrea says that's a chain of coffee shops in Georgia."

"Norman's with you?" Andrea asked in Hannah's ear, lowering her voice slightly.

"That's right."

"Does Mike know you took Norman home with you?"

"What does it matter? He gave up all rights when he didn't bother to show up for our date."

"I know, but you wouldn't want to get him too jealous. He's the lead investigator and he might decide to zero in on you. After all, you're the one with the most to gain."

"What's the matter?" Norman asked, noticing Hannah's disturbed expression when she hung up the phone.

"Andrea thinks I could be a suspect."

"That's ridiculous!"

"You know that and I know that, but Mike doesn't."

"Well, he should."

"Maybe, but you've got to admit I've got the best motive."

"You mean because she was cutting into your business?"

"That's only part of it," Hannah said, ticking the reasons off on her fingers. "One, she was my rival in business. Two, she was dating Mike and so was I."

"Was?" Norman interrupted her in mid tick.

"The way I feel right now, it's past tense. And three, there was no love lost between us and everyone in town knew it."

"But there must have been other people with motives. Who else would want to kill Shawna Lee?"

"The wife of almost every deputy at the sheriff's station for starters. She flirted with all the guys when she worked out there and she didn't seem to care if they were married or not."

"Are you going to try to find out who killed her?"

"I think I'd better," Hannah said with a sigh, "just to prove that I'm not the only suspect. Of course I might be cleared when Doc Knight declares the time of death. If I'm lucky, I was serving cake to a hundred-plus people when Shawna Lee was shot."

Hannah yawned and Norman took his cue. He stood up and smiled at her. "I'd better head for home. You look like you're going to pass out if I keep you awake any longer."

"It's been a long day." Hannah got to her feet and walked him to the door. "Are you available for a consultation tomorrow?"

"I'll *make* myself available. Is it a dental problem?"

"No, it's a murder problem." Hannah gave a little laugh. "Since Lisa's on her honeymoon, and Andrea's gone back to Lake Eden Realty to work part-time, I need someone to help me sleuth. I have to be at The Cookie Jar during the day, so we'll have to work at night. Do you mind spending a couple of nights with me?"

"I thought you'd never ask," Norman said. And he pulled her into his arms and kissed her.

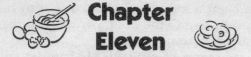

Chapter Eleven

Hannah filled the last of the display jars with the day's selection of cookies and placed them on the shelf behind the counter. It surprised her how much she missed Lisa. It wasn't the work. Hannah had handled the baking alone before Lisa had joined her. Although it was easier and faster with another set of hands, she could accomplish it herself. What she missed more than anything was Lisa's company.

Once she'd poured a fresh cup of coffee, Hannah sat down at her favorite table in the back of the coffee shop and tried to relax. She'd come in early on purpose, not knowing precisely how long it would take her to do everything alone. She'd erred on the side of caution and now she had almost an hour to wait until it was time to open.

As Hannah sat there sipping and sampling a new recipe she'd tried for the first time that morning, she wondered if someone at the sheriff's department had managed to contact Vanessa. Hannah felt sorry for Shawna Lee's sister. Vanessa had lost her husband in December and now, two months later, her sister was dead.

Hannah was about to get up and take another cookie, when a familiar car pulled up in front of The Cookie Jar. She watched as Andrea emerged, a vision in a dark purple suit and a matching cloak. She looked as if she could have been named fashionable female executive of the year with one small exception. The jarring note came from the pin she was wearing, a large, garish red flower.

As Hannah hurried to unlock the door, she noticed that the flower pin was decidedly lopsided and one of the petals appeared to be missing. "Tracey?" she asked, as she let Andrea in.

"What?"

"Did Tracey make your pin?"

Andrea nodded, slipping out of her cloak and hanging it up on the rack. "Of course Tracey made it. Do you think I'd go out and *buy* something like this?"

"No. As a matter of fact, I'm surprised you're wearing it. It doesn't exactly go with your suit."

"Look who's talking," Andrea said, giving Hannah an assessing glance. "You're black and blue."

"Where?"

"Your outfit. You're wearing a navy blue sweater with black jeans. That's a fashion no-no."

Hannah glanced down at her sweater. Andrea was right. "But I have an excuse," she said.

"What's that?"

"It was still dark when I got dressed and I thought I grabbed a black sweater."

Andrea laughed and so did Hannah. They were two sisters who enjoyed needling each other, as long as the barbs didn't get too sharp.

"They've got the whole bakery cordoned off," Andrea told her, gesturing toward the window.

"You can see part of it from here. There's crime scene tape on the front and it's on the back door, too. I drove down the alley to check. I just hope you baked lots of cookies, because everybody in town will be in."

"Because they can't go there?"

"That's part of it, but the other part is that they'll want to ask you what happened. Jake and Kelly mentioned on KCOW radio this morning that you found the body."

"Uh-oh," Hannah groaned, wondering if she'd baked enough cookies.

"You're going to try to find out who killed Shawna Lee, aren't you?"

"I think I'd better. You convinced me that Mike'll put me at the head of his suspect list."

"He will. Bill thinks so, too."

"Bill told you that?"

"Not exactly. He just didn't deny it when I asked him and that's the same as saying it. So what do you want me to do? I can nose around after I'm through showing houses and before I pick up Tracey."

Hannah thought about it for a minute. "Do you think you can find out the time of death? That's the first thing I need to know."

"I can try."

"Thanks. So Tracey asked you to wear her pin today?" Hannah asked, getting back to the subject.

"That's right. I just couldn't say no. She made it all by herself. Bill's mother took her out to the craft store and helped her pick out the kit."

"Do you ever get the feeling that your mother-in-law hates you?"

"All the time," Andrea replied with a laugh. "And

before you mention it, I know I could stash the pin in the car and put it on again before I go home. But it took Tracey hours to glue on all that macaroni and paint it. The least I can do is wear it."

Hannah stared at her sister in shock for a moment and then she reached out to pat her shoulder. "Good for you!"

"Thanks. Besides, it's going to be a great sales gimmick. If I tell all the clients that my daughter made it, they'll think I'm unselfish, caring, and honest. And then they'll believe everything I say about the property I'm showing."

"Right," Hannah said. So the fashion leopard hadn't changed her spots after all! "How about some coffee and cookies?"

When Andrea nodded, Hannah ducked behind the counter to pour another mug of coffee and put two cookies on a napkin.

"What are these?" Andrea asked, glancing down at the cookies when Hannah set them down in front of her.

"They're molasses raisin cookies. I just came up with the recipe this week, and I don't have a good name for them yet."

Andrea took a bite. "They're good. Very simple and you can really taste the molasses. Just look at this one."

"I'm looking," Hannah said, peering at the cookie that was left on Andrea's napkin. "What about it?"

"It's got three raisins on top, two for the eyes and one for the mouth. It looks a little like the pancakes you used to make me for breakfast. Remember?"

Hannah remembered. Andrea had been a picky

eater and she wouldn't touch a pancake unless it had a "face" of chocolate chips.

"Can you put just three raisins on each cookie?"

"Sure. They're not in the dough. They're just sprinkled on top."

"If you do that, they'll look like little doll faces. They're too scrunched up to be baby dolls, or fashion dolls, so they'll have to be old people dolls."

Hannah put on a perfectly straight face, even though she was screaming with laughter inside. "Somehow I don't think customers will buy them if we call them Old People Doll Cookies."

"I guess not!" Andrea started to laugh and Hannah joined her. When the laughter faded she said, "They look a lot like the Early American dolls with faces carved out of apples. You know the kind?"

Hannah knew the dolls well. She'd tried to carve a head for one in a college art class and ended up with several cuts on her fingers. "They do look a little like that, but I can't call them Apple Doll Cookies when there's no apple in the recipe."

"I know, but you can call them Doll Face Cookies. Everyone will love that. Each cookie will be a little different and they'll have to buy a couple to compare them."

"You've got a real talent for marketing," Hannah said, smiling at her younger sister.

"Of course I do! It's part of the training. I'm a real estate professional and we're expected to sell things that are overpriced and substandard every day." Andrea reacted to Hannah's frown and gulped audibly. "Of course that doesn't apply to your cookies. They're not overpriced and substandard. I was just speaking generically."

"You mean generally. And that was a good catch."

Once Andrea had left, Hannah finished her coffee and got up to switch to her serving apron. She still had fifteen minutes before it was time to unlock the door, but she was about to turn the sign from CLOSED to OPEN in the hopes that some early bird would come in and she'd have someone to talk to, when she heard a noise in the kitchen.

Hannah felt a prickle of unease. She was almost positive she'd locked the back door behind her when she'd come in. "Is anyone there?"

"Hi, Hannah!" a familiar voice called out from the kitchen, and a moment later, Lisa came into the coffee shop.

"Lisa!" Hannah was glad to see her partner, but she was also puzzled. "What are *you* doing here? Are you pining away for work after only one day with your new husband?"

Lisa gave a radiant smile. "Not exactly. It's just that Herb and I woke up early this morning and we turned on the *News At O'Dark-Thirty* to see what was happening in town. Jake and Kelly were talking about Shawna Lee's murder and they said you found the body."

"So you want to know all about it?"

"That, too. But Herb and I thought you'd need me to fill in here while you figured out who killed her."

"What about your honeymoon?"

"I'm still on it. We'll stay out at the Lake Eden Inn for a week, exactly as we planned, but I'm coming in to work until you get this whole murder business settled."

Hannah wanted to show her generous nature and tell Lisa to go back out to the Lake Eden Inn and enjoy herself. But what her partner had said was true. She really needed Lisa's help. Some of the confusion must have shown on her face, because Lisa reached out to touch her arm.

"Herb and I wouldn't be together anyway," Lisa said, doing her best to alleviate any guilt Hannah might feel about pulling her back from her honeymoon. "He volunteered to help Dick all week."

"Doing what?"

"Entertaining the men. Do you know about the Pretty Girl Cosmetics retreat that's starting today?"

Hannah shook her head. "This is the first I've heard of it."

"Their corporate headquarters reserved every room except the bridal suite. Sally and I talked about it, and she told me that if this one goes well, Pretty Girl might hold their corporate retreat there every February."

"That's good news. Now that the winter carnival's been moved to January, February's a slow month for Dick and Sally."

"It's the reason why Herb is helping Dick entertain the husbands while the wives hold their motivational meetings. He figured it was the least he could do after the incredible wedding gift we got from Gloria Travis."

Hannah felt like the fictional Alice after she'd fallen down the rabbit hole. "What incredible wedding gift? And who's Gloria Travis?"

"She's the personal assistant to the CEO of Pretty Girl. And she's also the person who picked the Lake Eden Inn as the site of this year's retreat. Do you happen to remember the dark-haired lady in the light blue silk dress who was sitting at the table with your mother during dinner?"

"I remember her very well," Hannah said. When she'd gone over to say hello to Mother and Winthrop, Gloria Travis had been friendly and nice.

"I'm surprised you remember her. She didn't say much and she left early."

"Right after dessert," Hannah said, recalling precisely when she'd left. "I noticed because I was paying particular attention to Mother's table."

"Why?"

"Because Mother was with Winthrop, and I hoped the wedding wouldn't give either one of them ideas."

"Oh." Lisa gave an understanding nod. "Well, Gloria was there for dinner, because she came in early. Since none of the other Pretty Girl executives are arriving until this afternoon, Sally asked if Gloria could attend the wedding."

"And you said, *That's fine with us. What's one more when practically the whole town is coming?*"

Lisa laughed. "That's exactly what I said! And it *was* fine with us, but we certainly didn't expect Gloria to give us a gift."

"You said it was an incredible gift?"

"And how! Gloria gave us a certificate for a champagne brunch for twelve at the Lake Eden Inn, paid in advance and redeemable any time we want to book it."

"Wow!" Hannah breathed, sounding a lot like Moishe when she opened the broom closet door and he caught a glimpse of the mother lode of kitty crunchies.

"That's exactly what Herb said when we opened the card. We never expected something that wonderful from someone we just met." Lisa glanced up at the clock and frowned. "Enough about the wed-

ding. We've still got five minutes. Tell me everything that happened last night and make it fast."

Hannah spent the morning answering questions with her stock phrase, *Sorry, I can't talk about
it, but the sheriff's department should be holding a press
conference any minute now.* Finally, when Lisa asked
her for the third time if she wanted a lunch break,
Hannah said yes and went home to fulfill the
obligation she'd made to Carrie and Norman.

It was ten minutes past noon when Hannah and
her loudly protesting feline passenger pulled up in
front of the Rhodes family home. "I'm just going
to check to make sure Carrie's here," Hannah
said, although she doubted Moishe could hear her
over his yowls. "I'll be right back."

Hannah hurried up the freshly shoveled walkway and rang the front doorbell. It was answered
almost immediately, but not by the person she'd
expected.

"Hi, Norman." Hannah gave him a big smile. "I
thought your mother would be here."

"They got really busy at Granny's Attic, and she
recruited me."

"Excuse me?"

"They got really busy at Granny's Attic, and she
recruited me. I don't have another appointment
until one."

"Sorry, I still can't hear you." Hannah frowned,
wondering whether Moishe's yowling had permanently damaged her eardrums. But then she remembered the precautions she'd taken before
she'd left the condo. "Hold on a second, Norman. I
forgot I was wearing earplugs."

Hannah removed the small pliable ear protectors Herb had given her the last time she'd gone to see Lisa compete in a Cowboy Shoot. Lisa had come in second after missing only two targets shaped like bank robbers, and nailing every one of the cattle rustler targets.

"That's better," Hannah said as she could suddenly hear again. Winter birds were twittering in the trees and traffic whooshed in the distance. "So you're here instead of your mother because . . . ?"

"They got really busy at Granny's Attic, and Mother recruited me. A couple of decorators drove up from The Cities and they wanted to know the provenance on everything. Luanne was looking things up on the computer, and the mothers were showing the decorators around the store."

"Sounds like a golden opportunity," Hannah said, remembering how her mother and Carrie had worked to attract decorators from Minneapolis and St. Paul.

"So, where's the rodent eradicator?"

"In the car. I'll go get him."

"I'll carry him," Norman offered, dashing out to the curb with her. They could hear yowling as they approached Hannah's cookie truck, but the yowls ceased and turned to purrs the moment Hannah opened the door and Moishe caught sight of Norman.

"Good heavens!" Hannah exclaimed, staring at Norman in shock. "He's obviously crazy about you."

"He knows what I've got for him."

"The shrimp?"

"That's from Mother," Norman said, lifting the

carrier and holding it while Hannah secured the truck. "I've got something else I bought for him this morning."

"What?"

"I'll show you after the massacre," Norman promised, leading the way to the front door. He carried Moishe down the hall to the guest bedroom and set the carrier down on the rug in front of the door. "The last time Mother saw the mouse, it was in here."

"There must be something about guest bedrooms that attracts them. That's where Mother's mouse is."

"*Is?*"

"Uh-oh," Hannah breathed, darting a glance at Norman. The less people who knew the better, but surely Norman could be trusted to keep the secret.

"Moishe didn't catch your mother's mouse?" Norman guessed.

"No. I mean, yes." Hannah stopped, realizing that her answer was confusing. "Let me start over. Moishe did not catch Mother's mouse."

"But according to my mother, you told your mother that he did."

Hannah shook her head. "Not exactly. That was an assumption on Mother's part, and I didn't bother to correct it. What I told her was that she didn't have to worry about her mouse any longer. What I *didn't* tell her was that I left the door to the guest room open, and I was hoping that just seeing Moishe scared her mouse away."

"So Moishe didn't kill it?"

Hannah pictured her cat in sphinx position, merely watching the mouse. "Are you kidding? He didn't even get close enough to breathe on it!"

"That's a relief," Norman said, reaching out to tickle Moishe's nose through the grate. "I thought I got over being squeamish in dental school, but I really wasn't looking forward to watching him hunt."

DOLL FACE COOKIES

Preheat oven to 375 degrees F.,
rack in the middle position.

(THESE COOKIES HAVE
NO EGGS)

½ cup melted butter *(1 stick)*
1 cup brown sugar, tightly packed
½ cup molasses***
1 teaspoon baking soda
½ teaspoon salt
½ teaspoon cinnamon
1 teaspoon lemon juice
½ cup milk
2½ cups flour *(no need to sift)*

1 cup *(approximately)* golden raisins, regular raisins, or currants to decorate

***Measuring molasses will be easier if you spray your measuring cup with nonstick cooking spray before pouring it in.

Melt butter in a large microwave bowl. When the butter has cooled to room temperature, stir in the brown sugar and molasses. Add the soda, salt, and cinnamon and mix it all up. Mix in the teaspoon of lemon juice.

Add half the flour to your bowl and mix it up. Slowly pour in the milk, a little at a time, and mix as you go. Add the rest of the flour and stir until it's thoroughly incorporated.

Drop the dough by rounded teaspoon onto UNGREASED cookie sheets, 12 to a standard-size sheet. Put three raisins on top of each cookie, two for the eyes and one for the mouth.

Bake for 10 to 12 minutes at 375 degrees F. Let the cookies cool on the sheet for 2 minutes and then transfer them to a wire rack to cool completely.

Yield: 4 to 5 dozen, depending on cookie size.

Immelda Giese, Father Coultas's housekeeper, ordered three-dozen Doll Face Cookies for Father's altar boys. When she came in to pick up the order, one of the cookies looked just like Sister Theresa. (She thought it did, not me!) The last I heard, Immelda was trying to talk Father Coultas into displaying the cookie in a glass case at St. Peter's.

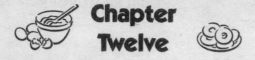

Chapter Twelve

Once Hannah had hung her parka on a hook and stashed her purse on a convenient stool at the workstation, she headed straight for the swinging door to the coffee shop. Lisa had been holding down the fort for an hour, and she could use a break.

"I'm back," Hannah said, stating the obvious as she ducked behind the counter to join Lisa. Their shop was crowded, but everyone seemed to be contentedly munching and sipping at the moment.

"Did he do his sphinx act again?" Lisa asked, and when Hannah nodded, she laughed. "Moishe's really a character."

"That's true. And now he's a quiet character."

"What do you mean?"

"I mentioned how loudly Moishe yowled when he had to ride in the truck, and Norman bought him a harness and a leash. He thought Moishe wouldn't mind the ride so much if he didn't have to be cooped up in his crate."

"And it worked?"

"Like a charm! Norman put on the harness and attached the leash to a hook in the back, so he wouldn't jump up in the front and distract me. That left Moishe free to roam around in the back, and I didn't hear a peep out of him all the way back to the condo."

"That's wonderful. But I didn't know they made harnesses and leashes for cats."

"I don't think they do, at least not cats Moishe's size. Norman bought a small dog harness at Cost-Mart and it had a picture of a miniature schnauzer on the tag. The thing that amazes me most of all is that Moishe let Norman buckle him in."

"That must have been a struggle."

"Not at all. Norman held up the harness, told Moishe that he'd look like a lean, mean killing machine if he wore it, and Moishe just stood there while Norman put it on him."

"Could Mike have gotten him in the harness?"

Hannah was surprised at the question, but it was intriguing and she thought it over. "I don't think so, not without excessive force, or maybe a tranquilizing gun. Why?"

"You should marry Norman. Your cat has spoken."

Hannah gave a snort of laughter and several customers at the counter swiveled to look at her curiously. "Sorry, just a little baking humor," she said to them, and quickly assumed a properly sober expression. It wouldn't do to be too jocular when her competition had just been shot out of the water, so to speak.

"I know I shouldn't give you advice," Lisa went on, "but Norman's reliable and Mike's not. Just think about what happened last night."

"You're right. And I *have* thought about it. I thought about it during the reception while I waited for him to show up. And then I thought about it later, when he told me that he called Shawna Lee a bunch of times to find out if she was all right. He called her, but he didn't bother to call me to tell me he wasn't coming. When I first started dating him, he was different. When he said he'd pick me up at seven, he picked me up at seven. And if something happened to delay him, he called to tell me. But ever since she moved up here from . . ." Hannah stopped speaking as Lisa made a cutting motion in front of her throat.

"Hi, Mike," Lisa called out, smiling politely.

Hannah swiveled around and by the time she faced Mike, she'd put on an exact duplicate of the smile Lisa was wearing. How much had he overheard? Enough to guess that she'd been talking about him? And did it really matter since everything she'd said was true?

"I need to ask you some questions, Hannah. Is the kitchen okay?"

"I guess," Hannah said. When a policeman said to do something, you said "Yes, sir" and did it. At least that was what her first grade teacher, Mrs. Chambers, had taught them. What she hadn't taught them was what to do when you were dating that policeman, you were as mad as blazes at him, and you didn't really want to be alone with him.

When she came around the corner of the counter, Mike put his arm around her shoulders and herded her toward the kitchen door. Hannah swallowed hard and tried not to think about how good it felt to be this close to him. Instead, she reminded herself that he'd stood her up and left her without a date for Lisa and Herb's wedding and reception.

Mike's arm slipped down to her waist when they entered the kitchen. By the time they'd crossed the floor to the island workstation, Hannah was a bit breathless, but she'd be darned if she'd let Mike know that. "Coffee?" she asked, proud that her voice didn't quaver.

"Sure. I really don't have any questions. I just wanted to talk to you alone."

"Oh?" Hannah managed to keep her hand steady as she set a steaming mug of coffee in front of the man who had many faults, none of which she could name at the moment.

"I came to apologize. I should have called you out at the reception and told you I didn't think I could make it. I'm really sorry I messed up."

Hannah busied herself pouring another cup of coffee, even though she didn't really want it. It was a way of preventing her from saying *That's okay. I understand.* It wasn't okay to make a date and not keep it. She had to let him know that.

"I really wanted to be there with you," Mike went on speaking when she didn't respond, "but there was this problem I had to settle with Shawna Lee. She was under the mistaken impression that I cared for her more than I did."

I wonder what gave her that impression? Hannah clamped her lips shut so she wouldn't say anything, but her mind formed the words she wished she could say. *Did it have anything to do with the fact your Hummer was parked outside her bakery overnight?*

"I guess I felt responsible for her, because I was the reason she moved here. All I did is talk to her on the phone and tell her how nice Lake Eden was and the first thing I knew, she was here applying for a job. Then, when she got it, I wanted to make sure she had a good time in Lake Eden."

A good time? Did that mean finding her an apartment in your complex, helping her move in, and going over there to do little fix-it jobs for her all the time? Did it include taking her out for pizza when she said she was hungry, and giving her rides everywhere when she said her car wouldn't start?

"Part of the problem was she never met anybody she connected with. It was really sad. I know she put people off because she was always flirting, but that was just her way. She really didn't mean anything by it."

She sure had you buffaloed! Hannah thought, using one of her father's favorite phrases. There was a moment of silence and Mike seemed to be waiting for a comment, so Hannah said the first innocuous thing that popped into her head. "Would you like a cookie?"

"No thanks. I don't think Shawna Lee had any friends except me. That's why I felt responsible for her."

If you can't say something nice, don't say anything at all. Thumper's line from *Bambi* flashed through Hannah's mind, and she didn't say anything at all. Mike was miserable, but she just wasn't in a supportive mood and there was no faking it with Hannah. He was asking the wrong person for comfort. She'd rather stand out in a blizzard in her underwear than let Mike cry on her shoulder!

"I know I shouldn't burden you with this," Mike said. And as so many other people did, he went on to do precisely that. "It's just that Shawna Lee was there for me when my wife died. I was so lonely, I didn't know where to turn, and she was my only friend when I needed one. I should have gone over there the second she didn't show up. If I had, she'd still be alive. I just feel so awful that I wasn't there for her when she needed me."

Hannah looked up into Mike's heartbreakingly handsome face, disregarded the suspicious moisture in his eyes, and spat out precisely what she thought. "Get over it, Mike! You've got a job to do. Quit feeling sorry for yourself and go do it."

Mike's mouth dropped open the way cartoon characters' do in comic strips. Hannah never thought real people did that, and she was amazed into absolute silence. But then Mike recovered, almost as quickly as the eye went to the next frame of the cartoon, and he reached out for her.

"You're right," he said, taking her hands. "I needed that. I guess that's why I came here. When I'm in trouble, you always give me what I need."

Hold the phone, the inner voice in Hannah's head cautioned her, as Mike came around the workstation and pulled her to her feet. And as he kissed her, the inner voice spoke again, *He's sandbagging you. Don't let him get away with it!*

"Gotta run," Mike said, breaking their embrace after a long moment. "I've got a job to do."

"Wait!" Hannah said breathlessly, willing her mind to start working again. There was something she had to ask him, something important.

"What is it?"

It took Hannah a split second, but then she remembered. "What was the time of death?"

"Doc Knight hasn't got back to us yet. But you don't need that information. And don't even think about trying to investigate. I'm sorry, but until I clear you, you're a suspect."

"Did you have to answer hundreds of questions?" Lisa asked, ducking into the kitchen where Hannah was baking another batch of Chocolate Chip Crunch Cookies.

"No, and remind me never to be alone with him again."

"Are you serious?"

"I'll let you know later. Mike warned me that I shouldn't investigate."

"He always does that." Lisa waved that away. "But you're going to, aren't you?"

"Of course. He admitted that I was still a suspect, so it's a matter of necessity." Hannah stopped speaking and listened to the level of noise coming from the coffee shop. "Sounds like we've got a crowd."

"We do, and it's a bigger crowd than we've had in a month. I told them you'll be bringing out hot cookies in less than ten minutes. They're all staying to have some."

"Of course they are. They saw Mike come in and they want to know what questions he asked me in the kitchen."

"That too," Lisa said with a grin. "What are you going to tell them?"

"I'll dazzle them with fancy footwork. First, I'll tell them about sitting here and wondering why the lights were on across the street. And then I'll describe how my heart pounded when I looked in the window and didn't see anything moving. Then I'll describe my walk around the building and how I stopped several times, thinking about hightailing it back to The Cookie Jar."

"Did you really?"

"No, but it makes for great drama. Then I'll describe how I peered through the window and saw Shawna Lee's shoe. And then I'll stop and say I can't tell them any more, because the sheriff's department is just starting their investigation and they don't want me to actually describe the crime scene. But I'll promise to tell them more the moment the sheriff tells me it's okay."

Lisa looked as pleased as punch. "Sounds like the cliffhangers my grandpa told me about when they used to show serials like *Deadeye Dick* in the movies. They always left you holding your breath."

"Precisely," Hannah said with a grin. "And everyone who's here today will be back tomorrow for the next installment."

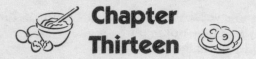

Chapter Thirteen

The Corner Tavern wasn't the best place in the world to discuss Shawna Lee's murder, but steak was what Hannah felt like eating, and Norman had agreed. She'd left her truck behind at The Cookie Jar, and now she was riding to the Corner Tavern in Norman's well-heated sedan. Andrea would meet them there since Grandma McCann was making supper for Tracey.

"This is heaven," Hannah said, unzipping her parka and luxuriating in the steady stream of warm air from the vents.

"You should get yours fixed." Norman turned onto the highway and flicked his lights to bright.

"I know. I'll do it one of these days." Hannah leaned back and watched the scenery roll by. There wasn't a whole lot to see, just massive snowbanks that were piled high at the edges of the asphalt with an occasional road sign sticking up from the crest like a stubby lollipop.

"I'm really looking forward to this," Norman declared, exiting the freeway on the access road that led to the Corner Tavern. "I'm going to have a steak, and onion rings, and garlic bread. Mother doesn't believe in red meat or deep fried food."

"How about the garlic bread?"

"She doesn't think that's healthy, either."

"I guess she hasn't compared health notes with *my* mother. Delores is convinced that garlic lowers your cholesterol."

"That's a good argument. I'll try it on her." Norman pulled into the parking lot and found a spot near the door. "Do you think this whole diet thing really matters in the long run?"

"Absolutely," Hannah said and waited until Norman walked around the car to open her door. Norman always opened doors for her. He was just that kind of a guy. "There's a lot of evidence that diet is related to longevity."

"So watching your cholesterol and limiting your carbohydrates are worth doing?"

"I didn't say that. You might live longer, but without any of the good stuff, it's not worth it."

Norman was still laughing as they walked in the front door of the rustic establishment that had been on the intersection of two county roads, one of which had become the interstate, for the past eighty years. There was a large cloakroom just to the right of the door that contained long benches for use in removing boots, a boot rack located in back of the benches, and hooks on the wall for coats. One wall was mirrored and as Hannah and Norman entered to hang up their coats, a woman in a blue velvet warm-up suit and silver tennis shoes was rearranging her hair. The cloakroom at the Corner Tavern had a scent that was particular to most Minnesota cloakrooms. It was a combination of damp wool, moist leather, drying rubber, and a hint of pine Hannah would have liked to think came from the knotty pine planks that lined the walls, but more likely originated with the cleaning solution they used to mop the floor.

Once Hannah had shed her parka coat and hung it on a hook, she sat down on the wooden bench to pull off her boots and placed them, like twin sentinels, on the boot rack. Then she reached into her extra-large, shoulder bag purse to get out the soft ballet-type slippers with rubber soles that she always carried with her in the winter months. Once those were on her feet, she ran her fingers through her hair to arrange it or disarrange it, depending on your point of view, and stood up. "I'm ready. Let's go eat."

"That's one of the things I like best about you," Norman said. "You never primp in front of a mirror like most women do."

"That's because it doesn't do me any good."

"No, it's because you don't have to. You always look good."

"Points," Hannah said. "Lots of points." And then she took Norman's arm as he held it out. Norman had a talent for saying the right thing at the right time.

As they neared the door to the main room of the restaurant, the noise level increased. There were sounds of silverware clinking, the low hum of conversation, and an occasional laugh. Hannah was smiling as Norman pushed open the door and she stepped through. The reservations desk was to the right and there was a line stretching all the way to the Corner Tavern mascot, a five-hundred-pound bear that was mounted standing on his hind legs.

"Hi, Albert," Hannah said. And then, unable to resist, she reached up to pat the bear's bristly broad chest.

"What's the story on this bear?" Norman asked, staring up at the glassy-eyed ursine.

"The official story is that the owner's great-grandfather shot the charging bear with a .22 rifle," Hannah related. "His name was Nicholas Prentiss and the Nick we know now is fourth generation. Great-Grandpa Nick realized that a .22 wouldn't do anything except make the charging bear angrier and his only hope was to hit a vital spot. Luckily, he was close to the bottom of a hill and bears don't run well downhill, so he hurried to the bottom to give him a few more precious moments. He remained motionless at the bottom and the charging bear didn't spot him, because a bear's eyesight isn't that keen. It took nerves of steel to wait there without moving or making a sound, but when the bear was close enough, he jumped to his feet, jammed the barrel of his rifle in the bear's mouth, and pulled the trigger. The bullet went straight into the bear's brain and it stopped him dead in his tracks."

"Is it true?" Norman wanted to know.

"Probably not, but it's a good story. Nicholas suffered a broken leg when the bear fell on him, but he knew he was lucky to be alive. He stayed with a family that owned a farm not far from where it happened until his leg healed. The family had a daughter, and he ended up marrying her."

"And this is the same bear?"

"So the story goes. The girl's father had the bear stuffed because it was such a fine specimen, and he gave it to the newlyweds as a wedding present. And when Nicholas and his wife built the Corner Tavern a few years later, the bear was installed inside the entrance to greet diners. Give him a pat, Norman. It's supposed to be good luck."

Norman gave the bear a pat. "Forty-two teeth. Twelve incisors, four canine, sixteen premolars, and ten molars."

"What?"

"I thought for a while I'd like to be a zoo dentist." They'd reached the front of the line and Norman stepped up to the reservations desk. "Norman Rhodes. I have a reservation. Three for dinner."

While the woman at the desk looked for Norman's name on her list, Hannah amused herself by adding up the inconsistencies in the story about the bear. For one thing, there hadn't been any grizzly bears in Minnesota for well over a hundred and fifty years. Back then grizzlies had only occupied a narrow area on the western border of the state. Lake Eden was in central Minnesota, where there were no known grizzly sightings.

Hannah might have believed the story if it had been about a black bear. Black bears, the kind one would encounter in the Lake Eden area, were approximately a hundred and thirty pounds. The black bear had a straight face profile, while the grizzly had a dish face. The black bear had no hump, while the grizzly did. The black bear didn't grow a ruff of long hair in the spring and the fall, and it had short, dark claws. The grizzly grew a ruff, and had long, lighter-colored claws.

This was a grizzly. It was as simple as that. And there were other inaccuracies in Nick's great-grandfather's story that had to do with bear behavior. Bears can run downhill easily. And bears can see as well as a man. Hiding at the bottom of a hill wouldn't have gained Great-Grandfather Nicholas any time. And thinking a bear couldn't see you because his eyesight was bad was just plain ridiculous.

Hannah patted Albert again. He was nearly three and a half feet across at the shoulders and that was even more proof that he was a grizzly. Hannah was willing to bet that the first Nicholas had bought the stuffed bear from a taxidermist, installed his ursine purchase in his new tavern, sworn his wife and in-laws to secrecy, and made up the whole story to pass on to future generations.

"Here it is," the woman behind the reservations desk said, flashing them a smile. "I'm sorry I didn't find it right away, but that's because your reservation's for three and three are already here. They requested two extra chairs though, so you'll be fine."

"Did you say *three* are here?" Norman asked, glancing at Hannah.

"Yes. The first one came in earlier and the second two joined her about fifteen minutes ago."

"Who are they?" Hannah quizzed the woman. "Were you here when they came in?"

"I don't know all the names, but Mrs. Sheriff Todd came in first."

"We were expecting her. She was the third on our reservation. Who are the other two?"

"I'm not sure, but one was wearing a fur coat. I remember her because it looked like one that my sister-in-law bought. She was a blonde and . . . uh . . ."

"If the word you're looking for is *plump*, it's my mother," Norman said.

"You're right. I was just trying to think of a nice way to say it. Very nice looking, and . . . she was plump. And the other lady had dark hair and wasn't at all . . . er . . . plump."

"*My* mother," Hannah said, locking eyes with Norman. "Batten down the hatches, Norman. The mothers have invaded."

The woman at the reservations counter started to laugh, but she sobered quickly. "I'm really sorry about that. How about if I seat you across the room in a private booth? And I don't let anyone know you're here?"

Hannah looked at Norman. Norman looked at Hannah. And both of them said, at the very same time, "It's tempting." And then they burst into laughter so infectious, the woman at the reservations desk couldn't help but join in.

Once the jocularity had passed, Norman made a decision. "Better not," he said. "Family, you know?"

"Believe me, I know!" The hostess gave them a parting smile and turned them over to a waitress, who shepherded them to a table across the room where Andrea, Delores, and Carrie waited.

"Okay," Andrea said, putting down her fork. "I didn't say anything while we were eating because you asked us not to, but I got the straight stuff from Doc Knight. Shawna Lee was killed between five and seven at night. Who do you think did it?"

Hannah took the last bite of her steak. It was blood rare, just the way she liked it, and she wasn't about to start talking about Shawna Lee until she'd enjoyed it. "Mmm. Just a sec."

Swallowing didn't take long, but Hannah milked it to the last millisecond. Then she turned to her sister. "I don't know who did it. All I can do right now is to look at the people who had a motive."

"Which people are . . . they . . . them . . . who?" Andrea sputtered, never the master of the objective case. And then she rephrased her question. "Who are you going to grill first?"

"I ought to grill *me* since I had a great motive, but I already know I didn't do it."

"Who else?" Andrea asked.

"You," Hannah said with a sigh.

"What!" Hannah's sister reached a new level of outrage. "What are you talking about?"

"Well . . . you didn't like the fact that Bill went to the Magnolia Blossom Bakery almost every day."

"That's true, but I wouldn't have killed Shawna Lee for that. If I'd killed anyone, it would have been . . . never mind. You can grill me if you want to. It's just not going to work out, that's all."

"I know that, but I had to say it to be fair. And then there are the deputies that Shawna Lee flirted with," Hannah went on. "Their wives and girlfriends certainly had a reason to want Shawna Lee out of the picture."

"Absolutely," Delores agreed. "And there's Ronni Ward."

"Ronni?" Hannah was surprised. "But I thought they were friends."

"They were until Shawna Lee decided she liked Ronni's boyfriend. Ronni caught them together in a booth at Bertanelli's and Ellie told me she thought Ronni was going to kill Shawna Lee before Bert and the dishwasher pulled her off."

"I wonder how I missed hearing about that," Hannah mused, jotting down Ronni's name. "I don't like doing it, but I've got to write down Barbara Donnelly's name. She was really angry with Shawna Lee for trying to take over her job when Sheriff Grant died and Barbara was out on compassionate leave."

Carrie's mouth dropped open. "But I know Barbara, and she'd never do something like that!"

"Of course not, but we can't discount it, not until we prove she couldn't have done it."

"And how do we do that?" Delores wanted to know.

"That's where you and Carrie come in if you want to help." When both mothers nodded, Hannah went on, "Andrea just told us that Shawna Lee died between five and seven. Lisa's wedding started at five. I looked at my watch when I heard the wedding march. What time did it end?"

"Six-fifteen," Andrea said, with the wedding consultant's voice of authority.

"Okay. Let's figure fifteen minutes to kiss the bride, and throw rice, and offer congratulations. How long does it take to get out to the Lake Eden Inn for the reception?"

"Fifteen minutes, maybe twenty," Norman said.

"Okay, that's ten to seven. The first people should have started to arrive a little before seven."

Hannah turned to the mothers. "Are you up for making some phone calls?"

"That's what we're best at," Carrie said, smiling at Delores.

"All right. I'm going to ask Lisa to give you the guest books. There was a guest book in the church, and another at the reception. I'll give you a copy of the suspect list and you'll check to see if they were at the wedding. If they were, you'll look for their names in the reception guest book."

"What good will that do?" Delores asked. "Someone could have left the church, killed Shawna Lee, and driven out to the Lake Eden Inn to attend the reception."

"That's true, but you can bracket the names," Hannah explained. "Nobody left early at the wedding. I know that for a fact. And one of Lisa's cousins was standing at the entrance to the dining room at the reception, asking people to sign the guest book when they came in."

"Of course," Delores said. "All we have to do is call the name ahead of a suspect and the name behind a suspect and see if they remember what time they got to the reception."

"That's right." Hannah smiled at her mother, who'd caught on instantly. "If the suspect took longer than half an hour between leaving the church and arriving at the reception, that suspect could have had time to kill Shawna Lee."

Delores turned to Carrie, who nodded. Then she turned back to Hannah. "We'll take care of it."

"Great! Now all we have to do is clear Mike."

"You mean Mike Kingston?" Andrea asked.

"Yes. He had an appointment with Shawna Lee at his apartment the night she was killed."

"An *appointment?*" Carrie looked as if she couldn't quite believe her ears. "What does that mean?"

"That's what he called it. He said he had to *get things straight* with Shawna Lee. After that, he said he planned to drive out to the reception to hook up with me."

There was silence for a long, long moment and then Andrea stepped into the breach. "Sorry, Hannah. We didn't mean to embarrass you. But do you believe him?"

"I don't know." Hannah swallowed hard. "I'd like to believe him, but I'm not sure I do. What if he wasn't telling the truth about the time of his appointment with Shawna Lee?"

"That's possible," Delores said with a shrug, "but he could simply be mistaken. Heaven knows men aren't good with time. Your father wasn't."

"Okay, let's give him the benefit of the doubt on that. But what if the appointment he told me about was really a date?"

Andrea looked shocked. "But he had a date with *you* for the reception!"

"I know that. Maybe he was planning to squeeze two dates into one evening. Whatever. But just for the purpose of discussion, let's say that Mike's appointment with Shawna Lee really was a date. And when he went to the Magnolia Blossom Bakery to pick her up, he found her with another man and shot her?"

Carrie was aghast. "But he's a sworn sheriff's deputy!"

"That's true," Norman said, "but not even sworn sheriff's deputies do the right thing all of the time. Mike could have seen Shawna Lee with another man and shot her in a jealous rage."

"But how about the other man? What happened to him?" Delores asked.

"He was probably just leaving. Mike was a couple minutes early and he stood there looking in the window, getting more and more jealous as Shawna Lee kissed this other guy goodbye. And then, once the other guy was out of the picture, Mike pulled out his gun and shot her."

Andrea gave a little laugh. "That's impossible. The first thing they do is check the ballistics, and all the department guns are on file. They'd know right away that Shawna Lee was shot with Mike's gun."

"How about his personal piece?" Hannah asked. "Is that on file, too?"

"What personal piece?"

"The handgun he carries in his body belt. It's a Colt Mustang."

Delores looked surprised for a moment, and then her eyes narrowed. "How do *you* know about his body belt?"

"He showed it to us when Norman and I went over to the gym at his apartment."

"Oh," Delores said, all smiles again.

"Do you really think Mike could have killed Shawna Lee in a jealous rage?" Andrea asked.

"It's possible," Hannah said immediately. "People in a jealous rage don't think, they just act. I really don't *want* to believe Mike could do something like that, but what I believe doesn't count. Let's just say I'm not a hundred percent sure he wouldn't do it." Hannah looked over at Norman and gave a relieved sigh. "At least you couldn't have done it, Norman. You were taking the wedding and reception pictures at the time."

"Only part of the time. The rest of the time, I was on the road. Everyone who's come into the dental clinic knows that I was upset that you and Lisa might have to close. Who's to say that I didn't stop by the Magnolia Blossom Bakery on the way to the reception and knock off your competition?"

Chapter Fourteen

The first thing Hannah did when she got home from the Corner Tavern was to fill her pathetically yowling feline's food bowl for the fourth time that day. The second thing she did was preheat her oven so that she could test the cookie dough she'd brought home with her. When Norman had dropped her off at The Cookie Jar to pick up her truck, she'd dashed in to get it. There were two bowls, a small one and a large one. The large one contained the cookie dough and the small one contained the frosting. The frosting was easier to work with if it was chilled, and Hannah had no qualms about simply putting it in the back of her vehicle and transporting it home to her condo kitchen. Keeping something chilled was not a problem for the owner of a drafty cookie truck who needed a new heater to reach the nether regions of her vehicle.

Once the oven had reached baking temperature, Hannah got out a cookie sheet, sprayed it with nonstick cooking spray, and assembled the cookies. She'd been working on this recipe for weeks, attempting to get it just right.

By the time the test sheet of cookies came out of the oven, Hannah's eternal craving for chocolate had grown into a hunger that could not be denied. The cookies she was testing were chocolate, but with chocolate it was always a case of more is better, and she went to the freezer for ice cream. She hadn't felt like having dessert after the mothers, Andrea, and Norman had thoroughly discussed several murder scenarios with Shawna Lee as the victim and Mike as her cold-blooded killer.

The cookies looked delicious, but looks were often deceiving in the pastry world. If they didn't pass muster, Hannah would be ruthless and they'd end up sweetening the malodorous depths of her condo building's Dumpster.

As she dished double chocolate fudge ice cream into one of the cut glass dessert dishes Delores had given her as a Christmas present, Hannah considered what they'd accomplished when they'd met for dinner. Everyone had wanted something to do and Hannah had given out assignments. Andrea would find out anything she could about Mike's whereabouts during the critical hours. Delores and Carrie would tackle the job of going over the wedding and reception guest books to see if someone on the suspect list had taken too long to get from the wedding to the reception. They'd also make a list of guests who'd attended the wedding only, guests who'd attended the reception only, and those people who'd been invited but hadn't shown up at either. Norman would talk about Shawna Lee's murder with his patients and gauge their reactions to her death. He'd ask probing questions and call Hannah immediately if he discovered someone who wasn't on the suspect list who'd had a motive for wanting Shawna Lee dead. He'd also hold himself available to help Hannah sleuth afterhours.

Hannah hadn't mentioned it at the dinner, but she had her own agenda. As far as she was concerned, Shawna Lee's death was a case of too many suspects. Instead of proceeding the way she usually did by making a list of the people with motives, checking their alibis, and eliminating them one by one, she had decided that putting practically every female in Lake Eden on her suspect list would be counterproductive. Hannah planned to concentrate on tracking Shawna Lee's movements on her last day.

Hannah had a starting point for a timeline. It was hours before the ceremony at St. Peter's had started, but it would have to do. She would go out to Bouchard's Bouquets and talk to Kyle. When he'd delivered her roses, he'd told her that he was also delivering roses to Shawna Lee.

"Rowwww," Moishe said, nudging her arm, and Hannah realized that she'd been frozen in the act of dishing up ice cream. Moishe wanted his, and she couldn't blame him. There was nothing like ice cream on a night that was twenty below zero, and she had the refrigerator magnet to prove it.

Hannah glanced at the magnet that was stuck to her refrigerator door. It read, "Lake Eden Snowmobile Rescue" and they'd come around the first winter after she'd bought her condo. The access road had been impassable and they'd wanted to know if she was out of any staples. Hannah had said yes, she was out of chocolate ice cream. She'd been deadly serious, but they'd thought she was joking and hadn't brought her the ice cream. Hannah had suffered through two days of sniffing an empty chocolate chip bag before the roads had opened up again and she'd been able to drive out for chocolate ice cream.

"Hold on, Big Guy," Hannah said, using Norman's nickname for her feline. "I'll get you a dish of vanilla and we'll have our dessert in the living room."

Hannah grabbed two cookies. They weren't quite cool, but she figured she might as well give them a three-part test. She'd try them warm, room temperature, and the next morning for breakfast.

Once Moishe's scoop of vanilla ice cream had been carried to the coffee table in an identical cut glass dessert dish, Hannah settled down to some serious eating and so did her cat. The cookies were good and Hannah was pleased. And the ice cream, a new designer brand that Florence at the Red Owl had recommended, didn't disappoint. It wasn't until the last cookie crumb was gone and the spoon scraped the bottom of Hannah's dish that either one of them spoke.

"I don't think Mike did it, do you?"

"Yowww," Moishe commented, extending his long pink tongue to reach the inside of the rim of his dessert glass.

"Is that a *yes?* I know you're crazy about Norman, but you like Mike too . . . don't you?"

"Rowww," Moishe said, looking up with a perfectly neutral expression.

"Forget I asked. I'll go get more cookies. I don't think chocolate's good for you, but you can have a little of the frosting."

Once she'd carried their dessert dishes back into the kitchen and come back with two more cookies,

Hannah applied herself to her role as official tester. The cookies were now at room temperature and they were delicious that way. Delores would love them. She'd always been especially fond of German Chocolate Cake, and these were German Chocolate Cake Cookies.

The phone rang and Hannah glanced at the clock. Only nine. It could be her mother. But Moishe wasn't bristling, and that meant it was probably someone else.

"Hello?" Hannah answered, swallowing her last bite of cookie.

"Hi, Hannah. It's Phil from downstairs, except I'm not downstairs, I'm at work." Phil sighed. "Did that make sense?"

"Sure. What can I do for you, Phil?"

"Well, I stopped by Granny's Attic this afternoon to pick up a painting that Sue really liked. It was a surprise for our anniversary. Your mother waited on me and she mentioned that Moishe was a really good mouser."

For one brief moment, Hannah wondered how that conversation had started. Then she placed her hand over the receiver and groaned. She knew what was coming and it was bound to entail a trip down the stairs in subzero cold for both woman and beast.

"I know it's late and you get up really early, but this is kind of an emergency. Sue just called me in a panic. She saw a mouse run into Kevin's bedroom closet and she's really afraid of mice. I told her I'd set a trap when I got home, but I know she won't sleep a wink all night. Do you think you could . . ."

"Sure," Hannah said, knowing that nine-tenths

of what Sue wanted was to be reassured. "Just let me slip on some boots and put Moishe into his harness, and we'll go right down there."

Much to Hannah's surprise, Moishe stood on the back of the couch and let her buckle him into his small-dog harness. She carried him down the stairs to save his footpads from the unaccustomed cold, and put him down when they entered the Plotniks' condo.

"I really appreciate this, Hannah," Sue said, looking extremely grateful. "I heard that Moishe liked shrimp and I've got a two-pound bag in the freezer to send home with him."

"You don't have to do that," Hannah protested, thinking about the other bags of shrimp that were already lying in state in her freezer. She'd only used one bag for the gumbo and that left the second bag of salad shrimp that Delores had given her, and the bag of medium tail-on shrimp that Carrie had contributed.

"I know I don't have to, but I want to. You have no idea how much I appreciate this, Hannah. I feel better about it already."

"But you're still shaking," Hannah said, noticing that her neighbor's legs were trembling. "Is there coffee?"

"In the pot. I'll just go and get you a cup."

"I'll get it," Hannah said, handing Moishe's leash to Sue. "You're shaking so hard, you'll probably spill it on the rug. Cream and sugar for you?"

"No, just black. The mugs are in the cupboard over the sink."

Hannah filled two mugs with coffee and carried them into the living room. She found Moishe sitting in Sue's lap. He was purring innocently as Sue stroked his fur, but his nose was inching closer and closer to the foil-covered plate Hannah had placed on the coffee table.

"Oh, no you don't!" Hannah grabbed her cat before he could commit cookie-cide. "We had our dessert already. These are for Sue."

"They look wonderful!" Sue said when Hannah removed the foil.

"They are. It's a new recipe, German Chocolate Cake Cookies, and I want you to eat at least two. The endorphins in the chocolate will make you feel better."

"That's the best excuse for pigging out that I've ever heard!" Sue said with a laugh, reaching for a cookie. She took a bite, smiled in pleasure, and took another bite. "So this doesn't count as breaking my diet, since they're medicinal."

"Absolutely right. Medicinal calories have no effect on the body." Hannah grinned to show she was joking and Sue laughed again.

"These are delicious, Hannah." Sue finished her first cookie and started in on the second. "And so were the wedding cakes you made for Lisa and Herb. Phil got chocolate and I got vanilla, and we switched plates halfway through. Between the candy at the hospital, the dessert buffet at the wedding, and these cookies, my diet's had a bad week."

"You'll get back on track," Hannah reassured her, and then she picked up on the first half of Sue's sentence. "You were in the hospital?"

"Just visiting. Phil and I went to see his cousin.

She slipped on her front steps and broke her ankle. Doc Knight's keeping her in the hospital for a couple of days because it's a bad break."

"That's too bad. I hope it's not too painful."

Sue shook her head. "They've got her all doped up and when we got there, she was chattering away a mile a minute with Ronni Ward. Ronni's all doped up, too."

"Ronni's in the hospital?" Hannah leaned forward slightly. This could be important.

"Ronni broke her ankle at almost the same exact time. Of course they were miles apart when it happened, but it's kind of a strange coincidence. Both of them were upset about missing Lisa and Herb's wedding, so we had to promise to bring them a piece of wedding cake."

Hannah made a mental note to call her mother and Carrie and tell them they didn't have to bother to look for Ronni Ward's name on the guest lists. Then she broached the rodent problem. "I'll let Moishe loose in Kevin's room, but I'm not sure he'll catch your mouse."

"I am. Phil said your mother gave him a glowing testimonial and so did Carrie. They said he was better than Professional Pest Control, or Mouse Be Gone."

"Well . . . that's nice to hear," Hannah said, wondering what in the world she'd gotten into when she'd assured her mother that Moishe had solved her problem. "Phil said the mouse was in Kevin's closet?"

"That's right. At least I had the presence of mind to shut the door so it couldn't get out. I wouldn't worry so much if it was in our closet, but Kevin's just a baby."

"I understand," Hannah said, gesturing for Sue to lead the way. And then she muttered, *sub rosa* to Moishe, "Did you hear that? We've got to get rid of this one!"

A moment or two later, Hannah was sitting on the rug in front of Kevin's closet, armed with a twenty-plus-pound cat. Kevin was sleeping the sleep of the angels, and Hannah wasn't about to disturb him. She whispered her instructions to Moishe.

"Try not to wake the baby. Just check to see if there's a mouse, and if it's here, get rid of it. You don't have to kill it if you don't want to. You can chase it off and that'll be fine. Just don't make a lot of noise so Kevin wakes up. And don't gross me out, okay?"

Moishe turned to stare at her with his perfectly blank expression again, and Hannah imagined she could read his mind. *Now you're going to tell me how to catch mice? Who's the cat here anyway?*

"Sorry," Hannah whispered. "I'm just a little nervous, that's all. I'll open the closet door and you can just do your thing."

Moishe waited until she opened the door and then he stalked to the closet. A second later, he was inside, burrowing in back of the packages of disposable diapers. And then he was out, grinning at Hannah, the tip of a tail protruding between his teeth.

"It's just a tail?" Hannah asked, feeling a bit anxious. "I mean . . . nothing's attached to it . . . right?"

Moishe didn't answer. He just sat down on his haunches and purred.

"So . . . what should I tell Sue?" Hannah addressed the only one who knew what had happened in the closet. "Did you get the whole mouse? Or just the tail? And is a tail something a mouse can live without?"

Moishe purred. He purred loudly, the loudest Hannah had ever heard him purr. Hannah assumed that was the only answer she was about to get and she led him out of the room.

"It's over?" Sue asked when they emerged.

"I think so. He was in the closet when the . . . uh . . . incident occurred. And I saw the tip of a tail peeking out between his teeth."

"That's good enough for me," Sue said, and reached out to give Moishe a pat. "How about some shrimp for your trouble?"

Even though Hannah protested and said that was what neighbors were for, Sue refused to let her leave without a two-pound package of frozen shrimp.

"What now?" Hannah asked as she trudged up the steps, carrying her purring feline. "Shall we put a notice in the *Lake Eden Journal* and rent you out as a community service?"

But Moishe just purred. And he continued purring as Hannah opened the door, took off her boots, and got the coffee ready to go off automatically in the morning. He purred as she washed her face and brushed her teeth, and put on the long, oversized sweatshirt that served as her winter nightgown.

Hannah set the alarm, switched off the light, and climbed into bed. Moishe was still purring when she upended him from her goose-down pillow and moved him over to the identical goose-down pillow she'd bought for him. He purred his permission as she cuddled him close and he didn't draw away and move down to the bottom of the bed.

"You're really mellow tonight," Hannah said, stroking his soft fur. It was highly unusual for Moishe to let her pet him this long. Usually three pats were all she was allowed before he moved out of reach.

Hannah was wondering if mice had endorphins that made cats happy, similar to the effect the endorphins in chocolate had on people, when Moishe opened his mouth. She let out a little gasp as she saw something small, and fast, and dark streak down to the foot of her bed. A second later, the small dark thing hurtled off into space, hit the floor scrambling, and hightailed it into her walk-in closet.

"No wonder you were purring!" Hannah gasped, sitting straight up in bed and flicking on the light in time to see her resident feline jump off the bed with a thump worthy of a much larger species, and set off in hot pursuit. "You brought Sue's mouse home to play!"

GERMAN CHOCOLATE CAKE COOKIES

Do not preheat oven yet—
make cookie dough first

COOKIE DOUGH:

1 cup butter *(2 sticks)*
1 cup milk chocolate chips
2 cups white *(granulated)* sugar
2 eggs
½ teaspoon baking powder
½ teaspoon baking soda
½ teaspoon salt
2 teaspoons vanilla
3 cups flour *(no need to sift)*

FROSTING:

½ cup firmly packed brown sugar
¾ cup tightly packed coconut
½ cup chopped pecans
¼ cup chilled butter *(½ stick)*
2 egg yolks, beaten

In a microwave-safe bowl, melt the butter and chocolate chips on HIGH for 2 minutes. Stir until smooth.

In another mixing bowl, mix the sugar and the eggs. Add the baking powder, baking soda, salt, and vanilla.

Stir the melted chocolate until it's fairly warm to the touch, but no longer hot. Add it to the mixing bowl and mix it in thoroughly.

Add the flour and mix well. *(Dough will be stiff and a bit crumbly.)*

Cover the dough and set it aside while you make the frosting.

Combine the sugar and coconut in a food processor. Mix with the steel blade until the coconut is in small pieces.

Add the chopped pecans. Cut the butter into four chunks and add them. Process with the steel blade until the butter is in small bits.

Separate the yolks, place them in a glass, and whip them up with a fork. Add them to your bowl and process until thoroughly incorporated. *(If you don't have a food processor, you can make the frosting by hand using softened butter.)*

Preheat the oven to 350 degrees F., rack in the middle position.

Chill the frosting while the oven's preheating. It'll make it easier to work with. This will be especially true if you've made the frosting by hand and haven't chopped the coconut into shorter shreds.

Pat the cookie dough into one-inch balls with your fingers. Place the balls on a greased cookie sheet, 12 to a standard sheet. Press down in the center of each ball with your thumb to make a deep indentation. *(If the health board's around, use the bowl of a small spoon.)*

Pat the frosting into ½-inch balls with your fingers. Place them in each indentation.

Bake at 350 degrees F. for 10 to 12 minutes. Let the cookies cool on the cookie sheet for 2 minutes, then remove them to a wire rack to finish cooling.

Yield: 5 to 6 dozen, depending on cookie size.

Chapter Fifteen

By the end of the day, Hannah's feet were aching. The customers had come in a steady stream, not even tapering off for their predictable eleven-thirty lull, a time when people thought it was too late for a breakfast cookie and too early for a lunch cookie. During the day, Hannah had manned the counter while Lisa had dashed back to the kitchen to mix up and bake a triple batch of Hannah's Bananas. When it was clear that they would sell out, Hannah left Lisa to man the counter while she mixed and baked a triple batch of Oatmeal Raisin Crisps.

Andrea had called in with her report. She'd driven out to the sheriff's station, intending to ask about the electronic gate card log for the time of the wedding, but she'd run into Marjorie Hanks in the parking lot. Marjorie had just picked up her check for cleaning the station on Valentine's Day. When Andrea asked her why she'd worked on a holiday, Marjorie had said that she preferred to work when most employees were gone, because then there were less people to get in her way. Further probing on Andrea's part had established that Marjorie had walked past Mike every ten minutes or so as she'd carried out trash and cleaned the various cubicles. He hadn't left the station. Marjorie had been sure of it.

"I served more coffee today than I've served in a week!" Lisa announced, coming through the swinging restaurant-style door that separated the coffee shop from the kitchen.

"How many urns did we go through?"

"I don't know. I stopped counting at a dozen. That's over . . . thirty times twelve . . . three hundred and sixty cups!"

"Is there any coffee left?"

"Just dregs. I'll dump it out and make a fresh pot here in the kitchen for your strategy meeting. Do you want me to sit in?"

"Of course, if you have time."

"I do. Herb isn't picking me up for another twenty minutes. I talked to him on the phone and he wanted me to ask you if there was anything he could do to help you. The Pretty Girl Cosmetic husbands are taking a bus to the Indian casino tomorrow, so Herb doesn't have to help Dick entertain them."

"Herb doesn't want to go to the casino?"

"Not really. He'd rather help you if you need him. He said this life of leisure is getting to him."

"The wedding was only two days ago," Hannah said with a laugh.

"I know. But Herb really loves his job and I think he misses the excitement of law enforcement."

Only because you're not there to provide another kind of excitement, Hannah thought, but she didn't say it. Lisa was a very private person and she considered some topics off-limits, even for friends and business partners.

Hannah's oven timer dinged and she went to take a final pan of cookies out of the oven. She'd finished baking the German Chocolate Cake Cookies and she was eager to try them out on her mother.

Five minutes passed while Hannah arranged cookies on a plate and Lisa made coffee in the kitchen pot. Then the two partners sat at the workstation for a moment, both of them lost in thought, until there was a knock on the back door and Lisa went to open it.

"Hi, Mrs. Beeseman," Norman said, chuckling when Lisa glanced around to see if Herb's mother was standing behind her. "That's you now, Lisa. Unless you'd prefer to be called Ms. Herman."

Lisa shook her head. "Mrs. Beeseman sounds nice. I'm just not used to it yet. I wonder how long it'll take me."

"At least a year," Andrea said, coming in the back door, "especially since you're working in a casual environment and everyone calls you Lisa anyway. If you worked in a big office and they called you Mrs. Beeseman all the time, you'd get used to the name in a hurry. Is there coffee? I'm dying of caffeine withdrawal here."

"Coming up." Lisa grabbed a mug and filled it. She added real cream and sugar, the way Andrea liked it, and set it down in front of her. "You look like you've been running all day."

Andrea took a big gulp of coffee. "That's right. I worked for three hours this morning entering listings in the computer, and then I went out to the sheriff's station and got the scoop on Mike. After that, I showed three houses, got another listing from the neighbor next door to one of the houses I showed, picked up Tracey and her friends from school, and dropped them off at dance class. Now all I have to do is run out to the mall to order some pens that Al wants to have made, and be home by nine to relieve Mrs. McCann so that she can watch *Hot Pix* on the Romance Network."

"What's that?" Lisa asked, expressing more interest than Hannah had expected. Perhaps marriage was widening her horizons.

"It's the most romantic movie of the week. The one tonight got five hot peppers and that means it really sizzles. *Hot Pix* is one of the reasons Mrs. McCann agreed to stay in our guest room and take care of Bethany for three months. She doesn't have a dish out at the farm and all she can get are the regular channels."

"I wonder if we should think about getting Mother a . . ." Hannah stopped and began to frown. Perhaps Delores would be better off *not* having a dish. It might give her even more romantic ideas about Winthrop. "Never mind," she said.

"Because it might . . . you know?"

"Exactly." Hannah exchanged an understanding look with her sister. "Did you say you were going out to the mall tonight?"

"Yes. Do you want to go along?"

"I'd love to," Hannah said, surprising everyone in the kitchen. She'd made it perfectly clear that she hated the mall and its myriad of shopping experiences back when it had first opened.

"Why?" Andrea asked, echoing the question that was in everyone's mind.

"I'm making a timeline for the day Shawna Lee was shot and I need to talk to Kyle."

"Who's Kyle?" Lisa wanted to know.

"The deliveryman for Bouchard's Bouquets." Hannah paused as she took in everyone's identical frown. "I know a timeline's never done us any good before, but maybe it'll work this time. It's just that . . . I'm really not sure what else to do. I'm stymied."

There was a moment of silence worthy of a great loss in basketball, or perhaps a presidential assassination. Norman was the first one to gather his wits about him. "*You're* stymied?"

"Yes."

Andrea reached out to pat Hannah's shoulder. "I know exactly how you feel. Unless Delores and Carrie come up with something, we're stuck in a canoe heading for the rapids without an oar."

"Canoes don't have oars, they have paddles!" Delores said, coming in the door with Carrie in time to hear Andrea's comment. "What's wrong?"

"Hannah's stymied," Norman repeated, turning around to explain to the mothers. "How about you? Have you come up with something?"

"I'm afraid not," Delores said, accepting the mug of coffee that Lisa brought to her. "We checked out all the names on our suspect list with the ones in the guest books and we only found one person who missed the service and came to the reception."

"Who was that?" Hannah asked, hoping against hope that it was someone with a motive.

"Gloria Travis," Carrie told her.

"She sat with us at the reception," Delores explained, "and she's with the Pretty Girl convention. She didn't know the area and this is the first time she's ever been in Lake Eden."

"No motive," Hannah said with a sigh. "And that was it?"

When both of the mothers nodded, Hannah got up to get the plates of cookies she'd prepared earlier and set them down in front of her mother. "Try one of these, Mother. I made them just for you."

"German Chocolate Cake!" Delores exclaimed after taking one bite. "I'm right, aren't I?"

"You're right."

"How did you make these, dear?"

"Baker's secret," Hannah replied, smiling at her mother.

"Well, they're simply marvelous! I think they're even better than your grandmother's German Chocolate Cake."

Hannah smiled widely, and she felt happy all the way down to her toes. Delores liked her cookies.

"The only thing that's different is the texture, and Mother's cake was always a little too light to suit me." Delores stopped speaking and began to frown. "You *did* write down the recipe, didn't you, dear?"

"Yes, Mother."

"And you can make more of these?"

"Yes, Mother."

"Well, that's a relief!" Delores pulled the plate of cookies toward her possessively. "I'll need you to cater the Lake Eden Ladies' Club meeting next Thursday and I want you to serve these."

"I'll be happy to, Mother."

"Excellent. You have other cookies you can serve now, don't you, dear? I want to take these home with me. They'll be perfect for tonight's bedtime snack."

Hannah and Andrea exchanged glances. This was a first. Their mother limited herself to one serving of dessert a day, and she'd often claimed that this minimum of sweets was her secret to maintaining a perfect figure. But now she had taken to snacking at bedtime? This revelation, so casually disclosed, made Hannah wonder if the newly instituted bedtime snack was Winthrop's idea. And if it was, did Winthrop share that snack with their mother?

"I'll put them in a bag for you," Hannah said, getting up to take the plate and transfer the contents to one of the miniature shopping bags she used for takeout orders. Then she put another dozen cookies on a plate and brought them to the workstation.

"Now what are these?" Delores wanted to know.

"I'm not quite sure. I think I'll call them Desperation Cookies. We had so many customers today, we ran out of cookie ingredients."

"Then what's in these?" Norman asked, reaching out for one.

"A little dab of this and a little dab of that. Whenever there's a little bit of something in the bottom of a bag, I save it. I don't know why, I just do. So when we ran out of things to put in cookies, I made a basic dough and used up all those bags."

"I like these!" Norman said, swallowing his first bite. "Every bite tastes a little different than the last."

Lisa took a cookie and tasted it. "This one has four different kinds of chips."

"Mine, too," Andrea said. "I got butterscotch and regular chocolate chips in the first bite."

Carrie tested a cookie. "I got white chocolate and milk chocolate. It's a nice combination. What kind of nuts do I taste?"

"I put in walnuts and pecans, and there were a few cashews thrown in."

"There's something chewy," Lisa said.

"That could be the coconut, or maybe a raisin. I threw in some of those. There might even be some dried cranberries in there. I'm just not sure."

"So could you make these again?" Norman wanted to know.

Hannah thought about it for a minute and then she laughed. "Not in a million years," she said.

"What are all these people doing here?" Hannah asked, dodging a young mother pushing a stroller with one hand and holding a toddler's arm with the other. They'd stopped off at her condo so she could feed Moishe and she found herself wishing she'd stayed there. The mall was noisy, a cacophony of sound, with hundreds of people talking at once. The concrete walls and ceilings, bare of baffles or any other means of muffling the noise, bounced the voices back and forth until no words were distinguishable and utterances of happiness, excitement, or dismay became one homogenous reverberation that resembled the lowing of a large herd of cattle.

"It's always crowded in the winter, especially at night. When people get off work, they come out here to do a little shopping, catch a bite to eat, and take in a movie. It's nice to be able to walk around without parkas and boots."

"I guess," Hannah said, although she'd much

prefer going home to her cat, heating something in the microwave, and watching a movie on television in the comfort of her own living room.

"Here's where I'm going." Andrea pointed to a small storefront with a sign that read, MR. LOGO. "Come on in with me. It's a fun store."

Hannah followed in her sister's wake, wondering when the word *fun* had become an adjective, and listened as Andrea placed an order for three hundred Lake Eden Realty pens. While her sister and the clerk were discussing font style and color, Hannah wandered away to look at a rack of bright purple T-shirts with white block lettering. They all bore the legend LAKE EDEN GULPS instead of LAKE EDEN GULLS, the name of Jordan High's sports team, and they had been discounted to a dollar apiece.

"Hello, my name is Tammy. Could I help you, ma'am?" asked a pretty brunette wearing a MR. LOGO golf shirt with the name *Tammy* embroidered in flowing script over the pocket.

"Yes," Hannah replied, wondering precisely when she'd reached the age where high school students called her ma'am. "Are these shirts really a dollar?"

"Not anymore. The manager just told me to mark them half off, because we need to hang something else on the rack. They're supposed to say, *Lake Eden Gulls.*"

"I'm from Lake Eden. I figured that out," Hannah said.

"Oh. Well, anyway, that's why they're so chea . . . um . . . inexpensive. Would you like to buy one?"

"No, I'd like to buy them all," Hannah said as a brilliant idea popped into her head. At the last town meeting, Mayor Bascomb had asked the business owners if they'd be interested in sponsoring softball teams to compete against each other in the summer. Both Lisa and Hannah were all for the idea, but part of the responsibility of a sponsoring business was to provide team outfits. Now the solution to The Cookie Jar's team uniforms had presented itself. Jeans and a *Lake Eden Gulp* T-shirt would be perfect, since The Cookie Jar was a bakery and coffee shop and their customers gulped coffee with their cookies.

"You want . . . *all* of them?" Tammy stared at her in surprise when she nodded. "Um . . . I know it's none of my business, but . . . why?"

Once Hannah had explained, Tammy was delighted. "Can I play on your team? I played softball in high school and I really miss it."

"You mean you're a graduate?"

"Two years ago from Eagle Valley High. I'm from Clarissa. I've been taking classes at the community college, but they don't have an athletic program."

"We'd love to have you play for us," Hannah said, making a manager's unilateral on-the-spot decision and handing over one of the cards Norman had made for her on his computer. "Call me next week and we should have everything set up by then."

"Thanks! I'm so excited! Now you stay right here and don't take anything up to the register. I'm going to talk to the boss and see if I can get you a bulk deal on these shirts."

Hannah stood and waited. And while she waited, she pondered another age-related question. At what point in her life had high school graduates started to look so young? As she got older and older, would everyone start to look younger and younger? Perhaps she should go out to the Lake Eden Convalescent Home and ask Grandma Walstrom, since she'd just celebrated her hundred and first birthday. There had been a picture of the celebration on the front page of the *Lake Eden Journal,* showing Grandma Walstrom sitting in a straight-backed chair, eating a piece of chocolate birthday cake and sipping a martini. When asked about the martini, the newspaper had quoted the centenarian as saying, *I always said I'd never touch strong spirits, not even if I lived to be a hundred. I lived to be a year over that, so now I'm trying this martini. Don't know what all the fuss is about. Tastes like turpentine to me!*

"Four for a dollar if you take them all," Tammy said, rushing up to Hannah's side with a piece of paper, and pulling her from her thoughts. "All you have to do is take this note to the register. And the best part is, we'll deliver! We've got a big order going to Jordan High next week, so the driver will drop yours off on the same run. There are eight shirts in each size and we have small all the way up to double extra large."

"Thanks, Tammy." Hannah gave the girl a big smile and reminded her to call in a week to find out more about The Cookie Jar team. Then she hurried up to the register to pay before the manager changed his mind.

"I saw you hand over a ten-dollar bill," Andrea said as they left the store. "What did you buy? And why didn't you take it with you?"

"Not it. Them. I bought more than one thing. Forty T-shirts, as a matter of fact."

Andrea turned to stare at her. "And I thought *I* was a good shopper! You really bought forty T-shirts for ten dollars?"

"That's right, and they're being hand-delivered next week. Somebody made a mistake in the lettering and it says Lake Eden *Gulps,* instead of *Gulls,* but that's perfect for The Cookie Jar's new softball team. We might even bring along iced coffee and pass it out to our fans."

"I didn't know you were sponsoring a softball team."

"Neither did I until I found those shirts. Lisa and I thought team shirts would be too expensive."

"Are you going to have cheerleaders?" Andrea asked, looking wistful.

"I don't know. The team's not even formed yet."

"Maybe I could find some cheerleaders for you. I could head up the squad. I still remember all the cheers. How about it?"

"Sure, if you think you'll have time," Hannah agreed.

"I'll *make* the time. It'll be a fun thing for me to do." Andrea glanced over at the flower shop. "So what do you need to find out at Bouchard's Bouquets?"

"I'll tell you while we're having a pretzel," Hannah said, pointing to a cart just past the entrance to the flower shop. It was selling hot salted pretzels, one of her favorite fast foods and the downfall of several low-carb diets she'd started.

"You go ahead. I have to eat dinner with Bill when he gets home." Andrea waited until Hannah had bought a pretzel and then they walked back to the florist shop. "So what do you need to know?"

"What time Kyle delivered Shawna Lee's flowers, whether he saw her in person, and what time he left. He's working the counter tonight. I called to ask. I also need to know anything else that Kyle knows about Shawna Lee's schedule for the rest of that day. I'm willing to bet that she offered him some of her peach cobbler and lots of personal attention."

"To generate more business?"

"No, to keep him there longer. Kyle's really cute."

DESPERATION COOKIES

Preheat oven to 350 degrees F.,
rack in the middle position.

2 cups melted butter *(4 sticks, one pound)*
3 cups white sugar
1½ cups brown sugar
4 teaspoons vanilla
4 teaspoons baking soda
2 teaspoons salt
4 beaten eggs
5 cups flour *(no need to sift)*
3 cups chips***
4 cups chopped nuts****

***Use any combination of regular chocolate chips, butterscotch chips, white chocolate chips, milk chocolate chips, vanilla chips, cherry chips, strawberry chips, peanut butter chips, or any other flavors you think will go together.

****Use any nuts you like including walnuts, pecans, cashews, almonds, even peanuts. If you don't have enough nuts to make 4 cups, fill in with crushed cornflakes, Rice Krispies, coconut, raisins, or any dried fruit.

Melt the butter. *(Nuke it for 3 minutes on high in a microwave-safe container, or in a pan on the stove.)* Mix in the white sugar and the brown

sugar. Add the vanilla, baking soda, salt, and mix. Add the eggs and stir it all up. Then add half the flour, the chips, and the chopped nuts. Stir well to incorporate. Then add the rest of the flour and mix thoroughly.

Drop by teaspoons onto greased cookie sheets, 12 cookies to a standard-size sheet. If the dough is too sticky to handle, chill it slightly and try again. Bake at 350 degrees F. for 10 to 12 minutes or until nicely browned.

Let cool two minutes, then remove cookies from the baking sheet and transfer to a wire rack to finish cooling.

Yield: Approximately 10 dozen.

Norman really likes these cookies. He says they're like life in Lake Eden because you're never quite sure what to expect.

Bouchard's Bouquets had an incredible display in the window and both Hannah and Andrea stopped to admire it. It was called Delicious Daisies and it consisted of pieces of fruit cut to look like daisies and other flowers. The flowers were held in place with long wooden skewers and arranged in a pretty basket.

Hannah stared in silent admiration for long moments. It was almost impossible for her to believe that such gorgeously succulent fruit could be found in Minnesota in the winter. There were daisies cut out of fresh pineapple with raspberries at the center of each flower. Red grapes and green grapes strung on wooden skewers looked like exotic ferns on long stems, and strawberries, point out, provided riotous splashes of color. Cheese wedges cut in fancy shapes and skewered in place served as a yellow, orange, and white accompaniment to the fruit, and the card that advertised the sumptuous bouquet stated that the whole arrangement, with the exception of the skewers and the basket, was entirely edible.

"It's got to cost a fortune," Andrea breathed,

and Hannah knew she was wishing she'd gotten one for Bill's inaugural party when almost everyone in town had shown up to see him sworn in as Winnetka County Sheriff.

"I'm sure neither one of us could afford it," Hannah said, hoping that Andrea wasn't going to order one just because it was pretty and put it on a credit card. "What we ought to do is take a picture. Lisa's so artistic, I'll bet she'll try to make one as soon as fruit is in season."

"I wonder where they get their fruit," Andrea mused.

"I don't know, but it's almost too beautiful to be real." Hannah stopped and began to frown. "Do you think it is?"

"Do I think *what* is?"

"The fruit. Do you think it's real?"

"I don't know. I'll ask." Andrea started to lead the way into the shop with Hannah in close pursuit. But then she stopped suddenly and turned in her tracks, nearly causing Hannah to mow her over.

"What?" Hannah asked, noticing her sister's intent expression.

"I think you should go sit on that bench over there, and eat your pretzel before it gets cold. You can't eat it inside anyway. I'll go talk to Kyle by myself. He already knows you, and he might clam up if both of us start asking questions. This way I'm just a talkative stranger who happened to drop in to ask about the fruit. I'll come out when I'm through pumping him for information and let you know what he said."

"That's fine with me," Hannah agreed, backing off and heading toward the bench without another word. Andrea was a wizard at getting people to talk and she'd be smart to go along with whatever her sister thought would work.

Ten minutes and most of a soft pretzel slathered with mustard later, Hannah was wondering what was taking her sister so long. She was about to get off the bench and wander past the window to see if she could spot Kyle and Andrea in the interior of the shop when a familiar voice called out her name.

"Mike?" Hannah whirled around and swallowed noisily. There he was across the mall from her with his reddish blond hair and mustache, piercing blue eyes, and six-foot-three-inch frame resplendent in his Winnetka County Sheriff Deputy's uniform. It was enough to take a girl's breath away, and Hannah was no exception even though she was no longer a girl. And even though she was still angry at him, her heart started the old familiar Mike Kingston drumroll in her chest.

Despite her resolve to ignore him, Hannah's hand had a mind of its own. It rose and her fingers waggled a greeting that Mike must have construed as an invitation, for he headed straight toward her across the steady stream of people filing into the movie theater.

Hannah knew she was a goner if she looked into his eyes, so she concentrated on the area right between his eyebrows instead. "Going to the movies?" she asked, with what she thought was just the right note of casual curiosity in her voice.

"Not unless there's something you want to see."

Hannah wasn't sure how to respond. Had he just invited her to the movies? Or was he merely asking if she approved of the lineup the six-plex was showing? If it was the former, she wasn't interested. If it was the latter, it was only polite to respond. The safest thing would be to treat it as a joke and Hannah settled for the first thing that popped into her head after a quick glance at the marquee. "I've already seen *Revenge of the Turtle Gods* three times. I guess I don't really need to see it again."

"*Revenge of the...*" Mike stopped and stared at her. Hard. Then he laughed. "You're kidding ... right?"

"Right."

"So why don't we go get something to eat? I'm not working tonight, and I'd really like to talk to you, Hannah."

"Sorry, but I'm out here with someone, and ..."

"Hi, Mike," Andrea interrupted Hannah in midexcuse. "What brings you out here? Crime in the mall?"

"Just checking out a couple of alibis. How about you?"

"Ordering pens for Al."

"Hannah and I were just talking about going to get something to eat. Are you interested?"

"No, you two go ahead. I have to be home by nine." Andrea ignored the dirty look her elder sister gave her. "I'll call you later, Hannah. The fruit's fake, and I found out more."

Mike gave Andrea a wave as she headed off and then he turned to Hannah. "Somebody's selling fake fruit?"

"No, it was just a window display. I said it looked too good to be real, and Andrea went in to ask."

Mike reached out to take Hannah's arm and tucked her hand in his. "So where are we going for dinner?"

"The Lake Eden Inn," Hannah said promptly, naming one of her very favorite restaurants. She figured that since she'd been shanghaied by Mike with the help of her sister, she might as well make it worth her while.

"Great dinner," Mike said, pulling up in back of The Cookie Jar. "Are you sure you don't want me to follow you home?"

"I'm positive," Hannah replied, not voicing the full sentence that ran through her head. *I'm positive I do want you to follow me home and I'm also positive I shouldn't let you do it.*

"So did you mean it when you said you've got it?"

"Got what?" Hannah asked, thoroughly confused by the question.

"The recipe for Orange Julius."

"I've got it. It might not be the recipe for the bona fide Orange Julius, but it tastes close enough to the real thing to fool everyone."

"Did I tell you why I need it?"

Hannah wondered whether the two glasses of wine Mike had consumed during dinner had somewhat altered his perceptions. But that was unlikely. She'd seen him drink much more than that and remain perfectly sober and lucid. "You said you knew a couple of people who were really disappointed when the stand at their mall closed."

"Right. And our mall doesn't have a stand, either. I checked the directory while I was out there. Do you think the Orange Julius company went out of business?"

Hannah shrugged, wondering why he was so interested. "I don't know."

"How about the recipe? Do you have it here at The Cookie Jar?"

"Yes, it's in my master file. We use it a lot for children's parties. I just made some for a birthday party we catered a couple of weeks ago."

"Then you've got everything you need to make it?"

"Sure. It's one of our staples. We offer lemonade, Orange Julius, milk, or punch."

"So you could make it anytime you wanted to make it?"

Hannah turned to look at Mike in the dim light that was coming from the dash of his car. He was acting very strange and she wasn't sure why. "I guess I could make it anytime. Why?"

"I'd really appreciate it if you'd go inside and make me some."

Hannah stared at Mike in bewilderment. "You want an Orange Julius right now?"

"Yes. I really need it, Hannah. Will you do it?"

"Sure," Hannah said, climbing out of Mike's car and leading the way to the back door of her shop. If she didn't know him so well, she'd swear Mike was having a nervous breakdown. Come to think about it . . . maybe she *didn't* know him all that well. In any event, he'd just bought her an incredibly good dinner and the beef Wellington she'd ordered hadn't come cheap. The least she could do was honor his request, throw the ingredients for Orange Julius in the blender, and zoop them up for him.

Once Mike was seated on a stool at the workstation, Hannah gathered the supplies she needed and plugged in her heavy-duty blender. "This is going to make almost two quarts and you're supposed to serve it over ice. Do you want to take it home with you?"

"Yeah. Except I'm not going home. I'm going across the street to Shawna Lee's."

Hannah stopped in the act of pouring the orange juice into the blender. "Vanessa's back?"

"Not yet." Mike glanced at the clock on the wall. "She's landing right about now. As soon as she picks up her luggage, she'll get her car from the airport lot and drive to Lake Eden. Traffic should be light, so I figure she'll get here by midnight at the latest."

"So . . . you know her schedule?"

"Yeah. I talked to her on the phone this morning. When she said she was driving back to town tonight, I said I'd meet her in the bakery."

"You've got a key?"

"Shawna Lee gave me one so I could, uh, check out the interior when they weren't home. You know, in case someone broke in."

"Right," Hannah said, instead of *Who do you think you're trying to kid here?*

"Anyway, I didn't think she should go into the bakery alone in the dark. I mean, with her sister being killed there and all. So I said I'd meet her."

Suspicion narrowed Hannah's eyes. Some people might think it was sweet of Mike to think of Vanessa's feelings, but he could have recommended that she stay at a hotel and drive to Lake Eden in the morning. Was there another reason why Mike had agreed to meet her inside when she got home? Local gossip had it that the two southern sisters traded boyfriends. When one would tire of a certain guy and stop dating him, the other sister would take over where her sibling had left off. Had Vanessa planned to step in with Mike when Shawna Lee tired of him?

Whoa! Hannah's mind shouted out a halt. Perhaps Vanessa really wanted Mike, wanted him so badly, she'd do anything to get him. And perhaps Shawna Lee hadn't wanted to give him up quite yet. Would Vanessa kill her own sister to get the man she wanted for herself? Had she really flown back to Georgia on the night that Shawna Lee was killed? Or had she shot her own sister and caught a later flight? It was a possibility that Hannah couldn't ignore.

"We're going to spend the night talking about Shawna Lee," Mike went on. "Vanessa wants it to be like a wake."

Hannah hadn't really thought about it before, but Quinn was an Irish name. "So they're Irish?"

"No. Their great-grandfather shortened the family name to Quinn because nobody could pronounce the real one."

"Okay. If Vanessa's not Irish, why does she want a wake for Shawna Lee?"

"Because she saw it in a movie and she thought it was a good way to remember someone. She said she's got lots of stories to tell me about when they were growing up. I'd invite you, but I know you didn't really like Shawna Lee all that well."

You got that right! Hannah thought, but of course she didn't say it. Instead, she asked, "So why did you want a pitcher of Orange Julius?"

"It was Shawna Lee's all-time favorite drink. Vanessa told me they used to spike cups of Orange Julius with vodka and walk around the mall sipping. Then, when they worked up the nerve, they'd go into the bridal store and try on the wedding gowns. Isn't that sad?"

"Isn't what sad?"

"That Shawna Lee loved to try on wedding gowns, but she never got to wear one."

"Mmm," Hannah said, figuring that a noncommittal response was her best bet. How could she be charitable toward Shawna Lee when the southern sister had been doing her utmost to wear that wedding gown with Mike?

"Anyway, I didn't want to go over there too early. Too many memories, you know? That's why I was so glad to see you at the mall. Going out to dinner with you was a great way to kill some time. I mean . . . we both had to eat, right?"

"Right." Any guilt Hannah might have felt about ordering something expensive vanished into thin air. Mike had used her, pure and simple.

"And then, when you said you knew how to make Orange Julius, it was just perfect."

"Perfect," Hannah repeated, gritting her teeth before she said something she might, or might not, later regret.

"I'll spike it with vodka just like they used to do, and if Vanessa wants to get smashed, I'll stay and hold her hand. There's only one problem with seeing her tonight. She's going to want to know how the investigation's coming along, and I don't know what to tell her."

Now's the perfect time to hit him with some questions! Hannah's inner voice prompted. Opportunity had knocked. While Mike was at low ebb, feeling sad about Shawna Lee's death, she could probe him about the murder investigation. He was far from his usual sharp self and he might tell her all sorts of useful information.

On the other hand, was it fair to take advantage of a man's grief? Hannah thought about that for a moment. Of course it wasn't, but he'd used her to kill time. And he'd used her to make Orange Julius for the woman who might convince him to spend the night with her. All was fair in love and war, and this was one of the above, or both of the above, Hannah wasn't quite sure which.

"So how *is* the investigation going?" Hannah asked in her best casual voice, dumping ingredients into the blender.

"It's not. Everyone who had a motive has an alibi."

"Including me?" she couldn't help but ask.

"Including you. I'm beginning to think that this was a random killing and the killer's long gone. That means we'll never solve it."

"It's possible, I guess," Hannah said, although she didn't believe it for a moment. "But do you really think a deranged killer would drive into Lake Eden, walk around to the back of the Magnolia Blossom Bakery, wipe a spot clean on the kitchen window, and shoot Shawna Lee for absolutely no reason when she was taking peach cobbler out of the oven?"

"Not really. Not when you put it like that. But there aren't any other suspects."

"How about someone from Shawna Lee's past? Did you look into that?"

"We knew the same people in the Cities and I checked with them. They couldn't think of anyone who'd want to kill her."

"How about before that? When she was living in Georgia?"

"Shawna Lee moved to Minneapolis five years ago. I don't think anyone would carry a grudge that long."

"You're probably right. But is it possible she made an enemy when she went back there in December for her brother-in-law's funeral? That was only two months ago."

"It's possible." Mike looked thoughtful. "I'll ask Vanessa about it tonight. Thanks for the idea, Hannah."

"You're welcome," Hannah said, and then she turned on the blender to discourage future conversation. Why had she given Mike a lead to investigate? He was getting information from her when it was supposed to be the other way around!

It didn't take long to make the Orange Julius. Hannah poured the mixture into a pitcher, added extra orange juice, and clamped on the lid. "Here you go. I want the pitcher back."

"You'll get it." Mike set the pitcher down on the stainless steel surface of the workstation and pulled her into his arms. He held her so tightly, Hannah could barely breathe, and her chances at normal respiration vanished when his lips met hers and he kissed her deeply.

When Mike released her, more than a couple of minutes later, Hannah felt as limp as the rag doll her mother had displayed in the front window of Granny's Attic. She reached up to touch her lips and was surprised they hadn't burst into flames and disintegrated.

"I'd better go now." Mike picked up the pitcher and headed for the door. "Thanks, Hannah. I really don't know what I'd do without you. You're the best friend I ever had."

Hannah stared at the door as it closed behind Mike. How could he walk away so nonchalantly? Were the kisses that turned her knees weak and made her heart pound like a trip-hammer just casual kisses to him? She felt like the world's biggest chump!

FAKE ORANGE JULIUS

3 cups orange juice
1 envelope dry Dream Whip *(the kind that makes 2 cups)*
1 package dry vanilla pudding *(the kind that makes 2 cups)*
3 more cups orange juice

Pour the orange juice into a blender. Add the dry Dream Whip and the dry pudding. Blend it for one minute on low and another minute on medium speed.

Pour the mixture in a 2-quart pitcher. Add another 3 cups of orange juice and stir well.

Serve over ice.

Yield: Makes almost 2 quarts.

Chapter Seventeen

Hannah was not in the best of moods when she drove to work the next morning. It had nothing to do with the report Andrea had given her last night. As usual, her younger sister had gotten the goods from someone who probably didn't even know he'd talked out of turn. Kyle had delivered Shawna Lee's yellow roses at eleven. At that time, the bakery had been open and packed with customers. But on Kyle's afternoon run, there had been another bouquet for Shawna Lee. When Kyle had delivered that, at four-thirty in the afternoon, the bakery had been closed and Shawna Lee had invited him in for a cup of coffee. Kyle had sworn to Andrea that Shawna Lee had been very much alive when he'd left her at five. And since Lisa and Herb's wedding had started at five and the guests were already seated by then, Shawna Lee's killer must have been someone who hadn't attended the ceremony at the church.

Of course Andrea had asked who'd sent Shawna Lee the second bouquet and the answer had set her back on her heels. Mayor Bascomb had sent it. Kyle remembered the card. It had read, *Southern*

Flowers for a Southern Flower, and it had consisted of magnolias, camellias, and hawthorn. Since it was February in Minnesota, and the flowers had to be flown in from hothouse growers, it had knocked Mayor Bascomb back to the tune of a hundred and fifty dollars.

All this had been interesting and most likely libelous, but Hannah knew Mayor Bascomb hadn't shot Shawna Lee. He had been sitting in a prominent front pew of St. Peter's Catholic Church with his wife during Lisa and Herb's wedding, and when it was time to start for the reception, Lake Eden's first couple had fallen into line right behind the limo that Hannah had been driving.

Hannah shook her head to clear it. Her bad mood was growing worse and the weather wasn't helping. Big wet flakes of snow splattered against her windshield and she was forced to use her wipers. Her windshield hadn't been washed for a while, and the blades left streaks in the shape of arches to obscure her vision. Hannah slowed to a crawl, pulled over to the side of the road, left the wipers on to dance their stately wintertime gavotte, and got out to remedy the problem.

It was quite a feat to find clean snow by the side of a busy road in February. The snow that was falling hadn't piled up enough to be of any use, and the hard-packed snowbanks the county snowplow had left were too dirty to clean anything. Hannah found a clear spot several feet away that was covered with a thin coat of ice. As she broke through the crust, pulled it apart with both hands, and scooped out the clean snow underneath, it reminded her of the way her father had broken open the crust of a chicken potpie to get at the meat.

Hannah filled both hands with snow and trudged back to her truck. She tossed the clean snow at her windshield, and smiled as she went back for more. Someone from out of state had once recommended that she carry a can of Coca-Cola in her cookie truck during the winter to clean her windshield. Hannah was sure it would work. Miss Bruder, her fifth grade teacher, had shown the class how to clean coins by dropping them into a glass of Coke. But if Hannah stored a can of Coke in her truck and the temperature dipped below freezing, the soda would expand and she'd end up with Coke-flavored ice all over her floorboards.

It took several more trips and at least two sets of wiper gavottes before her windshield was clean. Hannah dusted off her gloves, knocked the snow off her boots, and climbed back in behind the wheel.

As she drove toward town, Hannah forced herself to smile and pretend that everything was hunky-dory. Sometimes the simple act of smiling, no matter how forced, was enough to lighten a person's mood. It was as if the corners of the mouth told the brain what to feel. Unfortunately, the smile Hannah manufactured didn't affect her outlook one iota and it quickly drooped to a glower. Her feet were cold from tramping around in the snow and it was difficult to be upbeat when cold feet were part of the equation.

A glance at the clock on her dash, one feature of her truck that actually worked as advertised, told Hannah that she'd have to step on it if she wanted to get to The Cookie Jar by five. She didn't *have* to be there by five. Unless she had a special last-minute dessert to bake for a catering job, she seldom came in before six. But this morning she had an ulterior motive for arriving an hour ahead of schedule. Although she knew full well that people who spied on other people often discovered things they wished they hadn't, Hannah had decided to drive down the alley in back of the Magnolia Blossom Bakery to see if Mike's Hummer was still there.

Hannah took the turnoff into town with grim resolve. Mike had once told her that if he decided to marry again, he'd marry her. He'd also told her that he loved her. The three little words had passed his lips only twice, but Hannah was convinced he meant them. The important question for her had to do with loyalty. If Mike was still at the Magnolia Blossom Bakery, she wanted to know it. Comforting a grief-stricken sister shouldn't take all night.

What would she do if she saw Mike and Vanessa, silhouetted against the window, locked in a passionate embrace? Hannah groaned at the thought. She wasn't the morality police and she didn't have the authority to rap on the window and shout out, "Put your hands in the air! Step away from the cop! Now!" What she would do was drive quietly away and never tell anyone what she'd seen. But she wouldn't make the mistake of marrying Mike. If he ever asked her. Which was doubtful if he was still with Vanessa.

Hannah gripped the wheel tightly as she turned into the alley. She had the urge to fold her hands, shut her eyes, and pray that Mike's Hummer wouldn't be there. But not even Reverend Knudson, who was a great believer in prayer, advocated driving that way. Instead Hannah concentrated on the alley itself, keeping her truck rolling smoothly through the freshly fallen snow at the center of the pavement, and looking neither to the left nor the right.

As Hannah approached the parking lot for the Magnolia Blossom Bakery, something hit the side of her truck. She slammed on the brakes and turned just in time to see a snowball hit the passenger window.

Hannah peered out into the darkness to see a man in a parka standing at the side of the alley. He was forming another snowball and as she watched he pegged it straight at her windshield.

"Mike?" Hannah gasped, wishing that an alien spaceship would appear overhead and beam her up. But of course that didn't happen and when he motioned with his hand, she rolled down her window.

"What are *you* doing here?"

"Checking up on Vanessa." Hannah grabbed the first excuse that flashed through her mind. "I figured that if her lights were still on, I'd offer to make her some coffee, or something."

It was a lame excuse made even lamer by the blush that colored her cheeks, but Mike didn't seem to notice and he reached out to pat her hand. "That's nice of you, but Vanessa's okay. She fell asleep on the couch about an hour ago and I covered her up with a blanket. I think sleep's the best thing for her now."

"You're probably right," Hannah managed to

say despite the ton of guilt that settled on her shoulders. Not only had she been spying on Mike, she'd also lied about doing it.

"I was just going out for some breakfast before I got ready for work. Do you want to run out to the Corner Tavern with me?"

"I can't," Hannah said without regret. The last thing she wanted to do was manufacture more excuses and tell more lies. "I've got to get to work. We've got lots of customers, now that . . . you know. Vanessa's not going to reopen today, is she?"

"Not today. She's not in any shape to do the baking."

How hard can it be to open up a package of frozen peach cobbler and stick it in the oven? the mean little voice in Hannah's head asked. But Hannah didn't say anything. She knew better.

"Vanessa says she might not reopen at all. She was only doing it for Shawna Lee. See you later, Hannah."

Hannah gave a casual little wave as she drove off, but inside she was shaking. Thank goodness Mike hadn't put two and two together and realized that she'd been checking up on him, not Vanessa!

So what had she learned from her spying? Hannah asked herself that question as she parked behind The Cookie Jar, plugged in her head-bolt heater, and unlocked the back door. She'd discovered that Mike had still been with Vanessa at five in the morning, but she had no way of knowing if he'd acted as Vanessa's understanding friend, or if he'd played another, more romantic role. Hannah wanted to think he'd been the understanding friend and it did make some kind of sense. After all, what man would have the hubris to invite his girlfriend out for breakfast when he'd just finished romancing another woman?

Hannah flicked on the lights and groaned as the answer came to her. Only one man would have the nerve to do something like that. And that man's name was Mike Kingston.

Andrea pushed through the door the moment Lisa unlocked it and shivered as she hung up her coat. "There are times when I hate Minnesota!"

"What happened?" Hannah asked her.

"I got stuck in the school driveway and three boys from Drew Vavra's basketball squad had to push me out."

"But that's not so awful," Lisa commented, bringing Andrea a mug of coffee and two cookies without being asked.

"Yes, it is. It was really embarrassing. Everybody else was driving right in and out again, and I was the only one who got stuck!"

"So you hate Minnesota in the winter," Hannah reiterated. "How about the summer?"

"I don't like the summer, either. I hate mosquitoes. And those awful June bugs that bash against the screen and scare you half to death. I want to move to . . . I don't know where, but there's got to be someplace better."

"There's no place better," Hannah told her, feeling a bit like the Lake Eden Chamber of Commerce and the Minnesota Tourist bureau, all rolled up into one.

"But there must be!"

"There isn't." Hannah shook her head. "Minnesota's unique. It holds a special place in the lineup of states."

"You're kidding me!" Andrea accused her, but she was clearly interested in what Hannah had to say.

"I just don't know how you can even *think* of moving away from a state where you can warm up your hands by sticking them in your freezer."

Andrea, caught in the act of sipping her coffee, set the mug down with a thunk. "What did you say?"

"I said that in Minnesota, you can warm up your hands by sticking them in your freezer."

"That's what I thought you said. You're crazy, Hannah!"

"No, I'm not. It dipped down to twenty below last night. I heard it on the radio. And the freezer in my refrigerator is thirty degrees *above* zero. That means it was fifty degrees warmer in my freezer than it was outside."

"Yes, but . . ." Andrea stopped, frowning deeply.

"If I'd come in from the cold, I could have warmed up my hands by sticking them in my freezer."

Lisa was so delighted, she clapped her hands together. "I love it! Just wait until I tell Herb!"

"Okay," Andrea conceded. "That's pretty strange. But you said Minnesota was unique. You can do what you said in Alaska."

"True, but do they have all the church suppers we have?" Lisa asked, getting into the spirit of things. "I'll bet there are more church suppers and potluck fund-raisers within driving distance of Lake Eden than there are days of the year."

"You could be right," Andrea said, looking a little more cheerful. "What else?"

"Rhubarb," Hannah jumped in. "Do you think they ask, *Think the rain will hurt the rhubarb?* in any other state?"

Lisa started to grin. "I'll bet Minnesotans have more recipes for rhubarb than any other people in the world. I checked my mother's recipe file when we were working on the potluck cookbook and she had fifty-seven desserts using rhubarb."

"And the leaves are poisonous," Andrea pointed out. "I wonder which lucky person was the first one to say, *Let's eat the stalk, not the leaves.*"

Hannah nodded. "How about the first person to eat an artichoke? I'd love to know how many people tried, and failed. But getting back to rhubarb, do you remember when Carol Becker published the recipe for Rhubarb Custard Cake in the food column of the *Lake Eden Journal?*"

"There's no way I could forget it," Lisa said with a laugh. "My mother adored that recipe, and she made my father drive out to every deserted farmhouse to bring back their rhubarb. I had to go along to make sure he cut it off the right way. Then Mom and I cleaned it, cut it up, and froze it so we could have rhubarb cake all winter."

"We didn't." Andrea turned to Hannah. "Why not?"

Hannah shrugged. "Mother doesn't like rhubarb. But do you remember the Strawberry Custard Squares I made?"

"How could I forget? They were so good!"

"And how about the Peach Custard Squares?"

Andrea sighed and rolled her eyes.

"And the Cherry Custard Squares?"

"Incredible. You made them for Washington's Birthday, and I didn't even know he had his own birthday."

"What?" Lisa looked confused.

Hannah explained that people used to celebrate Washington's and Lincoln's birthdays separately back before Presidents' Day. After that, they had to share birthdays because everybody wanted a three-day weekend.

"Washington's probably spitting cherry pits at Johnson right now," Hannah quipped. And then because Andrea looked puzzled, she added, "Lyndon B. Johnson was president when they declared Presidents' Day a holiday. They rationalized it by claiming that Washington's birthday was under the old-style calendar and it could have been on February eleventh, instead of the twenty-second. That meant people were confused about when to celebrate it, so they lumped Washington and Lincoln together."

"You're so smart, Hannah." Andrea looked envious. "Sometimes I feel like a fool when you know all the answers and I don't."

"I don't know all the answers. And don't put yourself down like that," Hannah said, prompted by her sister's unusual candor. "You're a lot brighter than you think you are."

"I am?"

"Yes. How many other people pass the real estate broker's exam the first time they take it?"

"Not many. But that's my work. I'm supposed to do well at that. I still can't spell *possessions*. I know you quizzed me on it, Hannah, but I still have to write down *belongings* or *personal property* so I don't have to use it."

"But you know that *belongings* and *personal property* mean almost the same thing, and that's just as good."

"I do know how to spell *lutefisk*. You can't get out of grade school in Minnesota without knowing that."

They all laughed at that, including Andrea. And they were still laughing when the phone rang. Lisa hurried to get it and a moment later, Hannah turned to Andrea. "It's Herb."

"How can you tell?"

"She gets a glow, just like you do when you're talking to Bill." Hannah stopped and turned to her sister with an inquiring expression. "Do I get a glow when I'm talking to anyone? Like Norman? Or Mike?"

Andrea thought about it for a moment and then she shook her head. "I don't think so. At least not that I've noticed."

"That's what I thought," Hannah said with a sigh. Either her sister was unobservant, which would be highly unusual, or she wasn't head over heels in love the way Lisa and Andrea were.

"You can cross Vanessa off your suspect list," Lisa called out, hanging up the phone and hurrying back to the table. "That was Herb calling from the airport. A clerk at the airline check-in counter remembered her right away when Herb showed her picture. He said he watched her walk all the way up the ramp to the plane."

"I'll bet he did," Andrea said, not looking pleased at all. "There isn't a man alive who doesn't watch Vanessa. And the same went for Shawna Lee. They had all the men in this town acting like complete fools."

Hannah went on red alert. Her sister, one of the most trusting wives in Lake Eden, was jealous. And if Hannah hadn't known that Andrea's every second was accounted for during Lisa and Herb's wedding and reception, she might have added family to her suspect list.

"Oh! No! It's not possible!" Andrea gasped, clamping her hand over her heart. Her face turned as pale as the snow that decorated the branches of the pine across the street, and she looked ready to pass out in her chair. She was staring out the window and both Hannah and Lisa turned to see what had frightened her so badly. But all they saw was a deserted Main Street with snow piled on either side of the road.

"What is it?" both Hannah and Lisa asked in tandem, reaching forward to steady Andrea.

"Across the street! Shawna Lee!"

"Shawna Lee's dead," Hannah reminded her sister, taking Andrea's hands and rubbing them between hers. "There's no way you could have seen Shawna Lee."

"I know that. It was just . . ." Andrea stopped and took a huge gulp of air. "For a second there, I thought that I saw her walking outside the Magnolia Blossom Bakery."

"That must have been Vanessa. She came in last night," Hannah told Andrea, still patting her sister's hand.

"She's back?" Lisa asked, looking surprised.

"For a while. Mike talked to her and she said she doesn't know whether she's staying or not."

"Well, she nearly gave me a heart attack! She looked exactly like Shawna Lee," Andrea stammered, taking a deep gulp of air. "For a split second there, I thought I was seeing a ghost!"

Hannah was silent, deep in thought. Then her eyes narrowed as she faced her sister. "You saw Shawna Lee a lot when you went out to the sheriff's station?"

"Yes. She always made a big fuss over me, asking about when the baby was due and things like that. I think she was trying to get on my good side so I'd recommend her . . ."

"Never mind," Hannah truncated that train of thought. Everybody knew that Shawna Lee was an expert at playing politics. "And you met Vanessa several times?"

"More than several. Al asked me to show her our book of business properties for sale. I tried to talk her out of buying the building across the street. I really did."

"I know."

"I pointed out everything that was wrong with it, but she still insisted on buying it."

"You did your best," Hannah said. "Forget about that. There's something else I need to get straight. Just a second ago, when you went all green around the gills . . . you *really* thought you saw Shawna Lee?"

"I did! Ever since Shawna Lee got her hair cut like Vanessa's, they've looked like twins. I know Vanessa's taller and I could have told the difference if they'd been standing right beside each other, but . . . but they weren't."

Hannah was quiet for so long that Lisa reached out to nudge her. "What are you thinking, Hannah?"

"That maybe Andrea's not the only one who

can't tell the difference between Shawna Lee and Vanessa if they're not standing right next to each other."

There was a long, silent moment when no one spoke. And then Andrea broke the silence. "You mean you think that someone killed Shawna Lee because they thought she was Vanessa?"

RHUBARB CUSTARD CAKE

Preheat oven to 350 degrees F.,
rack in the center position.

1 package *(1 lb., 2.25 oz.)* lemon cake mix
3 to 4 cups peeled cut-up rhubarb***
1 cup white *(granulated)* sugar
2 cups whipping cream or Half 'n Half *(I use Half 'n Half)*

Sweetened whipped cream for a topping

***You can use frozen rhubarb. Just thaw it first and pat it dry with paper towels.

Prepare the inside of a 9-inch by 13-inch cake pan by spraying the bottom and sides with nonstick cooking spray and then dusting it with flour. Shake off excess flour.

Mix the cake according to the package directions.

Pour the batter into the pan you prepared.

Spread out the rhubarb on top of the batter.

Sprinkle the top of the fruit with the sugar.

Cover the sugar with the cream or Half 'n Half.

Bake at 350 degrees F. for 45 to 60 minutes. *(Mine took 50 minutes.)*

This cake won't "set up" exactly like a regular cake—the fruit and custard will sink to the bottom and have the consistency of a thick pudding, or a trifle. The top half of the cake will be like a regular cake.

Cool the cake completely in the pan. Cut it into squares, put them in wide dessert bowls, and top each serving with a generous dollop of sweetened whipped cream, or ice cream.

This pudding cake is good served warm, room temperature, or chilled.

STRAWBERRY CUSTARD SQUARES

Preheat oven to 375 degrees F.,
rack in the middle position.

1 cup flour *(no need to sift)*
½ teaspoon salt
½ cup chilled butter *(1 stick, ¼ pound)*
2 Tablespoons whipping cream *(⅛ cup)*
½ cup flour *(not a misprint—you'll use 1½
    cups in this part of the recipe)*
½ cup white *(granulated)* sugar
3 cups sliced strawberries***

TOPPING:

½ cup white *(granulated)* sugar
1 Tablespoon flour
2 eggs, beaten *(just whip them up in a glass
    with a fork)*
1 cup whipping cream
1 teaspoon vanilla extract *(or strawberry if
    you have it)*

***I've used sliced strawberries, peaches, or chopped
dark cherries.*

Spray a 13-inch by 9-inch cake pan with nonstick cooking spray.

In a small bowl, combine flour and salt. Cut in the half cup of butter until the resulting mixture looks like coarse sand. *(You can do this in the food processor with a steel blade if you like.)* Stir in the cream and pat the dough into the bottom of your cake pan.

Combine the ½ cup flour and the sugar. Sprinkle it over the crust in the pan and put the sliced strawberries *(or other fruit)* on top.

Topping: Mix the sugar and flour. Stir in the eggs, cream, and vanilla *(or other extract)*. Pour the mixture over the top of the fruit in the pan.

Bake at 375 degrees F. for 40 to 45 minutes, or until the top is lightly browned. Cool on a rack, and then refrigerate.

Serve warm or chilled, with sweetened whipped cream or ice cream for a topping.

Yield: 10 to 12 dessert squares.

Chapter Eighteen

"Hello, you've reached the Rhodes Dental Clinic. If this is a dental emergency and you need to page Dr. Rhodes, please press one. If this is a nonemergency call and you'd like to leave a message on the doctor's voice mail, please press two. If you need to make an appointment to see Dr. Rhodes for a consultation, please press three for our automated appointment desk. If you have a fax to transmit, please press four. If you'd like our mailing address, please press five. For handy tips to reduce tooth pain while waiting to contact Dr. Rhodes, please press six. To repeat these options, please stay on the line."

Hannah groaned. Several more options, the possibility of entering an endless loop with no way out except hanging up, some forgettable background music, and an irritatingly cheerful voice that told her that her call was important and she should stay on the line, and Norman's friendly one-dentist clinic could join the telephonic ranks of the conglomerates.

"What is it?" Andrea asked, noticing Hannah's disgruntled expression.

"Norman's new telephone system. It's got all these options."

"Press zero."

"That's one option it didn't give me."

"Just try it anyway. Sometimes a zero will bypass everything else and connect you with a live person."

Hannah pressed zero and she heard a ringing sound. A second later, Norman answered. "Are you live?" she asked.

"Last time I looked. What's up, Hannah?"

"I hate your new telephone system."

"So do I."

"Then why did you buy it?"

"I didn't. Mother decided I needed one and she signed me up for a month's trial subscription."

"Oh." Hannah gave a rueful smile. Their mothers often did things like that. "So you're not going to keep it?"

"No, they're coming in to take it out this afternoon. I canceled yesterday when it wanted me to put in a twelve digit alphanumeric code to retrieve my messages and it only gave me three seconds to do it."

"That sounds like a good reason to me. Are you really busy this morning?"

"Let's see." Hannah could hear pages rustling and she imagined that Norman was at the front desk, paging through his appointment book. "Not really. I've got a final fitting for caps, a broken upper plate, and a whitening appointment. The whitening's the only thing that'll take time. Did you need me to pull a couple of teeth?"

"No, thanks. I'm firmly attached to every one of

mine. I just need you to look up something on your computer, if you've got the time."

"I've got an hour between the caps and the whitening."

"Great. I need to know everything I can about Vanessa's background."

"That's easy. I'll run a search for Vanessa Quinn. Do you know her married name?"

Hannah turned to Andrea who'd just sat down at the kitchen workstation with the cookies she'd liberated from the baker's rack. "What name did Vanessa use when she bought the bakery?"

"Quinn. She said she went back to her maiden name when her husband died."

"Do you know his name?"

Andrea shook her head. "I don't think I ever heard it. She always referred to him as *my husband,* or *him.*"

"We don't know," Hannah reported, turning back to the phone, "but we will. I've got a real estate professional here who can get information from anyone. Just tell me what else you need to know to get the goods on Vanessa, and I'll call you back with the answers."

The moment Hannah hung up the phone, Lisa opened the swinging door from the coffee shop. "I just got a call on the other line. Vanessa wants you to come over. She said something about closing her bakery and getting rid of all the capital assets."

"She said *capital assets?*" Hannah was shocked.

"No, she said *stuff.* But I know what she meant. Anyway, she'll give you first pick if you want to buy something."

"Do I?"

"I think you do if the price is right. She's got a brand-new mixer and she said it was barely used."

Hannah snorted. If what she'd discovered about the Southern Peach Cobbler held true for their other desserts, everything Shawna Lee and Vanessa had served at the Magnolia Blossom Bakery had come straight out of the freezer.

"I know it's not fair to ask you to do it because you can't stand her because of Mike and all, but I think you should at least take a look."

"Andrea has to talk to her anyway, so I'll tag along," Hannah said, deciding on the spot. "We don't want to miss out on something good."

"Exactly. We could use another baker's rack, and who knows what else she's got? Not only that, she sounded . . . funny."

"Funny ha-ha, or funny peculiar?" Hannah asked, using her third grade teacher's question. Mrs. Carlson had still been teaching when Lisa was in school.

"Funny peculiar. It was like we were on a time delay, the kind you get when you talk to someone in a foreign country. I'd ask a question and there'd be this total silence for a couple of seconds, and then she'd answer."

"Great," Hannah said, turning to give Andrea a quick smile. "There are two possibilities. Vanessa's still half whacked from the wake, or she's got a killer hangover. Either way, we win."

Hannah and Andrea went out the back door and walked around the side of the building, rather than have all the patrons in The Cookie Jar ask what they were doing. Hannah wasn't looking forward to seeing Vanessa, but Norman needed information and it would be foolish to pass up a golden opportunity to get more baking supplies and equipment at a hefty discount.

"I still don't know why you wanted me to bring her a gift," Hannah grumbled, shifting the candy box she was carrying to her other hand. "It's not like we're paying a social call."

"I know, but if Vanessa's got a hangover from the Orange Julius Screwdrivers you told me about, Aunt Kitty's Rum Balls might make her feel better."

"Hair of the dog?"

"It's supposed to work. Where does that come from anyway?"

"Ancient Greece. The Asclepian dog. They believed he was magical and hair from his coat that was made into a potion cured disease."

"Well, your rum balls cure pain. I can testify to that. I had three at Lisa and Herb's reception and my feet stopped hurting."

"Maybe that's because you were sitting on a bar stool at the time," Hannah said.

"Maybe," Andrea conceded. "It was a stroke of genius to put them behind the bar with the champagne, instead of out on the dessert table. It made them even more special."

"That was Sally's idea, so the kids couldn't get into them."

"Well, it was a good one. Let's climb the snowbank."

"Okay," Hannah said, immediately feeling better. There was something exhilarating about climbing up a snowbank and racing down the other side. "Can you do it in those high-heeled boots?"

"Of course. I'm used to wearing boots with high heels and these are only medium high. Besides, they dig in and help me keep my balance."

Hannah wasn't taking any chances. Once they'd reached the top of the snowbank, she held out her hand to help Andrea down from the peak. "Vanessa's supposed to be waiting for us in front. When we knock on the bakery door, she'll let us in."

It only took a moment to dash across the street. Hannah knocked on the door while Andrea stomped the snow off her boots.

"Hello, Hannah." Vanessa greeted her cordially enough, but Hannah noticed that she was wearing dark glasses. Her hangover must have hit. "And Andrea! How is that handsome husband of yours?"

"Bill's fine," Andrea replied, and Hannah could tell that her sister's polite smile was twenty degrees below chilly.

"We're sorry for your loss," Hannah said, giving her sister a chance to regroup. "It must have been a terrible shock."

"It . . . was. Did you come to see the stuff?"

"Yes. And to bring you these." Hannah shoved the candy box into Vanessa's hands and saw that they were shaking slightly. She must have really tied one on last night.

"Candy?" Vanessa asked, several beats too late. Lisa was right. She was definitely on time-delay.

"Aunt Kitty's Rum Balls," Andrea pulled herself together enough to answer. "We thought you might like them."

"Oh. Well . . . thank you."

"What are you selling?" Hannah asked her.

"Um . . . everything. Even the stuff in the apartment. I . . . decided to go back to Georgia and it's like . . . why should I keep stuff I'm never going to use again?"

"Good point," Hannah said. "How about in here? Are the tables and chairs for sale?"

"Oh . . . well . . . they must be. I don't need them." Vanessa waved her hand at the table and chairs Hannah had envied when she'd looked through the front window.

"How about the cash register?" Andrea asked.

"Oh . . . that, too. I guess. I mean . . . why would I keep it? And all the cookie jars and everything else. I don't want to be in business again. It . . . was Shawna Lee's idea. I was just along for the . . . ride."

"What do you think you'll do after you go back to Georgia?" Hannah asked politely.

"Oh. Well . . . I might take acting lessons. You see . . . I really don't have to do anything. Mike thinks I should just . . . indulge myself. At least I think that's what he said. That way the people who need the jobs can . . . have them."

"Must be nice," Hannah said, deciding to change the subject before she gave in to the impulse to plant one between Vanessa's eyes just for fun. In her present state, she probably wouldn't even feel it. "How about the kitchen? What are you selling in there?"

"Everything. I already told . . . your girl about the mixer. Shawna Lee didn't use the kitchen things . . . much."

"Could we see the kitchen?" Andrea asked.

"Oh. Sure. Why not?" Vanessa reached out to

steady herself against the wall and led the way to the kitchen. "Everything in here is . . . up for grabs. I just want to . . . get away."

One glance around the kitchen had Hannah drooling. They could certainly use the mixer. Theirs was on its last legs. And their food processor was also getting ready to give up the ghost. Then there were the ovens. Hannah figured she'd probably commit a jailable offense to get her hands on the ovens. They were top-of-the-line models and the ovens at The Cookie Jar had been through two different owners before she'd purchased them used.

Hannah wanted to rave about the equipment, but she kept her mouth firmly closed. She had a theory about rich people. She believed that money was addictive. People who had it almost always wanted more of it, even if they had more than they could possibly spend. They hardly ever gave things away at a bargain if there was a profit to be made. It was to this end that she looked around and gave a little shrug. "I don't know. We're pretty well stocked already. I guess we could use a couple of those baker's racks, but let me think about it, okay?"

"Uh . . . sure. But don't wait too long. I want to go home soon. Come on. I'll show you the apartment."

"I'd love to see it," Andrea said. "Do you have a couple of minutes for coffee? You really should taste the rum balls that Hannah made. They're delicious."

"Rum balls? Oh, yes. These." Vanessa glanced down at the box she was holding. Then the question that Andrea had asked seemed to register and she led the way inside and started up the stairs to her apartment. "I didn't . . . make any coffee."

"I'll make it," Hannah said, heading up the stairs behind Vanessa. "I make great coffee. You have some, don't you?"

"I think . . . there's some in the kitchen."

Hannah turned to give Andrea a wink. It was clear that Vanessa's antenna wasn't receiving a full lineup of channels this morning. This would be almost like shooting fish in a barrel.

On her way up the stairs, Hannah thought about shooting fish in a barrel. What fun would there be in that? Had anyone actually done it? If they had, all it would take was one shot. Then all the water would run out of the barrel and you could just reach in and get the fish.

"Kitchen," Vanessa said, pointing to the room on the right at the top of the stairs. "Coffee should be . . . there."

"Don't worry. I'll find it," Hannah said, letting Vanessa lead Andrea into the living room.

"I can't believe this is the same building," Hannah heard Andrea say. "You must have had these rooms professionally decorated."

Hannah didn't stick around to hear Vanessa's answer. It was all too true, at least as far as Hannah could see. The bedroom across the hall looked absolutely perfect, as if it were part of a bedroom display at a furniture store, without a speck of originality or a trace of anything personal.

As she stepped into the kitchen, Hannah knew the same decorator had been at work. It was truly gorgeous with color-coordinated towels and pot holders that no one had ever used. Just to make sure, Hannah peeked in the oven. No spills, and the electric coils looked as if they'd never been heated. It was obvious that neither sister cooked, or if they did, they used the microwave.

Hannah busied herself opening cupboard doors, ostensibly looking for the coffee. She found it on the second try, but she pretended she hadn't and snooped her way through the southern sisters' kitchen.

There wasn't much to eat on the cupboard shelves unless you wanted to count a jar of coffee whitener and a half-empty and mostly petrified package of Fig Newtons. The refrigerator didn't yield much in the way of foodstuff, either. There was a squeeze bottle of catsup, a carton of menthol cigarettes, and a package of sliced cheese that had seen much fresher days. A jar of Miracle Whip with the top on crooked sat on the top shelf, and a six-pack of double-A batteries with three missing completed the picture.

She was supposed to be making coffee, Hannah reminded herself, and she hurried to put it on. While the coffee was dripping down into the carafe she'd had to scour before using, she glanced inside the dishwasher. There was her pitcher! Hannah washed that, too, and set it up on the counter to take back to The Cookie Jar with her. She was about to close the dishwasher door again, when she noticed that someone had put silverware in the basket.

Was that real silver? Hannah took out a spoon to examine it. It was Gorham silver flatware and it was expensive. Washing it in the dishwasher was a big mistake. Real silver should be hand washed and dried with a soft nonabrasive cloth, and very occasionally polished. Delores had taught her all about caring for silver at a very young age.

Disturbed by the casual lack of respect for fine collectibles, Hannah took another look. There were three Limoges china plates crusted with something that looked like cheese sitting in the dishwasher rack. On the rack above were several Waterford wineglasses. Crystal and fine china should also be hand washed and dried. Hannah was glad her mother wasn't with her. Delores would have a heart attack if she knew about the cavalier way Vanessa and Shawna Lee had treated their possessions. It seemed that both Quinn sisters were experts at spending money, but total fools when it came to caring for the fine things they'd purchased.

Hannah shut the dishwasher door and immediately felt guilty, even though there was no reason why she should. These weren't her china plates, crystal glasses, or silver flatware. She wasn't mistreating them. If they were ruined, the blame would rest squarely on the shoulders of the person who'd put the collectibles in the dishwasher in the first place. But she reached out to open the door again. She couldn't just stand by idly while someone mistreated these expensive items. It would be like watching a child step off the curb when a truck was coming and not grabbing his arm to haul him back to safety.

Even though she tried to banish the image, Hannah saw her mother's face in her mind. The imaginary Delores was wearing a disapproving frown and she was pointing her finger at Hannah. "Okay, okay," Hannah muttered, turning on the faucet and running dishwater into the sink. She'd wash these things and leave a note for Vanessa, telling her they had to be hand washed or they'd be ruined. That would absolve her of any responsibility and put a smile on the face of the mother in her mind.

When Hannah emerged from the kitchen, ten minutes later, she was carrying coffee on a tray she'd found in the cupboard. She stepped into the living room just in time to hear the answer to one of the questions they needed to ask, Vanessa's husband's first name.

"Neil wanted to be cremated," Vanessa said, dabbing at her eyes with a handkerchief. "I think he knew it would be easier for me. I just don't know what to do about poor Shawna Lee!"

"You don't have to decide that right now. Wait until you're thinking clearer," Andrea advised.

"Andrea's right. There's time to deal with all that later." Hannah passed Vanessa a cup of coffee, and offered her the whitener and the sugar substitute she'd found. There were three empty frilled cups in the box of rum balls and Vanessa was speaking faster, without the time delay. "Have another rum ball. Our Aunt Kitty used to make them and she said they made her *think more clearly*."

"I need to think clearer," Vanessa said, ignoring the little grammar lesson Hannah had done her best to impart. "I just never thought I'd be without my big sister!"

Hannah reached out to move the rum balls closer. Andrea had gotten the husband's first name and now they needed his last name. "It must be hard, especially since you just lost Mr. . . . I'm sorry. I don't know your husband's last name."

"Roper. Neil Roper. He was a lot older than me, but I just loved him to pieces, you know?"

Hannah gave a polite nod to indicate that she understood, but it made her wonder exactly how Vanessa's octogenarian husband had died. If Neil Roper had been hacked up into body parts by an intruder, Vanessa might very well have had a part in it.

"Neil was so wonderful to me! I had everything I ever wanted and you should see the showplace he left me. It's a real southern mansion, with magnolia trees and everything."

It was Andrea's turn to nod and smile. "I've always wanted to live on a southern plantation, ever since the first time I saw *Gone With the Wind*. Where is your mansion, Vanessa?"

"Just outside of Macon. That's where Neil's headquarters are." Vaness turned to Hannah and abruptly changed the subject. "I think you're very nice, Hannah . . . not at all like Shawna Lee said you were."

"Mmm," Hannah said, and prompted by a kick from Andrea, she managed to keep the smile on her face. Her grandmother used to say that you could catch more flies with honey than vinegar, and the whole purpose of this coffee klatch was to trap metaphorical flies. "Well, you're every bit as nice as Mike said *you* were."

"Isn't Mike just a doll?" Vanessa smiled so widely Hannah imagined she could see her tonsils. For one brief moment she wondered how much those perfectly straight teeth had cost, but that was a question only Vanessa, or a dental professional like Norman could answer.

"Mike told me you made the Orange Julius for our little party," Vanessa went on. "It was so good, just like the kind I used to drink out at the mall with Shawna Lee."

"You and Mike had a party last night?" Andrea asked, looking slightly shocked.

"It wasn't a real party, not like you have when you're happy. It was a . . . what do you call it?"

"A wake." Hannah supplied the word for the woman who most probably had romantic designs on Mike.

"That's it. It was Shawna Lee's wake. We talked about her a lot. And then Mike told me he was dating you, and that's why he couldn't spend the night with me."

"Really?" Hannah made a lightning decision to put words in Mike's mouth. It was one way she might be able to get at the truth. "That's really strange. When I ran into Mike this morning, he told me he spent the night with you."

Vanessa looked about as surprised as a woman with a hangover could look. "Well . . . I guess that's true in a way. Mike was here, but he didn't . . . you know."

"I'm afraid I don't know."

"Yes, you do. Anyway, nothing happened. If he said it did, he's just bragging. You know how men are. They want everyone to think they're so . . . what's that Mexican word?"

"*Macho.* It's Spanish."

"That's it. I remember it from *Man of La Macho.*"

"*Mancha,*" Hannah corrected.

"Whatever. Neil got front row tickets for me and my girlfriend. But really, Hannah, you don't need to worry. Mike and I didn't do a thing that I wouldn't have done in the front window of the bakery. I mean, really."

Andrea stood up, signaling the end of the visit. That was a good thing, since Hannah was ready to ask more probing questions that had nothing to do with the information they had set out to learn.

"It was nice to see you again," Andrea said, mouthing the polite phrases that Hannah found so difficult to utter. "I'm sorry it had to be under such sad circumstances."

"Likewise," Hannah said, using a word she'd vowed never to use because it was so utterly insipid.

"Thanks for the rum balls, Hannah. They're really good." Vanessa popped another in her mouth and stood up a trifle unsteadily. "I'll see you to the back door."

Hannah grabbed Vanessa's arm and guided her back down to the couch. "That's okay. We can see ourselves out. We'll just make sure the door locks behind us, okay?"

"Okay." Vanessa gave Hannah another of her wide smiles. "It's okay if you lock the door. Mike's got a key so he can let himself in later."

Andrea grabbed Hannah's hand and pulled her away from the woman who was clearly her rival. "We've got to go, Hannah. Now."

"Right," Hannah said, uncocking her fist and regretting that she hadn't been a trifle faster. "Okay. Let's go."

Vanessa gave a little wave of her fingers, and then she took another rum ball. "You don't have a thing to worry about, Hannah. Mike's just a friend, that's all."

Hannah was about to reply to that with a choice phrase one didn't usually associate with polite social occasions when Andrea's nails dug into her arm and she gave a little yelp of pain. Then her younger sister propelled her out of the room with a strength Hannah hadn't known she possessed, strong-armed her down the stairs, and out onto the snowy back steps.

"Why didn't you . . . I could have . . . I wish you'd . . ." Hannah sputtered, pulling away from her sister with a jerk.

"No way. You almost blew it up there. She was playing games with you, trying to make you jealous, and you almost fell for it."

"Really?" Hannah asked, desperately wanting to be convinced.

"I think so."

But something in Andrea's voice belied her words and Hannah could hear it. "No, you don't think so. You're just trying to make me feel better."

"Well . . . maybe," Andrea admitted, trudging around the side of the Magnolia Blossom Bakery toward Main Street. "But Vanessa did say she hadn't spent the night with Mike."

"I know. Several times. Methinks the lady doth protest too much."

"That's Shakespeare," Andrea announced, stopping at the curb to wait for a car that was driving by.

"I know. It's from *MacBeth*."

"Do you really think Vanessa reads Shakespeare?" Andrea asked, missing the point entirely.

"Not without moving her lips," Hannah said.

AUNT KITTY'S JAMAICAN RUM BALLS

DO NOT preheat oven—
these don't require baking!

4 cups finely crushed vanilla wafers *(a 12-ounce box is about 2½ cups crushed—measure after crushing)*

1 cup chopped nuts *(measure after chopping—I use pecans, but that's because I really like them—I've also used macadamia nuts, walnuts, and cashews)*

½ cup Karo syrup *(the clear white kind)*

½ cup excellent rum *(or excellent whiskey, or excellent whatever)*

2 Tablespoons Nestle's sweet dry cocoa *(I'm going to use Ghirardelli's sweet cocoa with ground chocolate the next time I make them)*

1 Tablespoon strong coffee *(brewed—liquid)*

COATING:

Dry cocoa
Powdered *(confectioner's)* sugar
Chocolate sprinkles

Crush the vanilla wafers in a food processor, or put them in a plastic bag and crush them with a rolling pin. Measure them and pour them into a mixing bowl.

Chop the nuts finely with a food processor, or with your knife. Measure them and add those.

Mix in the Karo syrup, rum *(or substitute)*, sweet dry cocoa, and strong coffee. Stir until thoroughly blended.

Rub your hands with powdered sugar. Make small balls, large enough to fit into a paper bon-bon cup. Dip the balls in cocoa, or powdered sugar, or chocolate sprinkles to coat them. Do some of each and arrange them on a plate—very pretty.

Refrigerate these until you serve them. They should last for at least a month in the refrigerator. *(I've never been able to put this to the test, because every time I make them, they're gone within a week.)*

Yield: At least 5 dozen, depending on how large you roll the balls.

Aunt Kitty's Jamaican Rum Balls make great gifts when they're packaged like fine candy. Most cake decorating stores stock a variety of frilly bonbon cups and decorative candy boxes for you to use.

To make these nonalcoholic, use fruit juice in place of the rum. This should work just fine, but make sure you refrigerate them and eat them within a week. You'll have to change the name to "No Rum Balls," but that's okay. Choose a fruit juice that'll go well with the chocolate, like peach, orange, or pineapple.

Note: I've always wanted to try these dipped in melted chocolate. I bet they'd be fantastic!

Chapter
Nineteen

It was the predictable noon break, the time of day when most people in Lake Eden thought it was too late for a midmorning cookie and too early for an after-lunch cookie. There was only one thing that made this noon break different from any other. It was that it wasn't much of a break. Contrary to custom, The Cookie Jar was still filled with sippers, dunkers, crunchers, and gulpers . . . and almost all of them wanted to know what Hannah had found out about Shawna Lee Quinn's murder.

Hannah had retired to the kitchen shortly after eleven, leaving Lisa with the message, *Hannah really can't say,* for anyone who wanted inside information. She'd baked another two batches of cookies and was finishing up on the third when Norman knocked on the back door.

"Smells good," Norman said, taking his usual place on a stool at the workstation.

"They *are* good. I'll get you one." Hannah poured a mug of coffee for Norman and set it down at the workstation. Then she took a cooled cookie from the baker's rack and handed it to him before she sat down beside him. "I'm calling this recipe Chocolate Almond Toast. Dunk it in your coffee. It's really good that way."

Norman dunked the end of the cookie into his coffee and tasted it. "Delicious," he passed judgment, giving her a nod. "It tastes a little like the chocolate biscotti I used to get in Seattle. It looks like it, too. Could you put some chocolate on the top?"

"I don't know why not. The next time I bake them, I'll dip the tops in melted chocolate chips."

"They'll be really good that way. And they're great plain, too."

"What's great plain?" Lisa came in from the coffee shop, carrying two empty glass display jars.

"Chocolate Almond Toast." Hannah motioned toward the baker's rack. "Fill up one of those jars and see how people like it."

"If it's chocolate, they'll like it," Lisa predicted, slipping cookies into the display jar.

Norman reached down for his briefcase and snapped it open on the stainless steel surface. He took out a thick sheaf of three-hole paper held together with a brass brad, and handed it to Hannah. "This is what I got when I ran that computer search."

"All this?" Hannah asked, thumbing through the three dozen or so pages.

"All that. Most of it's about Vanessa's husband. He was an important civic leader in Macon."

"Macon?" Lisa stopped in the act of filling the jar and turned to look at Norman.

"That's what it says. His company headquarters was in Macon, Georgia."

"I wonder if his building was anywhere near Pretty Girl Cosmetics. They have their corporate offices in Macon, too. They built a landmark building, and Gloria was telling us about it at dinner last night. It looks just like a lipstick with windows, and the CEO's office suite is all the way up at the tip of the lipstick."

"Hold on a second," Norman said, reaching out for the sheaf of papers. "I could be wrong, but when I was printing out the data for Neil Roper's financials, I'm almost sure I saw . . . here it is."

"Here *what* is?"

"Pretty Girl Cosmetics. Vanessa's husband was a senior member of the board."

"Hold the phone!" Hannah said, jumping up to do exactly what she'd just said. Within seconds she'd punched in her mother's work number and she paced impatiently until the phone was answered. "Hi, Carrie. Is Luanne working today?"

"Yes, dear. Shall I call her?"

"No. I need to talk to her, but not on the phone. If you're not too busy, could you ask her to run over here? I just baked a new cookie, Chocolate Almond Toast, and I'll send some back with her."

Carrie laughed. "Bribery will get you everywhere. I'll send her right over. Is it about Shawna Lee's murder?"

"Not directly. I just need some information about Pretty Girl Cosmetics that Luanne might know."

Hannah had just finished filling a takeout bag with Chocolate Almond Toast when Luanne knocked on the back door. Norman volunteered to relieve Lisa at the cookie shop so they could compare notes about Pretty Girl Cosmetics, and the three women were about to sit down with mugs of coffee when Andrea came rushing in.

"Norman sent me back here. He said you were having a meeting."

"We are." Hannah poured a mug of coffee for her sister and motioned her to a stool. Then she turned to Luanne. "I need to know some things about Pretty Girl Cosmetics. Did you ever go to their corporate headquarters in Macon, Georgia?"

"Yes. I qualified for a two-day seminar when I was selling Pretty Girl door-to-door and working at the café. Pretty Girl picked up all the expenses and Mom offered to take care of Suzie, so I went. It was great, almost like a mini-vacation."

"Did you get to meet any of the people on the board of directors?"

Luanne shook her head. "No, just the CEO when he welcomed us on the first day. I met all the other top salespeople from my region. They won trips to the seminar, too. And of course I met Gloria Travis. She arranged the whole thing."

"Do you know about the Pretty Girl Retreat out at the Lake Eden Inn?" Lisa asked.

"Sure. Gloria called me the first day she got to town and we're getting together tonight. I'm driving out to have dinner with Gloria and her husband."

"Her husband?" Lisa asked, looking surprised. "But . . . Gloria told us she wasn't married."

"She isn't? Oh, I'm really glad you told me! I probably would have stuck my foot in my mouth and asked some dumb question about why her husband wasn't there. I guess something must have gone wrong with her engagement and the wedding she was planning never happened."

"Hold on!" Hannah said, giving them the universal time-out signal. When everyone was silent, she turned to Luanne. "When did Gloria tell you she was engaged?"

"A year and a half ago, when I went to Georgia for the Pretty Girl Seminar. We got to talking and she said she was engaged to one of the board members."

"Neil Roper?" Hannah guessed, as some of the facts she'd been carrying around in the mixing bowl of her mind started to blend together.

"That could have been it. I'm pretty sure his name started with an N. It's been a while since I heard it, though."

"I know. Just try to think back, Luanne," Hannah encouraged her. "What did Gloria say about her fiancé?"

"Well . . . I don't remember, not exactly. But I did come away from our conversation with the impression that he was rich. And he was older, too. I'm almost positive that Gloria's fiancé was twenty years or so older than she was."

"So what are we doing here again?" Andrea asked, pulling up in the space marked for deliveries behind the back of the Lake Eden Inn.

"We're here to see if Gloria's ex-fiancé is Neil Roper, the same man Vanessa married. And then we're going to find out if Gloria knows that Neil married Vanessa."

"Okay. And we also need to know if Gloria picked the Lake Eden Inn for the site of the Pretty Girl Retreat so that she could follow Vanessa here, right?"

"Right. But you can't park here."

"Why not?"

"Because it's for deliveries."

"I'm delivering." Andrea drew a picture of Bethany out of her purse and flashed it at Hannah. "Sally asked me to bring a picture the next time I came out. Besides . . . which deputy is going to give the wife of the Winnetka County Sheriff a ticket?"

Hannah shrugged. Andrea was right. And Lord Acton was also right. Power did corrupt. She just hoped that Andrea never learned that absolute power corrupted absolutely.

"What are you waiting for?" Andrea asked, opening her door and climbing out of the driver's seat. They'd taken her Volvo because she'd refused to ride in what she called *Hannah's Traveling Ice Cube.* "Come on, Hannah. It's freezing out here. Let's get this show on the road!"

Once Andrea had shown Bethany's picture to Sally and Hannah had sighed enviously once again over the spaciousness of Sally's kitchen, they explained why they'd come out to speak to Gloria.

"You mean Gloria was engaged to Vanessa's husband?" Sally began to frown when Hannah nodded. "And you're thinking she might have something to do with Shawna Lee's murder?"

Andrea shrugged. "Maybe. We've got to check it out."

"Of course you do, but you're barking up the wrong tree. Gloria is the kind of person who'd work like the dickens to catch a moth in her living room and carry it outside. She wouldn't hurt anyone."

"You're probably right," Hannah soothed the woman who'd obviously become Gloria's friend. "But Gloria might be able to give us some leads.

Even if we're wrong and she wasn't engaged to Vanessa's husband, we know he was on the board of directors at Pretty Girl. Gloria must know something about him."

Sally shrugged. "Oh. Well . . . if you put it that way . . . come with me and I'll introduce you."

The afternoon session had just recessed for coffee and rolls in the dining room, and Sally ushered them to Gloria's table. "Hi, Gloria." Sally smiled at the Pretty Girl executive. "These are my good friends Andrea Todd and Hannah Swensen. They're Delores Swensen's daughters. You remember her, don't you?"

"Of course," Gloria said, smiling at both of them. "Your mother is just wonderful. She made me feel right at home. It gave me pause about going back to Macon, let me tell you!"

It gave her pause? Hannah thought, smiling in spite of herself. It seemed Miss Travis had a literary bent. If truth be known, Hannah liked her already, but she gave a little mental shake and told herself to keep an open mind.

"Hannah and Andrea would like to ask you a couple of questions about Pretty Girl. Do you have a few minutes for them?"

"Of course," Gloria said with a friendly smile, getting to her feet. She was an attractive woman of approximately their mother's age, dressed for success in a soft green pantsuit with a longer than average jacket. As she moved, the jacket parted slightly to reveal a cream-colored silk blouse with a high neck, and a few extra pounds around her waist. "Let's move to that small table over there. The ladies can get along without me for a few minutes . . . right, ladies?"

There were immediate responses of, *I don't know about that!* and, *How can we get along without you, Gloria?* but everyone was smiling as Gloria left the table. She led the way to a small table across the room, and waited until Andrea and Hannah were seated. "Okay, this must be serious. Neither one of you has cracked a smile. What is it?"

"Were you engaged to Neil Roper?" Hannah asked.

For a split second, Gloria looked as if she'd deny it, but then she sighed. "Yes. I should have known it would come out."

"And he's the same Neil Roper that Vanessa Quinn married?"

"That's right. Who told you about it? Luanne Hanks?"

Andrea stepped in quickly. "It doesn't matter. The important thing is, we know."

"What we don't know is how everything went down," Hannah jumped into the opening her sister had left for her. "Why don't you tell us exactly what happened after you and Mr. Roper broke up."

Gloria sighed deeply. "That's just it. We didn't break up. I thought everything was just fine. You probably know that Neil was older."

"We know," Hannah confirmed. And then she was silent as one of Sally's waitresses approached the table to bring them a carafe of coffee, three cups, and a plate of fresh cinnamon rolls. "Go on," she prompted, once the waitress had left.

"That's just it. I don't know exactly how all this happened, but I think it all started after Neil broke his ankle skiing."

"Skiing?" Andrea asked.

"That's right. He was very active for his age. He went off to visit an old friend in Aspen, and when he came back, his ankle was in a cast. That wouldn't have been so bad, but a week later the house-keeper who'd been with him for over thirty years died of a heart attack."

Hannah held her breath, waiting for the third incident. Her grandmother had always said bad things came in threes.

"Neil hired another housekeeper and both of us thought that things were looking up, but his ankle started to give him a lot of pain. It just wasn't heal-ing right. The doctor suggested a physical thera-pist and Neil hired someone through a medical registry. And that's really all I know. I spoke to him once on the phone after that, and . . . that's it."

"What!" Hannah gasped, not quite believing her ears. "You mean . . . you didn't see Neil again?"

"No. It sounds crazy when I say it, but every time I called the house, Neil was in therapy, or sleeping, or out of town, or whatever. He sent cards and flowers and things like that, but I didn't actually get to see him, or even talk to him except that once."

"Tell us about that," Andrea prompted.

"It was about a week after he hired the therapist. I called the house and Neil answered the phone. He didn't sound like himself at all. At first I thought he was drunk, but Neil didn't drink. Then, when he said something about how the nurse had gone to get his pill, I realized that he must be on some very strong pain medication. It really scared me. He was perfectly polite, but he didn't seem to be able to answer any questions and he sounded horribly confused. He asked me my name several times, but I don't think he knew who I was!"

"That's awful!" Andrea exclaimed, shivering slightly. "What did you do?"

"I called Neil's doctor, but he wouldn't give me any information. I wasn't a relative, you see. And then I called Neil's house again and asked to speak to his physical therapist. I told her how concerned I was about Neil's state of mind, and she said not to worry, that he'd been in a lot of pain and she'd given him the maximum dose of medication that the doctor had prescribed."

"And you bought her story?" Hannah asked, frowning slightly.

"Yes, I did. She seemed competent and pleasant, and I took her advice and stopped worrying. And the next morning a bouquet came for me at the office. It was from Neil and he said he was sorry I'd worried, but he was just fine, he loved me, and he hoped to be back on his feet soon."

"So you stopped worrying?" Andrea wanted to know.

"For a while. You've got to understand that Neil and I didn't see each other every day. He was still very active in his business and he traveled extensively. There were weeks when I didn't see him, but he'd always call or send flowers. My own job is very demanding, and I work extended hours. That's one of the reasons I planned to quit after we were married. Then, when he went to Paris, or London, or Beijing, I could go with him."

"So how much time passed between the time you spoke to Neil on the phone and when you started to worry again?"

"Three weeks. It was a busy time at Pretty Girl and I was distracted by work. And the flowers kept coming, my favorite daffodils every Monday morning. I really didn't think anything was wrong until I glanced at my calendar and realized that I hadn't actually spoken to Neil in almost a month. I'd called, but the physical therapist always answered and she said Neil was fine. It was almost as if she took over his life, which is exactly what happened."

"What do you mean?" Andrea's eyes narrowed.

"I mean, before I quite knew what was happening, Neil and the therapist were married."

"Vanessa Quinn?" Hannah asked, just to set the record straight.

"Yes. I kept calling, but I never got Neil on the phone. And I never spoke to him again." Gloria blinked back tears, and swallowed hard. "I'm convinced Vanessa killed him. I just wish I'd been able to do something to prevent it, but . . ."

"A woman scorned," Hannah quoted.

"You're absolutely right. I called the police and begged them to investigate, but they said there was no evidence that anything was wrong. I was just the jilted fiancée with a grudge. They wouldn't believe me when I said I thought the physical therapist had been drugging Neil to hold him hostage until she could marry him, and then kill him."

"Do you really think that's what happened?"

"I do. When I read about Neil's death in the papers, I got suspicious, especially since Vanessa inherited everything. Neil always told me he planned to leave part of his estate to his cousin's daughter, who was working two part-time jobs to get through college. But he didn't leave anything to her. Everything went to Vanessa, his bride of less than ten months. I'll eat my hat if Neil married her of his own free will. There's something really fishy about his death, and that's not just sour grapes on my part."

Hannah nodded, ignoring the fact that Gloria had used three figures of speech in one breath, and that had to be some kind of a record. "Let's move on to what happened when you got to Lake Eden. You came here because of Vanessa, didn't you?"

"Yes. Pretty Girl was looking for a spot for their retreat and it was the perfect opportunity for me to come to Lake Eden without arousing any suspicion. The inn is wonderful, by the way. We voted unanimously to hold our retreat here every year."

"Sally will be happy to hear that," Andrea said, and then she gazed at Hannah to show that she was through interrupting the questioning.

"Did you talk to Vanessa?"

"No, I didn't have the opportunity. The day I got here, I drove to the Magnolia Blossom Bakery. I intended to ask Vanessa about Neil."

"What time was that?" Hannah asked, her pen at the ready.

"I left the inn a little after five-thirty, so I must have gotten to Lake Eden around six. But the bakery was locked and no one answered when I knocked at the door."

"What did you do then?"

"I walked around the back. When I turned the corner of the building, I saw that the back door was standing open."

"Did you go in?"

"Yes, I walked to the stairs and shouted out Vanessa's name. Nobody answered me. The kitchen lights were on so I took several steps inside, and . . . and that was when I saw Vanessa lying there on the floor."

"But it wasn't Vanessa," Andrea broke in with an apologetic glance at Hannah.

"I know that now, but I didn't know it then. I never met Vanessa in person, and all I had to go by was the picture I clipped out of the paper when they ran their marriage announcement."

"So what did you do when you saw Shawna Lee?"

"I . . . I panicked. I knew if anybody figured out the connection between us, they'd think I killed her. She was dead. I could see that. And there wasn't anything anybody could do for her. So I . . . I just backed right out of there, pulled the door shut, and hurried back to my car."

"What time was that?"

"I don't know. I didn't look at my watch. All I remember was that church bells had started to peal and I figured that the ceremony was almost over. That meant I had to hurry and get back out to the inn so I could change to my dress clothes before the wedding party arrived."

"Truth?" Andrea asked, sliding in behind the wheel of her Volvo.

"I think so."

"So do I. And it just goes to show."

"Goes to show what?" Hannah asked, wincing at her own awkward sentence construction.

"That I'm not the only one who mistook one sister for the other." There was the sound of faint ringing and Andrea grabbed her purse. "Hold the wheel, Hannah. I've got to catch this call."

As Andrea drew her phone out of her purse and pressed the button to answer the call, Hannah peered through the windshield, guiding the car from the passenger seat. Was this legal? And if they got into an accident, would it be her fault, or Andrea's? Would they write it up as a cell-phone-related auto accident, even though she'd had her hands on the wheel? And did it really matter whose hands they were?

"Hi, Mother." Andrea held the phone to her ear with her left hand and took the wheel back with her right. "You can let go now, Hannah. I've got it."

"You're sure you can talk and drive at the same time?" Hannah asked, not willing to be a state highway statistic.

"I'm positive." Andrea proved it by cutting over a lane without signaling. "That's right, Mother. You did hear Hannah's name. We're just coming back from the Lake Eden Inn."

Hannah squeezed her eyes shut. It was always difficult to ride with Andrea at the best of times, and this obviously wasn't the best. And if she indulged her inclination to slip into the role of backseat driver, Andrea would be insulted.

"Of course we will, Mother." Andrea jerked the wheel to the right and took the turnoff for Lake Eden at the last possible second. "We'll be there in less than ten minutes. Just sit down and relax until we get there."

"We're going to Granny's Attic?" Hannah guessed when Andrea ended the call.

"No, to Mother's house," Andrea corrected. "She went home at noon today."

"Is she sick?" Hannah felt her heart start to pound in alarm. Delores never took a day off unless she was seriously ill.

"I don't think so. But there's something wrong with her."

"Did she say that?"

"Not exactly. She just asked both of us to come over because she needed some advice."

"She needs advice from *us?*"

"That's what she said."

"Then Mother must really be in trouble. She's never asked us for advice before."

CHOCOLATE ALMOND TOAST

Preheat oven to 350 degrees F.,
rack in the middle position.

1½ cups melted butter *(3 sticks)*
1 cup cocoa powder *(unsweetened)*
2½ cups brown sugar
5 large eggs beaten *(just whip them up in a glass with a fork)*
4 teaspoons baking soda
1 teaspoon salt
2 teaspoons vanilla
1 cup slivered almonds
6 cups flour *(not sifted)*

Melt the butter and mix in the cocoa. Add the brown sugar. Let it cool slightly and then stir in the beaten eggs. Add the soda, salt, vanilla, and slivered almonds. Stir until well blended. Add the flour in half-cup increments, mixing after each addition.

Spray two cookie sheets with nonstick cooking spray. Divide the dough into five parts, forming each part into a free-form loaf, 1 inch high, 7 to 8 inches long, and 3 to 4 inches wide. Place 2 loaves on one cookie sheet and 3

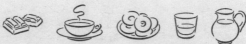

loaves on the other. Bake the loaves at 350 degrees F. for 35 minutes.

Cool the loaves on the cookie sheets for 10 minutes, but DON'T SHUT OFF THE OVEN. Transfer the loaves to a wire rack and cool for another 5 minutes. Slice them *(just like bread)* into ¾-inch-thick pieces with a sharp knife. *(The end pieces don't need more baking—save them to dunk in your coffee while the rest are baking.)*

Place the slices on their cut sides on the greased cookie sheets. Bake the slices for an additional 5 minutes, flip them over to expose the other cut side, and bake them for an additional 10 minutes. Let them cool on the cookie sheet for 5 minutes and then remove them to a wire rack to complete cooling.

These are great dunking cookies. If you want to make them look like biscotti, just dip the tops in melted chips *(I use milk chocolate)*, set them on a piece of waxed paper, and refrigerate them to set the chocolate.

Yield: Approximately 4 dozen, depending on cookie size.

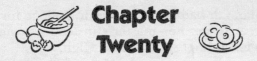

Chapter Twenty

When Delores answered the doorbell, Hannah had all she could do to hide her shock. Their mother looked old for the very first time. After a glance at Andrea, Hannah knew that their mother's appearance had also disturbed her sister. Something was drastically wrong.

"Hi, Mother. What's up?" Hannah tried for a note of levity, but it didn't work. She sounded flip and that's not what she meant at all. "Sorry. That came out wrong."

"It doesn't matter," Delores said flatly, stepping aside so that they could enter. "Come on, girls. I have coffee set out in the living room."

Hannah took a deep breath for courage as Delores led the way. Most family discussions were held in the kitchen around the circular oak table. That's where Delores told Andrea how much she could spend for her prom dress, and where they all sat around and discussed which college applications Hannah should fill out. The living room was only used for matters of gravity, like when Andrea announced that she wanted to marry Bill, and when Hannah had asked to stay in college for another year to get her master's instead of coming back to teach English at Jordan High.

"I'm worried about you, Mother," Hannah said the second she sat down. "Are you ill?"

"I'm not ill, just heartsick. I really thought Winthrop was the man for me. He was so perfect in every way. But now I've discovered that he has a . . . a fondness for other women."

Hannah glanced at Andrea, but she gave an almost imperceptible shake of her head that meant it was up to the oldest sister to handle this. "You knew that, Mother. Remember the night of the Christmas Potluck Dinner when he was flirting with Carrie, and Bertie Straub, and Florence Evans?"

"I remember. But that was harmless fun. I know that Winthrop would never have actually . . . well, you know . . . with any one of them. I know he has a . . . um . . . wandering eye. But this time I think more than his eye is wandering, if you know what I mean."

Andrea kept her eyes carefully lowered and Hannah read the signal loud and clear. Her younger sister was still out of her depth and it was up to her to counsel their mother.

"What makes you suspect that this . . . uh . . . current incident is more than a . . . an innocent flirtation?" Hannah asked, digging deeply into her store of euphemisms.

"It's the woman involved. I wouldn't be concerned about women like Carrie, or Florence, or Bertie. But in this case, there's her reputation to consider. And then there's the age factor."

"I see," Hannah said, surprised that she actually did. "So the woman you suspect of . . . er . . . dallying with Winthrop is younger and has a reputation for . . . um . . . dallying."

"That's right."

"Well, in that case, because of the age factor and . . ." Hannah stopped cold and stared at her mother. She'd just run out of euphemisms. "Why are we talking this way?"

"Which way?"

"Beating around the bush," Hannah said, aware that she'd just used another one. "You're afraid Winthrop is two-timing you with a younger woman who's got a bad reputation. Is that right?"

"Well. If you put it like that . . ." Delores took a bracing breath. "Yes, that's exactly right. And I don't know what I should do about it!"

Andrea raised her eyes for the first time since the conversation had opened and locked eyes with their mother. "Kill him," she said. "That's what I'd do to Bill if he cheated on me."

"But you're married, and I'm not."

"So how close to being married are you?" Hannah asked, taking over the questioning again. "I mean, Andrea and I don't want to know about your personal relationship or anything like that, but has Winthrop asked you to marry him?"

"Yes. Several times. And I said yes. I think you could say that we were unofficially engaged. He sent to England for his mother's ring several weeks ago."

Hannah came close to groaning, but she stifled that impulse. Their mother needed their help, not censure. "What made you suspicious? Did you see Winthrop with another woman?"

"Not exactly. It's just that Winthrop has a picture of Shawna Lee Quinn."

That was an act ender if ever there was one, and Hannah had the unfortunate impulse to applaud. If this were a play, she'd ring down the curtain. But their mother looked miserable. The strong woman who knew her own mind and would stop at nothing to get her way appeared utterly defeated.

"Get a handle on it, Mother," Hannah said, deciding that a dose of strong medicine was in order. "This isn't the time to play drama queen."

"I've never played drama queen in my life!" Two bright spots of color appeared in Delores's cheeks, and her eyes began to flash fire. "What are you talking about, Hannah?"

"You're worrying about Shawna Lee Quinn. She's no competition for you anymore. She's dead."

"I know, but . . ." Delores started to frown. "You're right. She's dead and I'm not. But I still want to know why Winthrop's keeping her picture."

"Why don't you just ask him?" Andrea suggested, causing both women to turn and look at her.

"Good idea." Hannah gave her sister a nod and then she turned back to Delores. "Just ask him, Mother. Maybe there's some sort of reasonable explanation. I mean . . . men carry all sorts of pictures in their wallets and they never think to update them. Maybe Shawna Lee had snapshots printed when her bakery opened and passed them out or something."

"It's not a snapshot. And it's not in his wallet."

"Okay." Hannah accepted that at face value. "Where is it?"

"It's a framed picture, a big one. And . . . well . . . it's in Winthrop's underwear drawer."

That was another act ender and after one look at her sister, Hannah snapped her own mouth closed. Their mother was full of surprises this afternoon. "Okay," she said, taking a deep breath. "I'll ask the question we both want to ask. What were you doing in Winthrop's underwear drawer?"

"Would you believe I was putting away Winthrop's laundry?"

"No," Hannah said unequivocally. "You don't even put away your *own* laundry. Marjorie Hanks does it when she comes in to clean."

"All right. I was . . . it doesn't really matter how I found the picture, does it? What matters is, I did. And because of the circumstances, I can't very well ask Winthrop why he has it!"

"Because then he'd know you were snooping?" Andrea guessed, starting to grin.

"Well . . . yes, if you want to put it that way. I prefer to think of it as . . . gathering more facts."

"Nice," Hannah said. "I may use that someday. But let's get back to the picture. Can you describe it?"

"Of course I can! I only got a quick peek before Winthrop came out of the shower, but it made a lasting impression."

Andrea gave Hannah a stricken look, and Hannah knew exactly what she was thinking. *The shower? What was Mother doing in Winthrop's bedroom when he was in the shower?*

"He was late getting dressed for us to go out, and I was supposed to be waiting in the living room. That's why I got only a quick peek."

Hannah glanced at Andrea and saw her relax

slightly. That was good. "Tell us everything you noticed in the photo."

"I think it was taken at a club, the kind of place where you can have your picture taken by a photographer who goes from table to table. Do you know the kind of place I'm talking about?"

"Expensive," Hannah said.

"That's right. And trendy. They were sitting in a booth and he had his arm around her. They looked very happy, and very . . . intimate."

"Are you sure it was Shawna Lee?" Andrea asked, after a glance at Hannah. "I mean . . . could it have been Vanessa? They look a lot alike."

Delores was thoughtful for a moment and then she gave a dainty little shrug. "It could have been Vanessa. I didn't even think of that. But she's still alive and that means I wasn't being a drama queen and I *do* have to worry! I'd better go right back over to Winthrop's and try to get another look at that picture."

"No," Hannah said, holding up her hand. "It's too much of a risk for you to do it, Mother. Winthrop might catch you snooping this time. Andrea and I will take care of it for you. We'll find out if it's Shawna Lee or Vanessa."

Andrea gave her older sister a look that said, *We will?* But she nodded in a show of sisterly solidarity. "Don't worry, Mother. We'll take care of it."

"All right," Delores said, sighing deeply. "You two are better at that sort of thing anyway. And if Winthrop comes back tomorrow and suspects that someone's been going through his things, I can say quite truthfully that it wasn't me."

"If Winthrop's coming back tomorrow, does that

mean he's out of town now?" Hannah asked, picking up on her mother's comment.

"That's right. It's some sort of investment seminar and he won't be back until six tomorrow evening."

"Perfect timing," Hannah said, turning to Andrea. "We'll break into his apartment right now and look for that picture."

Delores gave a smug little smile. "I just knew you'd say that. I can always count on my girls to help me." She reached down to pick up a key that was tucked next to her cup on the coffee table and handed it to Hannah. "You don't have to break in, dears. Just use my key."

"I don't want to know what this means," Andrea said, clutching the key in her hand as she drove. "I don't even want to think about it."

"Me neither. I hope he's got some rubber gloves under the sink. I don't want to dig around in that man's underwear drawer with bare hands."

"Hannah!" Andrea burst into giggles so infectious, Hannah had to join in. One giggle led to a gaggle and then, because Andrea's Volvo was beginning to wobble all over the road, they had to pull into Cyril Murphy's used car lot until they calmed down.

"You got a problem with that fancy foreign car of yours?" Cyril asked, coming over to see what was the matter.

"Yes, it needs a new driver," Hannah answered, sending them both into gales of laughter again.

By the time they pulled themselves together,

Cyril was chuckling, too. "I just called your place," he said to Hannah. "I need to work on your truck this afternoon."

"Why?" Hannah asked, hating to be without her vehicle even though she wasn't driving it at the moment.

"Factory recall. It won't cost you a cent. I'll have one of my boys run over there and get it, and he'll leave a loaner for you. I should have yours done by the time I close tonight."

"That's great." And it was until Hannah remembered that Cyril's garage was open until ten. "Do you want me to drive back to town and pick it up tonight?"

Cyril shook his head. "I'll have one of my guys deliver it to your condo. Just leave the key for the loaner under the floor mat on the driver's side. He'll drop your truck off and switch."

"Sounds good to me," Hannah said, agreeing quickly.

After a few more words with Cyril, Andrea pulled back out onto the road again. Hannah waited until they were on the highway, nearing the exit for Winthrop's apartment complex, and then she turned to face her sister. "So what do you say we go through his whole place while we're there?"

"You mean search it?"

"Right. I want to see if there's any other reason why Mother should ditch Winthrop."

"I would have been really disappointed if you hadn't suggested it," Andrea said, turning off the highway and onto the access road that led to Lakeside Villas, an apartment complex frequented primarily by working singles. "Take a look at

Mother's key," she said, handing it to Hannah. "It should be stamped with an apartment number."

"Two twenty-three," Hannah read the number.

"Okay. That's building number two on the second floor."

"You've been here before?" Hannah was curious.

"Every time I drive the dance class car pool. One of Tracey's friends lives in building number three. Those are the two-bedroom units."

Hannah looked out the window with interest as Andrea drove past the A-frame clubhouse with siding cleverly formed to look like logs, and around the side of building number two. There were designated parking spots for the residents under a sloping roof that jutted out from the back of the building, but the area for the visitors was uncovered. Andrea pulled into one of the visitors' spots and shut off the engine. "Okay. Let's go defend Mother's honor."

"It could be a little late for that," Hannah said, grinning impishly.

"I don't want to hear it. Let's go."

A sign announced that the front door was to be kept locked for security purposes and Andrea used their mother's key. It opened onto a foyer that contained another door with another sign that said it was to be kept locked.

"They're very security conscious," Andrea noted, sticking her key in the lock, pushing the door open, and stepping into the carpeted interior.

Hannah followed her, grinning widely. "No, they're not. Both of those doors had paper stuffed into the locks to keep them open."

"No!" Andrea backed up to take a look, and then she turned to Hannah in shock. "You're right! Absolutely anybody could have gotten in. Why did the sign say the doors were locked?"

"To keep out the people who can read," Hannah quipped, grabbing Andrea's arm as her sister started to giggle uncontrollably again and leading her to the elevator.

The two sisters were silent as they rode up in the elevator. It was the kind Hannah hated, a car with mirrored walls that made it seem as if twenty or thirty fashionably thin blondes were stuffed into an infinite number of elevator cars with the same number of plump, frizzy-haired redheads.

"Whew!" Hannah breathed, stepping out of the elevator with relief. "That was just too synchronized to suit me."

"Synchronized?"

"When I raised my hand to scratch my nose, all the redheads in the mirrors scratched, too."

"I know what you mean. I didn't like looking at that many me's."

Even though they didn't see any tenants, Hannah and Andrea were quiet as they walked down the hallway and stopped in front of Winthrop's door. Without being told, Andrea kept watch while Hannah unlocked the door and then they both stepped in and closed it behind them. Still perfectly silent, they tiptoed from kitchen, to bath, to bedroom, glancing in each door before Hannah finally spoke out loud.

"It's okay. He's gone. What do you think of the place?"

Andrea glanced around the living room and shrugged. "It's . . . generic. Just like Winthrop."

"Generic!" Hannah crowed, bursting into delighted laughter. "That's exactly the right word for him. Winthrop's a generic Englishman, typical in every way. It's like he took his personality straight from the pages of a book."

"A movie where he plays an English lord. He's not the type that reads."

"You're probably right." Hannah took a tour around the room. "This is much too tasteful to suit me."

"It's too tasteful to suit anybody. I don't know how Mother can stand it here." Andrea got up to look at the framed pictures on the mantel over the fake fireplace and gasped.

"What?" Hannah asked.

"These pictures. That's Pete and Daisy."

"You know them?"

"I know *of* them," Andrea corrected. "It's a kids' movie about a boy and his dog. I took Tracey and Karen to see it last year. I thought it was cute, but Winthrop must have liked it a lot to frame pictures of the characters."

"Not necessarily. Maybe he just wanted pictures on his mantel and he didn't want to use real photos."

"Why not?"

"Because . . . he didn't dare use pictures of real people from his past."

"Okay. But why didn't he dare to use real pictures?"

"Because he's running from the law?"

"Or *for* the law. Winthrop could be in the witness protection program."

"I suppose, but he doesn't look like the type. Then again, people in the witness protection program aren't supposed to look like the type to be in the witness protection program. Maybe you were right the first time and he just happened to love that movie. How about the rest of the pictures? Do you see any other famous movie stars?"

"I don't think so." Andrea went over for a closer look. "Pete and Daisy are the only ones, but . . ." She stopped at one picture and flipped it over.

"What?" Hannah asked.

"This is a Keep-It frame."

"What's that?"

"It's a brand name they carry at CostMart. I just bought a Keep-It frame for the picture Norman took of Tracey on The Cookie Jar float in the Fourth of July parade."

"Is that important?" Hannah asked, knowing that it sometimes took her sister a while to get to the heart of a story.

"It could be." Andrea walked over with the picture. "See this older couple in the frame?"

"I see them. Are they famous movie stars?"

"No, but they could be famous picture frame models. I'm almost certain it's the same couple that came in the Keep-It frame I bought for Tracey's photo."

"Winthrop bought these frames at CostMart and left the demo pictures in them?"

"I think so. I just framed Tracey's photo last night and I think the demo photo is still in the wastebasket. I'll look when I get home and call you."

"Okay." Hannah patted her sister on the back. "It's a good thing you're here. I never would have noticed."

"Thanks, but I don't think it's illegal to buy picture frames and leave the demo pictures in them."

"No, but it *is* suspicious. You start in here and see what else you can uncover. I'm going to look for those rubber gloves and tackle his bedroom."

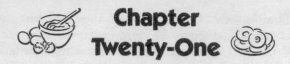

Chapter
Twenty-One

"**I**'m up. I'm up," Hannah groaned, sitting up in an evasive maneuver to avoid Moishe's sandpaper tongue. The raspy licks were Moishe's way of telling her that it was morning in the frozen tundra, she should hurry and shut off the alarm clock because it hurt his ears, and his food bowl was empty.

Hannah slapped the Off button on the alarm clock before it had time to do more than give the first electronic squawk, and shoved her feet into the soft fur-lined moccasins she used for winter slippers. "Come on, Moishe. I need coffee. There's no way I want to go back to sleep and dream that dream again!"

She slipped on her warmest robe, an ancient chenille that had faded so much Hannah could only guess at its original color. She'd found the robe at the Helping Hands Thrift Shop when she'd first come back to Lake Eden, and she'd gladly paid the dollar they'd asked for it. It reminded her of her Grandma Ingrid's robe and wearing it was almost like a hug from the grandmother she missed every time she baked one of her recipes.

"I dreamed about Shawna Lee and Vanessa," Hannah explained, on her way down the hallway toward the kitchen. "They were at Wimbledon playing tennis, and Winthrop's head was the ball."

"Roww!" Moishe commented, reaching out to give her slipper a halfhearted swipe.

"I know it could have been worse, but that was bad enough. I think I dreamed about them because I've got the picture Andrea and I borrowed from . . ."

"Roww!" Moishe interrupted loudly.

"Okay. You're right. We stole it. But I'm going to put it back this afternoon and that means it was only borrowed."

"Roww!" Moishe commented again, a little louder this time.

"All right. We borrowed it without permission. Will that do?" Hannah grinned down at him as he gave another yowl. Some people claimed that cats didn't understand what their people were saying, but Moishe meowed at the appropriate places and Hannah was willing to give him the benefit of the doubt. "Anyway, I've got the picture and I can't tell which sister it is. Neither can Andrea. Mike could probably tell, but there's no way I want to ask him!"

Once Moishe had been fed and the caffeine from her first cup of coffee was coursing through her grateful veins, Hannah headed off to the shower. She always tried to shower and dress before fully awakening, and this morning was no exception.

Less than ten minutes later, Hannah was sitting at her kitchen table. She was halfway through her second cup of coffee when full awareness hit and then she gave a tortured groan. "Mother," she said.

"Oww!" Moishe howled, arching his back.

"That's true, but I should have called to tell her about Winthrop's frames last night. Of course, maybe it's a good thing I didn't. We should have all our ducks lined up in a row before we shoot Winthrop down."

Moishe seemed to approve of that concept because he squinted before he returned to his food bowl, the closest he ever got to actually smiling. And to show his enthusiasm for shooting Winthrop down, or the ducks in a row, Hannah wasn't quite sure which, he crunched much louder than usual. Hannah was just hoping that he wouldn't break a tooth and need a kitty dentist when the solution to their problem hit her.

"Norman!" she exclaimed, causing Moishe to startle and look up at her. "I didn't mean to scare you, but you just gave me a great idea." Hannah grabbed the canister of fish-shaped salmon-flavored treats her feline adored and tossed a couple in his direction. "It's just like that forensic dentistry program we watched last week. Both Vanessa and Shawna Lee were Norman's patients. And the woman in the picture is smiling. Norman can probably tell which sister it is by comparing their dental records."

Hannah grabbed her steno pad and wrote down her plans for the day. *BAKE* went on the first line, *NORMAN & PIX* on the second, and *RETURN PIX* on the third. Then she flipped to the pages she'd used to jot notes about Shawna Lee's murder to see if any lightbulbs would go on over her head.

She'd listed the suspects on the first page and

Hannah reviewed them. The first was Mike and the motive listed was a lovers' quarrel. Hannah had crossed his name out when Andrea had cleared him by talking to Marjorie Hanks. There was no way Mike could have murdered Shawna Lee when he'd been within sight and sound of Marjorie's vacuum at the sheriff's station the whole time.

Next on the list were the wives of several deputies that Shawna Lee had flirted with blatantly. Their motives were jealousy. But every single wife had an alibi and so did their deputy husbands. They'd all attended Lisa and Herb's wedding and they'd arrived at the reception in a group.

Ronni Ward's name was next on her list, but Hannah had crossed it out. While it was extremely unlikely that Ronni had hobbled around the back of the bakery with her ankle in a cast to shoot Shawna Lee, Hannah had called to make certain that Ronni had spent the whole day and night at Lake Eden Hospital.

Barbara Donnelly's name was next on the list and it was also crossed out. Hannah had done that after Norman's report. He'd cleaned Barbara's teeth and she'd mentioned that she'd gone to the wedding and the reception with Nettie Grant. One call to Nettie had confirmed that and Barbara was in the clear.

Farther down on the page, right after the horizontal line Hannah had drawn to denote a change in her thinking, was the word *VANESSA* in block letters. At this point, Andrea had raised the question about whether the killer might have mistaken Shawna Lee for Vanessa, and they'd talked about new motives and new suspects. Gloria Travis was listed, but after they'd met with Gloria, Hannah had added a question mark behind her name. Gloria didn't have an alibi and she'd admitted that she had good reason to kill the woman she'd thought was Vanessa, but neither Hannah nor Andrea thought she'd done it.

Hannah picked up her pen and tapped it lightly against the paper. Should she? Or shouldn't she? She debated that question for a moment and then she wrote down Winthrop's name. She didn't know if he had a motive, but the picture of Vanessa or Shawna Lee in his underwear drawer must mean something. It was true that he'd been at Lisa and Herb's wedding, but not for the entire ceremony. He'd left to get the rice Delores had left in the car. Perhaps he'd only been gone for a few minutes, but it only took a few minutes to dash up to the Magnolia Blossom Bakery, shoot Shawna Lee through the window, stash his gun in the car, and race back to the church with the rice.

Moishe yowled again and Hannah turned to look at him. "I know. I'm probably not being fair. But there's something strange about Winthrop. Why would an English lord come to Lake Eden anyway?"

Another yowl from Moishe caused Hannah to reconsider. "I know the fishing's good, but it's not summer and Winthrop hasn't mentioned word one about fishing. And it's not like he crash-landed here from another planet, or something. He's got to have come to Lake Eden for a purpose . . . but what?"

Moishe yowled for the third time and Hannah was about to praise him for his scintillating morning conversation when she noticed that his food bowl was empty. Moishe wasn't having a stimulating dialogue with his mistress. He was yowling for more food. Hannah filled his bowl again, stuck her steno book in her shoulder bag purse, slipped into her parka coat, and headed out the door.

The cold air hit her like a blast in the face and Hannah pulled her knit watch cap down low over her ears. She hurried down the stairs, grateful for the roof over the outside staircase that kept the snow and ice off the treads, and dashed across the sidewalk to the concrete steps that led down to the garage.

Her cookie truck was in her spot, just as Cyril had promised. The mechanic who'd brought it had plugged it in and it was sparkling clean. It was one of the things Hannah loved about taking her truck to Cyril's garage. He always washed it after his mechanics had done their work. Hannah unplugged the cord, wrapped it around her bumper, and slid behind the wheel. It was time to drive to work.

Once she'd backed out of her parking spot, Hannah drove up the ramp and onto the winding road that led through her condo complex. Except for the lovely old-fashioned globe streetlights, darkness surrounded her. It was only four-thirty in the morning and not that many people were awake at that hour. Hannah saw one light on in a unit that she knew belonged to a couple that had a small baby, but the rest of the complex was deep in sleep.

A flick of her card in the slot, and the bar rose to grant her exit. Hannah pulled out and turned onto the access road. There must have been an ice storm during the night, because the wind was still and the world was painted with a film of silver ice.

The glaze of silver sparkled in her headlights and dazzled the photons that swept over the snow. The gem of the morning was diamonds and they glittered in strings from the power lines that she passed.

Not a creature was stirring as Hannah plowed through a deep drift to get onto the highway. She stepped on the gas and snow blew up on either side of her truck in plumes that drifted down to powder her windshield. The early morning was still, so still that Hannah felt as if she were the only living person in Winnetka County. Everyone else had been beamed up to a distant planet, but they'd left her behind because she'd been sleeping when the spaceship had come instead of standing out on Main Street in Lake Eden with everyone else. Now she was alone and she had to somehow contact the distant planet and convince the leader to send another . . .

Hannah's mental journey into woo-woo land disappeared abruptly as a Cozy Cow Dairy truck passed her and the driver honked his horn. Other people were awake and everything was perfectly normal except . . . Hannah crinkled her forehead, deep in thought . . . there was one thing that was unusual about her commute this morning.

"Whoa!" Hannah breathed, partly to test the theory and partly because she was so thoroughly discombobulated. She'd puffed the word out, straight at the inside of the cold windshield, but she couldn't see her crystallized breath in the air.

"Whoa!" Hannah tried it again and still there was no visible sign. She wiggled her left hand out of her winter glove and tentatively touched the tips of her fingers to the plastic designed to look like leather that covered the console between the seats. Warm. Her console was slightly warm to the touch. And so was her steering wheel, and the dashboard, and even the frame around the rearview mirror. Her heater was working! Hannah let out a joyous yelp that would have done a bull moose proud. The object of the recall must have been the heater, and Cyril had fixed it!

Hannah smiled all the way to the turnoff for Lake Eden. She smiled as she drove through town, and she was still smiling when she pulled into her parking spot at The Cookie Jar. She was about to smile her way out of her truck and into her shop when she noticed that there was a pitcher on the passenger seat.

"That's my pitcher!" Hannah said to no one at all and then felt silly for talking to herself. But it *was* her pitcher, the same pitcher she'd washed and left on the counter in Vanessa's kitchen. What was it doing here in her truck?

Hannah picked it up and saw that someone had stuffed a note inside. She opened the lid, pulled out the note and read, *Hannah—thanks for the Orange Julius. Vanessa washed the pitcher.*

"No, she didn't," Hannah muttered, and then she went on reading. *I knew you'd never get that auxiliary heater, so Bill and I hatched this plan with Cyril and we installed it for you. I found the leak and fixed it, so you shouldn't be freezing your foot off anymore. I just wanted to say thank you for cutting me some slack the other night with Vanessa and I figured this was one way to do it.* And the note was signed, *I love you, Mike.*

Hannah knew she should be angry. A woman with principles, an independent woman who didn't need to rely on a man for her comfort and well-being would have been angry. She did her best to work up a snit, but she was just too thankful to feel annoyed. So what if Mike had tricked her by faking a factory recall? So what if he'd decided what would be best for her and done it without consulting her? Her heater was fixed. Basking in the glow of being warm following a winter commute for the very first time since she'd bought her truck, Hannah suspected that if Mike suddenly appeared and begged her forgiveness for two-timing her with both Shawna Lee and Vanessa, she'd come within a cat's whisker of doing it!

Ten dozen Orange Snaps, twelve dozen Chocolate Chip Crunch Cookies, eight dozen Oatmeal Raisin Crisps, six dozen Boggles, nine dozen Black and Whites, and fourteen pans of various cookie bars, and Hannah was through baking for the morning. Her next task was to make preparations for lunch. The main ingredient would be shrimp. With two pounds of salad shrimp, two pounds of medium-size tail-on, and two pounds of jumbo colossal shrimp overloading her condo freezer, she'd decided that something had to give. She was going to use the salad shrimp for Shrimp Bisque and offer it to friends who dropped in around noon. Trudi Nash, a former art teacher at Jordan High, had given Edna Ferguson the recipe for her "cheat" collection. These were recipes that weren't made entirely from scratch, but as Edna said every time she used one, *Only a real food snob could tell the difference.*

Hannah thawed the shrimp in running water and chopped it with a knife. Then she got out the "cheat" ingredients, a can of condensed tomato soup and a can of condensed green pea soup. She dumped the soups in the blender, turned it on low, and combined them with the milk. Then she poured the resulting mixture in a saucepan that she carried to the walk-in cooler. The shrimp went in a separate container that she placed right next to the saucepan, and she was all ready to heat it when lunchtime rolled around.

She shut the cooler door, poured herself another cup of coffee, and carried it to her favorite booth at the back of the coffee shop. It was still dark outside and nothing was moving. That wasn't surprising, considering that it was six forty-seven in the morning. Lisa, who was an early riser, wouldn't even get up for another few minutes. Of course now that she was married . . .

Hannah steered her mind away from those possibilities and zeroed in on her tasks for the day, not nearly as interesting, but much, much safer for a single woman who wanted to stay that way, at least for a while.

TRUDI'S SHRIMP BISQUE

*Note: You can also make this bisque
with crab meat, or with a
combination of shrimp and crab.*

10¾ oz. can condensed tomato soup
  (I used Campbell's)
11¼ oz. can condensed green pea soup
  (I used Campbell's)
3 cups whole milk *(or light cream, if you
  want it richer)*
2-pound package salad shrimp, roughly
  chopped
½ cup sherry *(optional)*

Mix the tomato soup and the green pea soup together. *(It has to be green pea—don't use split pea.)* The green pea soup is lumpy, so use a blender if you have one. Add the milk or light cream.

Heat the soups and the milk in a saucepan over low heat, stirring occasionally, while you thaw and chop the shrimp. When the mixture is warm, add the chopped shrimp and stir it in.

When the soup is heated thoroughly, add the sherry and serve.

Yield: Makes approximately 6 servings.

Lisa said this bisque is even better than the bisque she had at the very fancy, very expensive restaurant in Minneapolis where Herb took her last year on Valentine's Day. Herb agreed, and not just because it's a whole lot cheaper.

Chapter
Twenty-Two

"**D**id you know that Bill and Mike fixed my heater?" Hannah asked, climbing into the passenger seat of Andrea's Volvo.

"I knew," Andrea admitted, "but they swore me to secrecy. That's why we pulled into Cyril's garage yesterday. It was supposed to seem like a big coincidence when he told you about the fake recall."

"It was really great being warm on the drive to work this morning."

"How about your feet? Bill said Mike was still trying to find the leak when he left last night."

"Mike found it. When I got out of the truck this morning, I could actually feel my toes."

"So . . . is he forgiven?"

"Bill?" Hannah asked, deliberately misunderstanding.

"No, silly. Mike. He's sorry, Hannah. He told Bill he wished he could take it all back."

"Take *what* back?"

Andrea looked very nervous. "Um . . . all the time he spent with Shawna Lee."

Hannah didn't say a word, but the goodwill

she'd felt toward Mike for fixing her heater vanished like free soft serve at the Fourth of July picnic.

"He told Bill absolutely nothing happened between them."

"Of course he did. He knew that Bill would tell you, and you'd tell me."

"I guess. But it's like you told Mother... Shawna Lee's dead and she's no competition anymore."

Hannah remembered saying that, but what was sauce for her mother's goose was not necessarily sauce for hers. "So Bill saw them together a lot?"

"Of course. I mean, they work together and they go to the same places to eat lunch. If Mike took Shawna Lee to lunch, Bill saw them. But you don't have to worry. Nothing happened. Mike told Bill that every time Bill mentioned he'd seen them together."

"Makes me wonder why Shawna Lee was after him. With all those *nothing happeneds*, why did she bother?"

"Don't tell me," Norman said when he opened the sliding glass panel between his waiting room and the receptionist's desk. "You're here to see the forensic dentist."

Hannah grinned. Norman was always a quick study. "That's right," she agreed. "How did you know?"

"It's unlikely both of you would have a dental emergency at the same time. And since neither of you look as if you're in any pain, that can't be it anyway. Of course I'd like to think you came to see me because you find me incredibly intelligent, and attractive, and sexy, and . . ."

"That, too," Hannah said, interrupting what would surely be a list of Norman's sterling qualities. "We'd like you to take a look at a picture. We need your expert opinion."

"Hand it over."

Hannah shoved the framed photo they'd taken from Winthrop's apartment through the open glass panel. "We really need to know whether the woman in this picture is Shawna Lee, or Vanessa."

"Vanessa," Norman said, giving the photo a quick glance.

"But . . . don't you have to compare it to dental charts or something?" Andrea asked.

"No. It's Vanessa."

"How do you know that for sure?" Hannah tapped the photo with her finger. "It looks just like Shawna Lee to me."

"This woman's left incisor is perfectly formed. Shawna Lee's left incisor had a chip."

"But maybe this picture was taken before she chipped it," Hannah suggested.

"No. She told me that happened in kindergarten when she fell off the swings."

"So you know for sure that this is Vanessa?"

Norman nodded. "I'd stake my license on it. I can go get the dental records if you want me to, but there's no doubt in my mind."

"That's good enough for me," Andrea said, turning to Hannah. "We'd better not tell Mother. You just got her calmed down and this'll rile her up all over again."

"You're right, especially since Vanessa is still alive.

We'll have to tell her sooner or later, but I agree that it should be later."

Norman looked like a guy who'd just gone down for the second time and was about to feel the water close over his head again. "I don't get it. Why would this picture upset your mother? It's a perfectly ordinary picture. Winthrop and Vanessa are sitting at a table in some kind of a restaurant or club, and they're smiling for the photographer."

"But Winthrop never said a word about knowing Vanessa, and Mother thought he'd told her everything."

"Maybe he didn't think it was important, especially if they didn't know each other that well. I can understand why your mother would be curious, but it's not exactly incriminating."

"Oh, yes it is," Hannah said.

"How? Professional photographers take pictures like this all the time."

"I know, but Winthrop must have known Vanessa pretty well because Mother found this photo hidden in his underwear drawer."

"Oh," Norman said, and then he was silent. To his credit, he didn't ask what Delores had been doing in Winthrop's underwear drawer. Perhaps, like Hannah and Andrea, he didn't really want to know.

"Now all we have to do is find out exactly where it was taken," Hannah told him. "Mother will want to know."

"That's easy," Norman said, shoving the photo back to Hannah's side of the glass. "It's obviously taken by a professional. Just look at the back and see if it's stamped with the studio name."

"You do it," Hannah said, shoving the picture over to her sister.

"Okay," Andrea agreed, turning the frame, glass side down, on Norman's counter. "Everybody cross their fingers . . ."

Hannah and Norman watched as Andrea bent back the prongs that kept the backing in place and lifted out the cardboard. The photo was backside up and there was a stamp in the lower left-hand corner.

"Peachtree Photo," Andrea read aloud, turning to them with a pleased expression. "There's a phone number and the photographer's in Macon, Georgia. Do you want me to call?"

"Absolutely," Hannah said. "Call now."

Andrea, who was always ready for any assignment that tested her information retrieval skills, snatched her cell phone from her purse and punched in the number. Hannah rummaged through her purse, pulled out her steno notepad, flipped it to a blank page, and handed it to her sister.

"Oh, hi!" Andrea said, when the call was connected. "I'm calling about this incredible photo of a friend of mine. I was wondering if I could order another copy, or get the negative, or something. You see, we're having a surprise party for her birthday, and we want blowups of all her flattering photos to put up in the restaurant. And since this is such a good one . . ."

Andrea started to doodle a smiling face and Hannah took heart. It was a promising sign.

"It's taken at some kind of restaurant, or club," Andrea releated, "and it's of Vanessa and a guy she met while she was living in Georgia. She looks so good in it. It's probably the best picture I've ever seen of her."

Another smiling face doodle joined the first, and Hannah felt a smile break out on her own face. Andrea was working wonders with the person on the other end of the line.

"Yes, it's a two-shot," Andrea confirmed, glancing over at Hannah and winking. "Tropical decor, peacock chairs, and glass-topped tables on rattan bases. There's a caged parrot in the background, if that helps."

Andrea was silent for a moment and then she bent down for a closer look at the photo. "A number in the lower left-hand corner? Yes! I see it. It's really small. Hold on a second and I'll read it off to you."

Hannah and Norman listened as Andrea read the number to the person at the other end of the line. "Okay. I'll hold on."

"She's going to look in the files," Andrea said, shaking her head like a runner after a tiring race. "She wants to help me, so that's a plus."

Time passed in a series of breaths in and out. Norman exchanged glances with Hannah and Andrea, and they exchanged glances with him. And then Andrea turned back to the phone. The assistant at Peachtree Photos had come back on the line.

"Hi. Yes, I'm still here. Bobby Joe Peters bought the negative? Who's he?"

Another moment passed and Andrea laughed. "Right. I should have known you wouldn't have that information. But he paid for the photo and the negative?"

Andrea and Hannah exchanged glances. Who was Bobby Joe Peters?

"You're right! I don't know why we didn't think of that! All we have to do is scan it and take it to a copy place to make a blowup. Thanks so much for suggesting it."

"Bobby Joe Peters?" Norman asked, when Andrea had hung up the phone.

"That's right," Hannah answered, reading from Andrea's notes. "Vanessa and Winthrop must have been out with another couple, and the other man paid for the photos."

Andrea frowned slightly. "I guess that makes sense. We really didn't learn much, did we?"

"We learned enough to do another search on the Internet," Norman said. "Why don't you two go back to The Cookie Jar while I find out all I can about Bobby Joe? I'll start a search and let it run during my next appointment. I've got somebody coming in at one, but then I'm free for an hour. I can walk up and bring you the printout."

"Good heavens!" Lisa said, staring down at the framed photograph. "Does your mother know about this?"

"No. I mean, yes . . . but not really. That is, she knows, but . . ." Andrea stopped trying to explain and turned to her sister. "Hannah!"

It was the same desperate tone Andrea had used in high school when she'd encountered a math problem she couldn't solve. Hannah responded as she had back then. "Relax. I'll explain." And then she proceeded to do it. "Mother's seen the photo, but she thinks the woman is Shawna Lee. It's not. It's Vanessa."

"And Winthrop."

"That's right. And a man named Bobby Joe Peters paid for the photo. Norman's checking him out on the Internet right now and he'll be here around two with a printout."

"Do you think this Bobby Joe Peters is important?" Lisa asked.

"I don't know. If we're operating under the assumption that Shawna Lee was killed because she looked like Vanessa, he could be very important." Hannah stopped and took a deep breath. "Really, it's a long shot, but we don't have any other clues," she admitted. "Besides, Mother will probably want us to contact Bobby Joe Peters to find out exactly what Winthrop was doing with Vanessa."

Chapter
Twenty-Three

"**Y**ou're early!" Hannah exclaimed when she opened the back door of The Cookie Jar in response to a series of quick, hard knocks and found Norman standing there. "Do you want some Shrimp Bisque? It's really delicious."

"I'm sure it is. Can I take some with me and heat it in the microwave?"

Hannah ladled a generous helping into a take-out container. "Here you go," she said, handing it to him.

"Thanks. The reason I'm here is because I took a quick peek at the printout while I was waiting for Mrs. Kuehn's X rays. She's in the chair and I've got to get right back."

"What's so important in the printout?" Andrea asked, shutting the door behind Norman to keep out the cold.

"Bobby Joe Peters. There's a picture of him on page five. I think he's Winthrop. At least he looks exactly like Winthrop without the mustache."

"Uh-oh!" Hannah swallowed hard. "But . . . can't you tell by his teeth? The way you did with Vanessa?"

"He's not smiling. They don't let them smile in

mug shots. Read it, you'll see. I've got to get back before Mrs. Kuehn thinks I deserted her."

After Norman had left to rush back to his patient, Hannah and Andrea sat down at the workstation and read every word of the printout. Bobby Joe Peters did look exactly like Winthrop, but that wasn't the most frightening part. Bobby Joe Peters had escaped from a minimum-security prison in Georgia last August. He'd been sentenced to ten years for scamming an elderly woman out of her retirement money.

"Do you think Bobby Joe is Winthrop? And do you think that's why he's dating Mother?"

"I don't know what to think," Hannah said, handing her sister the next page of the printout. "Read. There's more."

By the time the two sisters were through reading, they knew everything about Bobby Joe Peters except his shoe size. The upshot was that he was a con artist who'd gone by various aliases in the past and he'd been known to work with a female accomplice.

"But Winthrop didn't bring a woman to Lake Eden with him," Andrea pointed out.

"Maybe she's still in prison. Or maybe this time he decided to work alone. Do you think we should show this to Mother right away?"

"Yes," Andrea said, getting up to get her coat.

"I'll be right with you," Hannah called out, grabbing a bag and stuffing it with Twin Chocolate Delights. "Mother's going to need chocolate after she finds out that Winthrop isn't Winthrop."

A cold wind was blowing as the two sisters rushed the short distance between the buildings and ducked in the back door of Granny's Attic. As usual, there was barely room to turn around since the mothers were using the back room for a storeroom. Andrea slid around the back of an oval mirror and hopped over a footstool with clawed feet. Hannah followed her sister's lead and eventually they beat a circuitous route to the inside door.

"Hi, Carrie," Andrea greeted Norman's mother, who was manning the front counter. "Where's Mother?"

"You just missed her by a half hour or so. She said she had an errand to run and it could take most of the afternoon. She'll be back before closing, though."

"Do you know what the errand is?" Hannah asked, hoping that Carrie had been her usual nosy self.

"Not completely, but I know she checked to make sure she had her bankbook, so I assume she went there. And I *think* it had something to do with Winthrop, but I'm not entirely positive about that."

"Why do you think it had something to do with Winthrop?" Hannah followed with the obvious question.

"Because she said something about how people in love had to trust one another and it was a good thing she knew where he hides his extra key. I figured she had to be talking about Winthrop, since he's the only man she's been serious about since your father died. I just hope my best and oldest friend doesn't get hurt. There's something about Winthrop that's just too . . . too . . ."

"Slick," Hannah supplied the word and then she handed over the cookie bag. "Don't worry, Carrie.

We'll find her. In the meantime, have a couple of these cookies. They'll make you feel better."

After warning Carrie to keep Delores at Granny's Attic if she came back, and making sure Lisa would do the same at The Cookie Jar, Hannah armed herself with another bag of Twin Chocolate Delights and climbed into the passenger seat of Andrea's Volvo. Their destination was the First National Mercantile Bank. The bank was only a stone's throw away, but Andrea had insisted on taking her Volvo so that they could chase after their mother if they saw her.

The lines at the bank were impossible and Hannah headed straight for Doug Greerson's office instead of waiting. Doug was a hands-on bank president. He knew everything that happened at First National Mercantile and he'd know if Delores had come in. That was one of the reasons Hannah hadn't asked Doug for a loan to bail out The Cookie Jar. Doug wouldn't have talked, but all the loan applications had to be run past the board and it was a cinch that someone would have mentioned it.

"Hannah." Doug stood up to greet them when Hannah tapped on his open office door. "And Andrea. Would you like a cup of coffee? I've got a nice French roast from Guatemala."

"Not this time, Doug," Hannah answered for both of them. "We're in a real rush."

"We just came to see if Mother's been in," Andrea entered into the conversation.

"She was here earlier. She left about fifteen minutes ago."

"Did she happen to say where she was going?" Hannah asked.

"No. And I didn't ask. What's wrong?"

Hannah exchanged glances with Andrea. Doug could be trusted. "Please don't say anything to Mother about this, but we think someone she knows may be conning her out of a large sum of money. We want to make sure that doesn't happen."

"An investment scheme?" Doug asked.

"It's probably something like that. We were just hoping she didn't withdraw a lot of money."

"I can't tell you what she withdrew," Doug said, shaking his head. "All I can do is tell you that she needed a manager's approval to make the withdrawal."

"And a manager has to approve any amount over . . . ?"

"Two thousand dollars. And I have to personally approve any amount over fifty thousand. Just in case you're interested, no one's asked for my approval today."

"Thanks, Doug," Hannah said, realizing that he'd just told them that their mother had withdrawn over two thousand dollars and under fifty thousand dollars.

"At least she didn't have to ask for Doug's approval," Andrea said as she slid back behind the wheel of her car.

"That's true, but she could have withdrawn forty-nine thousand dollars."

"That's a lot! What should we do? Go and look for her?"

"Drive past the house and we'll see if her car's there."

Andrea turned the corner and drove to their mother's house. Hannah rang the bell, but there was no answer and the sisters let themselves in. A check of the garage revealed that it was empty. Their mother was out somewhere in her car.

"I'll leave a note," Hannah said, scrawling on a piece of cardboard she found in the kitchen, and propping it up by the staircase that faced the front door. "She's bound to see that when she comes in."

"Unless she comes in through the garage."

"Which she probably will, since she's driving. Thanks, Andrea. I'm so rattled, I'm not thinking clearly." Hannah moved the note to a kitchen chair and placed the chair directly in front of the inside door to the garage. "That ought to do it. She can't get in without moving that chair. What do you think?"

"Winthrop is a convict using a false name. Dangerous. Call Hannah and Andrea right away!" Andrea read the message out loud. "That's good, but do you think she'll believe it?"

"I don't know. I hope so. Let's go check Winthrop's apartment. That money she withdrew was for him. I'm almost sure of that."

"But he won't be back until dinnertime tonight. I don't think Mother would just sit there and wait for him, do you?"

"Not in a million years. Mother's not a patient person. She probably dropped off the money for him in an envelope, just like she used to do with us when she wasn't home to give us our allowances."

"A sealed envelope," Andrea reminded her. "That was so you couldn't tell how much I was getting and I couldn't tell how much you were getting. Remember?"

"Of course. So how much *were* you getting?"

"I'll never tell."

"Neither will I. Come on, let's go. If Mother's left an envelope with Winthrop's name on it, I'll just take it and that'll solve the problem."

It was starting to snow again as Andrea turned onto the highway, and Hannah thought about how she'd rather be driving than riding with Andrea. "We could have taken my truck this time, now that the heater's fixed."

"Your truck's too distinctive. If the envelope's there and you take it, we don't want someone saying they saw your cookie truck behind his building in a visitor's spot."

"True," Hannah said. Andrea had a point. "So do you think Winthrop is really Bobby Joe Peters? Or do you think Bobby Joe is Winthrop's evil twin?"

"He's Bobby Joe Peters. Remember when I said everything about him was too generic and he acted like someone playing an English lord in a movie?"

"I remember."

"Well, that's what he's been doing. He's Bobby Joe Peters all right. And we've got to keep Mother from giving him our inheritance."

"Our *inheritance?*" Hannah was shocked.

"I didn't really mean that the way it sounded, but Mother promised to do things for Tracey and Bethany."

"What things?"

"Like putting them through college. And that's getting more expensive every year. If she gives Winthrop almost fifty thousand dollars, there may not be enough."

"Oh," Hannah said, not commenting one way or the other. Since she was the one who'd moved back in with their mother after their father died, and Delores had never even balanced a checkbook before, Hannah had assumed the role of her mother's accountant. That made her privy to information that Andrea and Michelle didn't have. Hannah knew that her mother had enough in securities and investments to live off the interest the rest of her life and not even touch the principal. But no one knew that except Hannah and Delores, and neither one of them was talking.

"Mother's not going to go broke, is she?" Andrea asked, the worry plain in her voice.

"It's not likely," Hannah said. "Even if she withdrew a fairly large hunk of cash, she'll be okay. But there's no way I want to see that snake get anything from her except the back of her hand."

"Right!" Andrea said, stepping on the gas.

"Slow down, Andrea. We can't stop Winthrop, or Bobby Joe, or whoever he really is from taking Mother's money if we're a highway statistic."

"True."

Andrea slowed down a bit, but she was still traveling too fast to suit Hannah. Hannah reminded herself that her sister had never been involved in an accident and tried not to watch as the speedometer headed upward again. They'd make it. They had to. And they'd save the day. Delores would be there, stuffing an envelope with money for Winthrop. And Hannah would spirit her mother and the cash off to safety before the rat came back to collect his ill-gotten gains.

Chapter Twenty-Four

"Park right here," Hannah advised, pointing to the space right across from the one allotted to apartment number 223. "If Winthrop drives in, honk three times."

"But . . . he'll see me!"

"That's fine. Let him think you were honking at him and keep him talking for a couple of minutes, just long enough for me to get out of the building. Then drive around the back by the Dumpsters and pick me up. You'll have to dream up some sort of story to explain why you're here."

"No problem, I've got it."

"Already?" Hannah was surprised.

"I'm a real estate agent. I'm good at things like that. I'll just say I have a client who's looking for a one-bedroom rental until her new house is built. And I'll ask him questions about his apartment and what he thinks about the management. I can keep him talking for at least five minutes, maybe ten."

"Great. Now don't get worried if it takes me a while. If Mother left the money, it might not be in plain sight."

"Take as long as you want," Andrea said, reaching in back for the bag of cookies Hannah had brought. "I'll just eat some chocolate and wait for you."

Hannah headed for the front of the building at a fast clip, hoping that all the Twin Chocolate Delights she'd packed for Delores wouldn't be gone by the time they found her. She dashed up the walkway to the front door and pulled it open, not bothering to use her mother's key. The same applied to the second door. It was still unlocked and Hannah had no doubt it would remain unlocked until some security-minded tenant complained to the management.

There was no way she wanted to brave the elevator with the mirrored walls today, especially since she was wearing her parka coat. She'd look like a gang of chubby, redheaded trolls straight from a Scandinavian ice floe. And even though she knew it would be an optical illusion, it was too much for her to handle right now. Hannah pulled open the door to the stairs and took them two at a time. She was in a hurry. She wanted to replace the photo in Winthrop's underwear drawer, find the envelope with her mother's money, and get back out to Andrea's car before she hit any kind of a snag.

Hannah took a moment to catch her breath once she burst out of the stairwell and into the carpeted corridor of the second floor. She walked sedately to apartment 223 and glanced around to make sure that no one was watching. Then she slid the key in the lock, turned the knob, and stepped quickly inside, locking the door behind her.

Clutching the picture in one hand, Hannah glanced around for the envelope. It had to be here somewhere. It wasn't on the mantel with the demo pictures in their new frames, and it wasn't propped up on the coffee table. Hannah was about to head for the bedroom to look there when she heard a sound that made her freeze. Someone had opened a drawer in the bedroom. It had to be Winthrop! But before she could turn and run back outside, the bedroom door opened and Winthrop emerged.

"I thought I heard someone," he said, staring at her with a frown on his face. "What are you doing here? And how did you get in?"

Hannah thought fast and said the first thing that popped into her mind. "I just came to ask you some questions. And I figured you were here since the door was unlocked. I guess you didn't hear me knocking."

"No." The frown remained on Winthrop's face and it was clear he didn't believe her. "What questions did you want to ask me?"

Hannah took a deep breath and went for broke. Maybe she could throw him off base and make a run for it. "Why are you pretending to be Winthrop Harrington when your real name is Bobby Joe Peters? And what do you want with my mother?"

"Oh, my dear. I'm so sorry you found out about that," Winthrop said, losing his English accent in the process. And then he reached into his pocket and pulled out a gun, pointing it directly at her. "Sit down. Right there on the couch."

Hannah sat. What else could she do? It was as her father, and Mike, had told her repeatedly. If someone points a gun at you, do exactly as they say.

"You think you're a pretty smart little cookie, don't you?"

Hannah kept mum. It was a rhetorical question and he didn't really want an answer. And all the while her mind was spinning, trying to think of some means of escape.

"I assume you figured out that I planned to meet up with Vanessa in Lake Eden after her husband was killed?"

"Killed?" Hannah couldn't help asking. Her only chance was to keep him talking and perhaps some escape route would open up for her. "I thought her husband died of natural causes."

"Oh, he did." Winthrop laughed a mean little laugh that didn't bode well for Hannah. "The pillow Vanessa put over his face was filled with goose down, and you can't get more natural than that."

Hannah came very close to groaning out loud. Winthrop was admitting too much and there was no way he was going to let her go. If she couldn't figure out some clever way to stop him, she'd wind up as dead as the goose who'd given up the down that had smothered Neil Roper.

"Vanessa wouldn't cut me in. I thought that was pretty rotten, considering we'd hatched up the whole scheme together. She said she should get all the money since she'd had to put up with the old man for almost a year."

Hannah judged the distance between Winthrop's gun and her own position. Too far. Even if she were a martial arts expert, which she wasn't, she still wouldn't be close enough to kick the gun out of his hand.

"The first day she got to town, I went right over to see her. I figured everything was just fine, you know? We had long-range plans in place and both of us had done our part. But all that money had changed her. She thought she was too good for me. She actually had the nerve to threaten to turn me in as a fugitive if I didn't get out of town right away."

Hannah knew it was risky, but she risked a comment. "But you *didn't* get out of town. You're still here."

"That's because it was a standoff between us. She couldn't turn me in, because I knew exactly how she killed her husband. And I couldn't turn her in, because she knew I'd escaped from prison."

"So why didn't you let it go on like that, a standoff with nobody getting hurt?"

"Because we had a deal, that's why! And because she was trying to get out of it!" Winthrop's eyes glittered with hatred and Hannah was sorry she'd asked. "There was no way I was going to let my partner get away with that!"

The words flashed before Hannah's eyes, *been known to work with a female accomplice.* Vanessa Quinn Roper was the female accomplice mentioned in the printout Norman had given them.

"I kept my end of the bargain. They would have reduced my sentence if I'd named her, but I didn't."

Hannah was reminded of a phrase her Grandma Ingrid had used. There was no such thing as honor among thieves. Once the code of ethics had been broken in one area, it was weakened and that much easier to break in another area.

"I couldn't let her get away with threatening me, not after I taught her everything I knew and helped her get started. It was just a question of waiting for the right time."

"The wedding," Hannah breathed, remembering how Winthrop had gone to get the rice for her mother.

"That's right. I let everybody see me at the church with your mother. And then, when I forgot the rice in the car, I told her I'd run right out and get it."

"And you did. But not until after you'd taken a little side trip to the Magnolia Blossom Bakery."

"That's right," Winthrop said, beaming at her like a teacher rewarding a bright pupil. "You catch on fast. Too bad you're so honest. You would have made a great partner."

Hannah wasn't sure if she should thank him or not. Being considered for the position of accomplice to a con man wasn't exactly a compliment. She felt around behind her for something to use as a weapon, but the only things that came to hand were soft pillows. And then she heard honking. Andrea was honking her horn in the parking lot, but she wasn't supposed to honk unless Winthrop drove up. And Winthrop, or Bobby Joe, or whatever his real name was, was right here pointing a gun at her. "But Vanessa wasn't at the bakery that afternoon," she said, still stalling for time.

"That's right, but I didn't know that."

Hannah looked down at the package in her lap. It was the framed picture of Winthrop and Vanessa, and the frame had sharp edges. It wasn't much, but it would have to do if she couldn't find anything else. She just hoped that Andrea wouldn't try to come up here and walk straight into trouble. "So what happened when you got to the Magnolia Blossom Bakery? It was snowing, right?"

"That's right. It was snowing pretty hard by

then. I went around to the back of the shop and I saw Vanessa taking something out of the oven."

"But the woman you saw wasn't Vanessa."

"I know that now, but I didn't know it then. The window was steamy and I wiped it a little on the outside. That didn't help much. Then I fired the first shot through the window, but I missed her."

"You fired two shots?"

"That's right. She turned and I nailed her. I didn't realize I'd killed Shawna Lee until the next day. That was when Delores told me that Vanessa had gone to Georgia for a couple of days."

"So you killed the wrong sister," Hannah said.

"It's just a temporary setback. I'll get Vanessa when the time is right. I just have to wait until your disappearance blows over." Winthrop gestured at her with the gun. "Get up. We're going to the basement. There's a little room next to the furnace and I'll put you there. It's noisy and nobody can hear you scream."

"You're going to . . . kill me?" Hannah asked, still stalling for time. Shouldn't the cavalry arrive about now? Or shouldn't her sister start honking the horn again to distract him?

"Of course I'm going to kill you. You're smart enough to know I can't let you live."

"How about Mother?" Hannah asked, her heart beating hard at the thought that Winthrop might harm her mother. "You won't hurt her, will you?"

"No reason to hurt her. She's a foolish old lady, but that's the way I like them. The old ones are grateful for the attention." Winthrop stopped and frowned. "What's that?"

"What's what?" Hannah asked, although she'd

heard something, too. It had sounded like some-one was outside in the hallway, but she wasn't about to mention that.

"I thought I heard something."

"I didn't hear anything," Hannah said, praying that the cavalry, any cavalry, was coming.

"Whatever it was, it's gone now. You're actually doing me a favor, you know? The old lady's been worried that you don't like me. Now you'll be out of the way. I'll give her lots of love and comfort when she hears about her daughter's tragic acci-dent and she'll give me even more money."

Hannah clutched the picture frame. She'd learned something. Winthrop was planning to dis-guise her death as an accident. That meant he wouldn't shoot her unless he had no choice, be-cause there was no way he could explain away a gunshot as a tragic accident.

"Get up. Now!" Winthrop waved the gun again.

Hannah stood up, watching his eyes. The slight-est evidence of inattention and she'd lunge with the picture frame, and pray for the best. That was when something happened that shocked both of them. The front door to the apartment flew open and a whirling dervish blew in.

"You unmitigated scoundrel!" Delores shouted. She grabbed an umbrella from the stand next to the door, held it in front of her like a foil, and hur-tled it at Winthrop full bore.

"Mother!" Hannah screamed, lunging for Win-throp's arm with the picture frame and succeed-ing in knocking the gun out of his hand.

Winthrop yelped in pain as the point of the um-brella plunged into a soft spot near his shoulder. It wasn't a killing blow, but he was down and Hannah jumped on him before he could get back up. "Find something to tie him up with, Mother."

"Certainly," Delores said, recovering some of her equilibrium. "How about an extension cord? There's one behind the television set."

"That'll be fine. Just unplug it and hand it to me. And then call the paramedics."

"Why?"

"Because he's bleeding. The point of the umbrella went into his chest."

Delores shrugged. "He's not bleeding that much. I'll call the sheriff's department and tell them to come. They can decide if he needs the paramedics."

"Okay," Hannah said, bowing to the higher authority of a woman who'd been insulted. It was obvious that Delores had heard what Winthrop had said about her.

Since it was a long extension cord, Hannah bound Winthrop's hands and his feet, trussing him like a Christmas goose. Then she spotted his robe on the back of the bathroom door and took the belt to gag him. There was no way she was going to let him insult her mother again!

"Why do you have him gagged, dear?" Delores asked, coming back from the kitchen where she'd gone to use the wall phone.

"He's said enough. I don't want to hear any more."

"Very good." Delores gave Hannah an approving nod. "The dispatcher said a squad car should be here any minute."

"It can't be soon enough to suit me. Thank you, Mother."

"For calling the sheriff's department?"

"No, for getting here in the nick of time. You saved my life."

Delores gave a little shrug. "Perhaps I did, but you were very good with that picture frame."

"Thanks, Mother. What were you doing at the door? Coming in to give Winthrop money?"

Delores looked nonplussed for a moment and then she gave Hannah a questioning look. "That doesn't really matter now, does it?"

"Not really. Not the way it turned out. The bad guy's down and the good women won."

"That's the way it should be." Delores perched on the arm of Winthrop's sofa. "So what did you think of my technique, dear?"

"What technique?"

"I took fencing in high school. Of course we used foils and not umbrellas, but the concept's the same."

"Your technique was perfect, Mother. You won the match."

"Yes, I did, didn't I?" Delores gave a pleased smile.

Chapter
Twenty-Five

Hannah signed her statement and passed the pen to her mother, who signed hers. They were sitting in one of the interrogation rooms at the Winnetka County Sheriff's Department and they'd been there for the better part of an hour, waiting for their statements to be typed. Since Andrea had been in her car the whole time and not party to what had happened in the apartment, Mike had told her to go home to her children, and Bill would take her statement in the morning.

"We're clamping a lid on this," Mike warned them. "I don't want either one of you to say a word about what happened."

Hannah started to frown. "But Winthrop . . . I mean Bobby Joe, told me that Vanessa killed Neil Roper. He said they planned the whole thing together. Isn't that enough to arrest her?"

"It would be in most circumstances, but this one's a little tricky. Bobby Joe Peters is an escaped felon. His word isn't highly credible. And the alleged murder took place in Macon, Georgia. That's way out of our jurisdiction. I think we could get away with arresting her and getting the warrant from Macon later, but I don't want to take the chance that some smart lawyer could get the case dismissed on a technicality."

"That makes sense," Delores said, sipping the coffee that one of the deputies had brought her. She made a face and Hannah sympathized. The coffee at the sheriff's station was awful.

"I guess I can understand how you'd have to be careful to follow procedure," Hannah said, "but aren't you afraid Vanessa's going to hear that Bobby Joe was arrested and take off?"

Mike shook his head. "Not if you ladies don't talk. Bill already warned Andrea, and now I'm warning you. Mum's the word."

"Mum's the word," Hannah repeated, because Mike seemed to expect it. "But we're not the only ones who know you made an arrest. How about the secretary who typed our statements? And the other deputies who saw you bring him in cuffed? They know, so we're not the only ones who know, you know?"

Hannah gave a little groan as her last sentence replayed in her mind. She'd always prided herself on having decent grammar and a good command of the English language, but she'd just used the word *know* three times in one sentence.

"That's not a problem. The only other people who know are sheriff's department employees. They *can't* talk."

"You mean *mustn't*. If they *can't* talk, they're mute," Hannah mumbled under her breath.

"What was that?" Mike asked.

"Nothing. Just talking to myself. Are we through? I still have some things to do today."

"We're through."

"Thank goodness!" Delores looked very grateful. "I'm going to tell Andrea that she should do something with this room now that Bill is the sheriff. This institutional tan paint is dreadful. Perhaps she could put a nice pale yellow on the walls, since there aren't any windows. That would make it a lot more cheerful. And new furniture, of course. I'll never understand why they bothered to bolt down these chairs. No one in their right mind would want to steal them!"

Mike smiled at her and Hannah could tell he was amused. "You're absolutely right. This furniture is pretty bad, but it's an interrogation room and it doesn't have to look good. See that rub mark on the arm of your chair?"

"This?" Delores touched a spot where the paint had worn off and the metal showed through.

"Yes. Those scratches are from handcuffs. We leave one hand free so the suspect can write, and the other is cuffed to the arm of the chair. That's why the chairs have to be bolted down."

"Oh," Delores said. "I didn't know."

"I wouldn't expect you to know. I really doubt that you've been in an interrogation room before."

"You're right."

Delores gave a little laugh and Mike joined in. So did Hannah. She was glad Mike was handling her mother so well. Delores had suffered a big shock this afternoon and her pride was bound to be at low ebb.

"Thank you very much for your cooperation," Mike said, smiling at both of them. "I know giving your statement hasn't been fun, but it was necessary."

"I bet you say that to all the girls," Hannah quipped, but she quickly sobered when Mike didn't laugh. "Sorry. We'll be going then. And don't worry about us saying anything. We won't."

Mother and daughter were silent as they headed out to Delores's car. Once they were buckled in, Delores turned to Hannah. "Do you have to go straight home, dear?"

"Not really," Hannah said, reacting to her mother's expression. Delores looked dejected.

"Do you have time to get a cup of coffee somewhere?"

"Of course I do," Hannah said, because if she didn't have time, she'd make time. Then she glanced at her watch in the light from the dash. It was five forty-five and winter darkness had closed in. "Let's go back to The Cookie Jar and I'll put on a fresh pot. Lisa's gone, but there's bound to be some cookies left. I had a whole bag for you when I started out this afternoon, but Andrea ate them all while she was waiting for me in the car."

Instead of the outraged expression Hannah had expected, or the good-natured laugh that would acknowledge her middle daughter's love for Hannah's cookies, or even a comment about how Andrea had best start watching her weight, Delores just nodded. That made Hannah worry. And what made her worry even more was the fact that her mother didn't ask what kind of cookies they'd been. Delores always asked. At least, she had always asked in the past.

Delores drove through the silent streets to The Cookie Jar. There was only the swoosh of an occasional car as it passed by on the other side of the road, heading home to hearth and family. When

Mike had first moved to Lake Eden, he'd commented that they rolled up the streets at six o'clock in the winter. Except for bright lights spilling out of the front window of the Cut 'n Curl signifying that Bertie Straub had a late customer, all the businesses on Main Street were closed. And since it was such a cold night, no one was out on the sidewalk, walking.

"I hope Carrie remembered to turn on the alarm," Delores said, turning in the alley and driving past the back of her building.

"Do you want to stop and check?" Hannah asked.

"No, that's okay. She's usually pretty good about that."

Delores pulled into the small parking lot in the back of The Cookie Jar and took the spot right next to Hannah's truck. "I could just go home if you're busy, or something."

"I'm not busy. And I'm not something, either." Hannah tried for a laugh, but she didn't get it. "Come in, Mother. You need some chocolate to perk you up."

Five minutes later, mother and daughter were sitting at the back table in The Cookie Jar, sipping coffee and dunking Chocolate Almond Toast.

"Wonderful," Delores said, looking much relieved. "You're right, Hannah. Chocolate does improve one's mood. I'm sure that's why men have given women chocolates over the ages. They had chocolate in Regency England, you know."

"They did?"

"Yes. They primarily used it in beverages. A young woman would have chocolate for breakfast."

"Was it like our hot chocolate?"

"It was similar, but much less sweet. Marge Beeseman gave a report on it last year." Delores stopped and raised the corner of a paper napkin to her eyes. "I'm sorry, Hannah. I'm just so depressed. I keep thinking of Winthrop's favorite saying."

"What was that?" Hannah asked, not reminding her mother that Winthrop was really Bobby Joe Peters, the con man, and that his favorite saying, if he had one, would be, *Never give a sucker an even break.*

"He used to say, *Life is not measured by the number of breaths we take, but by the moments that take our breath away.*"

"Didn't work for Neil Roper," Hannah said, before she could stop herself.

"What do you mean?"

Hannah came close to groaning. Her mother was depressed. The man she'd trusted, the man she'd been about to marry had betrayed her. She needed tender loving care, but Hannah had stuck her foot in it. "I mean, he had his breath taken away. Literally. And I don't think he enjoyed it."

"Hannah!" Delores rebuked her, but a smile was hovering at the corners of her lips. "That's awful."

"I know. It's just the way my mind works. I must have gotten it from Dad."

"Or me," Delores said, the smile peeking out. "I had a pretty good sense of humor at one time. I lost it after your dad died."

"Maybe you'll get it back," Hannah said, hoping that was the right thing to say. Careful, sensitive counseling wasn't her thing. She tended to say it like it was.

"I hope so. I miss being able to laugh at myself. Change places with me, Hannah. I don't want to look at myself in the mirror."

"Okay." Hannah got up and changed places with her mother. "Why don't you want to look at yourself?"

"Because I look awful."

"No, you don't!" Hannah stared at her mother in shock. Delores was wearing a sleek dark green pantsuit that showed off her perfect figure, her makeup was flawlessly applied, and her hair looked fabulous. "You look great, Mother. That pantsuit is terrific on you. I'd kill for a figure like yours."

"You would?" Delores looked pleased at the compliment.

"Absolutely."

"It's simple to improve your figure, dear. All you have to do is watch your diet and get plenty of exercise."

"I know. But I won't do it."

"But . . . you said you'd kill for a figure like mine."

"Oh, I'd kill for it. I just won't diet and exercise for it."

Delores laughed, a bit hysterically, Hannah thought, and then she reached up to dab at her eyes again. "I'm terribly ashamed of myself, Hannah. Winthrop was right. I'm just a foolish old lady."

"No, you're not!" Hannah crossed her fingers and hoped she could think of the right thing to say.

"I *am* foolish. What else would you call a fifty-year-old woman who falls for a fake English lord who's more than ten years younger than she is, just because he's handsome and he can dance the tango?"

Hannah took heart. Her mother was fifty-seven, not fifty. If Delores could still lie about her age, she still had some hope left for the future. Of course there was another possibility, one that negated any positive spin that Hannah had attempted to generate. It was possible that her mother had lied about her age for so long, she'd actually lost track.

"Well? What would you call her?"

"A romantic," Hannah said. "I admire that about you, Mother. You're not afraid to dream. And once you find that dream, you go for it. I wish I had your nerve."

"But not my gullibility," Delores said, smiling slightly.

"No, not that," Hannah agreed, reaching out to give her mother a hug. "Although . . . it beats being bored for the rest of your life."

"Are you bored, dear?"

"Not me. Just when I think I might be, there's always something."

"That's true. I was just saying to . . ." Delores stopped in mid-sentence and started to frown. "I swear that was Vanessa's Corvette I just saw."

"Are you sure?"

Delores gave a short laugh. "Of course I'm sure. How many gold Corvettes are there in Lake Eden?"

"You've got a point," Hannah said, turning to look at the taillights that were disappearing around the corner of the block. "She must be just getting home."

"Well, I hope she stays put."

Delores stared at Hannah and Hannah stared

right back. Hannah had no doubt that the mother-daughter radar was working and the same thought was running through their minds.

"You think somebody's going to call and tell her that her former partner's been arrested? And she's going to take off before Mike can get that warrant from Georgia?" Hannah asked.

"That's exactly what I think. How about you?"

"Me, too. There are no secrets in Lake Eden. Mike should have realized that. What do you think we should do about it?"

"Watch her."

"Surveillance. That's good. And what shall we do if she leaves?"

"Follow her. And call the sheriff's department. We're supposed to do that, aren't we?"

"Yes, we're supposed to do that. I don't have a cell phone, do you?"

"No. I was going to get one, but . . . she's leaving!" Delores pointed out the window at the car that was inching out of the alley that led to the Magnolia Blossom Bakery. "She must have heard about it wherever she was, and she made a quick trip back here to pick up money, or her passport, or something."

Hannah got up for a better look. "You're right. That's Vanessa. She's just checking out the street to make sure the coast is clear. Let's go!"

"This is exciting," Delores said, sipping the mug of coffee she'd grabbed to take with her. "Are you sure your truck can keep up with her?"

"She's not driving fast."

"That's because she really *is* from the South.

They just don't know how to deal with the weather we have up here. Do you think she knows we're behind her?"

"Maybe, but it really doesn't matter. I've got a full tank of gas and we'll follow her as far as we have to."

Hannah and Delores were silent as they tailed Vanessa through the silent streets. The only sound was the slap of Hannah's windshield wipers against the glass. It was snowing again, very lightly, but just enough so that she needed to clear the glass. Why was it that snow, or rain for that matter, always fell at a rate that was just between the set speeds of the windshield wipers?

"What if she sees us behind her and stops?" Delores asked. "Do you have a weapon?"

"Only cookies. We could force-feed her chocolate, but I don't think that would do much good."

"I've got my coffee cup," Delores said. "I could throw that at her."

"But could you hit her?"

"Of course I could hit her. I used to be the pitcher on my high school softball team."

"Whoa!" Hannah gasped, turning for a quick look at her mother. "Will you play for The Cookie Jar? I'm going to have a softball team this summer and I need a pitcher."

Delores looked as excited as Hannah had ever seen her. "I'll do it! You've got a pitcher!"

"Thanks, Mother," Hannah said and then she gasped as Vanessa did something she hadn't expected. She hung a U-turn in the middle of the road and headed straight back toward Hannah's truck.

"What is she doing?" Delores asked.

"I don't know. Brace yourself, Mother. I'm going to try to run her off the road. I think she'll go in the ditch rather than hit us."

Even if Vanessa had opted for toughing it out, it wouldn't have been much of a collision. Vanessa's Corvette was low to the ground, and Hannah was driving the American SUV that some car magazines had compared to a tank. As Hannah bore down on Vanessa's car, and Vanessa tried to move out of the way, the Corvette hit a patch of ice and skidded off the road into the ditch.

"We got her!" Delores exulted, as the Corvette sank into the snow so far that its wheels were covered. "There's no way she can drive out of that!"

"You're right. But I wonder why she . . . Look!"

Hannah pointed to what had caused Vanessa's abrupt reversal. Four sheriff's squad cars were waiting at the entrance to the freeway with their lights flashing.

"There's more back there!" Delores exclaimed.

Hannah turned to see what looked like a phalanx of squad cars coming up behind them.

Sirens screamed as the squad cars descended upon them, and Hannah and Delores covered their ears. A brace of deputies headed for Vanessa's Corvette, and radios crackled commands in the icy night air.

"Are you okay, Mother?" Hannah asked, tearing her eyes away from the multitude of red lights that were dancing across the face of the snow.

"I'm fine," Delores said, her eyes sparkling. "I haven't had so much fun in years."

Once Hannah made sure her mother was comfortable with coffee and the bag of cookies she'd grabbed on her way out the door, she got out of the truck and headed for the scene of the action. She climbed a slight rise and peered down the embankment at Vanessa's car buried in the snow. Two sheriff's deputies had Vanessa in handcuffs and Mike was supervising her arrest. When he finished, he turned, saw Hannah, and motioned for her to wait as he climbed the bank.

"Why were you following Vanessa?" Mike asked when he arrived at her side.

Hannah swallowed hard. Mike didn't sound pleased at all. "Well . . . Mother and I thought that maybe . . ."

"That maybe I was so dumb I wouldn't stake out her apartment?" Mike finished the thought for her.

"Not exactly. It's just . . ."

"It's just that you didn't trust me to do my job?" Mike interrupted again.

"No! Mother and I were in The Cookie Jar having coffee. And we saw Vanessa leaving in her car. You didn't tell us you were going to have her under surveillance, or stake out her apartment, or anything like that. If you had, we wouldn't have bothered to chase her."

"So you just underestimated me," Mike said.

"I . . . I . . ." Hannah struggled to think of some way to go on the attack, but Mike was right and the only fair thing to do was admit it. "I *did* underestimate you. I'm sorry, Mike."

Mike didn't say anything. He just stared at her for a long minute. And then he asked, "Did I just hear you apologize?"

"Yes." Hannah nodded, and then she decided she'd better qualify it. "I apologize for underestimating you, not for anything else."

Mike grinned. "Good enough."

There was a moment when Hannah thought Mike was going to kiss her, but he just slipped one arm around her waist and gave her a little hug. "You must be tired. It's exhausting to try to run the world, isn't it, Hannah?"

"I don't . . ." Hannah stopped in mid-sentence. Now wasn't the time to light into Mike, not when she had a favor to ask. "Can I talk to Vanessa for just a second? We have some unfinished business."

"Yes, as long as you don't scratch her eyes out, or maim her in any way."

"You don't have to worry about that. I wouldn't attack her in front of witnesses."

Mike laughed and Hannah felt better. Laughter was better than apologies.

"Hold up a second," Mike called out to the two deputies who were about to climb into their squad car. Then he turned back to Hannah. "Come with me. You've got one minute."

Mike escorted Hannah to the squad car and opened the back door. "Someone to talk to you, Vanessa," he said.

"You!" Vanessa glared at Hannah. "You ran me off the road!"

"Of course I did. I couldn't let you get away. Do you want me to find you a lawyer?"

Vanessa's mouth dropped open in surprise. "You'd do that for me?"

"Absolutely . . . if you'll sell me everything in your bakery. I've decided I want it all."

"Take it. I don't care. Take everything that's there. It's a gift. Just find me a lawyer."

"A gift that big isn't legal. Not when you're under duress. Set a price and I'll pay it."

"A thousand dollars for everything. Take it or leave it. But you have to find me the best lawyer in town."

"Are you sure?"

"I'm sure."

"Deal," Hannah said, smiling. And then she turned to Mike. "You heard that?"

"I heard it."

"Okay. I'm out of here then. I have to go get Vanessa a lawyer."

When Hannah got back to her cookie truck, the smile was still on her face. It had been a very productive night.

"You look happy," Delores said.

"I am." Hannah climbed in behind the wheel and turned around to drive back to town. Howie Levine was the best lawyer in Lake Eden. He was also the only lawyer in Lake Eden, but that didn't matter. She'd call him the moment she got home and tell him about his new client. That would fulfill her part of the bargain, and once she sold off Vanessa's crystal, silver, and china, she would completely recoup the business losses they'd suffered at The Cookie Jar.

"So why are you smiling like that?" Delores asked.

Hannah considered telling her about the incredible deal she'd made on Vanessa's possessions, and how she thought she'd arrived at some kind of a truce with Mike, but all that was complicated. It had been a long day, and she was too exhausted to explain. She summed it all up as best she could in one simple sentence. "I'm always happy when the good guys win," she said.

Chapter
Twenty-Six

Hannah glanced at her reflection in the mirror. She looked good, really good. Her hair was behaving, and her skin was glowing. The former was due to a new gel that Andrea had picked up for her, and the latter had been caused by the icy wind she'd braved when she'd dashed out this morning with the garbage.

The outfit Hannah was wearing was pure Claire. Claire Rodgers from Beau Monde Fashions, the upscale boutique next to The Cookie Jar, had called Hannah in to show her a suit from her newest shipment. It was a color called barleycorn, a shade of brown with a bit of orange in it that picked up the highlights in Hannah's red hair. The fitted jacket and circle skirt were cut from a woven material that Claire said would accentuate her figure assets and minimize her figure faults. Since Hannah figured she had more faults than assets, she'd bought the outfit on the strength of Claire's conviction.

Today was a special occasion. Lisa and Herb had decided to use the complimentary champagne brunch gift that Gloria Travis had given them for their wedding. Sally's champagne brunches, at the Lake Eden Inn, were legendary, and Hannah hadn't eaten a speck of food in twenty-four hours to prepare for the event. They were celebrating the arrest of Bobby Joe Peters, aka Winthrop Harrington the Second, for the murder of Shawna Lee Quinn. And they were also celebrating the arrest of Vanessa Quinn Roper for the murder of her husband, Neil Roper. There was even more to celebrate because Hannah had given Lisa and Herb a second wedding gift. Now that she owned all the durable goods in the Magnolia Blossom Bakery, she'd told them to go through the apartment on the second floor and take any furnishings they liked for their home.

Hannah had just picked up the earrings she was planning to wear, an unusual accessory for her and a testament to the importance of the occasion, when she happened to glance in the mirror. What she saw made her stop with her hand halfway up to her ear, and stare.

Moishe had just come into the bedroom and it was clear he was carrying kitty crunchies in his mouth. He often did this, transporting food to a more comfortable place to consume it. But instead of sitting down to eat it on the floor, or hopping up on the bed to have his snack, he snagged the sliding door to the closet with his paw and pulled it open.

Strange, Hannah thought, continuing to watch as her resident feline disappeared into the jumble of shoes, boxes, and other things she simply couldn't throw out that were stored on the floor of her closet. A few moments later, Moishe came back out, pushed the closet door shut, and headed back to the kitchen for another bite.

Even stranger, Hannah thought. *What is he doing? Feeding the mice he keeps in the closet?*

Hannah chuckled as she put on one earring. That was patently absurd. Cats fed mice in an occasional cartoon, never in real life. In real life, mice fed cats. Literally. Perhaps the closet was the scene of a particularly tasty former meal involving small rodents and dust bunnies, and Moishe had decided to treat it thereafter as his private dining room.

Hannah had put on her second earring and was struggling with the clasp on her necklace when Moishe came back into the room. Again, he was carrying kitty crunchies in his mouth, and again, he opened the closet door with his paw. Hannah listened carefully, but she didn't hear the sound of crunching. Moishe wasn't eating. She was almost sure of that. But she did think she heard a small squeak. Could she have been right the first time? Could Moishe actually be feeding the mice he was keeping in the closet? If so, there must be a reason and only two occurred to her. Either the mice had become Moishe's friends and he was feeding them to keep them alive, or he'd taken a hint from the farmers in the Lake Eden area and he was fattening them up for the kill.

She had to find out. Hannah waited until Moishe had headed back to the kitchen again, and then she opened the closet. What she saw surprised her. It was a mound of kitty crunchies with no mice in sight.

"Stranger and stranger," Hannah intoned, hurrying to the kitchen. Moishe was still there, but he was just disappearing into a hole he'd eaten in the side of the broom closet door, a hole that led straight to the twenty-five-pound bag of kitty crunchies. He'd tunneled through the door and he hadn't wanted Hannah to know that he'd done it until he'd moved the mother lode to a safe place!

"I just couldn't!" Hannah said, shaking her head as Sally came to the table with a fresh basket of popovers. "I've already eaten way too much."

"Are you sure?" Sally asked, holding the basket out so that Hannah could see the puffs of golden pastry nestled in the napkin.

"Well . . . maybe one. With butter. And apricot jam."

Everyone laughed including Norman, who was sitting to her right, and Mike, who was sitting to her left. Hannah grinned good-naturedly and looked around for the dish of butter and the pot of homemade apricot jam.

"Here's the butter," Mike said, and he passed the dish so that Hannah could take it with her left hand.

"And here's the jam," Norman added, zooming in from the other side so that Hannah could take the pot of jam with her right hand.

"How about some more coffee to go with that?" Norman asked, grabbing the carafe. "Or orange juice?" He picked up the pitcher of orange juice with his other hand.

"I could make you a Mimosa," Mike offered, taking the bottle of champagne from the ice bucket.

"Thanks, but I don't want a Mimosa," Hannah said, answering Mike. "But I'll have a little more champagne." Then she turned to Norman. "And I'll have more coffee, but I don't want more orange juice."

And there Hannah sat, holding butter in her left hand and jam in her right, as Norman filled her cup with coffee and Mike poured champagne in her glass. She was hemmed in by two men who were falling all over themselves to serve her and it made her feel ridiculous. She really had to talk to the person who arranged the next extended family gathering in advance. She was tired of feeling like the white filling in Norman and Mike's Oreo.

The whole gang was here and they were all in marvelous moods. Andrea and Bill looked as happy as Lisa and Herb, and so did Marge Beeseman and Jack Herman. Evidently their living arrangements were working out just fine. Mike was happy at having solved two cases, and Norman was proud of the fact that he'd helped her sleuth. Carrie and Delores were sitting on either side of Tracey, who'd been invited to attend her very first champagne brunch. She was drinking sparkling apple juice out of a champagne glass and she had both Carrie and Delores laughing at something she'd said.

"And here's Hannah's contribution to the brunch," Sally announced, passing a silver tray filled with Chocolate Overload Cookie Bars, the rich confections Hannah had made to celebrate the fact that two killers were behind bars.

For a long moment, there was no talking, and that was the greatest compliment a baker could receive. Hannah watched the rapturous expressions of her friends and relatives as they ate the rich, creamy, chocolate cheesecake cookie bars. In no time at all, the tray was empty and everyone was smiling.

"Hannah?" Mike grabbed his opportunity as Norman went over to talk to Bill. "Have you got a minute? I really need to talk to you alone."

Hannah wanted to say no, but that wouldn't be polite. Not only that, she was curious. She reminded herself that curiosity had killed the cat, but it didn't deter her the way she'd hoped it would.

Once they'd excused themselves to the group, Hannah and Mike walked out of the restaurant and down the carpeted hallway to the lobby. Mike led her toward a couch near the huge granite fireplace and waited until she was seated.

"I just wanted to tell you that I'm sorry," Mike said as he took her hand and sat down on the couch with her. "I've been a terrible fool. Can you ever forgive me?"

"I'm not sure," Hannah replied quite honestly, doing her best to maintain her objectivity. Having Mike this close must be a bit like getting hooked on drugs. She felt that without him, she'd be a shell. And with him, she could be anything she wanted to be. The feeling scared her and she fought it. This wasn't love; this was addiction.

"I've been doing a lot of thinking." Mike took both of her hands in his. "I realized how much I love you . . . really love you. And I promise I'll never look at another woman again. You're the only one in the world for me."

Hannah couldn't breathe. And that meant she couldn't speak. Did this mean what she thought it did?

"I wasn't ready before, but I am now," Mike declared. "Everything's changed. I want to put the past behind me and start a new life with you. If you're willing, that is. Be willing, Hannah... please."

Hannah tried to move, or breathe, or speak, but she couldn't. She was frozen like a deer in the headlights, waiting for her rescuer, or killer, or captor... whatever the case might be... to release her.

As she sat there wondering how long she could exist without oxygen, Mike got down on one knee and took a small velvet jeweler's box out of his pocket.

"I wanted to give this to you at Lisa and Herb's reception, but... well... you know what happened. I remember when you said you didn't really like diamonds, that they were colorless."

"That's true," Hannah said, surprised that she'd managed to squeeze any words out of the throat she thought was permanently blocked.

Mike flipped the velvet-covered cask open so that Hannah could see the ring inside. "I bought you an emerald engagement ring, because the green matches your eyes. Will you marry me, Hannah? Please?"

Hannah gazed down at the ring and was rendered speechless yet again. She couldn't say yes, or no, or even maybe. Her heart felt like it would burst out of her chest and race free as Mike took the ring out of the cask and held it out. A proposal at last, from Mike! All she had to do was accept, and she would be Mrs. Michael Kingston.

Then, out of the corner of her eye, she saw Norman approaching and the *yes* that was about to escape her lips caught on the lump in her throat. Norman saw Mike down on his knees in the lobby and he held up his arms in a *time-out* signal.

Hannah started to grin, even though the moment was fraught with emotion. Norman was wheeling his arms in circles and she couldn't help herself.

"What?" Mike asked, noticing Hannah's inattention.

"Nothing," Hannah said, and Norman beat a hasty retreat. What was Norman doing? Wasn't he even going to fight for her?

"Hannah? Will you marry me?" Mike asked again, beginning to frown slightly.

"An urgent telephone call for Mike Kingston," the loudspeaker intoned. "Please report to the front desk immediately."

"Uh-oh," Mike said, jumping to his feet. "Hold that thought. This could be important. I'd better take it, okay?"

Hannah didn't have time to answer before he was gone, but she had the feeling that her whole life would be that way if she married Mike. She would never come first. She was really sorry that Norman hadn't . . .

"Hannah!" Norman rushed to her side. "Don't marry Mike! Maybe he loves you, but he's going to break your heart. Marry me instead. I love you and I promise to make you laugh every day. Our life together will be great, you'll see."

Hannah glanced at the phone banks against the far wall. One phone was hanging from its cord and she realized that Norman had placed that urgent phone call to Mike. What a dirty trick! And how delightfully diabolical!

"Hannah?" Norman asked, pushing his luck just

a little too far. "Will you marry me and live with me in our dream house?"

Hannah thought about it for a second or two before she realized that she was being railroaded. There was only one thing to do to gain some thinking time.

"I'll let you know really soon," Hannah said, leaning down to place a fond kiss on Norman's lips. "And when Mike comes back, you can tell him the same thing."

CHOCOLATE OVERLOAD COOKIE BARS

Preheat oven to 350 degrees F.,
rack in the middle position.

FOR THE CRUST:

1½ cups flour
¼ cup cocoa powder
¾ cup sugar
¾ cup softened butter *(1½ sticks)*

Mix the dry ingredients together and then cut in the softened butter. *(You can also do this in a food processor with a steel blade, using chilled butter that's been cut into chunks.)*

Spread the mixture out in the bottom of a greased 9-inch by 13-inch cake pan and press it down with a spatula.

Bake at 350 degrees F. for 15 minutes. *(Don't shut off the oven—you'll need it for the second step.)*

FOR THE FILLING:

2 eight-ounce packages softened cream
   cheese *(the block type, not the whipped
   type)*
1 cup mayonnaise

1 cup sugar

4 eggs

2 cups melted chocolate chips *(12-ounce bag)*

2 teaspoons vanilla

You can do this by hand, but it's a lot easier with an electric mixer. Soften the cream cheese and beat it with the mayonnaise until it's smooth. Gradually add the sugar. Add the eggs, one at a time, beating after each addition. Melt the chocolate chips in a microwave-safe bowl for 3 minutes. *(Chocolate chips may retain their shape, so stir them to see if they're melted.)* Let them cool for a minute or two, and then gradually add the chocolate, mixing thoroughly. Then mix in the vanilla. Pour the finished mixture on top of the crust you just baked.

Bake at 350 degrees F. for 35 minutes. Let it cool to room temperature and then chill for at least 4 hours.

Cut into brownie-size bars. Garnish the bars with strawberries, whipped cream, or powdered sugar if desired.

Baking Conversion Chart

These conversions are approximate, but they'll work just fine for Hannah Swensen's recipes.

VOLUME:

U.S.	Metric
½ teaspoon	2 milliliters
1 teaspoon	5 milliliters
1 Tablespoon	15 milliliters
¼ cup	50 milliliters
⅓ cup	75 milliliters
½ cup	125 milliliters
¾ cup	175 milliliters
1 cup	¼ liter

WEIGHT:

U.S.	Metric
1 ounce	28 grams
1 pound	454 grams

OVEN TEMPERATURE:

Degrees Fahrenheit	Degrees Centigrade	British (Regulo) Gas Mark
325 degrees F.	165 degrees C.	3
350 degrees F.	175 degrees C.	4
375 degrees F.	190 degrees C.	5

Note: Hannah's rectangular sheet cake pan, 9 inches by 13 inches, is approximately 23 centimeters by 32.5 centimeters.

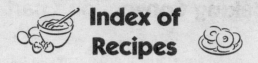

Index of Recipes

Hannah Swensen and her bakery, The Cookie Jar, bask in the glow of Hollywood glamour when Main Street becomes a movie set. And although tensions simmer as the cameras roll, no one expects the action to turn deadly ... until it's too late ...

There's no such thing as privacy in Lake Eden, but Hannah never thought things would go this far. Everyone has been telling her what to do ever since she got not one but *two* marriage proposals. The votes are evenly divided between Detective Mike Kingston and town dentist Norman Rhodes.

Movie mania takes over and Lake Eden locals turn into Hollywood wannabees. Even Hannah's cat wants a shot at stardom! Hannah's marriage dilemma becomes more complicated as she re-meets producer Ross Barton, an old college crush who is now handsome, famous, and single. The Cookie Jar serves as snack central with Main Street rented out for the week, and Hannah stirs up fresh gossip as she caters to Jeff, whipping up treats for cast and crew, including demanding director Dean Lawrence's favorite—cherry cheesecake.

Everything's on schedule until Dean demonstrates a suicide scene with a prop gun that turns lethal. Now there's a real body on the set and Hannah's on the case in a flash. There are plenty of suspects to go around, starting with lead actress Lynne Larchmont—one of a slew of female visitors to Dean's trailer—whose husband, Tom, is financing the film. Then there's Tom Larchmont himself, forty years his wife's senior, and smitten enough to be motivated by jealousy. Ross Barton was constantly keeping Dean out of trouble . . . could he have had enough? Lake Eden local Winnie Henderson publicly threatened to kill Dean if he moved the statue her brother sculpted because it was blocking his shot. And what about male star Burke Anson? He'd argued with Dean about something mysterious the morning of the murder.

As filming continues, Hannah sifts through the clues, hoping against hope that the person responsible for Dean's death is half-baked enough to have made a mistake. When it happens, Hannah intends be there—ready to rewrite a killer's lethal script with the kind of quirky ending that can only happen in Lake Eden.

Please turn the page for an exciting
sneak peek at
CHERRY CHEESECAKE MURDER
coming next month!

# Prologue

Lake Eden, Minnesota
Wednesday, the Second Week in March

"Cut!"

Dean Lawrence had directed on plenty of locations, but Lake Eden was the worst. These yokels raised boredom to a whole new level. The chubby broad who ran the bakery made a great cherry cheesecake, and that was the only good thing he could say about Podunk Central.

Nothing was working today. They were never going to get this scene. The local lethargy must be catching, and it was time to kick some butt.

"What's with you, Burke? You're supposed to make people weep for you! Get up. I'll show you what I want here." Dean pushed Burke out of camera range and got ready to play the scene himself.

Midway through the scene, he noticed that the redhead who baked his cheesecakes was staring at him with new respect. Maybe she'd be a little more receptive, now that he'd impressed her with his talent. He opened the center desk drawer, pulled out the prop gun, and stared at it while he waited for Lynne's line.

"I love you, Jody! Don't do this to me!"

It was a perfect reading of the line and Dean was glad he'd decided to use her in his next movie. He put on a tortured expression as the camera came in for his close up, and gazed at Lynne with tears welling in his eyes. "I'm not doing it to you, Li'l Sis. I'm doing it *for* me."

He raised the gun to his temple. Lynne looked horrified, exactly as she should, and he gave her a last, sad smile. Then he squeezed the trigger.

The gun went off and Lynne screamed for real. Their director was dead.

Chapter One

Two Weeks Earlier

Hannah Swensen did her best to convince her sleep-logged mind that the insistent electronic beeping she heard was in the soundtrack of her dream. A huge semi-tractor-trailer was backing up to the kitchen door of her bakery, The Cookie Jar, to deliver the mountain of chocolate chips she'd ordered for the gazillion Chocolate Chip Crunch Cookies she'd promised to bake for her biggest fan, Porky Pig, who'd finally overcome his stutter with the help of a voice coach and was now being sworn in as president of the United States . . .

The dream slipped away like the veils of Salome, and Hannah groaned as she clicked on the light. No doubt her dream was the result of watching Cartoon Network until two in the morning and eating two dishes of chocolate ice cream with a whole bag of microwaved popcorn. She silenced the alarm and threw back the covers, sitting up in bed in an effort to fight her urge to burrow back into her warm blankets and pull them up, over her head.

"Come on, Moishe," she said, nudging the orange and white lump that nestled at the foot of her bed. "Daylight in the swamps, dawn in the desert, and sunrise in Lake Eden, Minnesota."

Moishe's yellow eyes popped open. He looked out the window into the darkness beyond, then swiveled his head to stare at her accusingly. While most people didn't think cats could understand "human-speak," Hannah wasn't most people. But this was primarily because Moishe wasn't most cats. "Sorry," Hannah apologized, backpedaling under his unblinking yellow gaze. "It's not really daylight in Lake Eden, but it will be soon and I have to get up for work."

Moishe seemed to accept her explanation. He opened his mouth in a wide yawn and gave the little squeak in the middle that Hannah found endearing. Then he began to stretch.

Hannah never tired of watching her previously homeless tomcat go through his morning calisthenics. Moishe rolled onto his back and gazed up at the bedroom ceiling. His right front leg came up in a fascist salute and after a slight pause, his left leg shot up to join it. Then his back legs pushed toward the foot of the bed and spread out in a tensely inverted "Y," like the handholds of a witching rod. Once his whole body was stretched taut, he began to quiver like the proverbial bowlful of Jell-O.

The kitty quiver lasted for several seconds and then Moishe flipped from back to stomach. This was the position Hannah called "shoveled," because it was about as flat as a cat could get without the aid of a steamroller. All four legs were stretched out to the max and Moishe's chin was perfectly parallel to the worn nap on the chenille bedspread Hannah had rescued from Helping Hands, Lake Eden's only thrift store.

The part that came next was Hannah's favorite. Moishe's back legs moved forward, first the left and then the right in what her first grade friends had called "giant steps" in their games of *Captain, May I.* This continued by awkward measure until Moishe's rear was up in the air, his hips so high it turned him into a kitty teepee. Once the apex had been reached, he gave a little sigh, a little shake, a little flick of both ears simultaneously, and then he made a big leap to the floor to follow Hannah down the hallway.

"Hold on," Hannah said, hopping from foot to foot as she pulled on her fleece-lined moccasin slippers. "You know you can't open the Kibble Keeper by yourself."

After a short trip down the hall spent dodging Moishe's efforts to catch the laces on her slipper, Hannah reached the kitchen. She flicked on the bank of fluorescent lights and winced as the walls shimmered dazzling white to her sleep-deprived eyes. Perhaps it was time to paint her walls a darker color, a color like black, especially if she kept operating on three hours sleep. Last night had been another night in a long string of nights spent in her living room, stretched out on the sofa with a twenty-three pound cat perched on her chest, watching television until the wee small hours of the morning and wrestling with a decision that would have stymied even Solomon.

An indignant yowl brought Hannah back to matters at hand and she opened the broom closet to lift out the Kibble Keeper. It was a round gray bucket-type container with a screw on lid that was guaranteed to keep out even the most persistent pet. Hannah had found it at the Tri-County Mall after Moishe had defeated every other means she'd tried to keep him from helping himself to his own breakfast. It wasn't that she begrudged him food. It was the cleanup that made feline self-service dining unfeasible. Hannah had swept up and dumped out the last kitty crunchy she was about to sweep and dump, and the salesclerk at the pet store had assured her that no living being that lacked opposable thumbs could open the Kibble Keeper. It was made of a resin that was impervious to biting and scratching, knocking it over and batting it around had no effect at all on its sturdy exterior, and it had been tested on a tiger at the Minnesota Zoo and come through with flying colors.

Even though Hannah knew that Moishe was physically incapable of unscrewing the lid, she still concealed her actions from him It wasn't wise to underestimate the cat who was capable of so much more than the ordinary tabby.

"Here you go," she said, scooping out a generous helping and dumping it into his bowl. "Finish that and I'll give you some more."

While her feline roommate crunched, Hannah poured herself a cup of steaming coffee and sent a silent message of thanks to whoever had invented the automatic timer. She took one sip, swallowed painfully, and added a coffee ice cube from the bag she always kept in the freezer. A regular ice cube would dilute what her grandmother had called "Swedish Plasma," and that was why Hannah kept one ice cube tray filled with frozen coffee. She needed her caffeine full-strength in the morning.

Several big gulps and Hannah felt herself beginning to approach a wakeful state. That meant it was time to shower and dress. The lure of a second cup of coffee would make her hurry, and she was awake enough not to doze off and turn as red as a lobster under the steaming spray.

Hannah reentered the kitchen eleven minutes later, her red hair a damp mass of towel-dried curls, and clad in jeans and a dark green sweatshirt that proclaimed CHOCOLATE IS A VEGETABLE—IT COMES FROM BEANS in bright yellow script. She'd just poured herself that second cup of coffee when the phone rang.

Hannah reached for the bright red wall phone that hung over the kitchen table, but she stopped in mid-stretch. "What if it's Mike? Or Norman?"

"Rrowww!" Moishe responded, looking up at the phone as it rang again. "Yowwwww!"

"You're right. So what if they both proposed? And so what if they're waiting for me to choose between them? I'm thirty years old, I run my own business, and I'm a sensible adult. Nobody's going to rush me into a decision I might regret later . . . including Mother."

As Hannah uttered the final word, Moishe's ears flattened against his head and he bristled like a Halloween cat. He despised Delores Swensen and Hannah's mother had a drawer full of shredded pantyhose to prove it..

"Don't worry. If it's Mother, you don't have to speak to her."

Hannah took a deep breath and grabbed the phone, sinking down in a chair to answer. If it was her mother, the conversation would take a while and there were bound to be unveiled references to her unmarried state. If it was her younger sister, Andrea, the conversation would include the latest about Hannah's two nieces, Tracey and Bethany, and it would also take a while. If it was Michelle, Hannah's youngest sister, they were bound to have a discussion about college life at Macalister College and that would also eat up the minutes Hannah had left before she had to go to work. "Hello?" Hannah greeted her caller, hoping mightily that it wasn't either of the two men in her life.

"What took you so long? I was almost ready to give up but I knew you wouldn't leave for work this early."

It was a man, but it wasn't either of the two in question and Hannah breathed a sigh of relief. It was Andrea's husband Bill, the only other early riser in the Swensen family. "Hi, Bill. What's up?"

"I am. I'm out here at the sheriff's station and we've got a problem."

Hannah glanced at the clock. It was only five-fifteen. Bill kept regular hours now that he was the Winnetka County Sheriff. He never went to the office until eight unless there was an emergency. "Is there anything I can do to help?"

"You bet there is. And you're the only one who can fix this mess!"

"What mess?" Hannah had visions of homes burglarized, motorists carjacked, public buildings vandalized, and murder victims stacked up like cordwood. But if crime was running rampant in Lake Eden, she certainly hadn't heard about it. And how could she possibly be the only one who could fix it?

"It's Mike. You really did a number on him,

Hannah. One minute he's on top of the world, telling everybody that you're bound to choose him. The next minute he's all down in the mouth, absolutely sure that you're going to ditch him and marry Norman."

Hannah did her best to think of something to say. It wasn't *her* fault that Mike couldn't handle the stress of waiting while she made up her mind which proposal to accept. It had been only a week. A girl, even one whose mother thought her old enough to qualify as an Old Maid, was entitled to all the time she needed for such an important decision.

"Look, Hannah. I know it's not totally your fault, but I've got a dangerous situation here."

"Dangerous?"

"That's right. Mike's supposed to be my head detective, my right hand when it comes to solving crime. The way he's acting right now, he couldn't catch a perp even if the guy stood in front of his desk holding a sign that said *I did it.* I mean, what if we have a real murder, or something like that? What'll happen then?"

Hannah let out her breath. She hadn't even realized she'd been holding it. "So what do you want me to do?"

"Make up your mind so Mike can get back to work. Fish, or cut bait . . . you know?"

"But I can't rush my decision. It's just too important."

"I understand," Bill said with a sigh, "and I'm not really trying to influence you. I just know it'll be Mike in the long run. If you love him as much as I think you do, you'll accept his proposal today and put him out of his misery. He's the right one for you and that's not just my opinion. Everybody in the department thinks so, too."

"I'll . . . uh . . . think about it," Hannah said, settling for the most noncommittal reassurance in her arsenal.

"Think fast. And keep your fingers crossed that we don't need Mike for anything until you give him a yes."

Hannah promised she would and hung up the phone. She could understand Bill's point. A week was a long time to keep anyone on hold, but she was no closer to making a decision than she'd been on the day both men had proposed. Mike was handsome and exciting. Norman was dependable and endearing. Mike made her stomach do flips when he kissed her, and Norman's kisses made her feel warm and tingly all over. She wished she could have both of them, but she couldn't. And there was no way she could give up one for the other.

Before Hannah could take another swallow of her coffee, the phone rang again. She grabbed it in mid-ring, certain that it was Bill who'd forgotten to tell her something. "What did you forget, Bill?"

"It's not Bill, it's Lisa," Hannah's young partner replied. "I just wanted you to know that you don't have to hurry to work this morning."

"Why not?"

"Because I'm down here at The Cookie Jar already."

Hannah glanced up at the clock. It was five thirty and Lisa wasn't due at work until seven. "Why so early?" she asked, hoping that Lisa hadn't had a fight with her new husband.

"Herb had to get up at four and after he left, I couldn't go back to sleep."

"Why did he have to get up at four?"

"He's driving to Fargo for the Traffic Tradeshow."

"What's that?" Hannah asked, although she suspected that if she'd remained silent, Lisa would have gone on to tell her.

"It's everything to do with traffic and parking, like signs, parking meters, and traffic signals. Mayor Bascomb called us at home last night and he wants Herb to check out the price on parking meters."

"Parking meters?" Hannah was shocked. Parking had always been free in Lake Eden.

"That's right. He told Herb to find out how much it would cost to put them up on Main Street."

"On Main Street?"

"Yes, but Herb thinks it's a smokescreen."

"A smokescreen?" Hannah repeated, feeling more and more like an obedient myna bird.

"There's a group that wants Lake Eden Liquor shut down. They say the city shouldn't be making a profit on the sale of alcohol."

Hannah gave a little snort. Every few years someone organized a group to close down the municipal liquor store. "I wish people would learn that you can't legislate morality. Closing the liquor store isn't going to cut down on drinking."

"I know, but his time they're really serious. They're collecting signatures to get it on the next ballot. Herb's sure that's why Mayor Bascomb wants an estimate on those parking meters."

Hannah took another slug of coffee, but she still didn't see the connection. "What do parking meters have to do with the liquor store?"

"Herb thinks the mayor's going to give them a choice. Close the liquor store and put parking meters on Main Street to make up for the lost revenue, or keep it open and forget about the tax increase they'll have to pay to get the parking meters installed in the first place."

"That ought to work," Hannah said with a smile. The mayor was almost as devious as her mother.

"I think so, too. Everybody wants to park for free and nobody wants to pay more taxes. Anyway, I'm here and you don't have to come in until you want to. You need some time to think."

"Think?"

"About Mike and Norman. Mayor Bascomb asked Herb if you'd made up your mind yet."

"He did?" Hannah was surprised. "I didn't know he cared one way or the other."

"Well, he does. He wants you to marry Norman. He says it's your civic duty."

"What?!"

"That's exactly what Herb said, but Mayor Bascomb explained it. He said that they can always hire a new detective, but finding a dentist to take over the clinic will be a lot harder."

"Wait a second . . . the mayor thinks the man I don't marry will leave town?"

"Yes, and he's not the only one. Herb says Mike's not going to stick around and feel like a loser if you end up marrying Norman. He's too proud to eat crow in front of the whole town. And Norman's not going to stay here and watch you live happily ever after with Mike. He really loves you and it would be too painful for him. Not only that, if Norman leaves, Carrie will probably go with him, because he'll be all depressed and she'll think he needs her. And then your mother will end up losing a partner."

"Oh, boy!" Hannah groaned under her breath. This was a whole new set of problems to consider. She'd been thinking about how her choice would affect her own happiness, but now it seemed it could have ramifications on the whole town of Lake Eden!

"Anyway, take your time about coming in. I'll see you when you get here."

Hannah said goodbye and turned to look at Moishe. "I wish I'd known sooner. Turns out we could have slept in."

"Rrrow!" Moishe replied, and Hannah thought he looked disappointed. Sleeping in while nestled at the foot of the bed, half buried in the fluffy comforter, was one of Moishe's favorite activities.

"Oh, well. I guess I might as well carry out the garbage and . . ."

Before Hannah could finish telling a disinterested feline her plans, the phone rang again and she snatched it up. "Hello?"

"Hi, Hannah. It's Barbara Donnelly. I know it's early, but I wanted to catch you before you left for work."

"Hi, Barbara." Hannah grabbed the steno notebook she kept on the kitchen table. Barbara was the head secretary at the sheriff's station and she always ordered cookies for the staff meetings she held on Monday afternoons. "Did you want cookies for this afternoon?"

"Yes. Give me three-dozen Black and Whites. I'll send one of the girls in to pick them up. On second thought, better make it four-dozen. They're our favorites. But that's not the reason I called. I need a favor."

"What's that?" Hannah asked, wise enough not to agree before she heard what Barbara wanted.

"I'm begging you to put an end to this whole thing today."

Hannah was ninety-five percent certain she knew what Barbara meant, but she went for the remaining five percent. "What whole thing is that?"

"The whole thing with Mike. He's driving us all nuts. I had to assign three different secretaries to him in the past week."

"Why so many?"

"Because after a day with him, they come to my office and ask for reassignment. It's just too stressful working for a boss that's walking around whistling one minute and chewing his fingernails the next. Of course I hope you choose Mike, but that's up to you. I just want you to make a decision today and put my secretaries out of their misery."

"I'll try," Hannah promised and signed off. She'd no sooner hung up the phone than it rang again. "Okay, okay," she plucked the receiver from its cradle. "Hello?"

"It's Doc Bennett, Hannah."

In one fluid motion, Hannah stretched out the phone cord, poured herself another mug of coffee, and sat back down in her chair. "What's up, Doc?"

"Wery funny," Doc Bennett responded in his Elmer Fudd voice, the same voice that had taken the fear out of going to the dentist for so many Lake Eden children. "Seriously, Hannah, what's up is Norman."

"What do you mean?"

"That poor boy isn't getting any sleep and he called to ask me to fill in for him again today. It's a real pity, Hannah. I don't know how much more of this Norman can take. So far, he hasn't made any dental mistakes that I know of, but it's only a matter of time before he fills the wrong tooth, or something even worse. What's taking you so long, anyway? If you love Norman as much as I think you do, you should accept his proposal today and let him get some sleep!"

Hannah was stymied. She didn't know what to say. "I . . . I'm . . ."

"I know it's an important decision, but you've taken long enough. Will you try to decide today?"

"I'll try," Hannah agreed, doubting that she'd be successful.

"Good. I've got to go. Mrs. Wahlstrom is here for a cleaning."

Doc Bennett hung up abruptly and Hannah was left holding a dead line. As she hung up on her end, she uttered a phrase she'd never use within Tracey or Bethany's hearing, even though Bethany was too young to understand it and Tracey had probably heard it before, and then she turned to Moishe. "They're ganging up on me. What am I going to do?"

Moishe gave her a wide-eyed look that Hannah interpreted to mean he didn't have the foggiest idea. She reached down to pet him, but before she her hand connected with his orange and white fur, the phone rang again.

"Uh-oh," Hannah breathed as Moishe's ears flattened against his head and he started to bristle. Her kitty caller I.D. wasn't infallible, but nine times out of ten that bristle meant her mother was on the phone. When Moishe's tail started to switch back and forth like a metronome, Hannah reached for the phone. Her mother was nothing if not persistent. If she didn't reach Hannah at home, she'd wait and call her down at The Cookie Jar. "Hello, Mother."

"You really shouldn't answer the phone that way," Delores gave her standard greeting.

"I know, but you'd be disappointed if I didn't."

"Perhaps," Delores conceded. "I need to talk to you about something important, Hannah. And I want you to know that normally I'd never interfere . . ."

But, Hannah provided the next word. She knew it was coming, although she chose to say it aloud.

"But Carrie just called me and we have a situation on our hands. Do you know that Norman's down at Hal and Rose's Café right now, slogging down coffee as fast as Rose can pour it?"

"No," Hannah answered truthfully.

"Well he is. Rose called Carrie to tell her. She said she tried to get Norman to go easy on the coffee, but he said this could be the most important day of his life and he wasn't about to sleep through it."

Hannah groaned. "Norman thinks I'm going to give him an answer today?"

"It's not just today. Carrie says he's been like this every day since he proposed. And to make matters even worse, Mike's down there, too. He's sitting right across from Norman in the back booth, matching him cup for cup."

"At least it's not beer for beer," Hannah commented, grinning slightly.

"Shame on you, Hannah Louise! That's not one bit funny and you know it. I've done my very best to keep mum, but this time you've gone too far. I didn't raise you to be cruel!"

"Cruel?" Hannah was shocked.

"What else would you call it? I'm serious, Hannah. Enough is enough and it's time for you to stop dithering. You should choose which man you want to marry, tell him so, and let the other down gently. That's what a lady would do under the same circumstances. Drawing it out the way you've done is unkind to everyone concerned."

Hannah was silent for a long moment, considering what her mother had said. Delores did have a point. "You're right, Mother."

There was a crash as Delores dropped the phone. And then a scrabbling noise as she picked it up again. "I'm sorry. Did you say I was *right*?"

"That's what I said."

"Well . . ." Hannah's mother sounded slightly breathless and extremely shocked. "Does that mean that you agree to settle this once and for all?"

"Yes, I'll settle it."

"And you'll do it today?"

"I'll do it right now. Talk to you later, Mother."

Hannah hung up the phone to cut off any further questions, filled Moishe's food bowl one last time, grabbed her coat and car keys, ignored the phone that was frantically ringing again, and headed out the door to keep her date with destiny at Hal and Rose's Café.